Im
Great Priest Imhotep

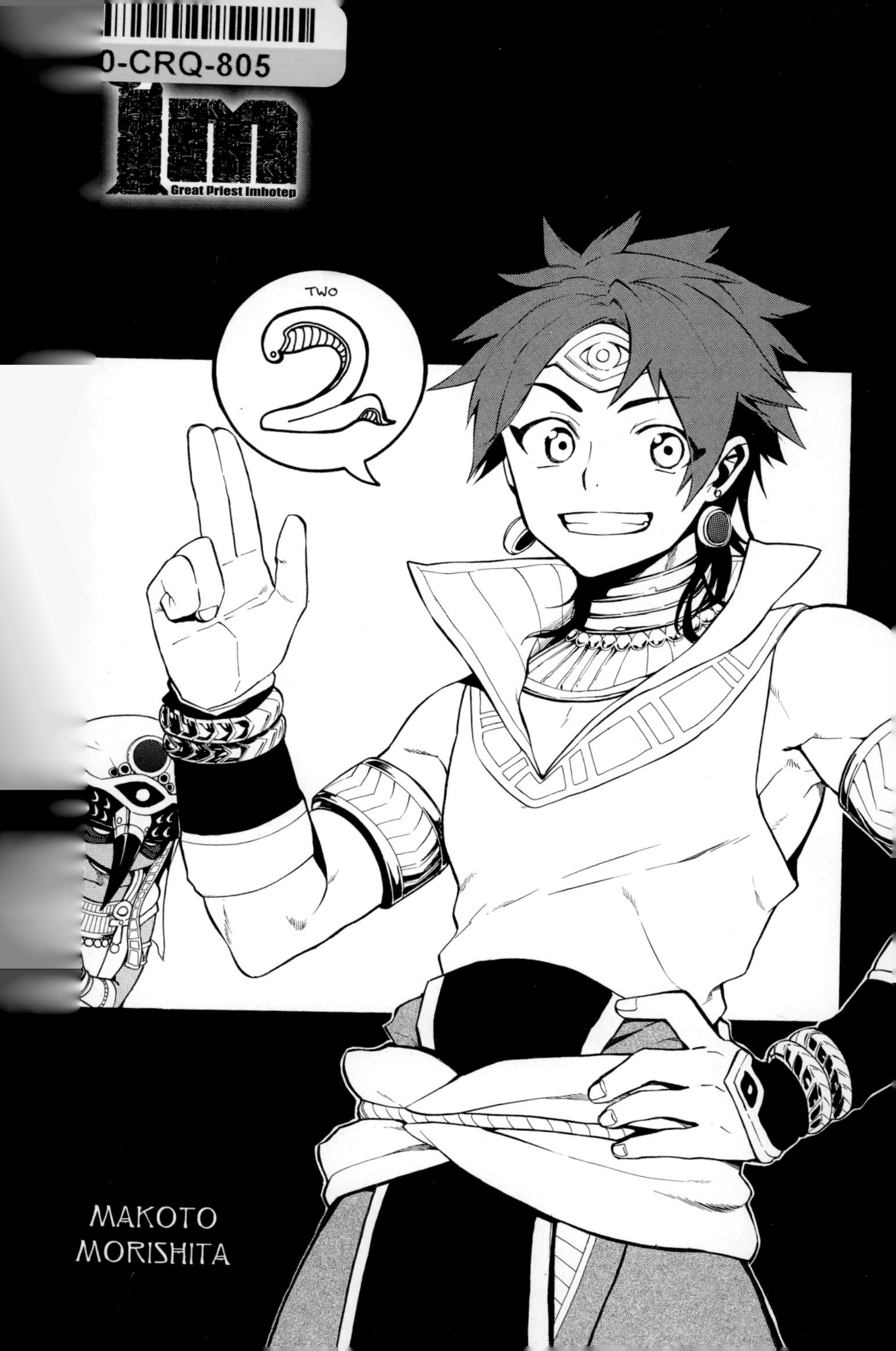
TWO
2

MAKOTO MORISHITA

Im

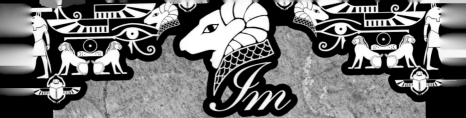

Great Priest Imhotep

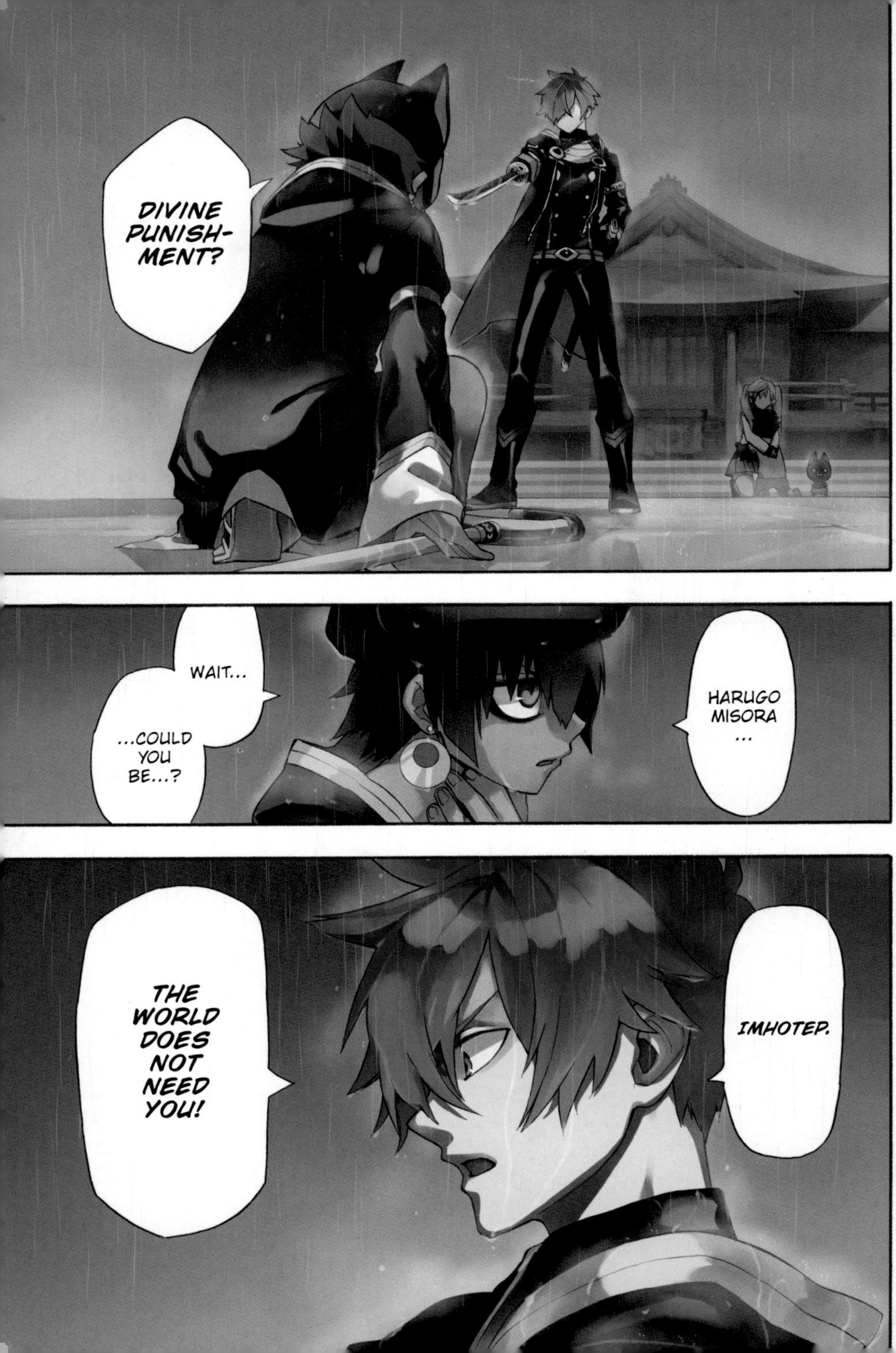
DIVINE PUNISH-MENT?
HARUGO MISORA ...
WAIT...
...COULD YOU BE...?
IMHOTEP.
THE WORLD DOES NOT NEED YOU!

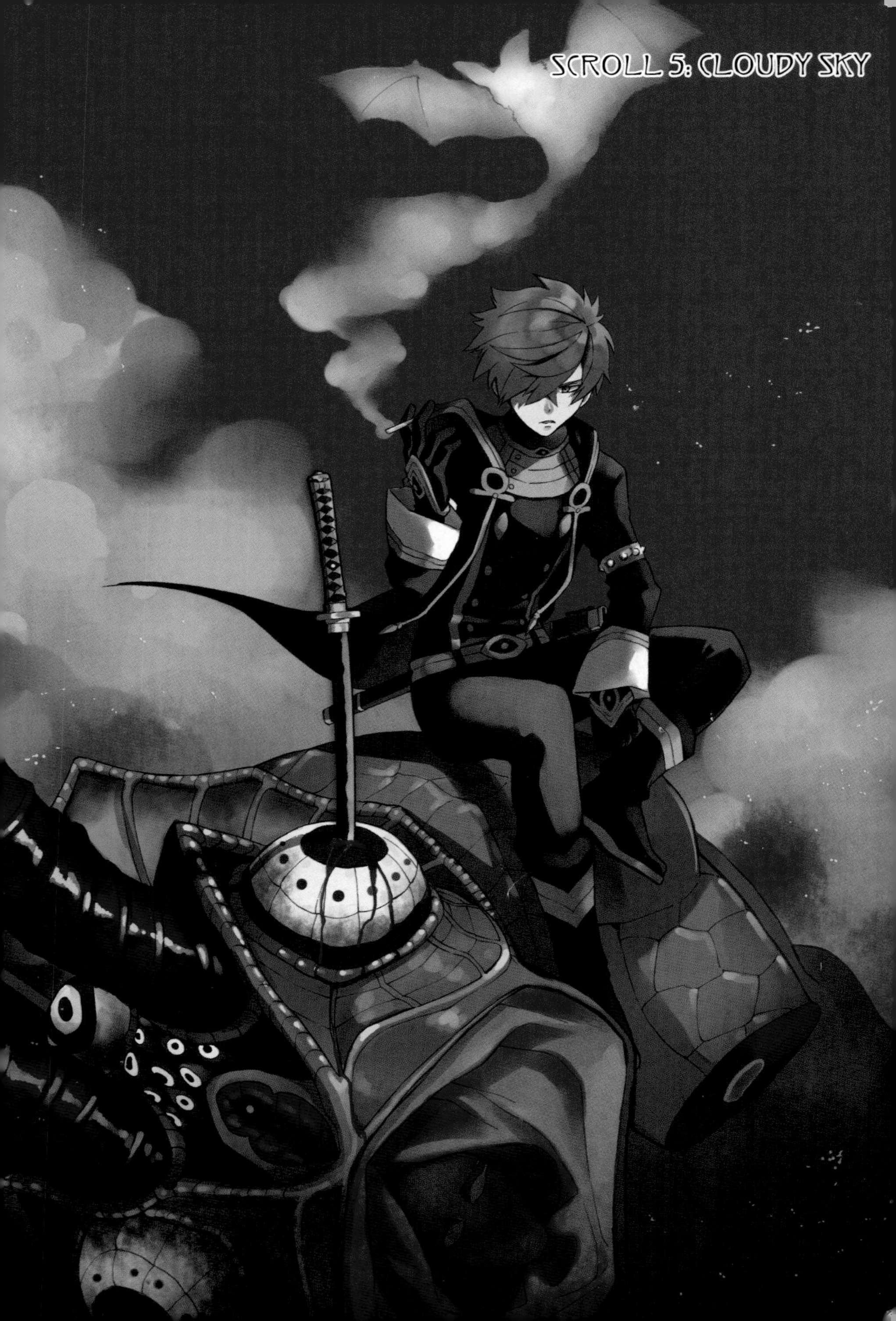
SCROLL 5: CLOUDY SKY

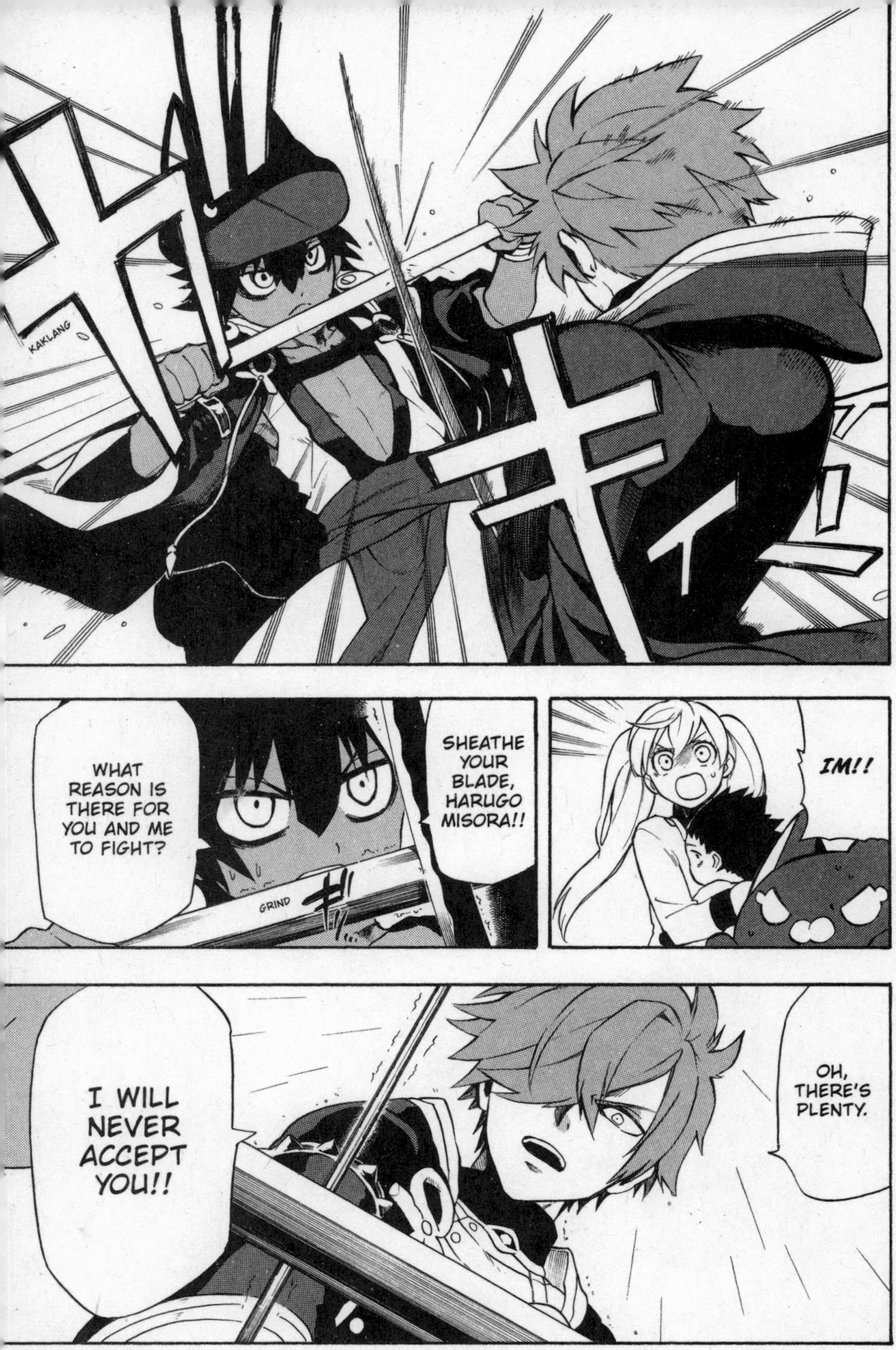
KAKLANG
IM!!
SHEATHE YOUR BLADE, HARUGO MISORA!!
WHAT REASON IS THERE FOR YOU AND ME TO FIGHT?
GRIND
OH, THERE'S PLENTY.
I WILL NEVER ACCEPT YOU!!

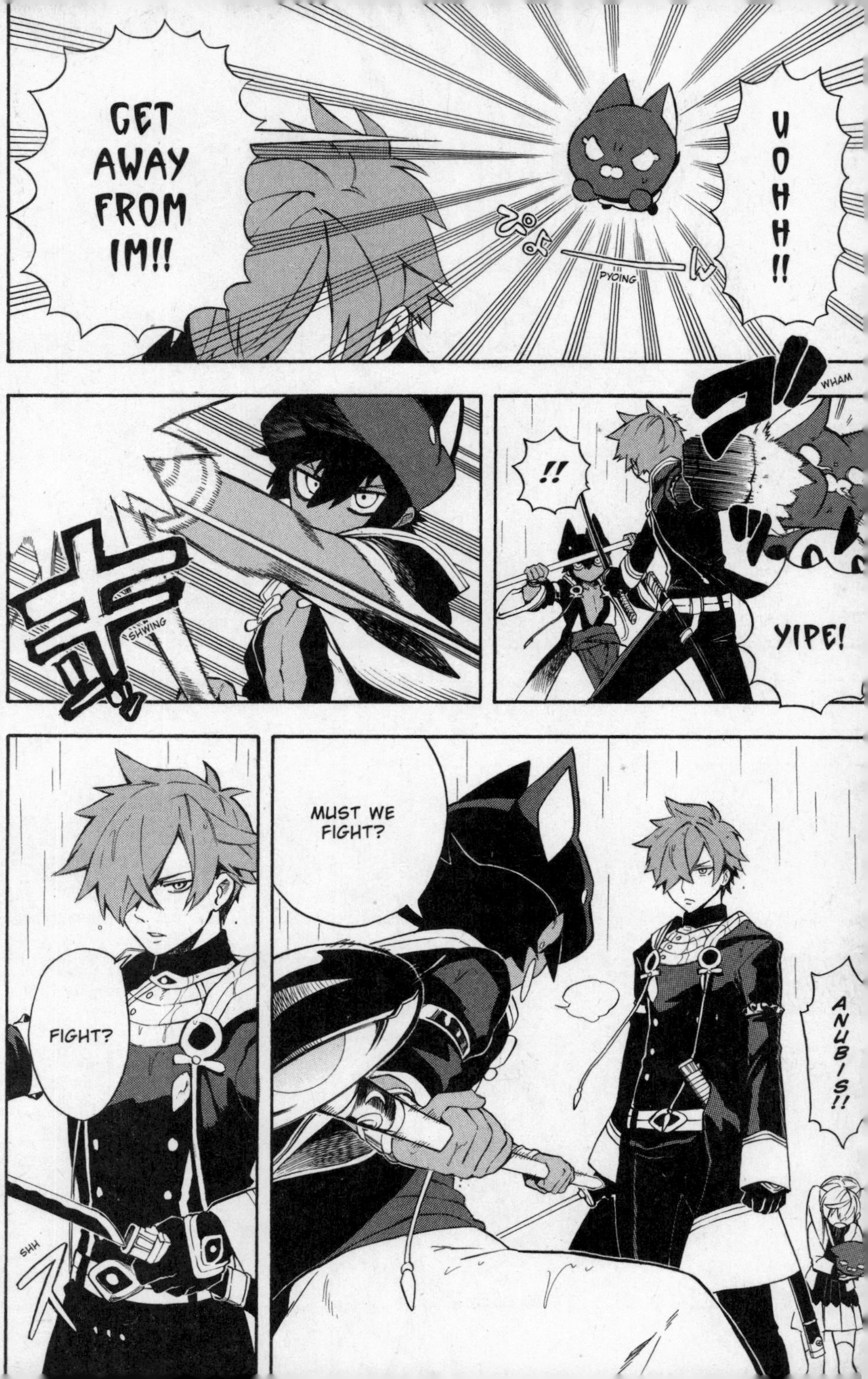
UOHH!!
ぴょーん
PYOING
GET AWAY FROM IM!!
WHAM
!!
YIPE!
SHWING
ANUBIS!!
MUST WE FIGHT?
FIGHT?
SHH

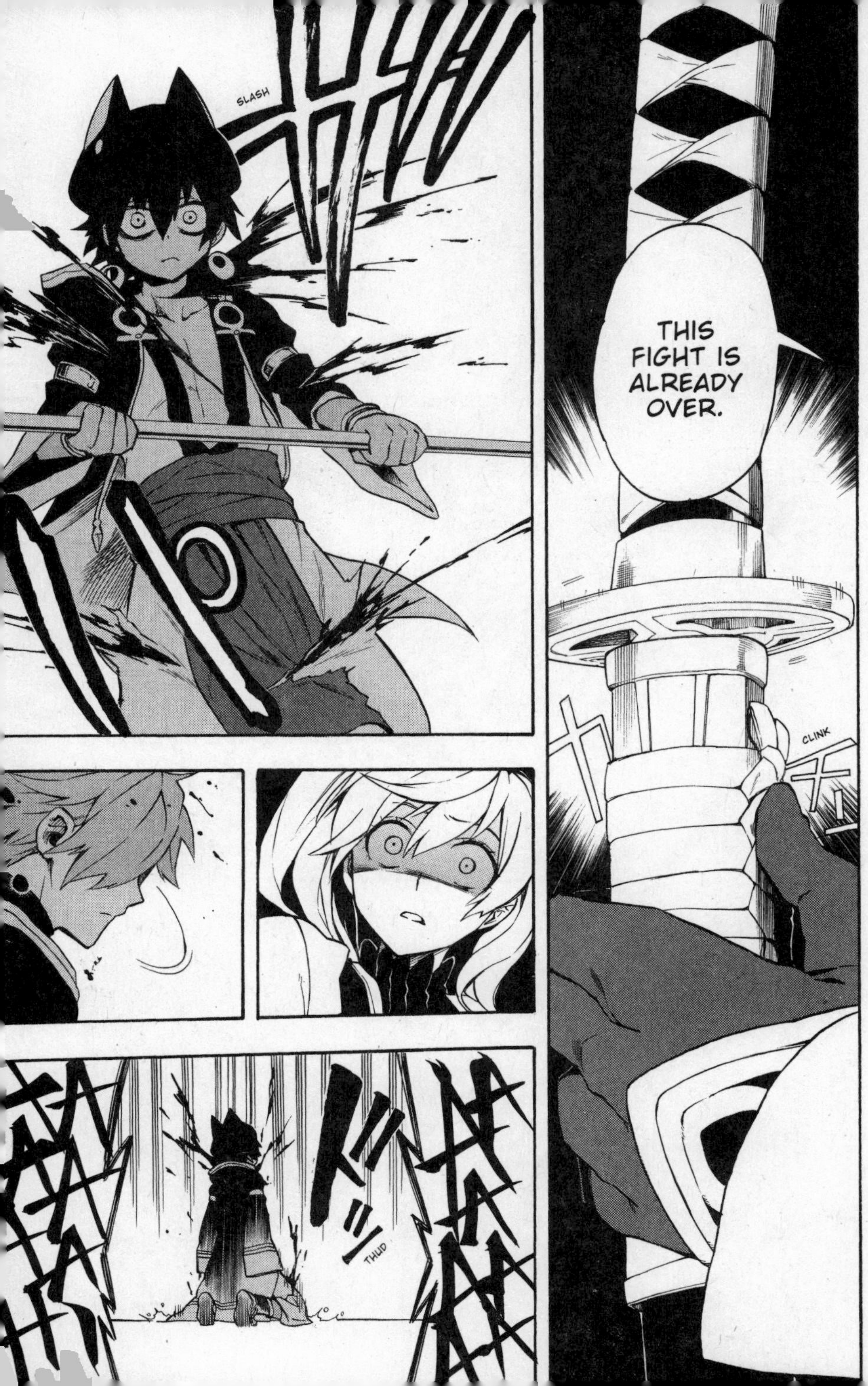
THIS FIGHT IS ALREADY OVER.
CLINK
SLASH
THUD

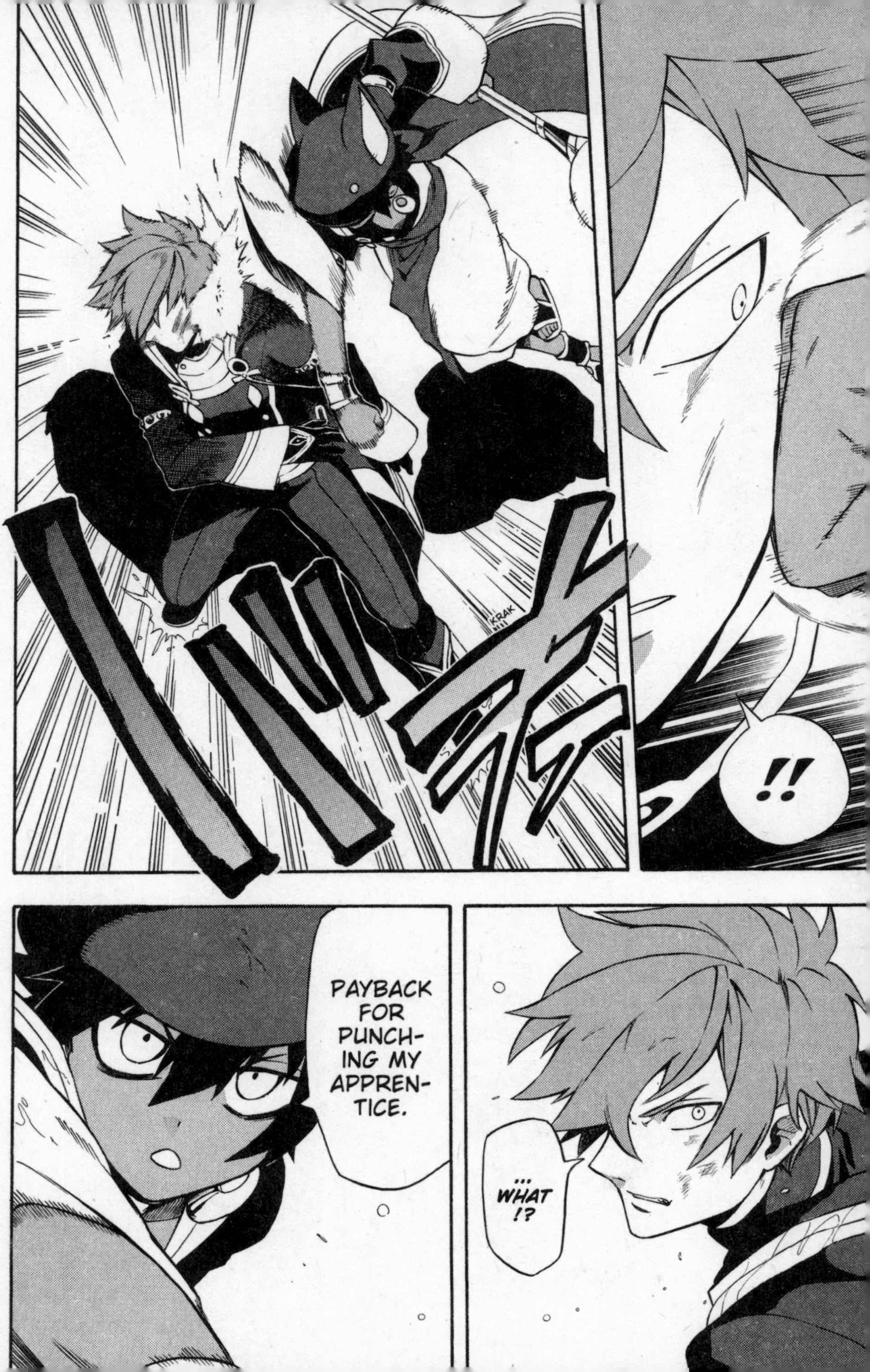
!!
KRAK
...WHAT!?
PAYBACK FOR PUNCHING MY APPRENTICE.

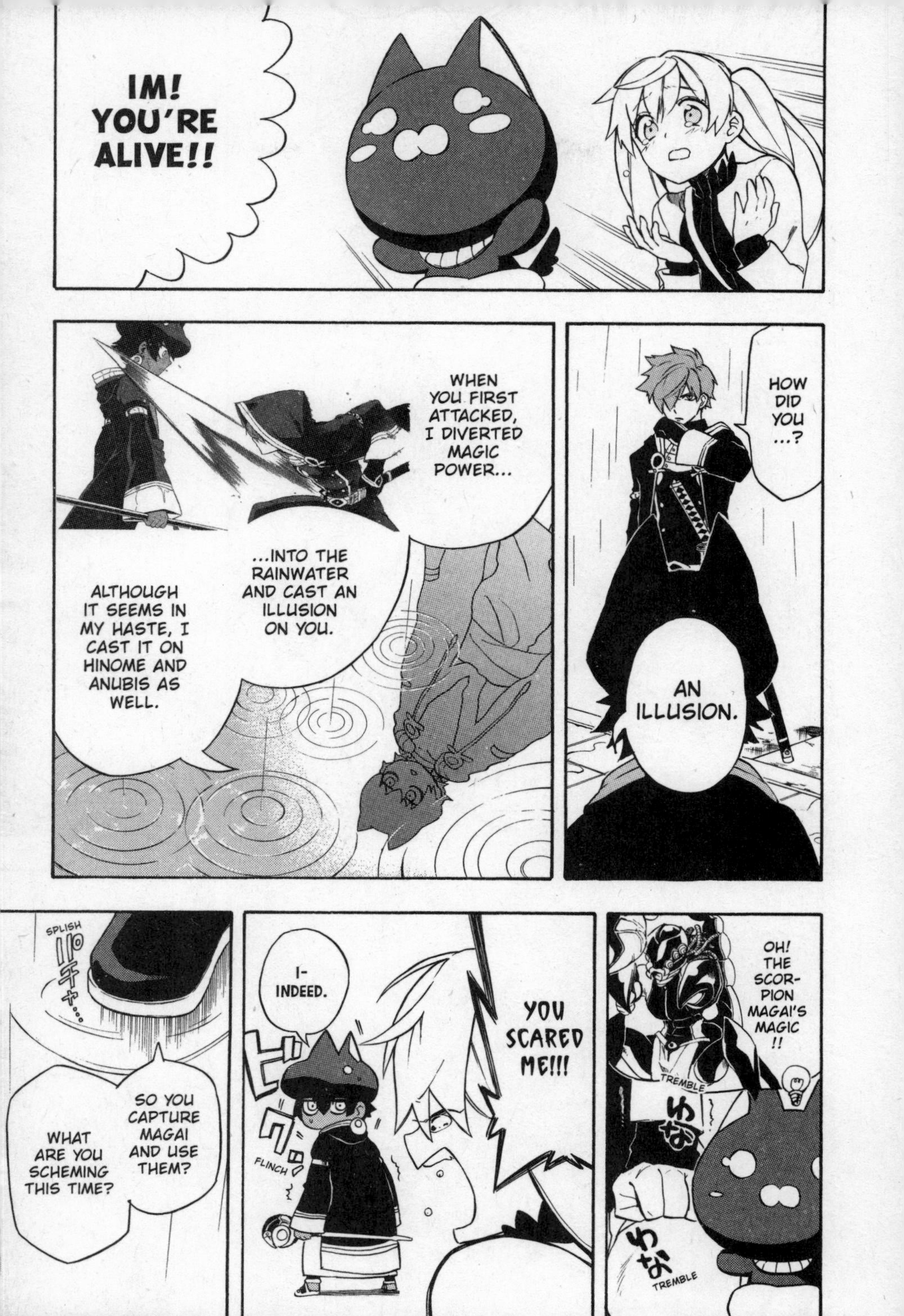
IM! YOU'RE ALIVE!!
HOW DID YOU ...?
AN ILLUSION.
WHEN YOU FIRST ATTACKED, I DIVERTED MAGIC POWER...
...INTO THE RAINWATER AND CAST AN ILLUSION ON YOU.
ALTHOUGH IT SEEMS IN MY HASTE, I CAST IT ON HINOME AND ANUBIS AS WELL.
OH! THE SCORPION MAGAI'S MAGIC!!
TREMBLE
TREMBLE
YOU SCARED ME!!!
I- INDEED.
FLINCH
SPLISH
SO YOU CAPTURE MAGAI AND USE THEM?
WHAT ARE YOU SCHEMING THIS TIME?

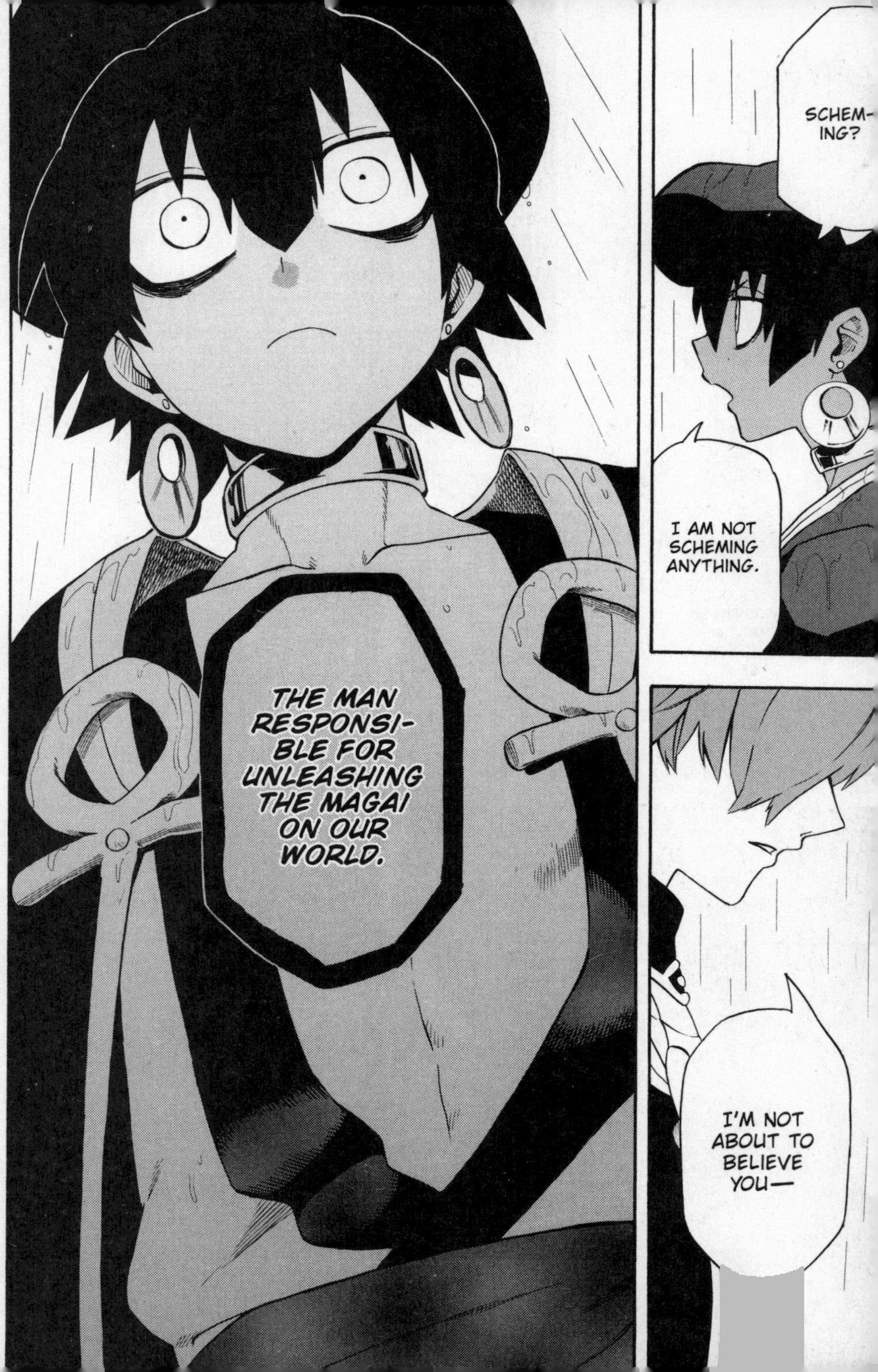
SCHEMING?
I AM NOT SCHEMING ANYTHING.
I'M NOT ABOUT TO BELIEVE YOU—
THE MAN RESPONSIBLE FOR UNLEASHING THE MAGAI ON OUR WORLD.

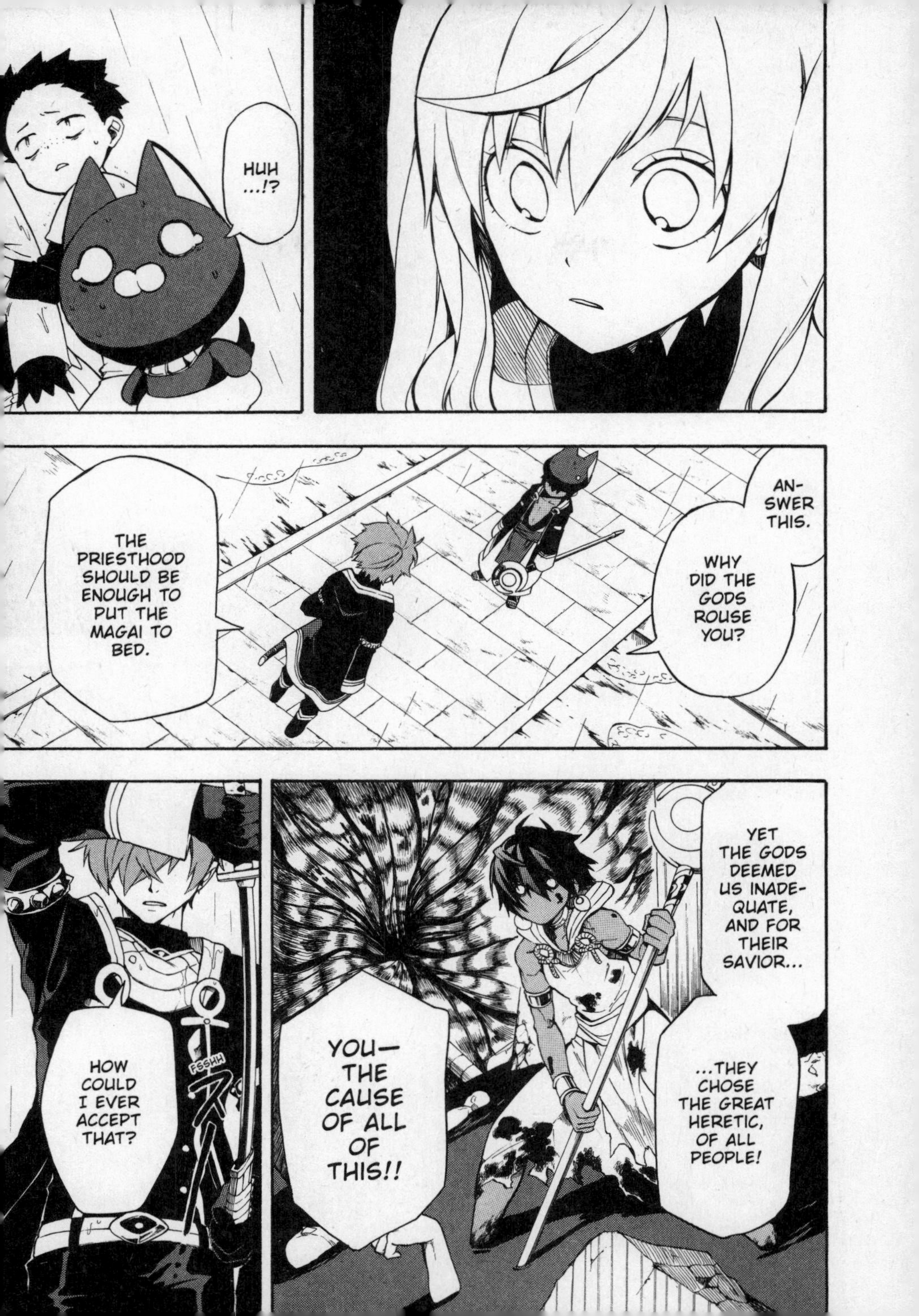
HUH ...!?
AN-SWER THIS.
WHY DID THE GODS ROUSE YOU?
THE PRIESTHOOD SHOULD BE ENOUGH TO PUT THE MAGAI TO BED.
YET THE GODS DEEMED US INADE-QUATE, AND FOR THEIR SAVIOR...
...THEY CHOSE THE GREAT HERETIC, OF ALL PEOPLE!
YOU— THE CAUSE OF ALL OF THIS!!
FSSHH
HOW COULD I EVER ACCEPT THAT?

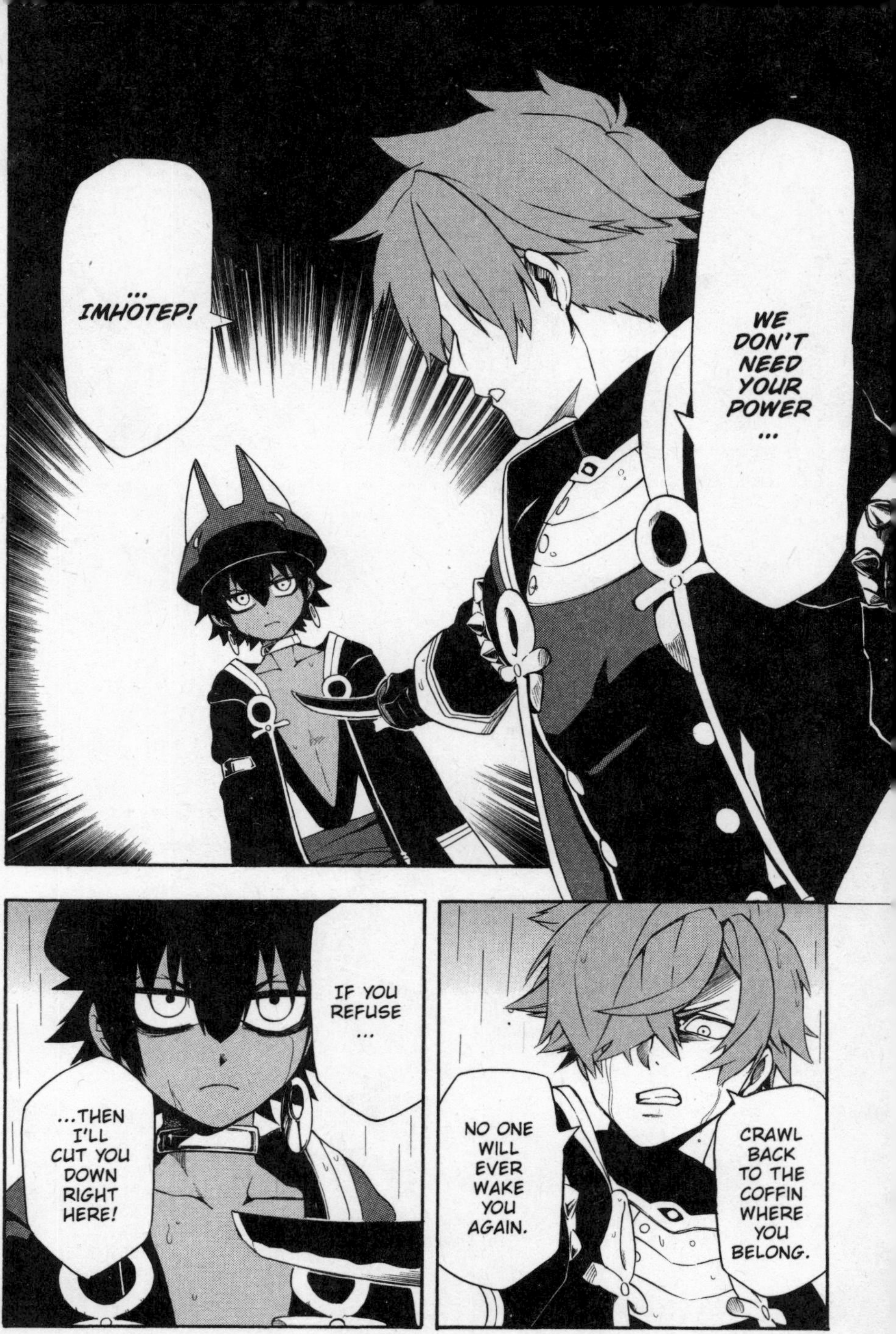
WE DON'T NEED YOUR POWER...
...IMHOTEP!
CRAWL BACK TO THE COFFIN WHERE YOU BELONG.
NO ONE WILL EVER WAKE YOU AGAIN.
IF YOU REFUSE...
...THEN I'LL CUT YOU DOWN RIGHT HERE!

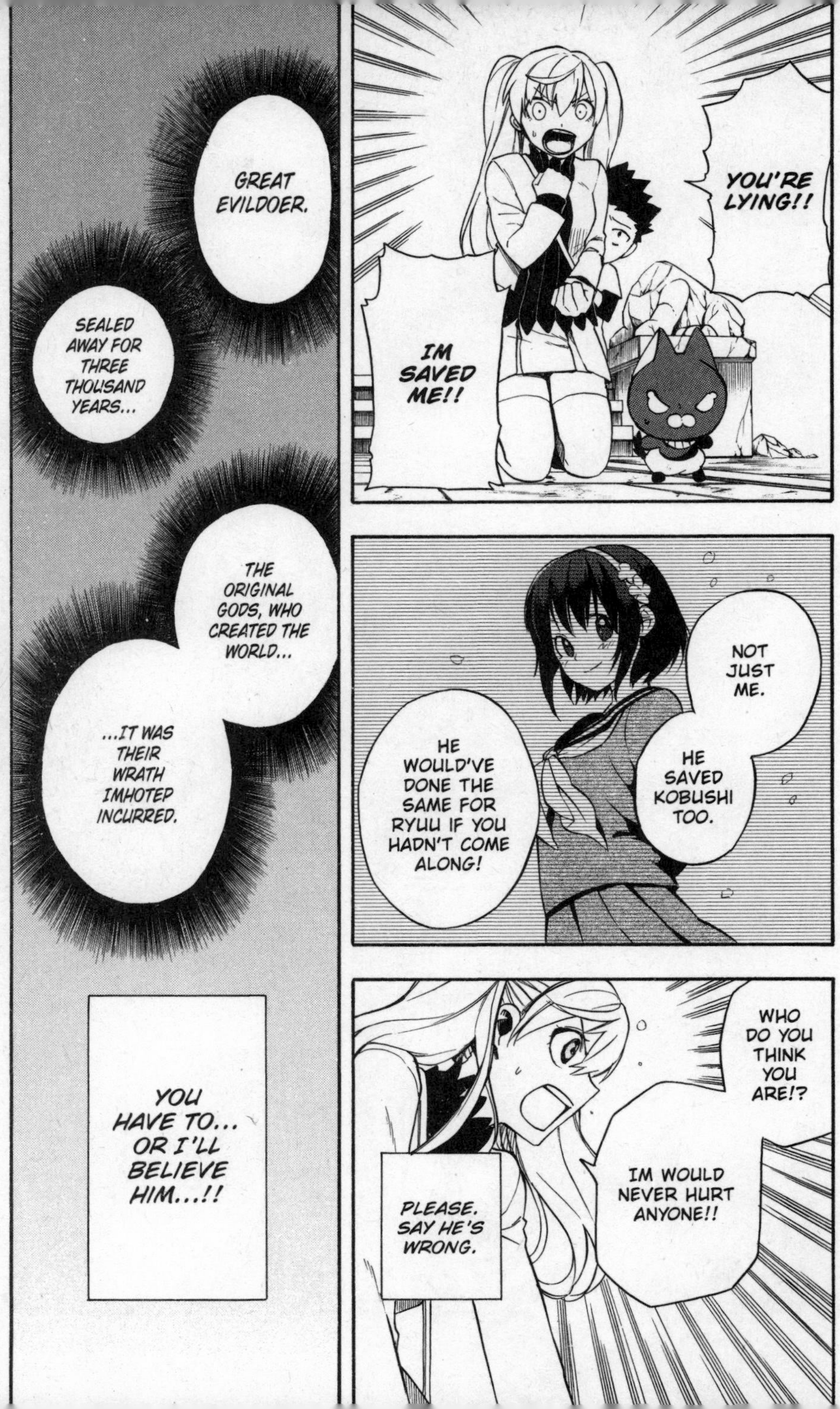
YOU'RE LYING!!
IM SAVED ME!!
NOT JUST ME.
HE SAVED KOBUSHI TOO.
HE WOULD'VE DONE THE SAME FOR RYUU IF YOU HADN'T COME ALONG!
WHO DO YOU THINK YOU ARE!?
IM WOULD NEVER HURT ANYONE!!
PLEASE. SAY HE'S WRONG.
GREAT EVILDOER.
SEALED AWAY FOR THREE THOUSAND YEARS...
THE ORIGINAL GODS, WHO CREATED THE WORLD...
...IT WAS THEIR WRATH IMHOTEP INCURRED.
YOU HAVE TO... OR I'LL BELIEVE HIM...!!

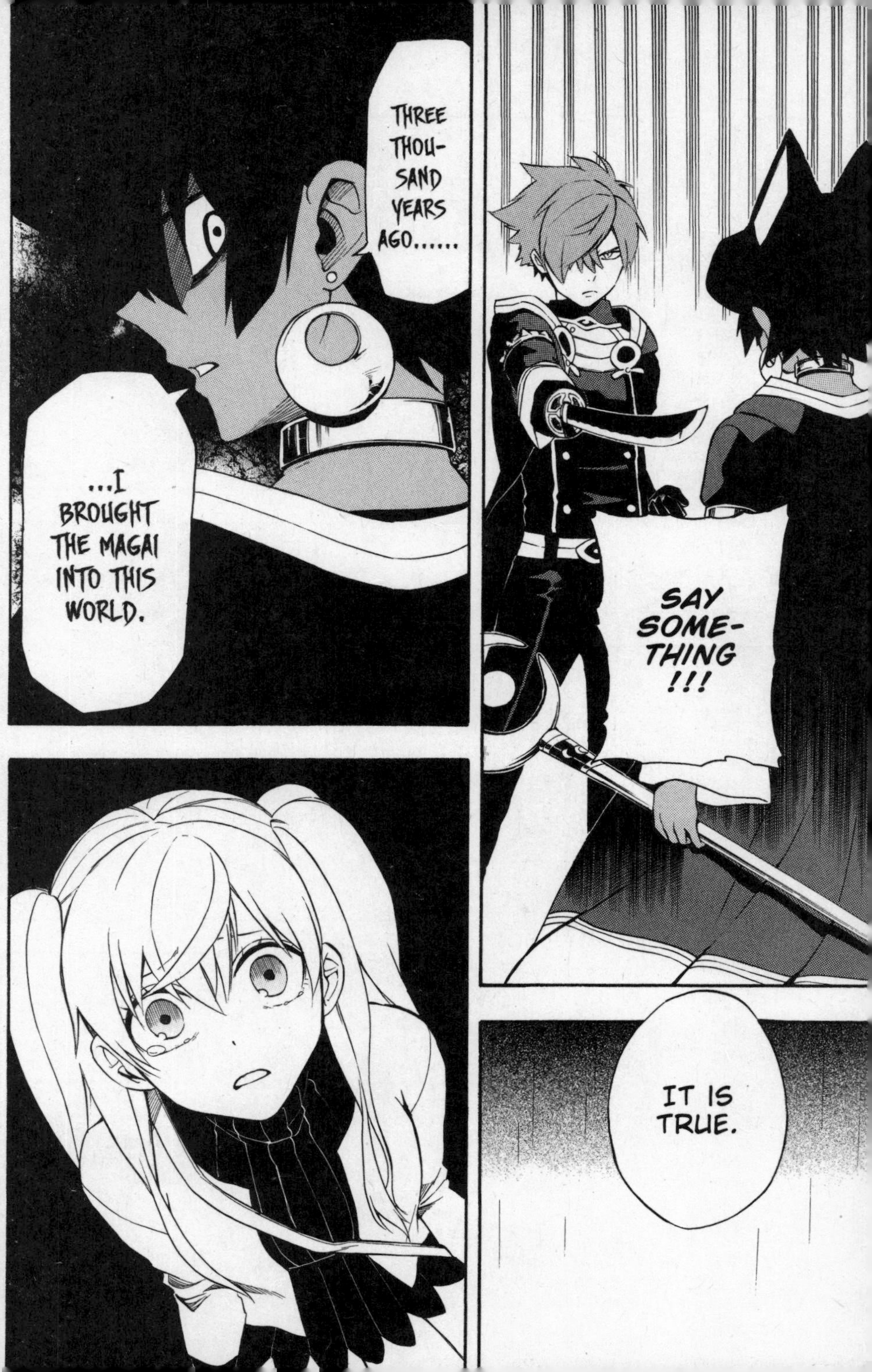
SAY SOMETHING!!!
THREE THOUSAND YEARS AGO......
...I BROUGHT THE MAGAI INTO THIS WORLD.
IT IS TRUE.

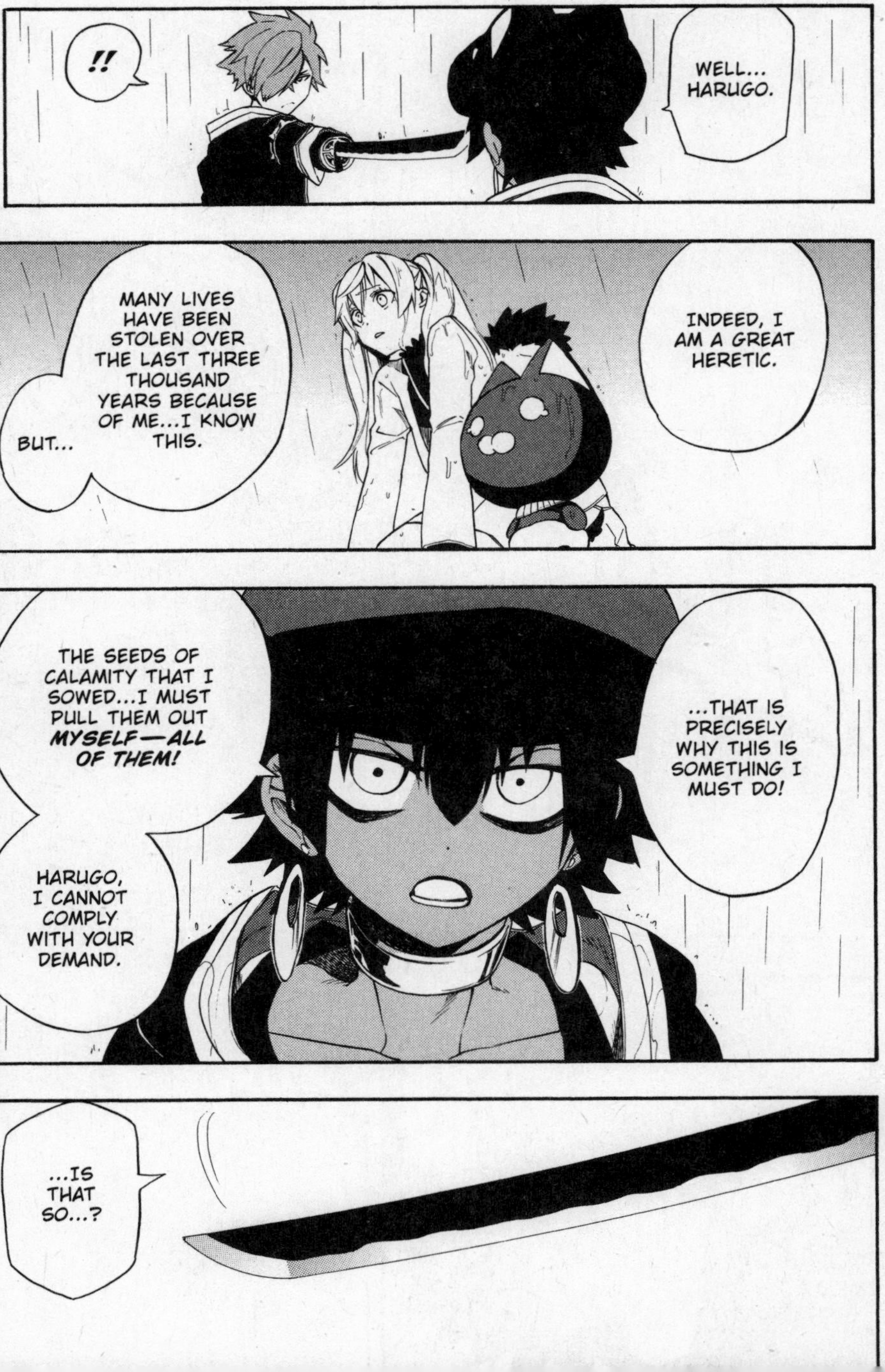
WELL... HARUGO.
!!
INDEED, I AM A GREAT HERETIC.
MANY LIVES HAVE BEEN STOLEN OVER THE LAST THREE THOUSAND YEARS BECAUSE OF ME...I KNOW THIS.
BUT...
...THAT IS PRECISELY WHY THIS IS SOMETHING I MUST DO!
THE SEEDS OF CALAMITY THAT I SOWED...I MUST PULL THEM OUT *MYSELF—ALL OF THEM!*
HARUGO, I CANNOT COMPLY WITH YOUR DEMAND.
...IS THAT SO...?

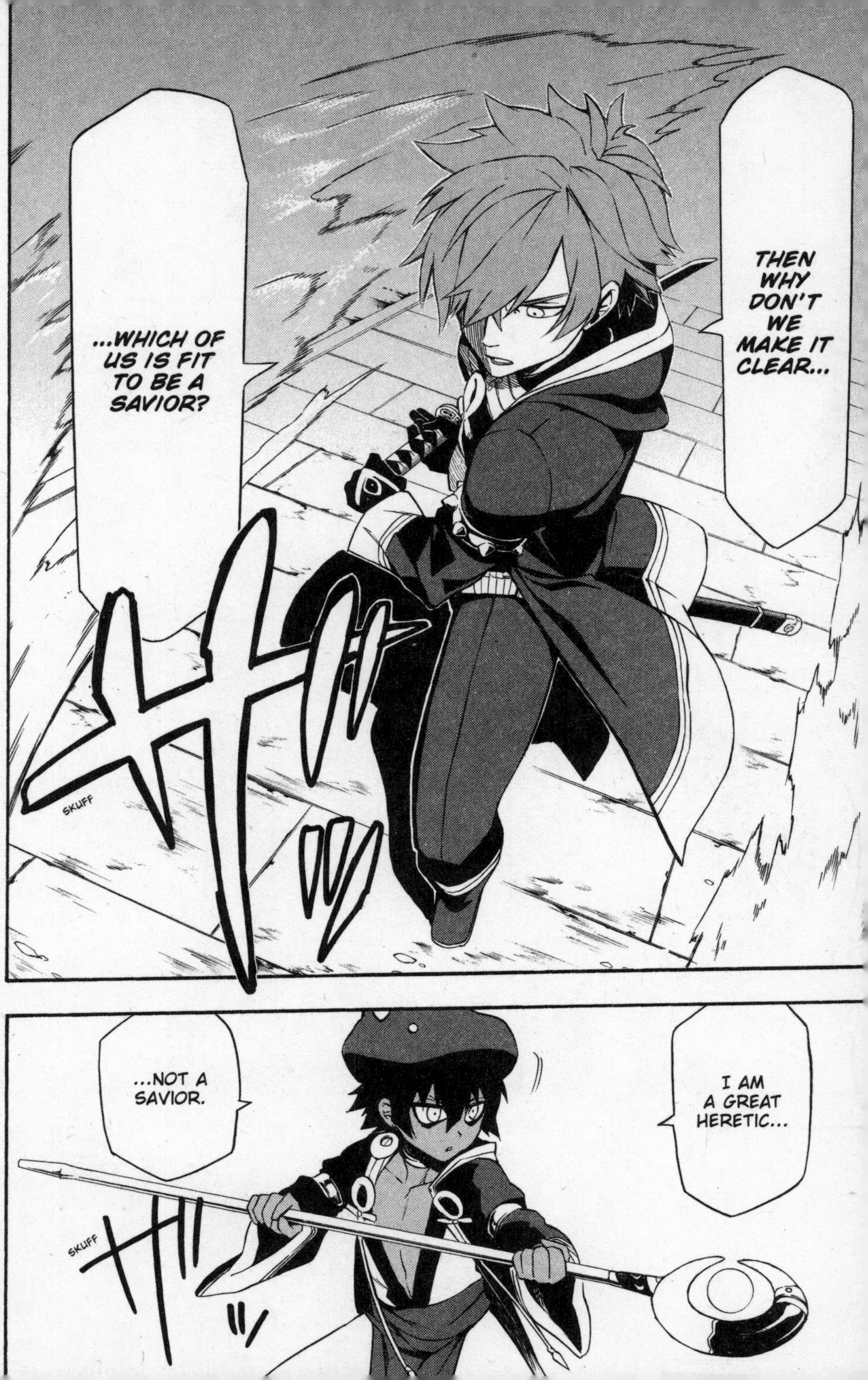
THEN WHY DON'T WE MAKE IT CLEAR...
...WHICH OF US IS FIT TO BE A SAVIOR?
SKUFF
I AM A GREAT HERETIC...
...NOT A SAVIOR.
SKUFF

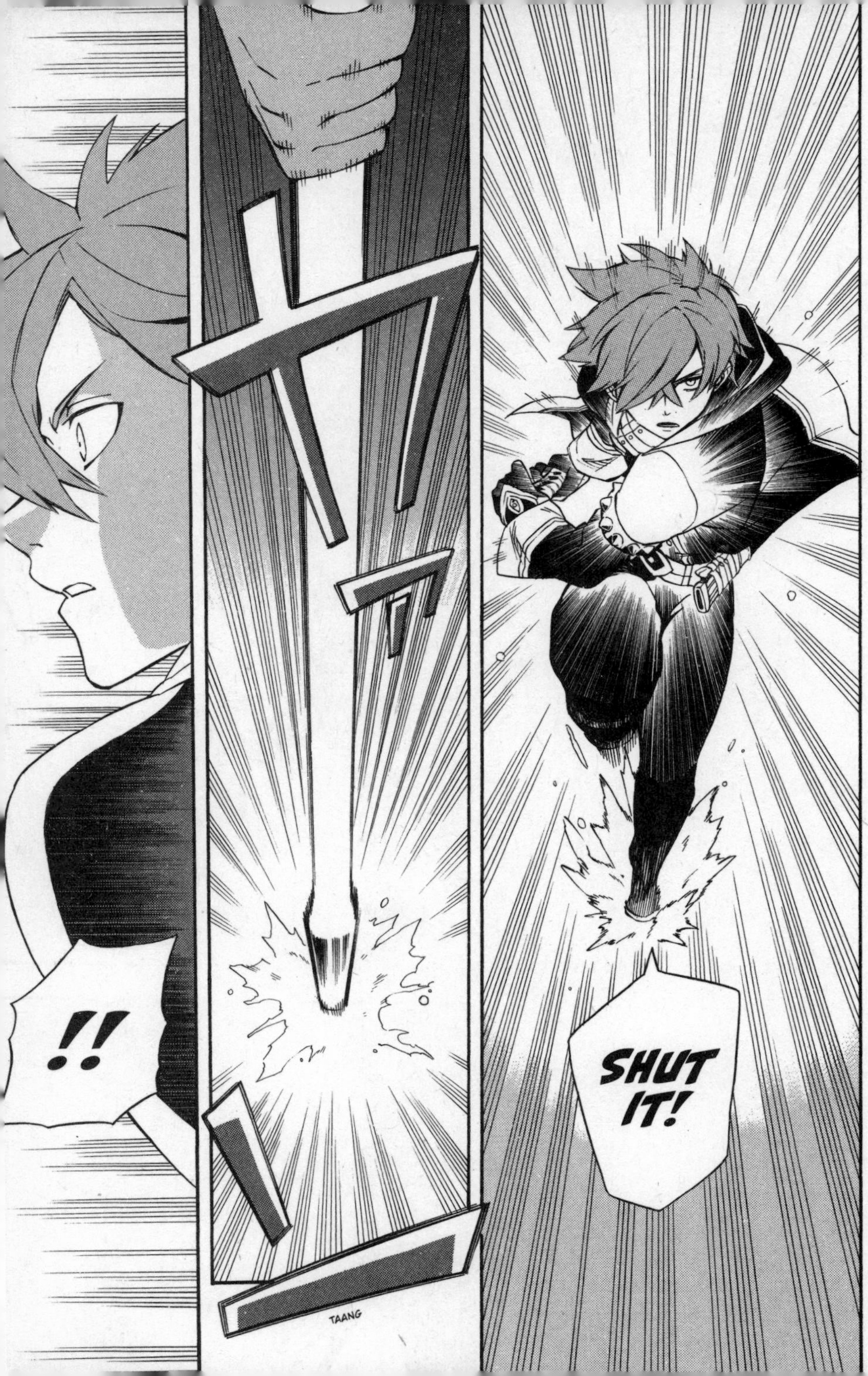
SHUT IT!
TAANG
!!

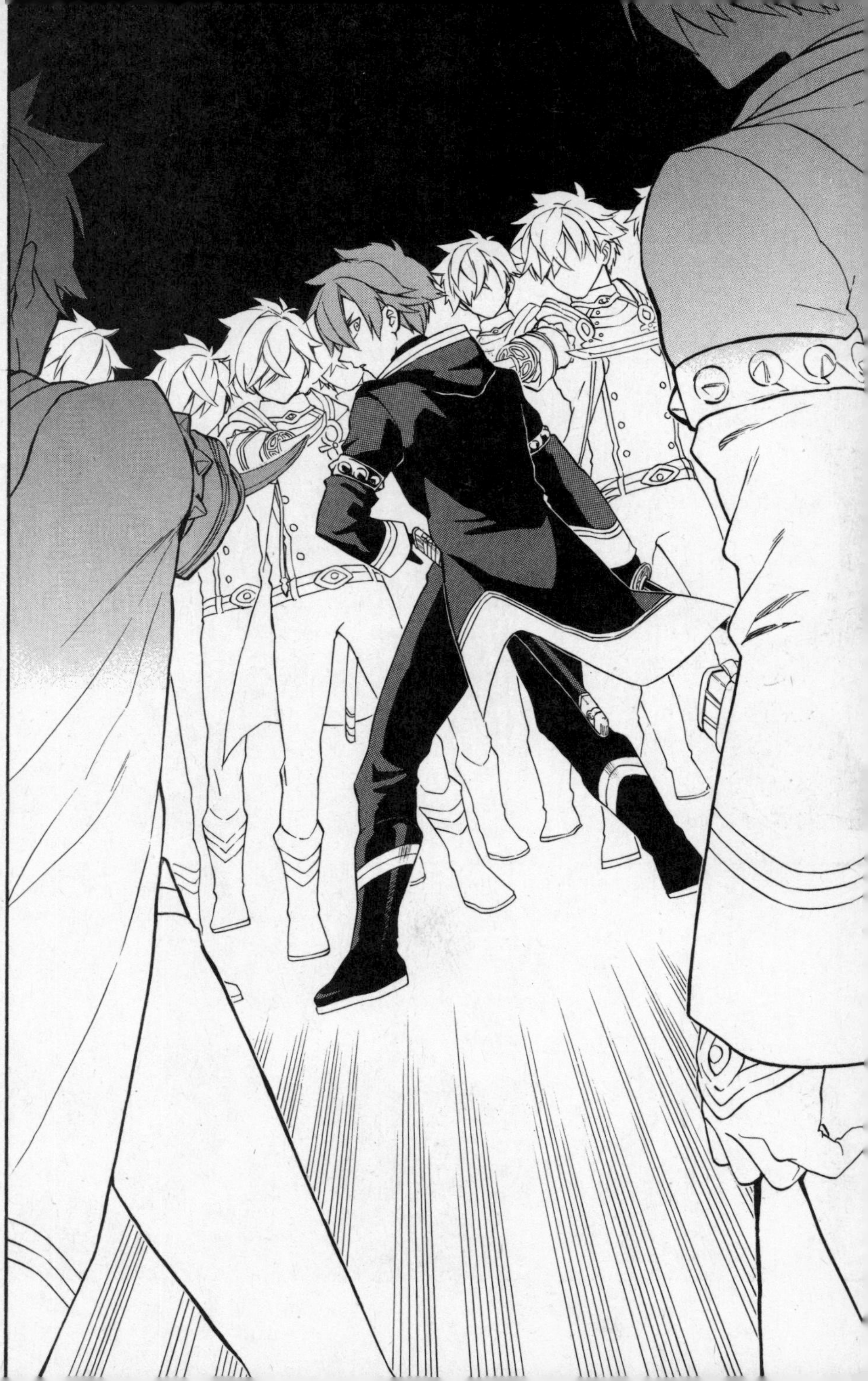

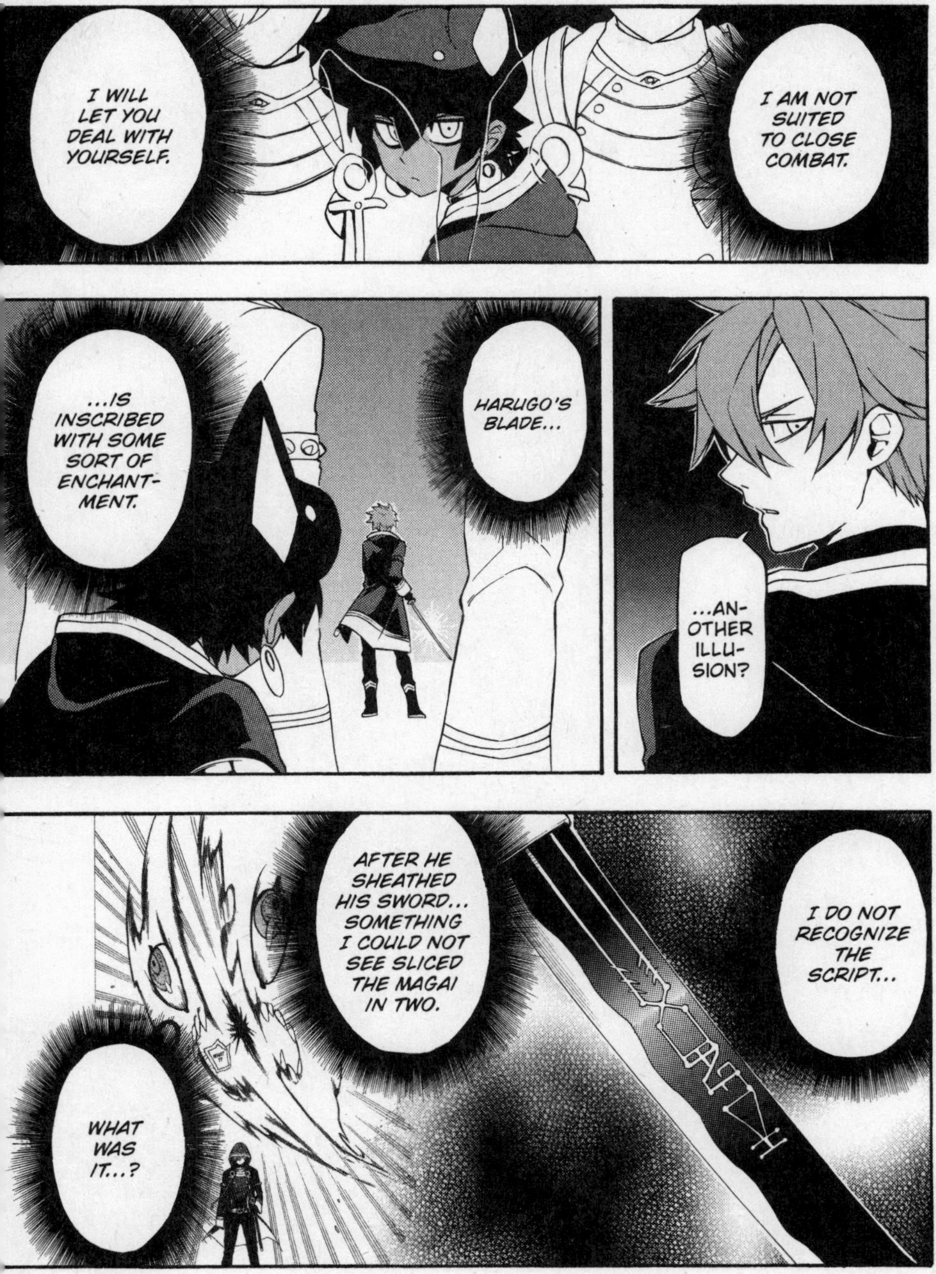
I AM NOT SUITED TO CLOSE COMBAT.
I WILL LET YOU DEAL WITH YOURSELF.
...ANOTHER ILLUSION?
HARUGO'S BLADE...
...IS INSCRIBED WITH SOME SORT OF ENCHANTMENT.
I DO NOT RECOGNIZE THE SCRIPT...
AFTER HE SHEATHED HIS SWORD... SOMETHING I COULD NOT SEE SLICED THE MAGAI IN TWO.
WHAT WAS IT...?

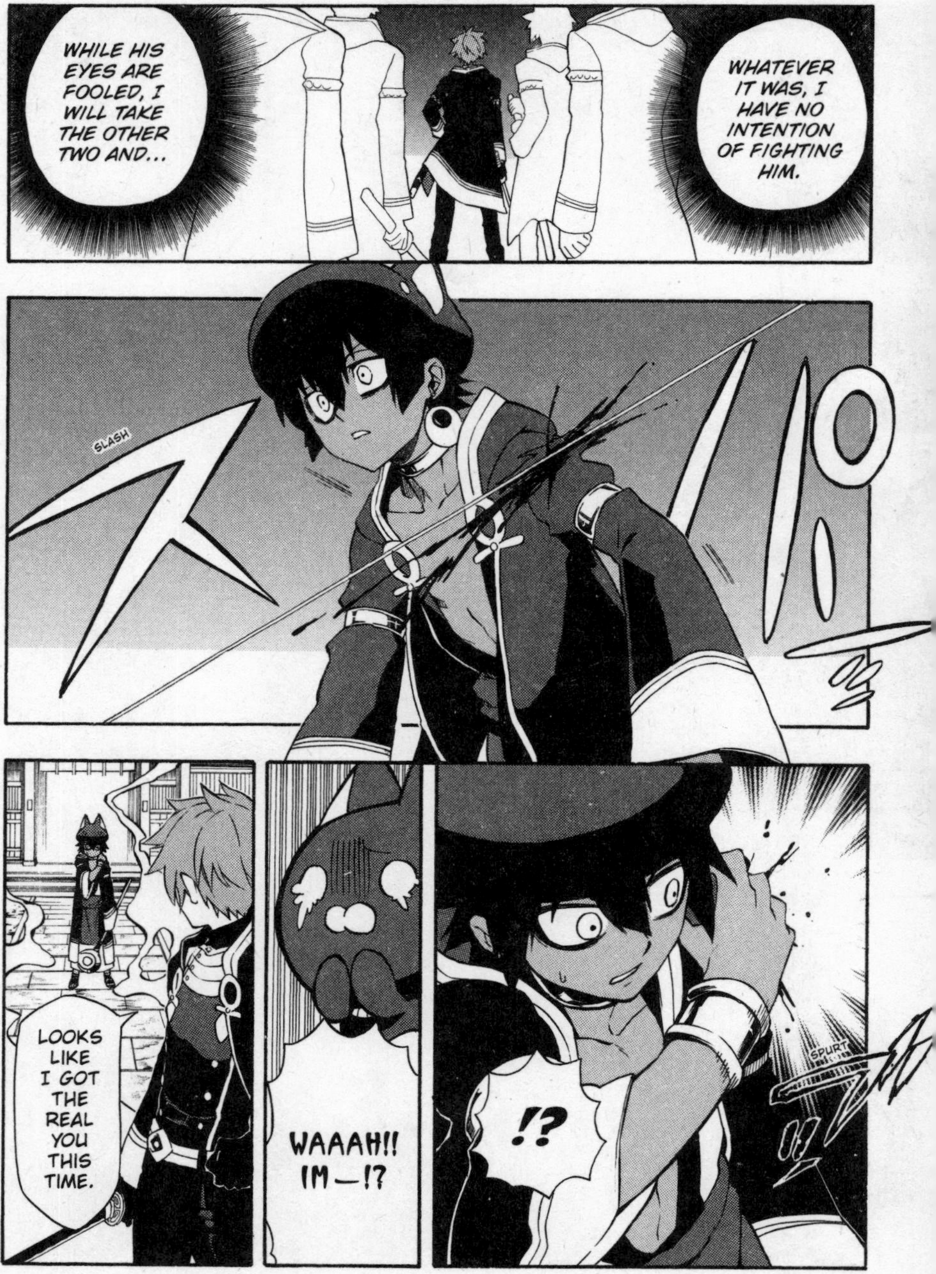
WHATEVER IT WAS, I HAVE NO INTENTION OF FIGHTING HIM.
WHILE HIS EYES ARE FOOLED, I WILL TAKE THE OTHER TWO AND...
SLASH
SPURT
!?
WAAAH!! IM—!?
LOOKS LIKE I GOT THE REAL YOU THIS TIME.

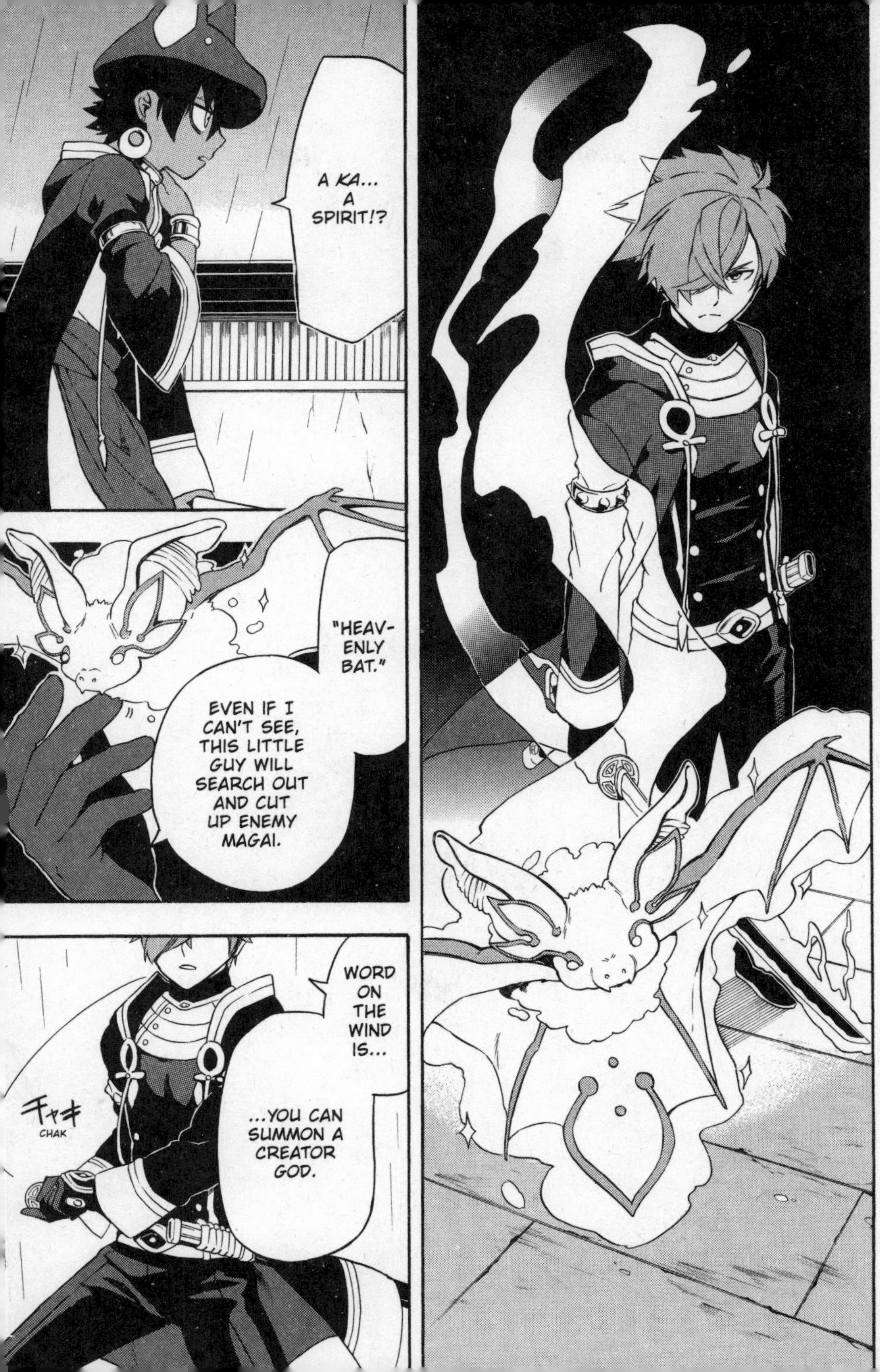
A KA... A SPIRIT!?
"HEAVENLY BAT."
EVEN IF I CAN'T SEE, THIS LITTLE GUY WILL SEARCH OUT AND CUT UP ENEMY MAGAI.
WORD ON THE WIND IS...
...YOU CAN SUMMON A CREATOR GOD.
チャキ
CHAK

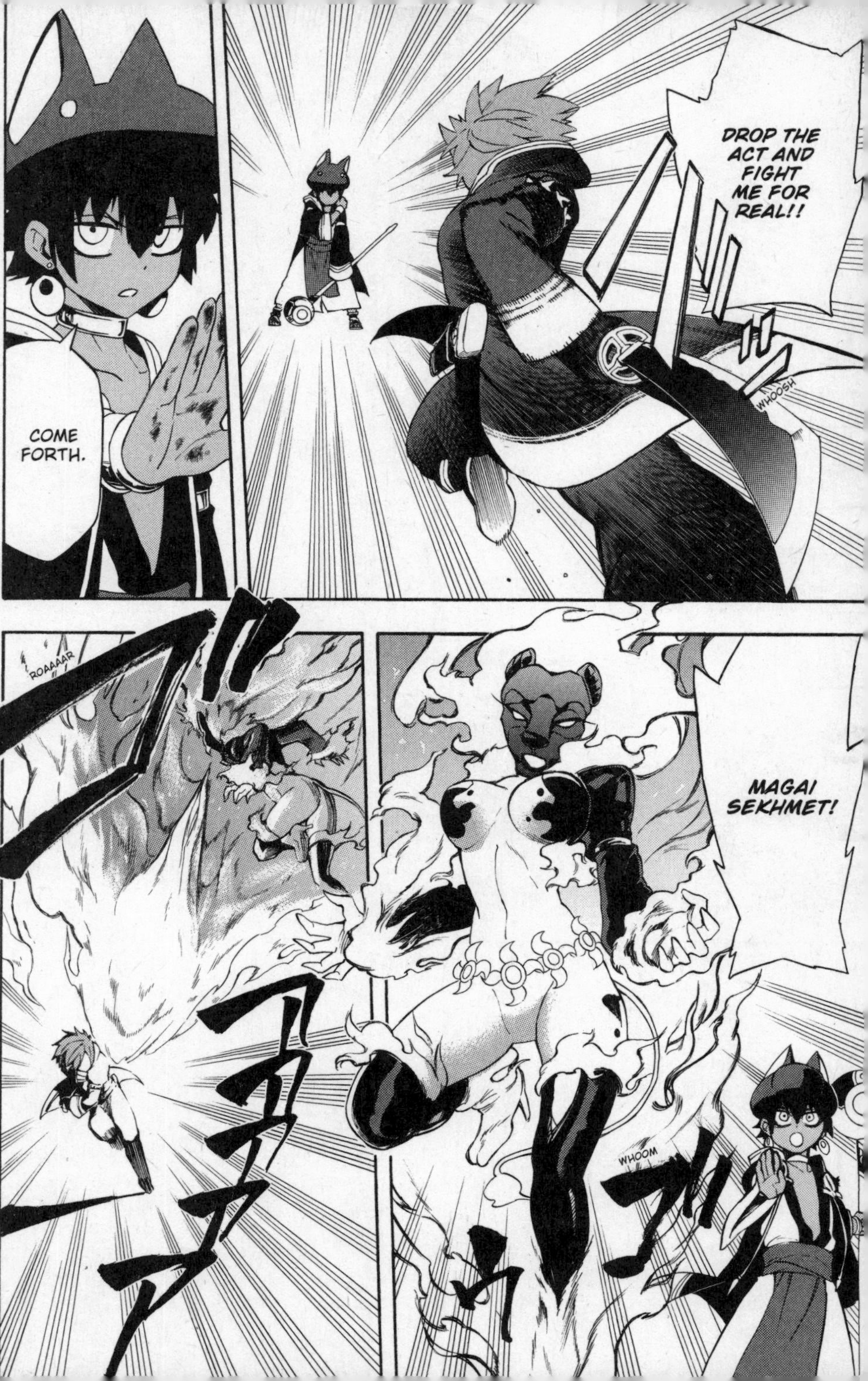
DROP THE ACT AND FIGHT ME FOR REAL!!
WHOOSH
COME FORTH.
MAGAI SEKHMET!
WHOOM
ROAAAAR

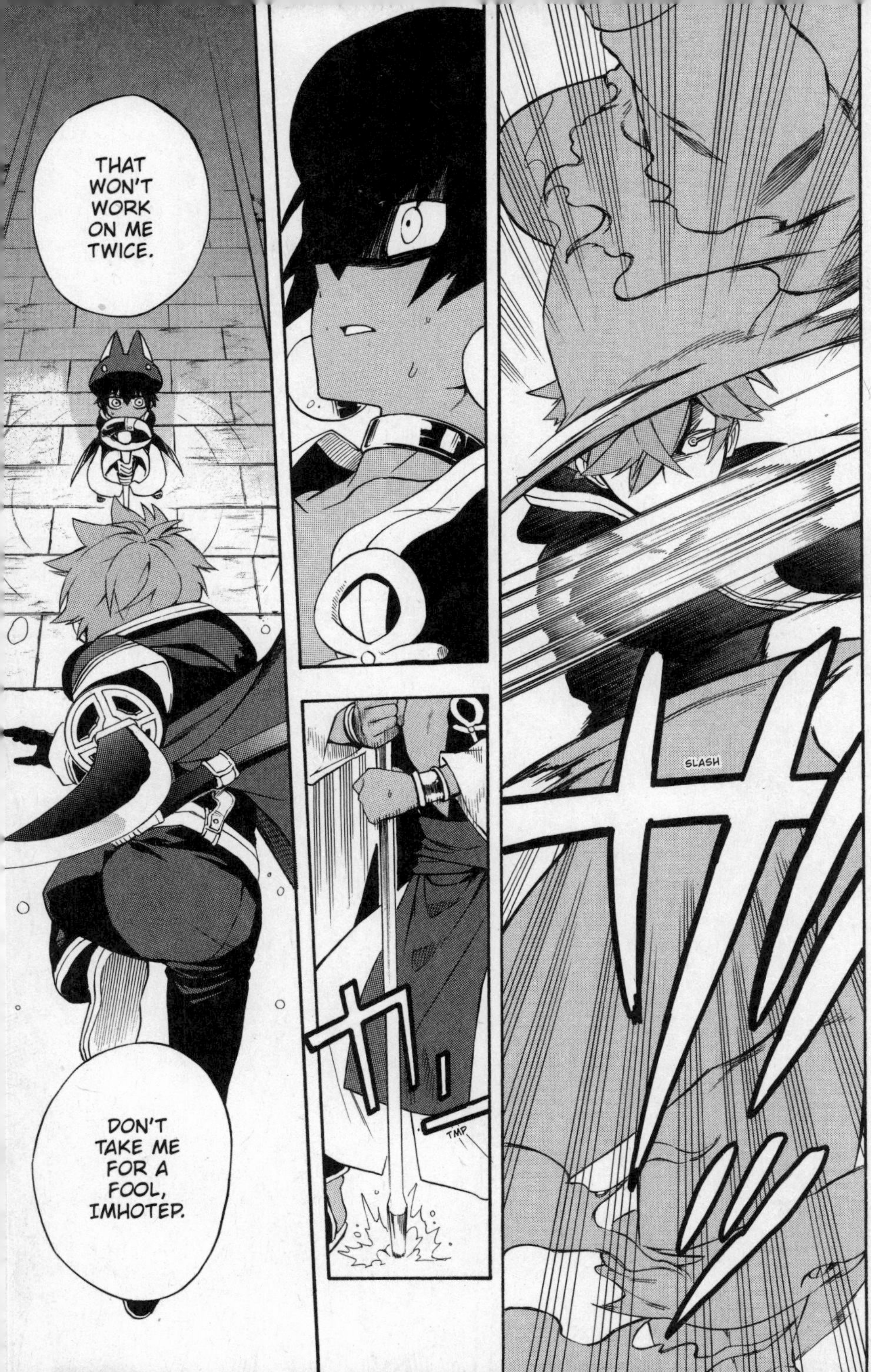
SLASH
TMP
THAT WON'T WORK ON ME TWICE.
DON'T TAKE ME FOR A FOOL, IMHOTEP.

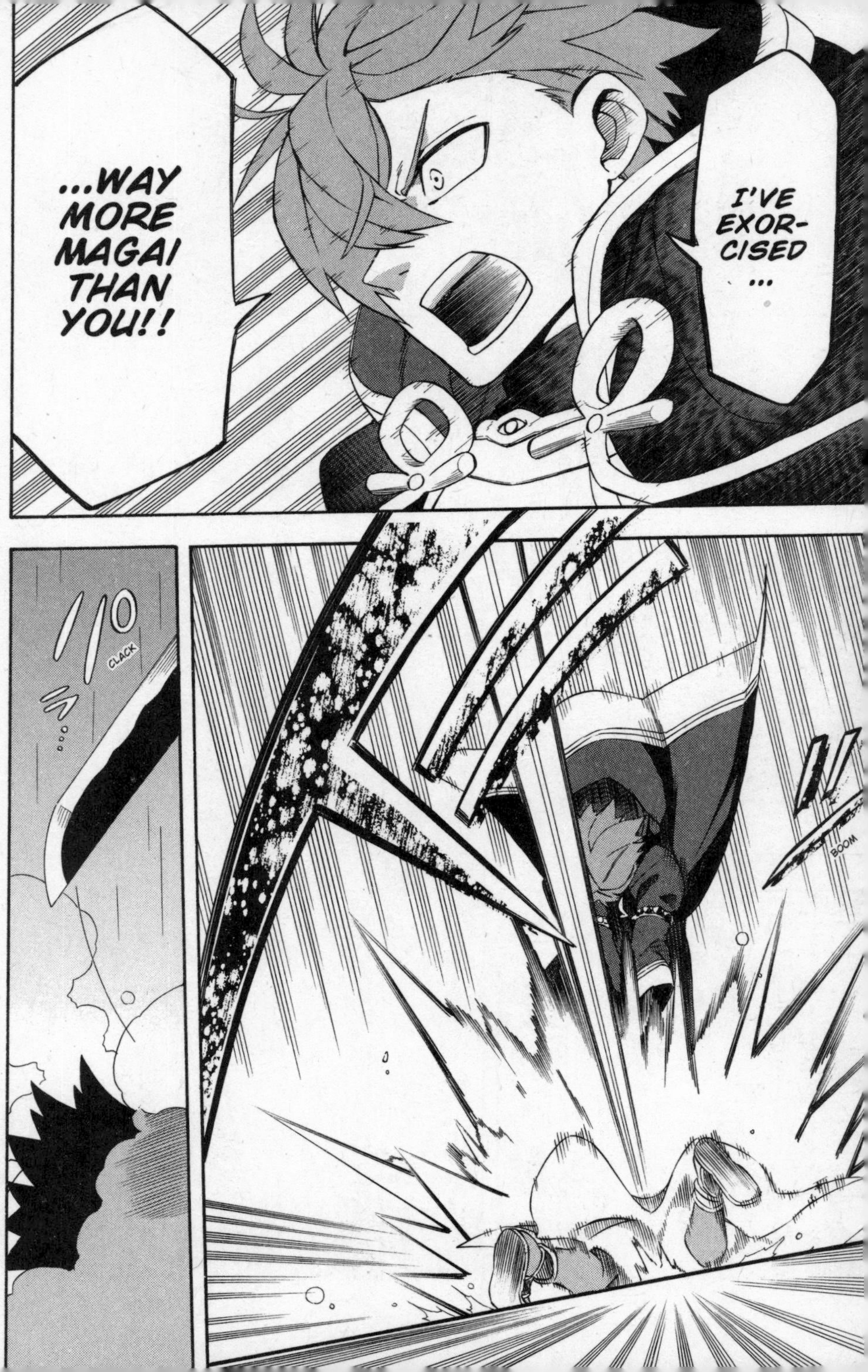
I'VE EXORCISED...
...WAY MORE MAGAI THAN YOU!!
BOOM
CLACK

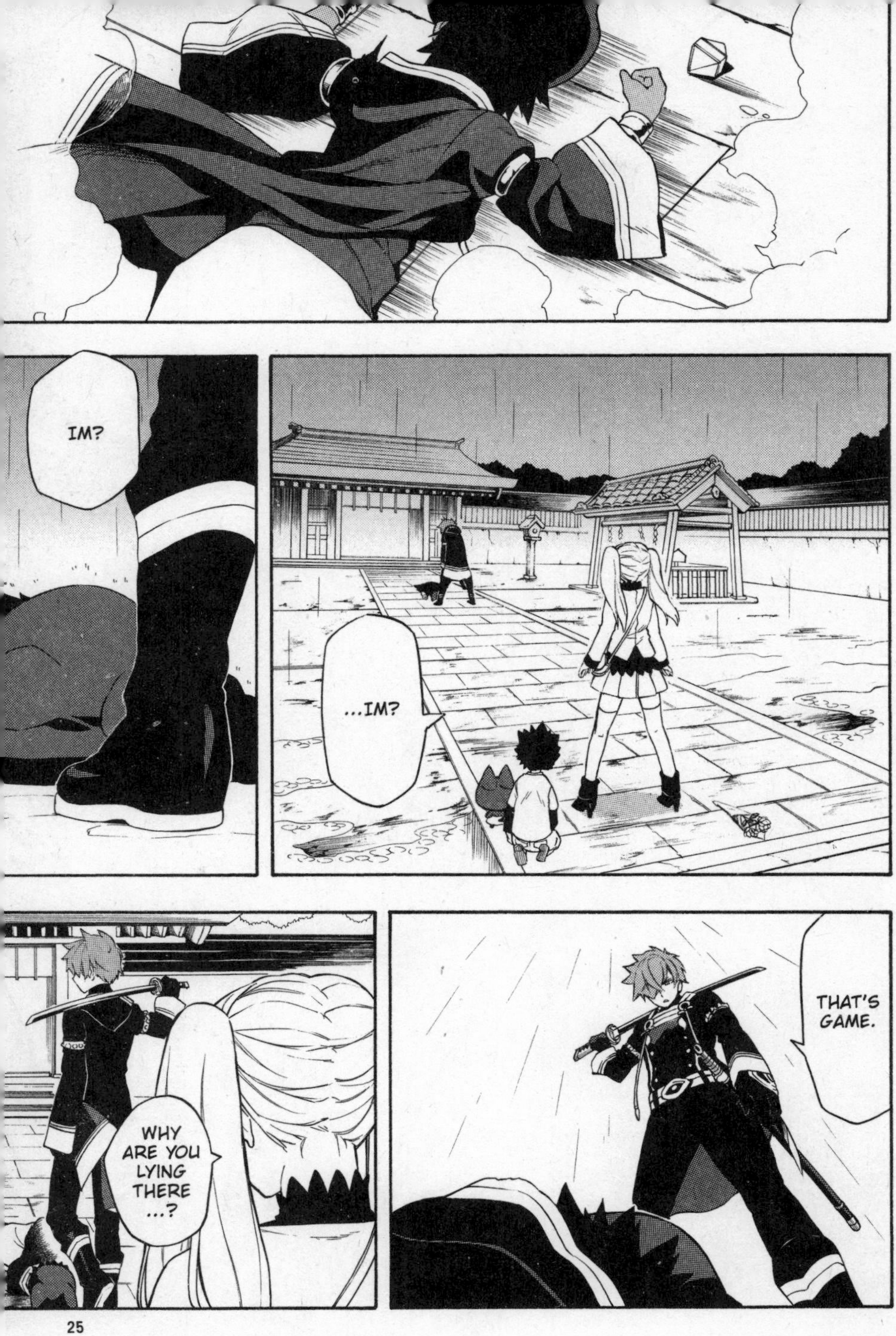
...IM?
IM?
THAT'S GAME.
WHY ARE YOU LYING THERE ...?

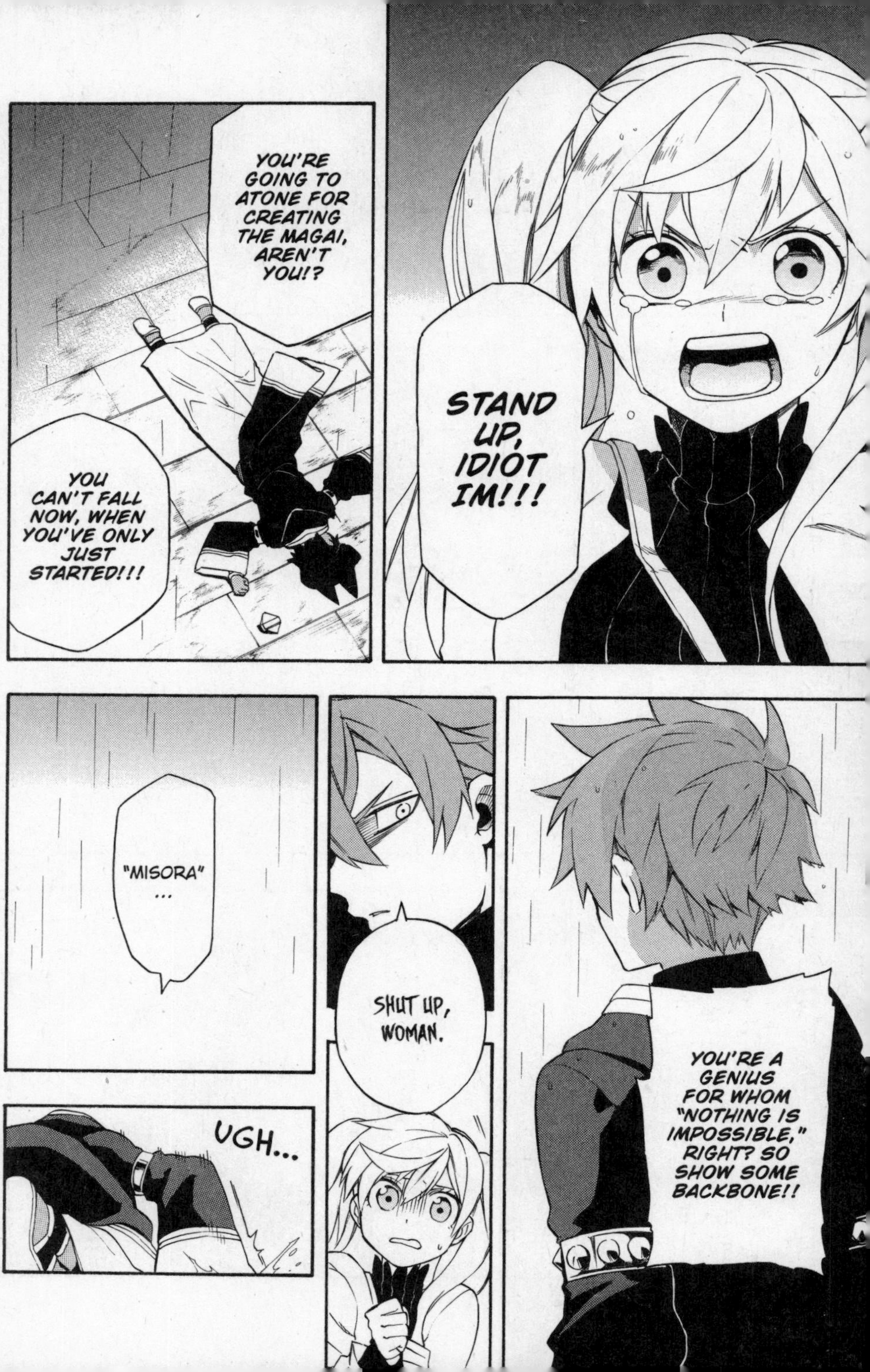
STAND UP, IDIOT IM!!!
YOU'RE GOING TO ATONE FOR CREATING THE MAGAI, AREN'T YOU!?
YOU CAN'T FALL NOW, WHEN YOU'VE ONLY JUST STARTED!!!
YOU'RE A GENIUS FOR WHOM "NOTHING IS IMPOSSIBLE," RIGHT? SO SHOW SOME BACKBONE!!
SHUT UP, WOMAN.
"MISORA" ...
UGH...

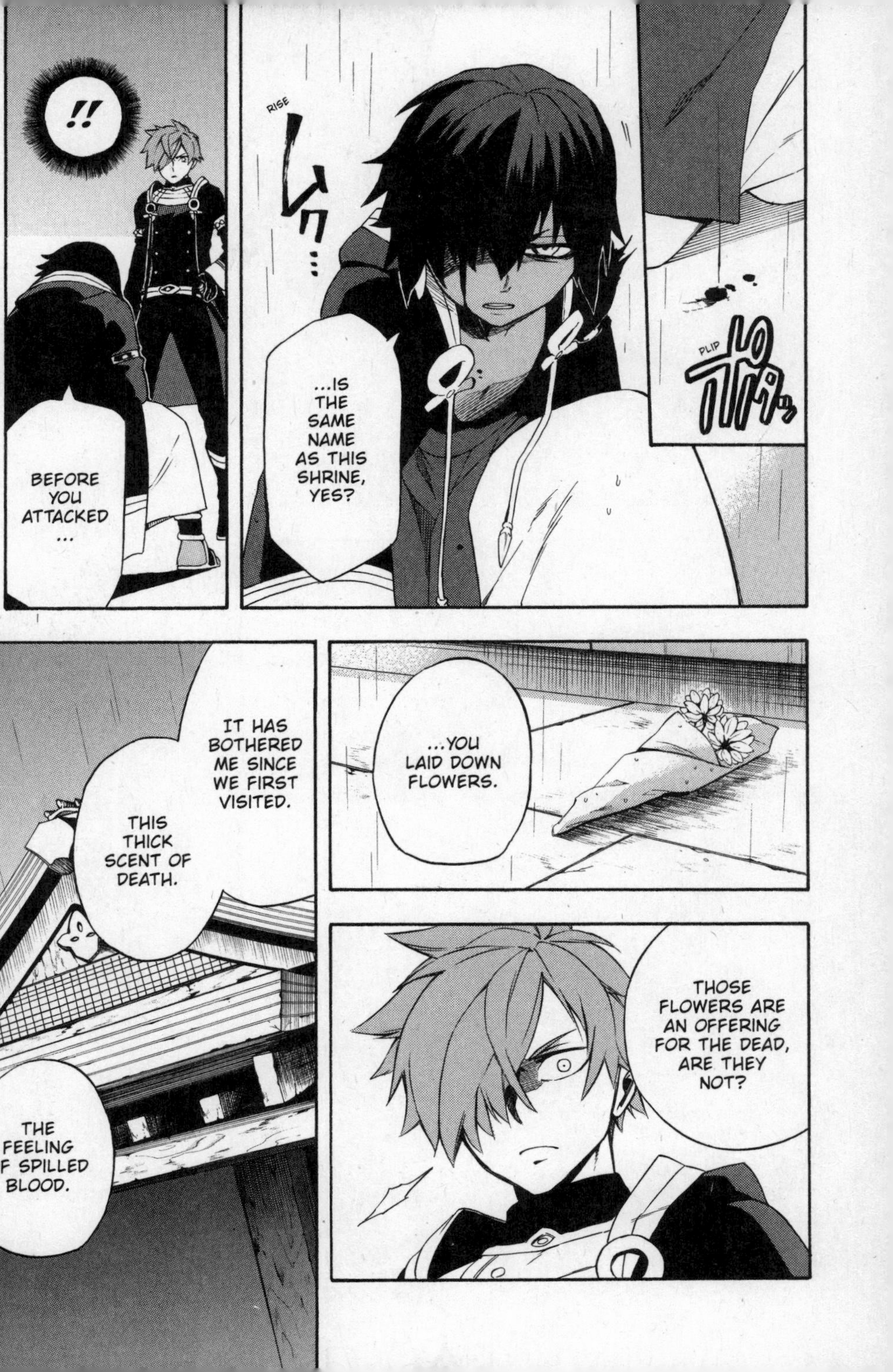
PLIP
RISE
...IS THE SAME NAME AS THIS SHRINE, YES?
!!
BEFORE YOU ATTACKED ...
...YOU LAID DOWN FLOWERS.
THOSE FLOWERS ARE AN OFFERING FOR THE DEAD, ARE THEY NOT?
IT HAS BOTHERED ME SINCE WE FIRST VISITED.
THIS THICK SCENT OF DEATH.
THE FEELING OF SPILLED BLOOD.

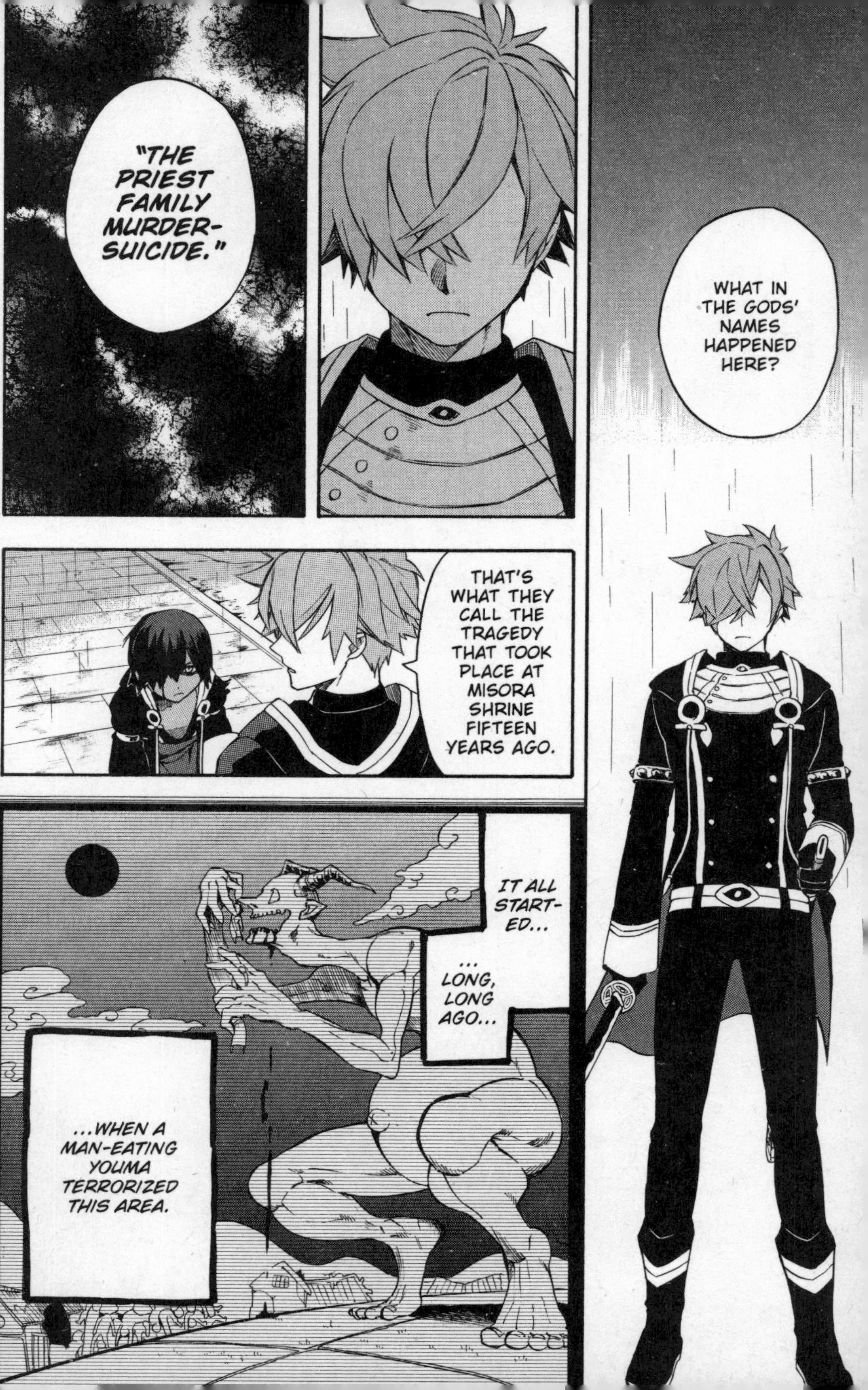
WHAT IN THE GODS' NAMES HAPPENED HERE?
"THE PRIEST FAMILY MURDER-SUICIDE."
THAT'S WHAT THEY CALL THE TRAGEDY THAT TOOK PLACE AT MISORA SHRINE FIFTEEN YEARS AGO.
IT ALL STARTED...
...LONG, LONG AGO...
...WHEN A MAN-EATING YOUMA TERRORIZED THIS AREA.

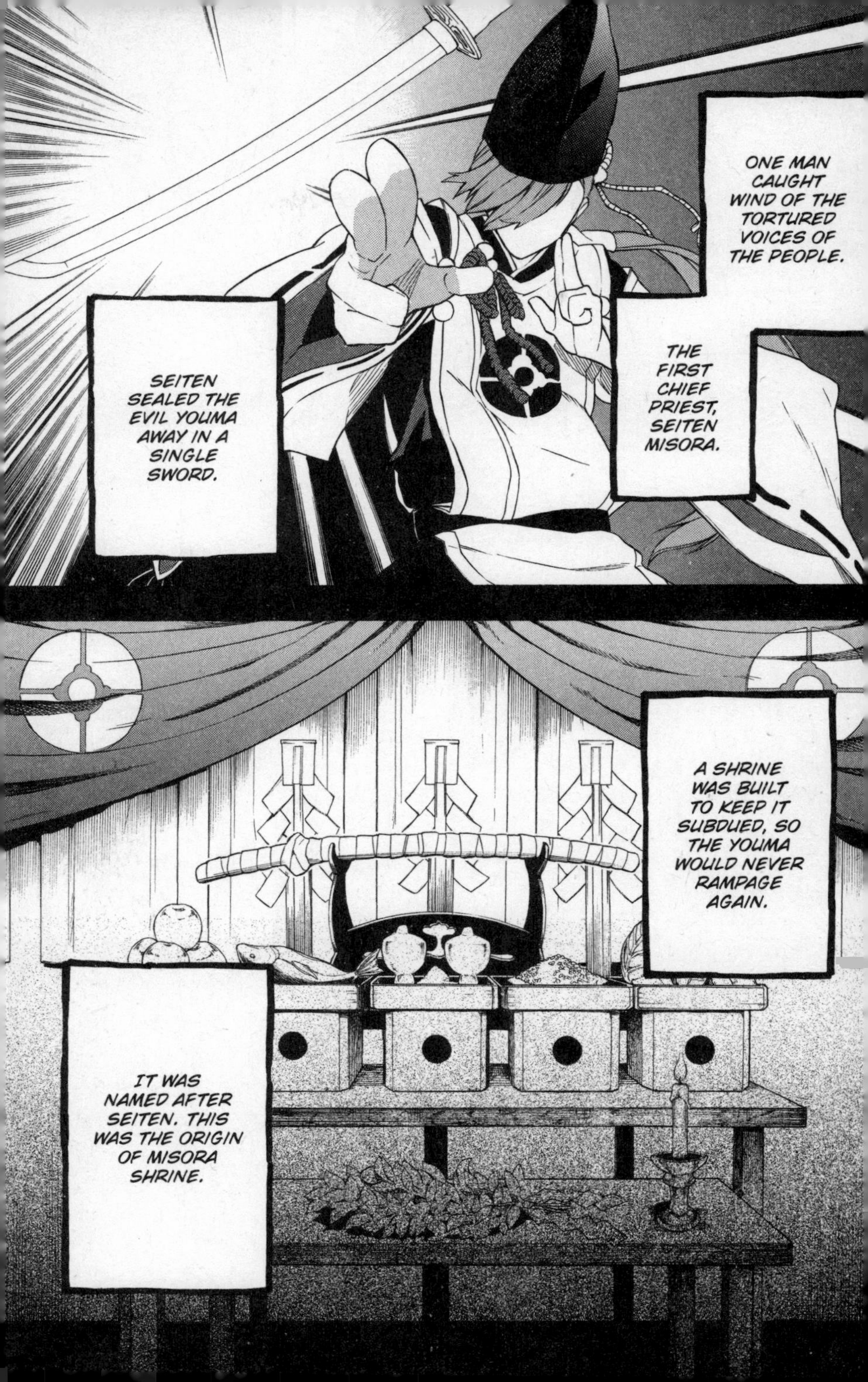
ONE MAN CAUGHT WIND OF THE TORTURED VOICES OF THE PEOPLE.
THE FIRST CHIEF PRIEST, SEITEN MISORA.
SEITEN SEALED THE EVIL YOUMA AWAY IN A SINGLE SWORD.
A SHRINE WAS BUILT TO KEEP IT SUBDUED, SO THE YOUMA WOULD NEVER RAMPAGE AGAIN.
IT WAS NAMED AFTER SEITEN. THIS WAS THE ORIGIN OF MISORA SHRINE.

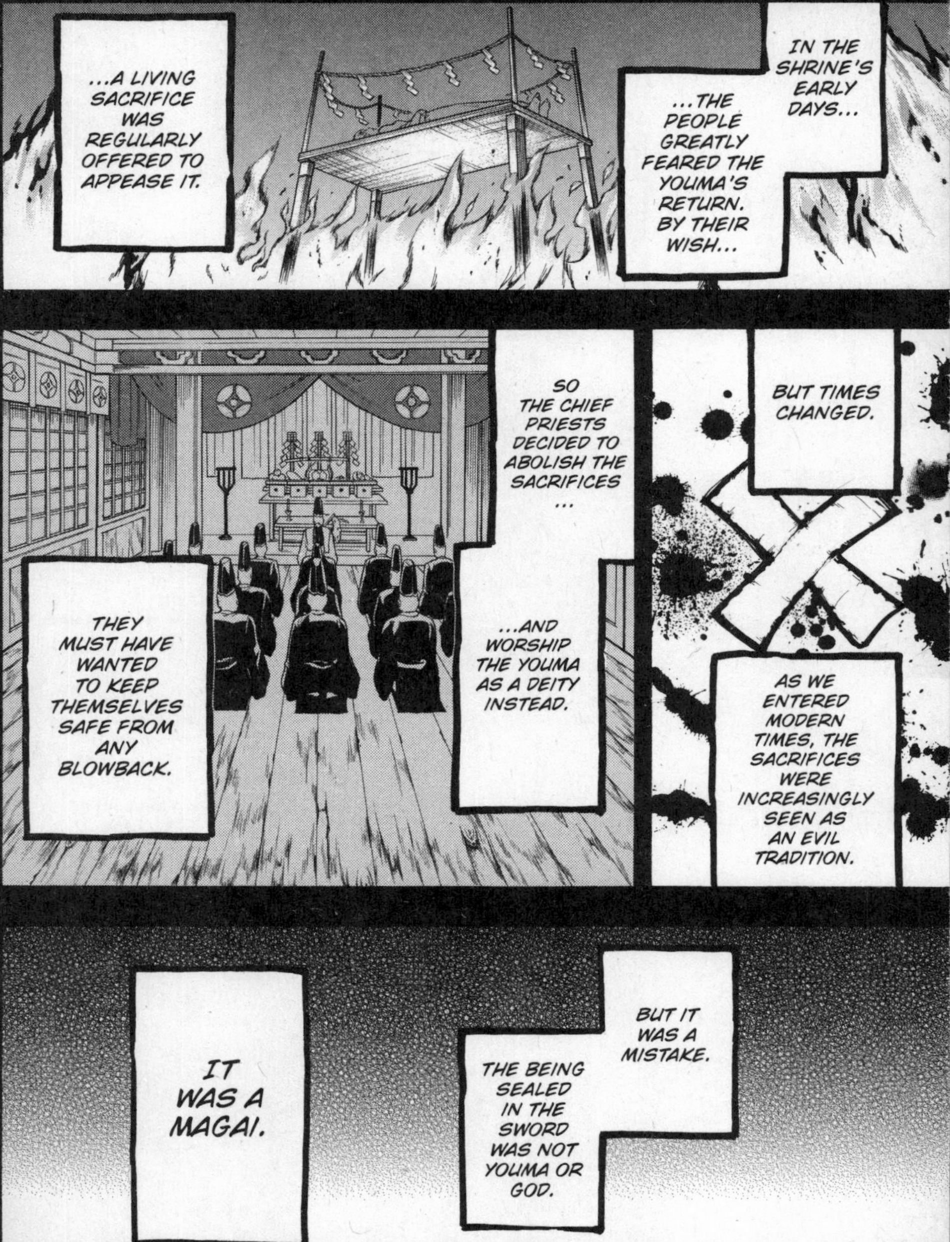
IN THE SHRINE'S EARLY DAYS...
...THE PEOPLE GREATLY FEARED THE YOUMA'S RETURN. BY THEIR WISH...
...A LIVING SACRIFICE WAS REGULARLY OFFERED TO APPEASE IT.
BUT TIMES CHANGED.
AS WE ENTERED MODERN TIMES, THE SACRIFICES WERE INCREASINGLY SEEN AS AN EVIL TRADITION.
SO THE CHIEF PRIESTS DECIDED TO ABOLISH THE SACRIFICES...
...AND WORSHIP THE YOUMA AS A DEITY INSTEAD.
THEY MUST HAVE WANTED TO KEEP THEMSELVES SAFE FROM ANY BLOWBACK.
BUT IT WAS A MISTAKE.
THE BEING SEALED IN THE SWORD WAS NOT YOUMA OR GOD.
IT WAS A MAGAI.

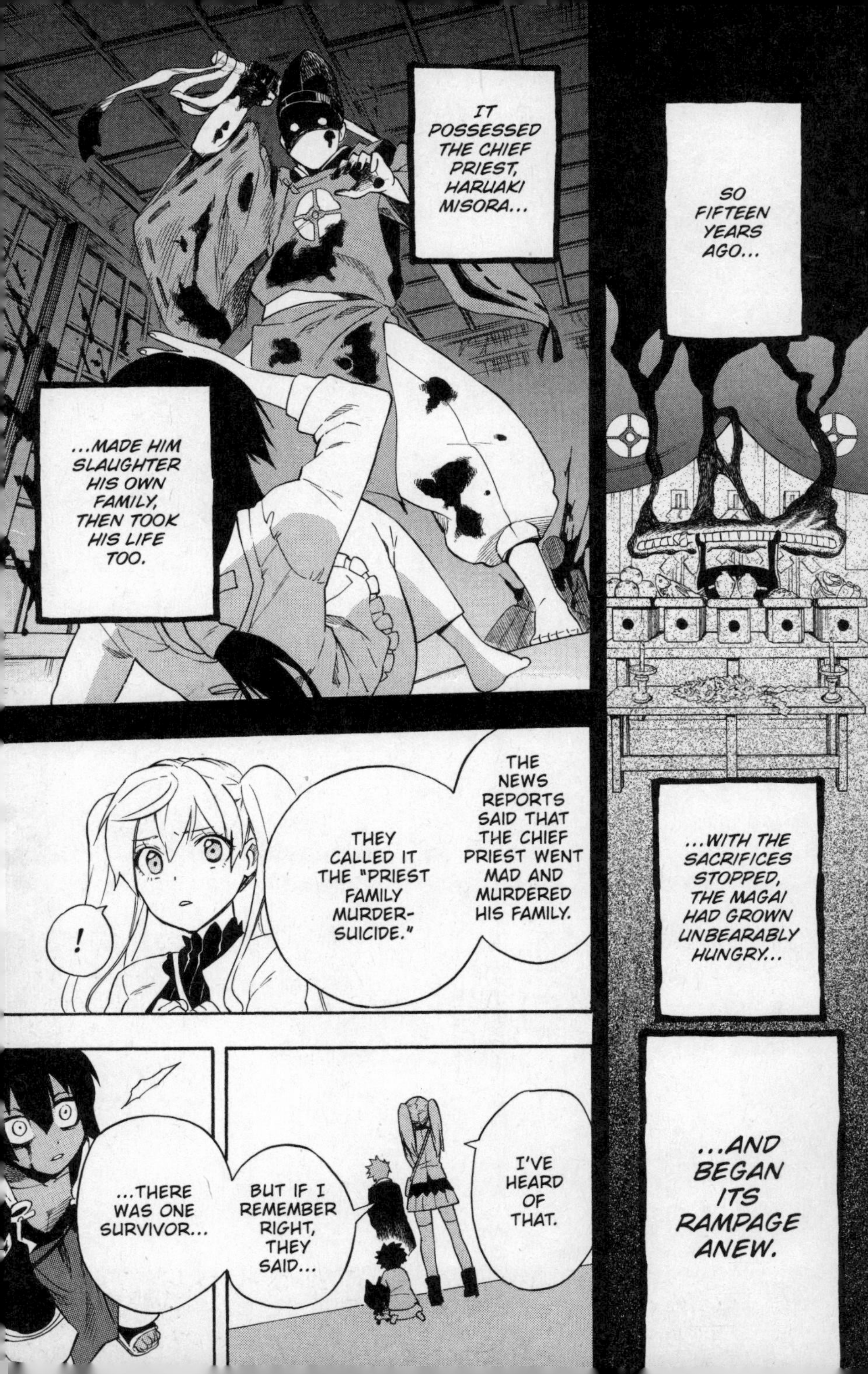
SO FIFTEEN YEARS AGO...
...WITH THE SACRIFICES STOPPED, THE MAGAI HAD GROWN UNBEARABLY HUNGRY...
...AND BEGAN ITS RAMPAGE ANEW.
IT POSSESSED THE CHIEF PRIEST, HARUAKI MISORA...
...MADE HIM SLAUGHTER HIS OWN FAMILY, THEN TOOK HIS LIFE TOO.
THE NEWS REPORTS SAID THAT THE CHIEF PRIEST WENT MAD AND MURDERED HIS FAMILY.
THEY CALLED IT THE "PRIEST FAMILY MURDER-SUICIDE."
!
I'VE HEARD OF THAT.
BUT IF I REMEMBER RIGHT, THEY SAID...
...THERE WAS ONE SURVIVOR...

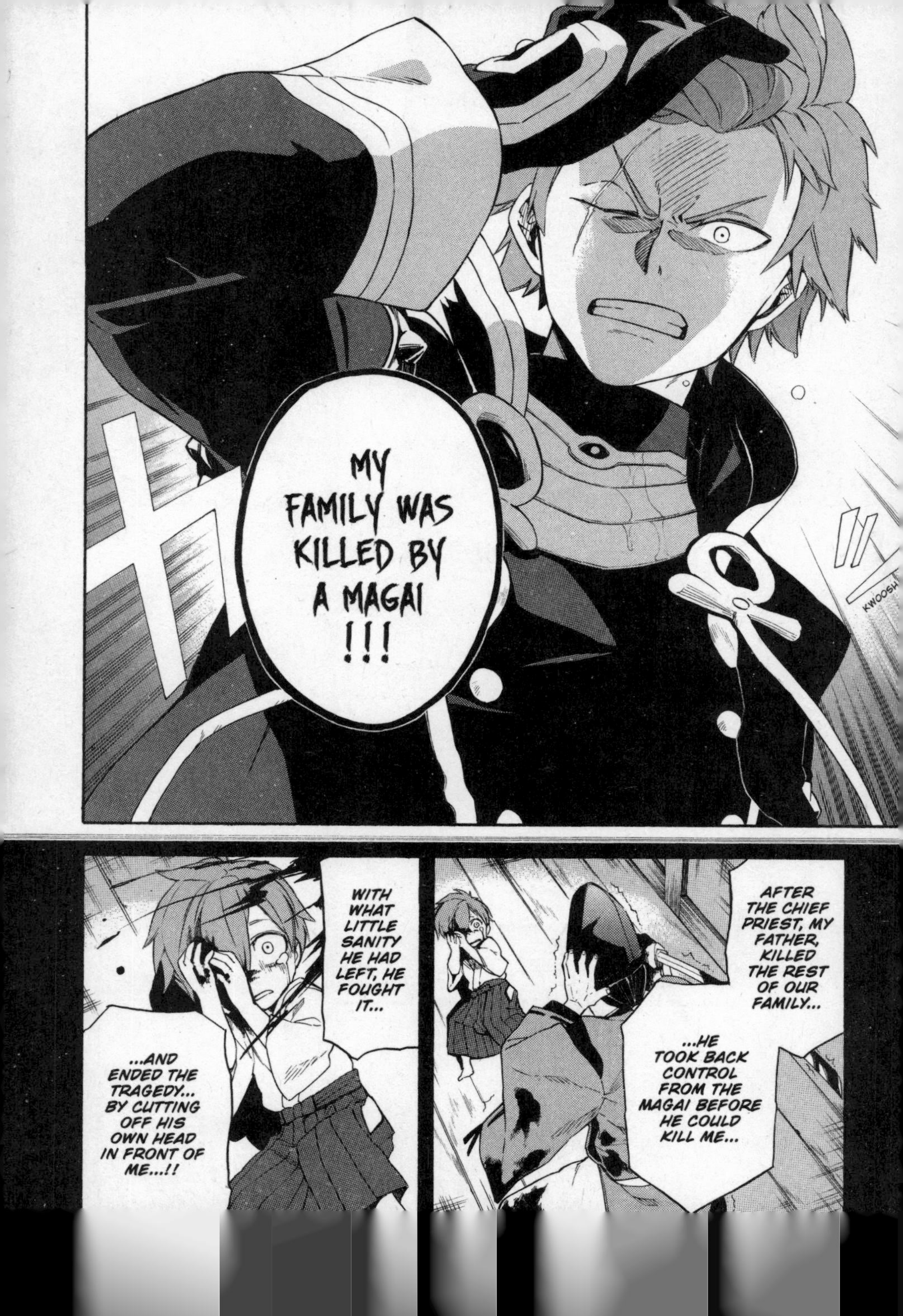

MY FAMILY WAS KILLED BY A MAGAI !!!
KWOOSH
AFTER THE CHIEF PRIEST, MY FATHER, KILLED THE REST OF OUR FAMILY...
...HE TOOK BACK CONTROL FROM THE MAGAI BEFORE HE COULD KILL ME...
WITH WHAT LITTLE SANITY HE HAD LEFT, HE FOUGHT IT...
...AND ENDED THE TRAGEDY... BY CUTTING OFF HIS OWN HEAD IN FRONT OF ME...!!

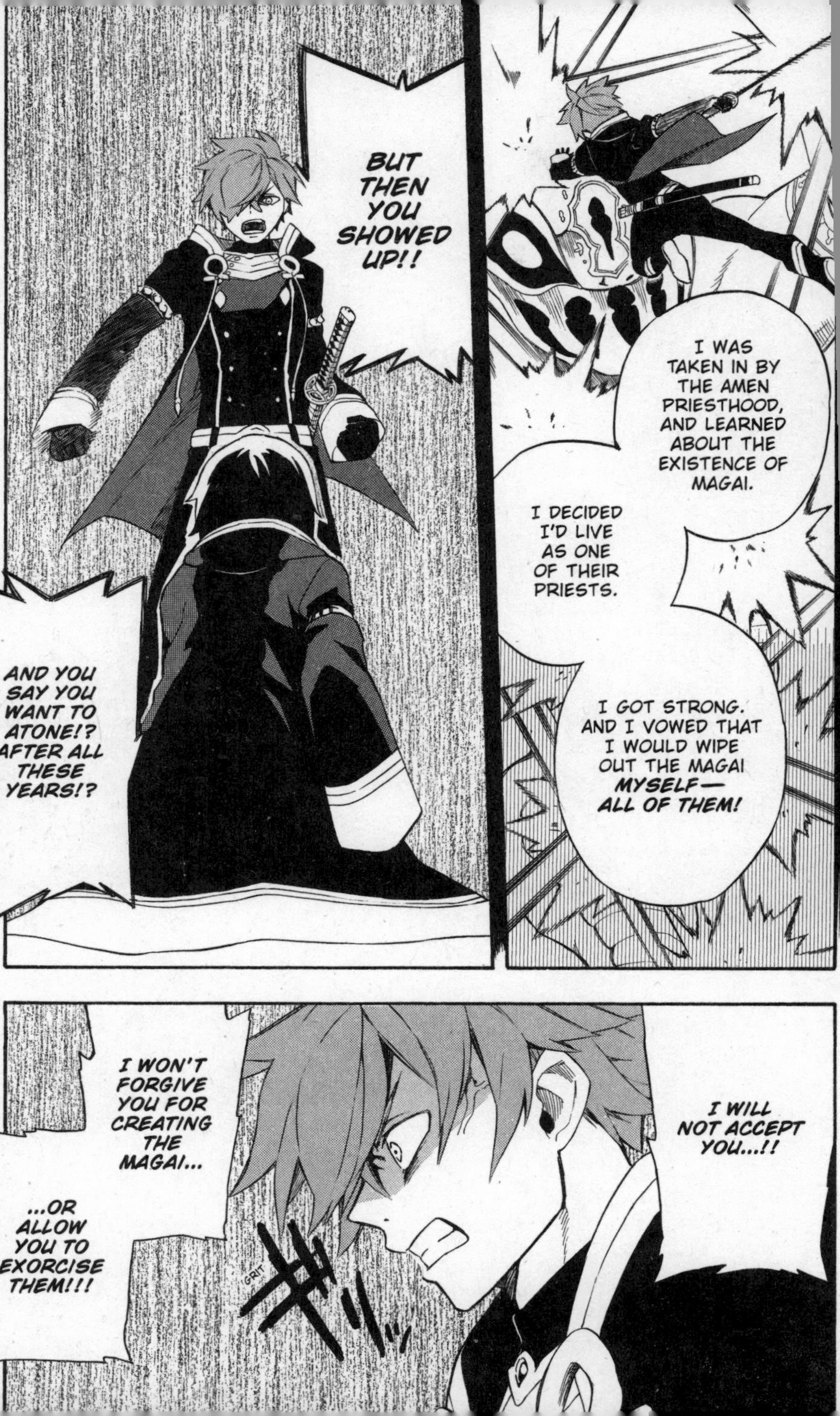
I WAS TAKEN IN BY THE AMEN PRIESTHOOD, AND LEARNED ABOUT THE EXISTENCE OF MAGAI.
I DECIDED I'D LIVE AS ONE OF THEIR PRIESTS.
I GOT STRONG. AND I VOWED THAT I WOULD WIPE OUT THE MAGAI MYSELF—ALL OF THEM!
BUT THEN YOU SHOWED UP!!
AND YOU SAY YOU WANT TO ATONE!? AFTER ALL THESE YEARS!?
I WILL NOT ACCEPT YOU...!!
I WON'T FORGIVE YOU FOR CREATING THE MAGAI...
...OR ALLOW YOU TO EXORCISE THEM!!!
GRIT

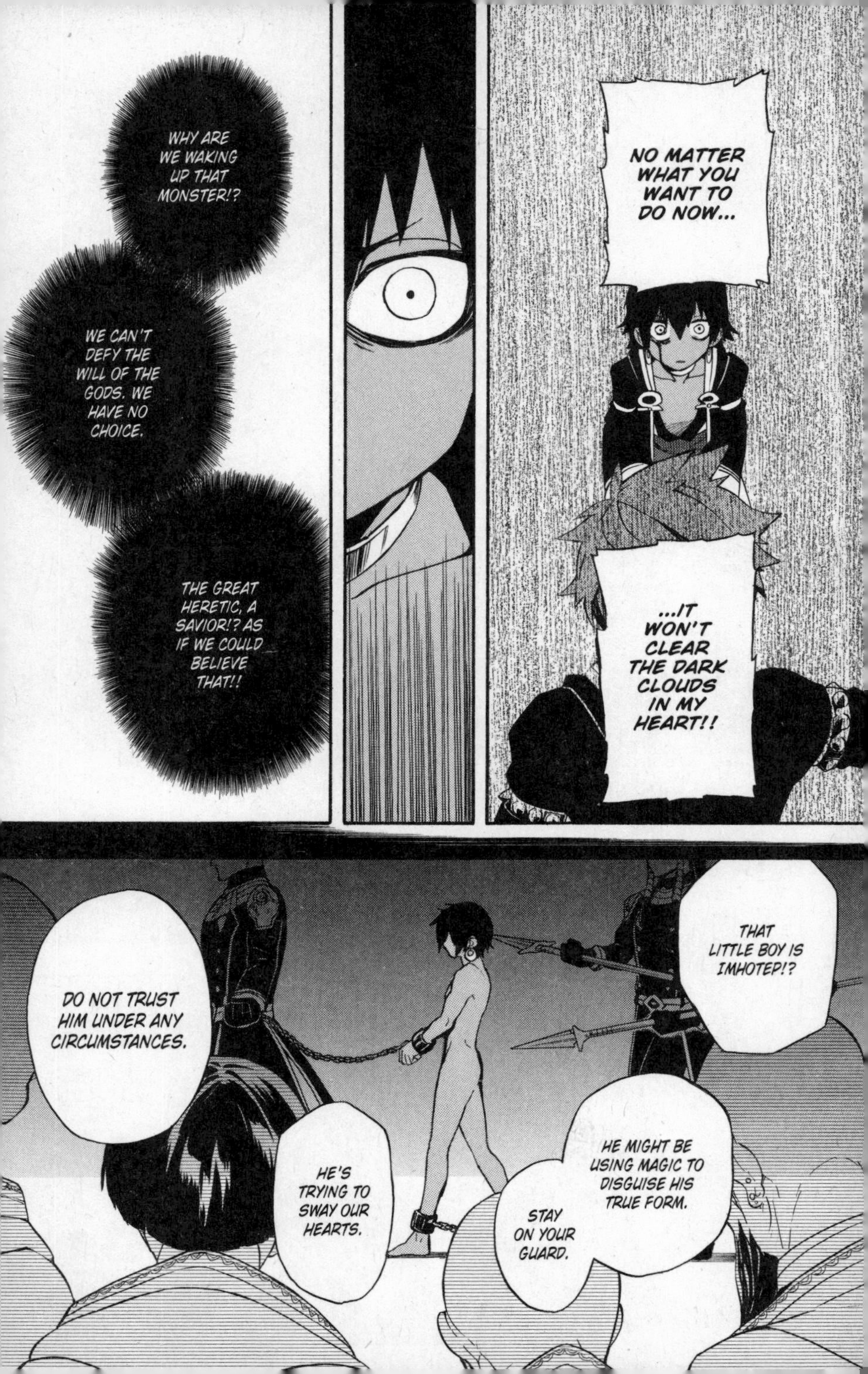

NO MATTER WHAT YOU WANT TO DO NOW...
...IT WON'T CLEAR THE DARK CLOUDS IN MY HEART!!
WHY ARE WE WAKING UP THAT MONSTER!?
WE CAN'T DEFY THE WILL OF THE GODS. WE HAVE NO CHOICE.
THE GREAT HERETIC, A SAVIOR!? AS IF WE COULD BELIEVE THAT!!
THAT LITTLE BOY IS IMHOTEP!?
DO NOT TRUST HIM UNDER ANY CIRCUMSTANCES.
HE MIGHT BE USING MAGIC TO DISGUISE HIS TRUE FORM.
STAY ON YOUR GUARD.
HE'S TRYING TO SWAY OUR HEARTS.

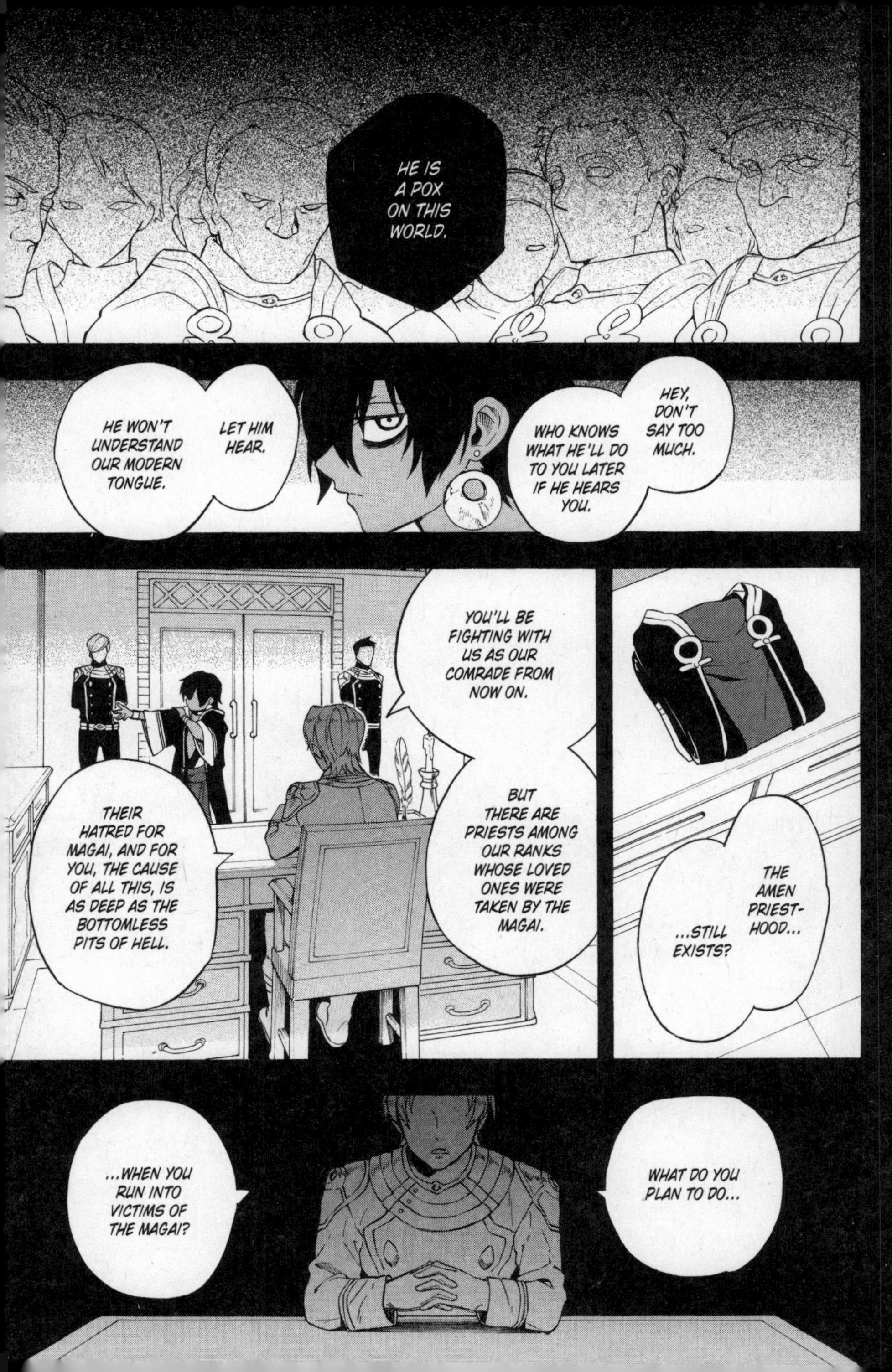
HE IS A POX ON THIS WORLD.
HEY, DON'T SAY TOO MUCH.
WHO KNOWS WHAT HE'LL DO TO YOU LATER IF HE HEARS YOU.
LET HIM HEAR.
HE WON'T UNDERSTAND OUR MODERN TONGUE.
THE AMEN PRIEST-HOOD...
...STILL EXISTS?
YOU'LL BE FIGHTING WITH US AS OUR COMRADE FROM NOW ON.
BUT THERE ARE PRIESTS AMONG OUR RANKS WHOSE LOVED ONES WERE TAKEN BY THE MAGAI.
THEIR HATRED FOR MAGAI, AND FOR YOU, THE CAUSE OF ALL THIS, IS AS DEEP AS THE BOTTOMLESS PITS OF HELL.
WHAT DO YOU PLAN TO DO...
...WHEN YOU RUN INTO VICTIMS OF THE MAGAI?

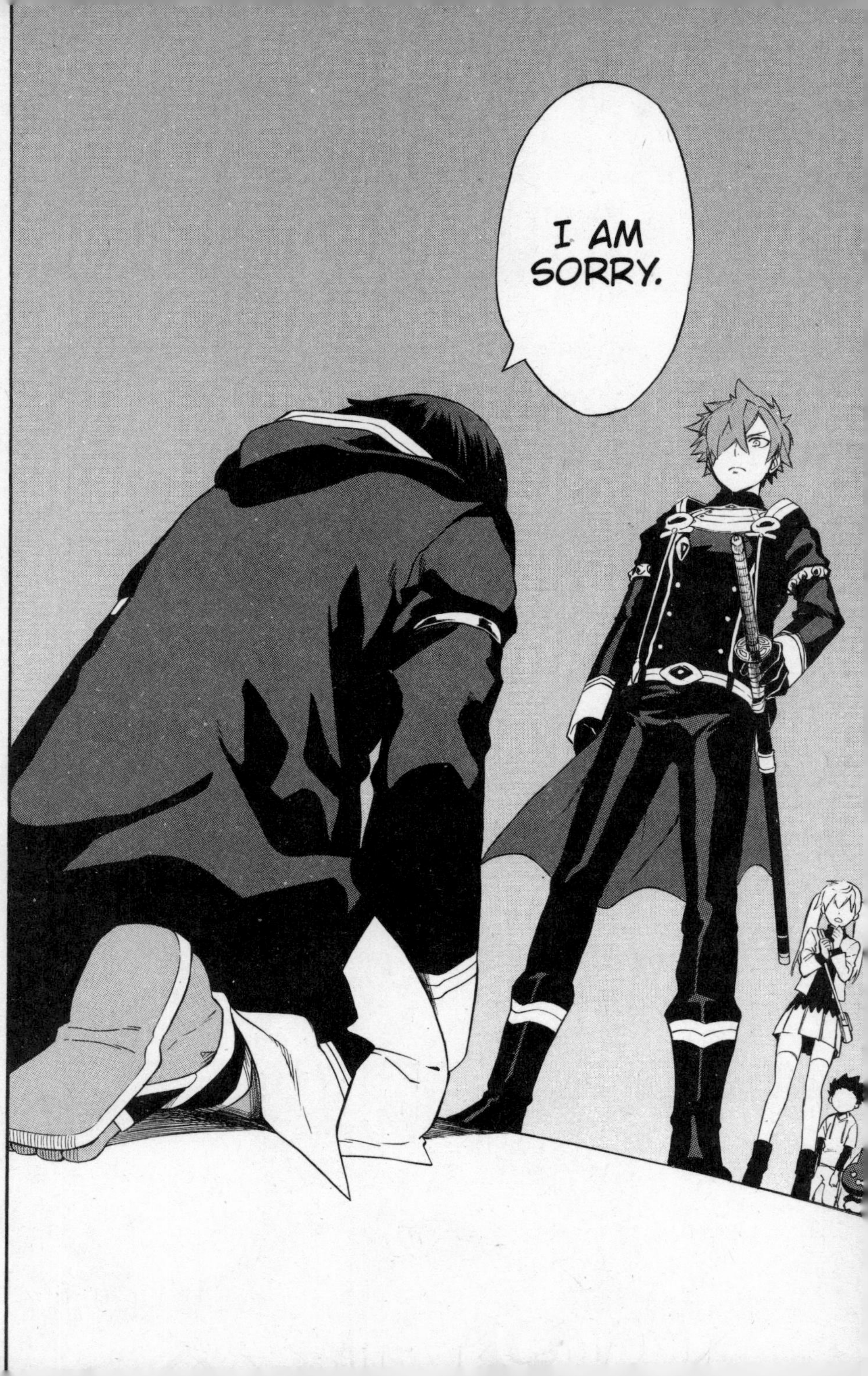
I AM SORRY.

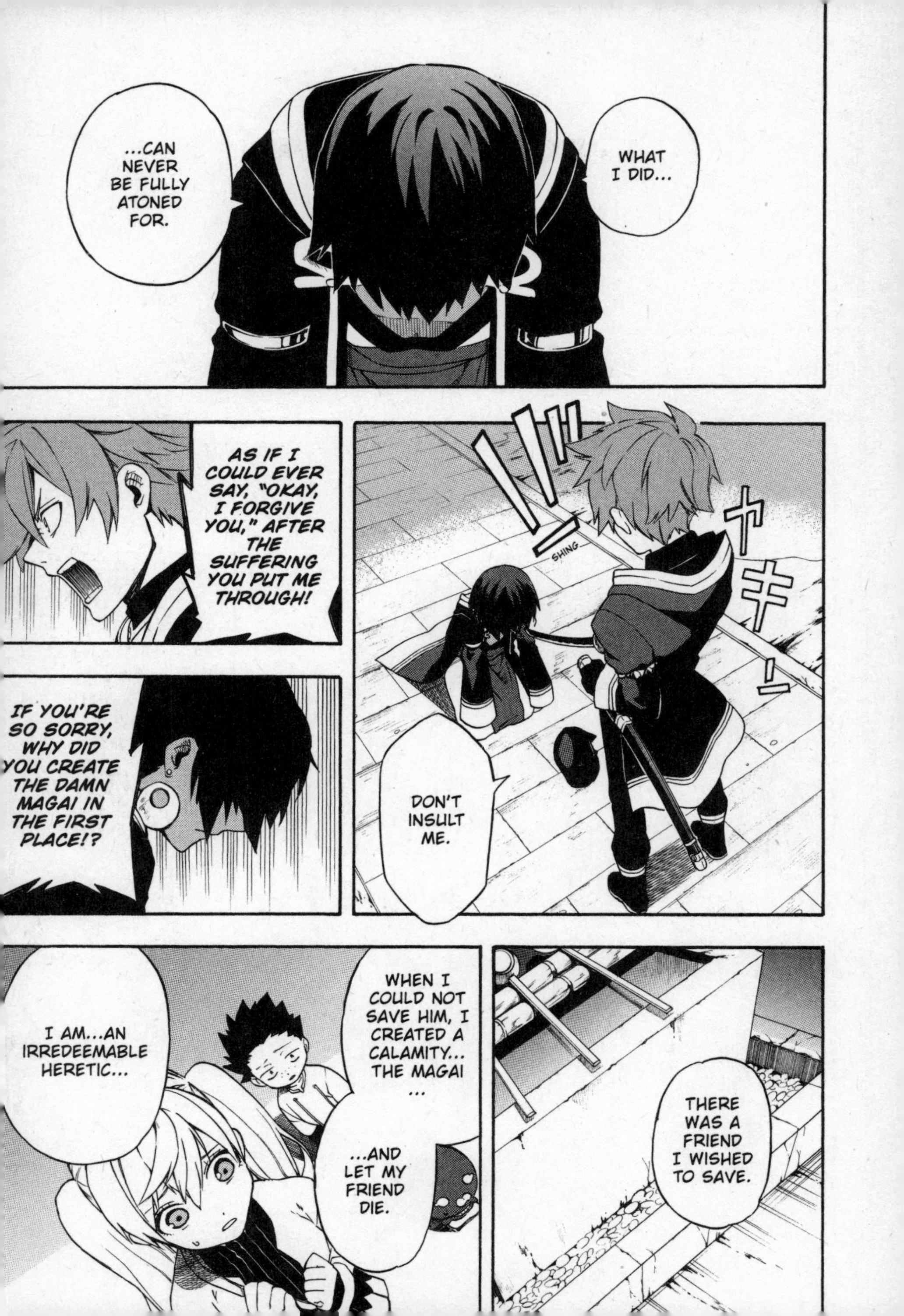
WHAT I DID...
...CAN NEVER BE FULLY ATONED FOR.
SHING
DON'T INSULT ME.
AS IF I COULD EVER SAY, "OKAY, I FORGIVE YOU," AFTER THE SUFFERING YOU PUT ME THROUGH!
IF YOU'RE SO SORRY, WHY DID YOU CREATE THE DAMN MAGAI IN THE FIRST PLACE!?
THERE WAS A FRIEND I WISHED TO SAVE.
WHEN I COULD NOT SAVE HIM, I CREATED A CALAMITY... THE MAGAI ...
...AND LET MY FRIEND DIE.
I AM...AN IRREDEEMABLE HERETIC...

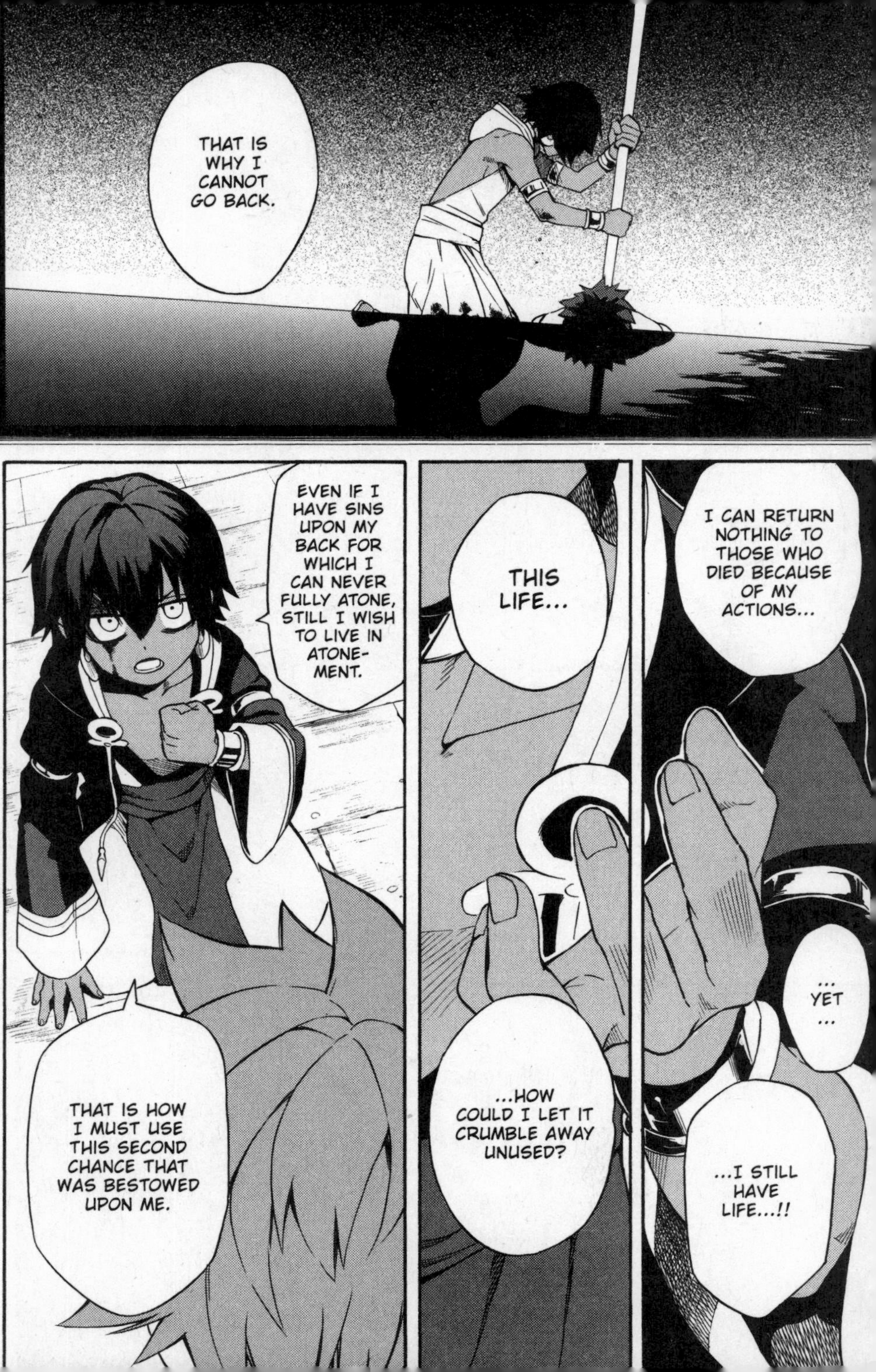
THAT IS WHY I CANNOT GO BACK.
I CAN RETURN NOTHING TO THOSE WHO DIED BECAUSE OF MY ACTIONS...
... YET ...
...I STILL HAVE LIFE...!!
THIS LIFE...
...HOW COULD I LET IT CRUMBLE AWAY UNUSED?
EVEN IF I HAVE SINS UPON MY BACK FOR WHICH I CAN NEVER FULLY ATONE, STILL I WISH TO LIVE IN ATONE-MENT.
THAT IS HOW I MUST USE THIS SECOND CHANCE THAT WAS BESTOWED UPON ME.

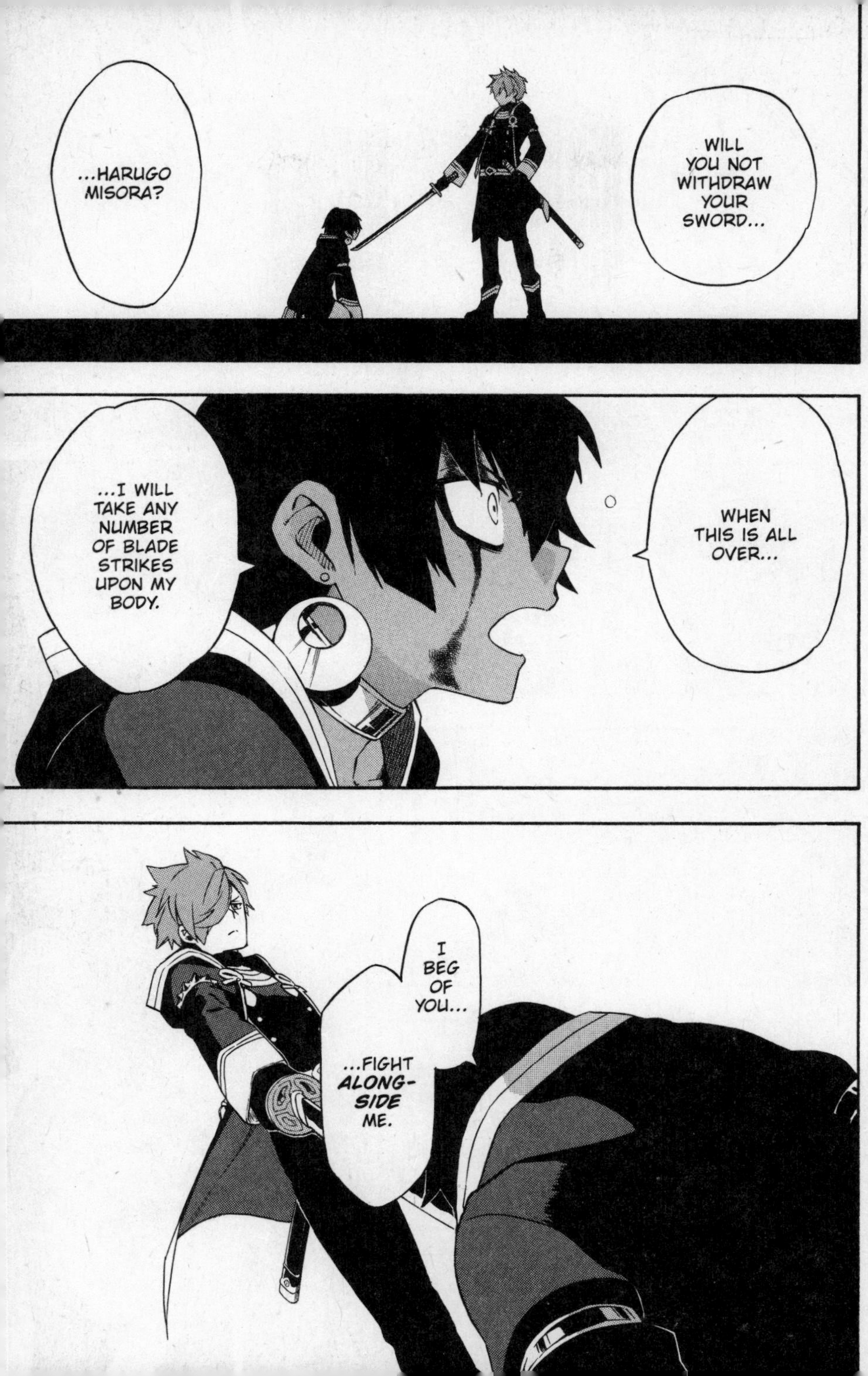
WILL YOU NOT WITHDRAW YOUR SWORD...
...HARUGO MISORA?
WHEN THIS IS ALL OVER...
...I WILL TAKE ANY NUMBER OF BLADE STRIKES UPON MY BODY.
I BEG OF YOU...
...FIGHT ALONG-SIDE ME.

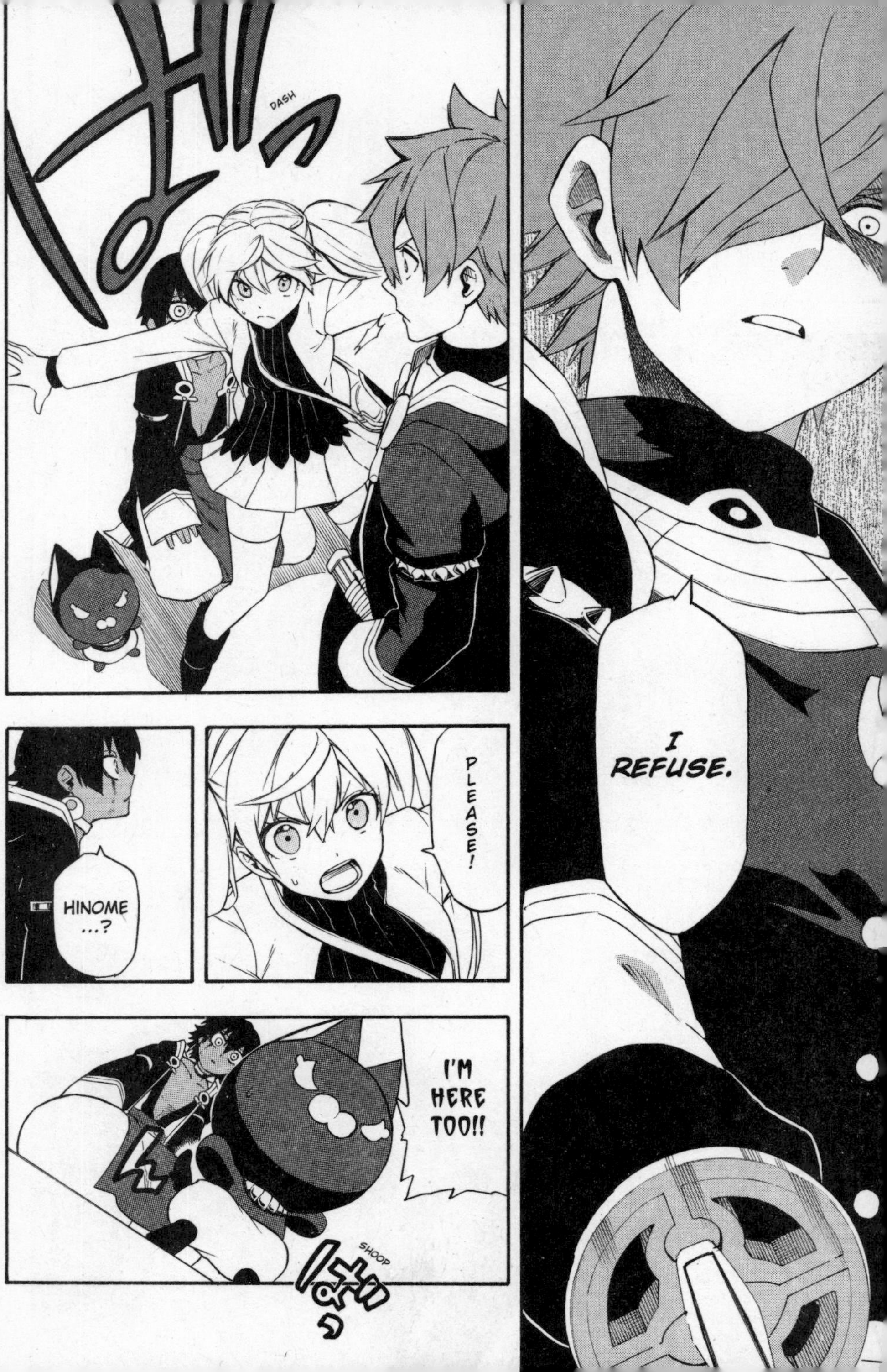
I REFUSE.
DASH
PLEASE!
HINOME ...?
I'M HERE TOO!!
SHOOP

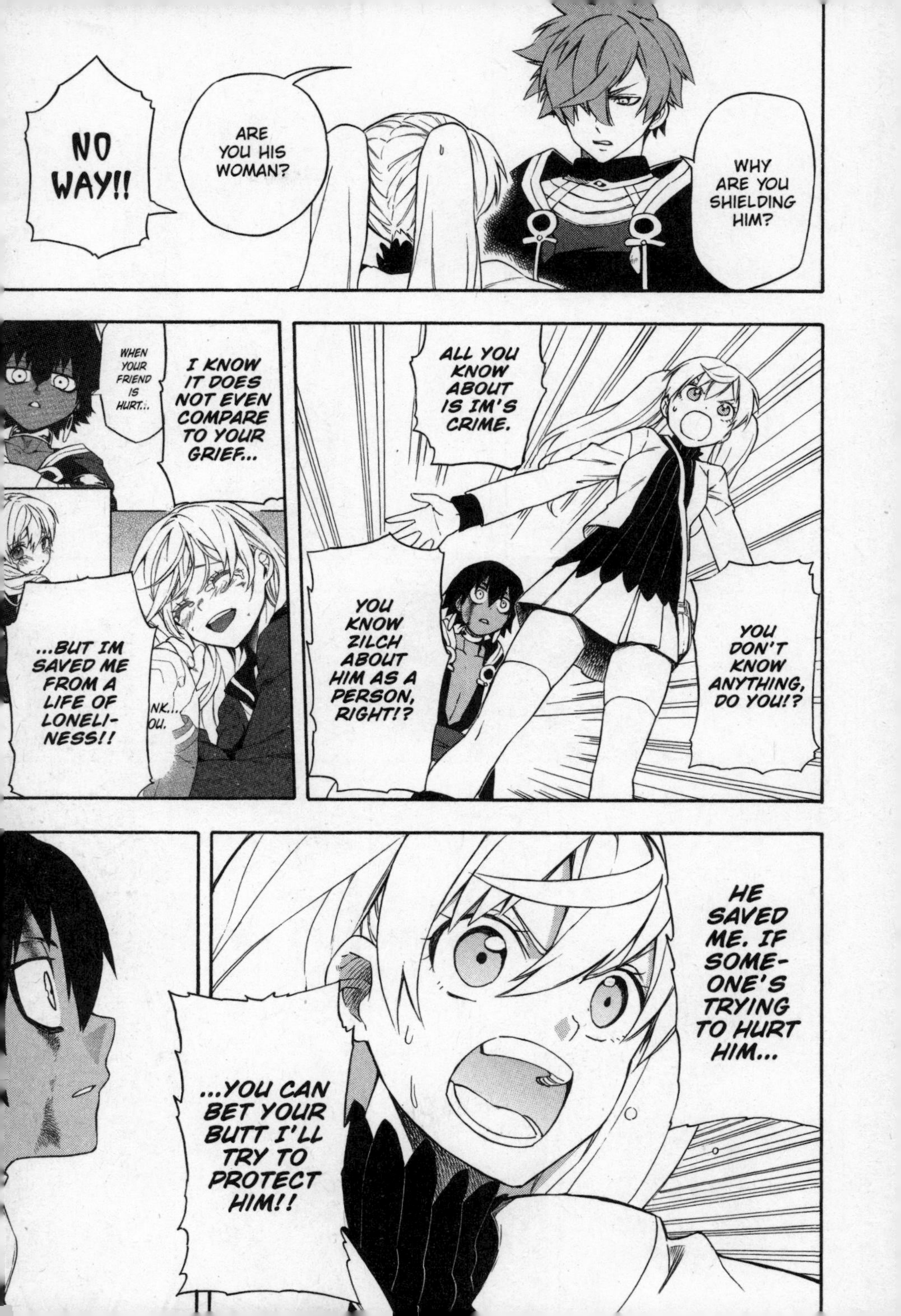
WHY ARE YOU SHIELDING HIM?
ARE YOU HIS WOMAN?
NO WAY!!
YOU DON'T KNOW ANYTHING, DO YOU!?
ALL YOU KNOW ABOUT IS IM'S CRIME.
YOU KNOW ZILCH ABOUT HIM AS A PERSON, RIGHT!?
I KNOW IT DOES NOT EVEN COMPARE TO YOUR GRIEF...
WHEN YOUR FRIEND IS HURT...
...BUT IM SAVED ME FROM A LIFE OF LONELI-NESS!!
HE SAVED ME. IF SOME-ONE'S TRYING TO HURT HIM...
...YOU CAN BET YOUR BUTT I'LL TRY TO PROTECT HIM!!

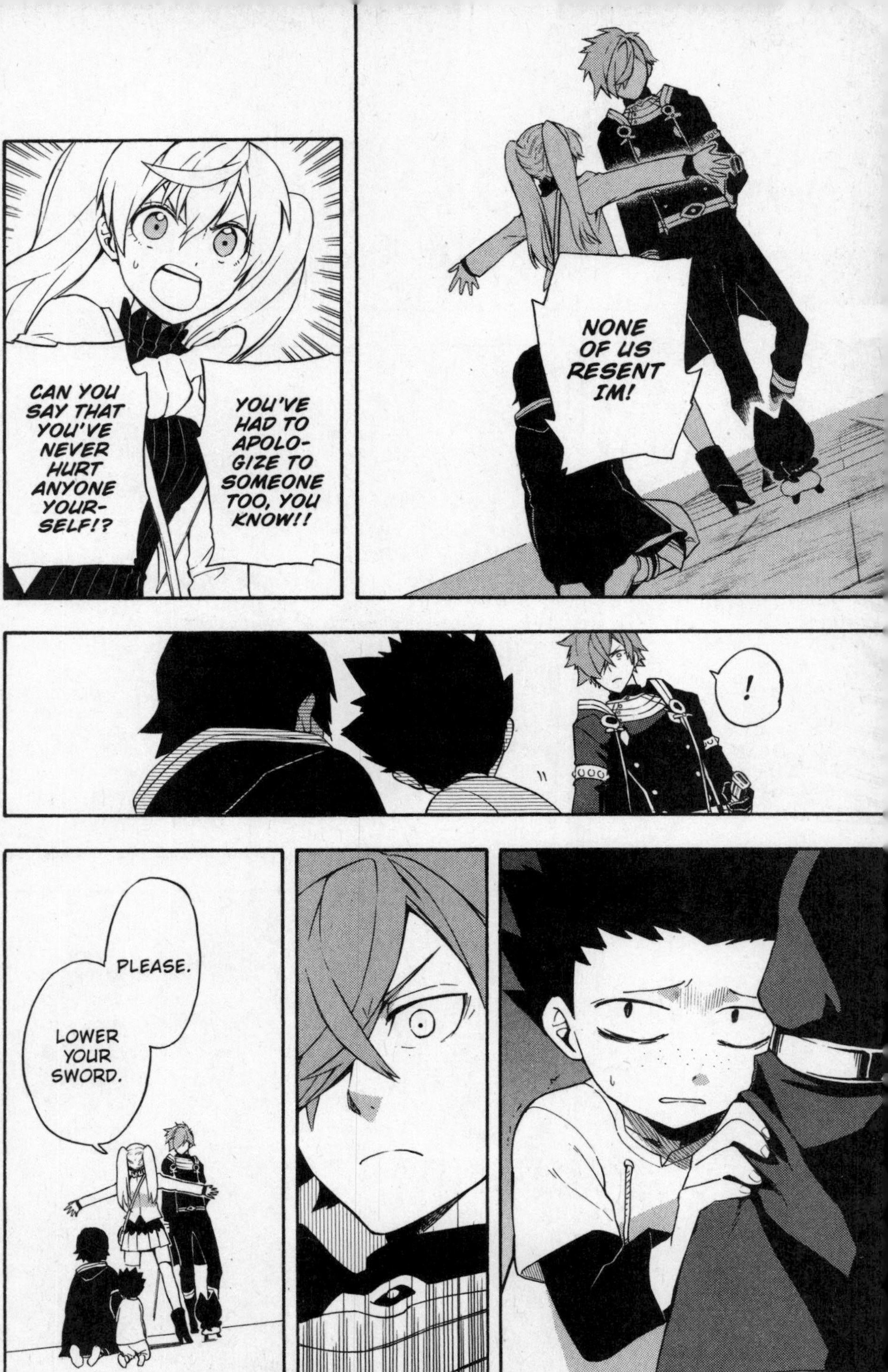
NONE OF US RESENT IM!
YOU'VE HAD TO APOLOGIZE TO SOMEONE TOO, YOU KNOW!!
CAN YOU SAY THAT YOU'VE NEVER HURT ANYONE YOURSELF!?
!
PLEASE.
LOWER YOUR SWORD.

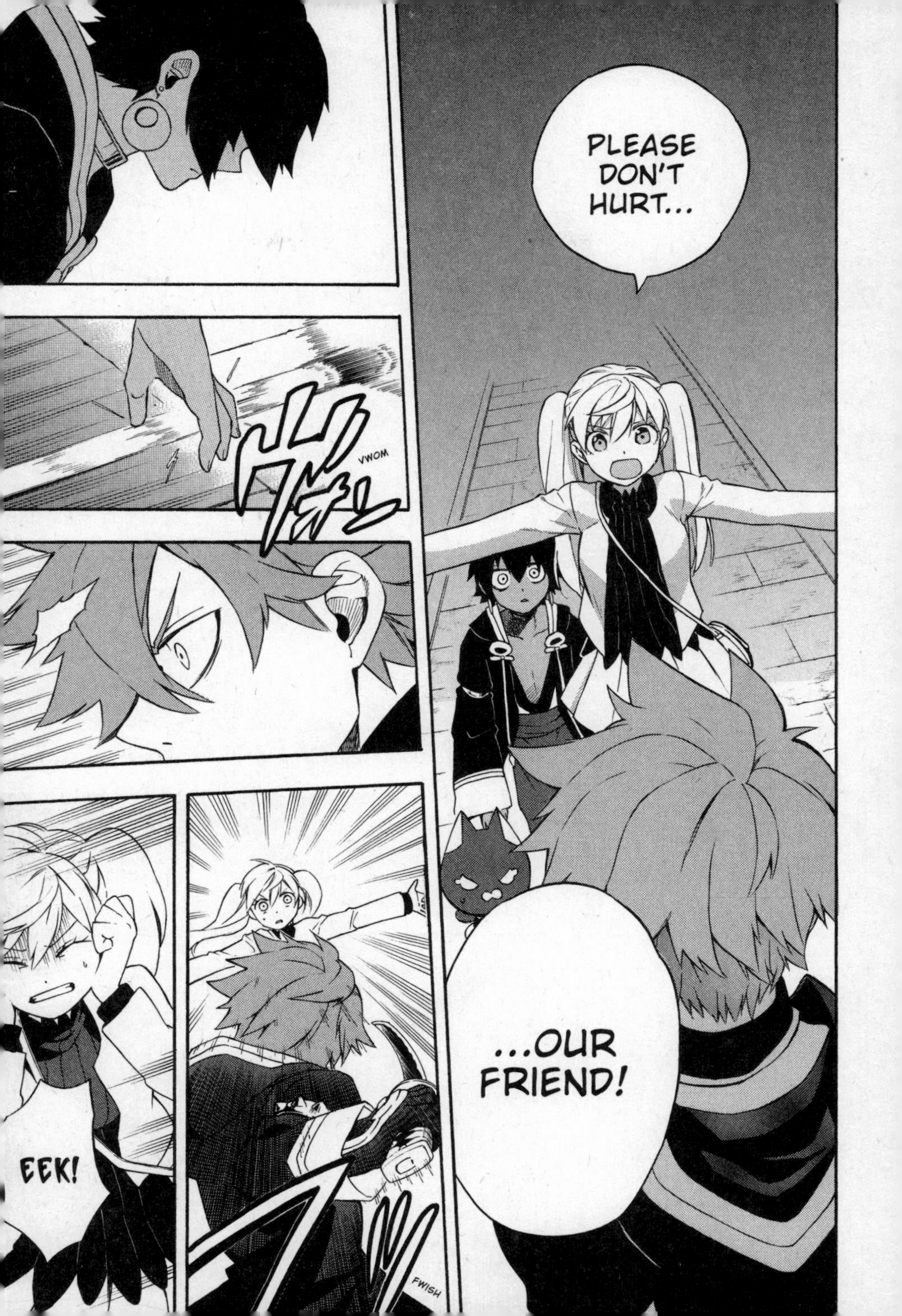
PLEASE DON'T HURT...
...OUR FRIEND!
VWOM
FWISH
EEK!

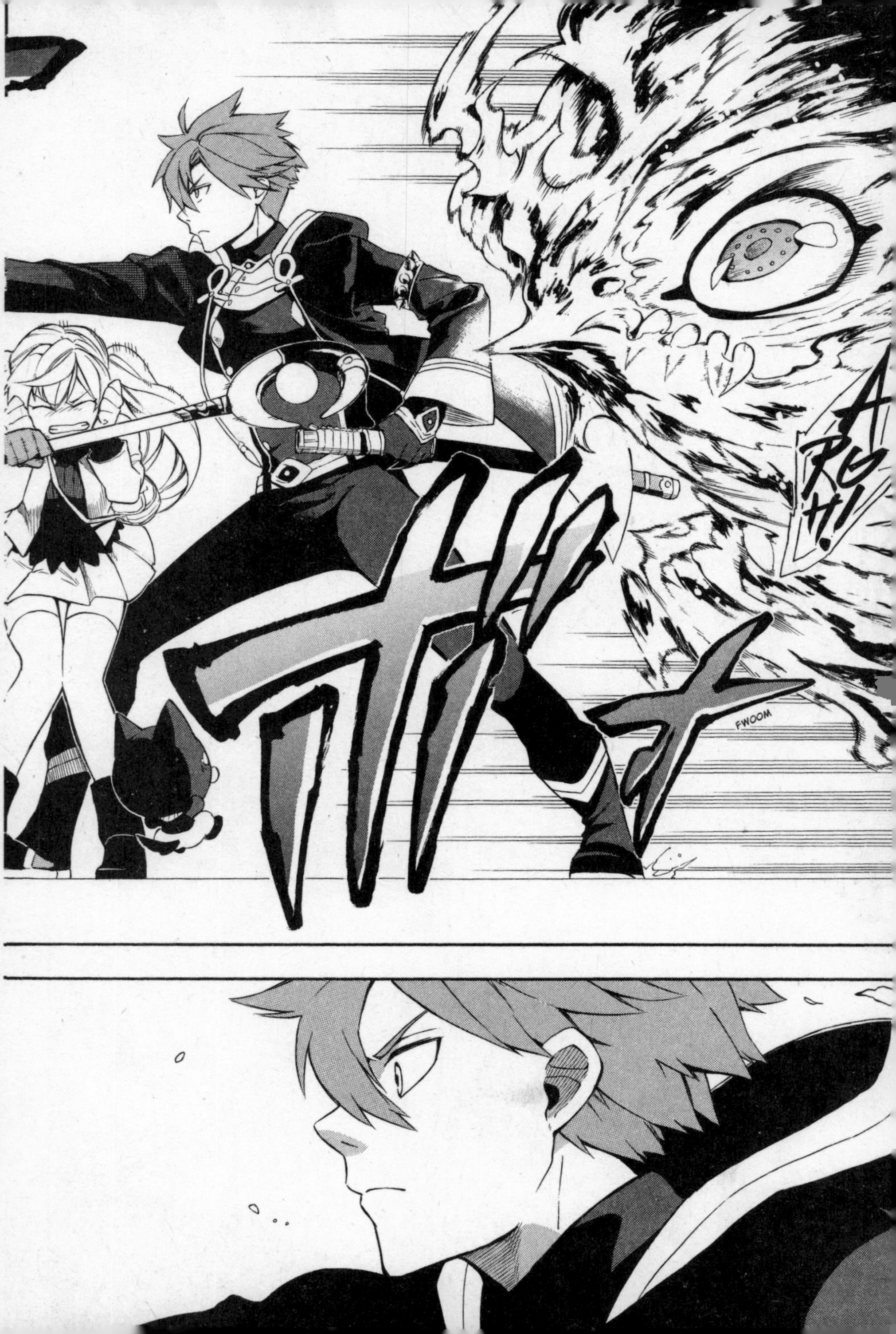
ARGH!
FWOOM

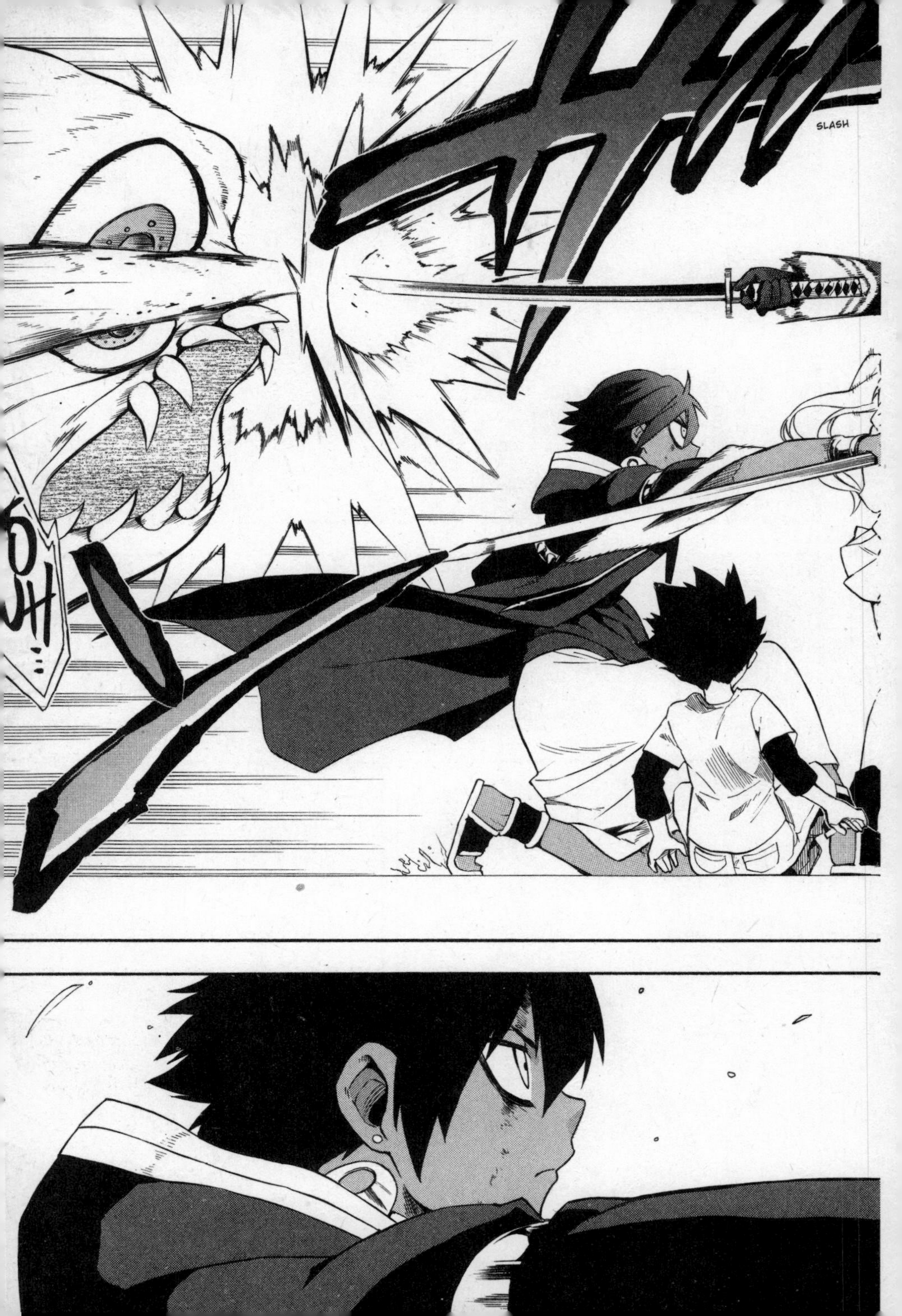
SLASH

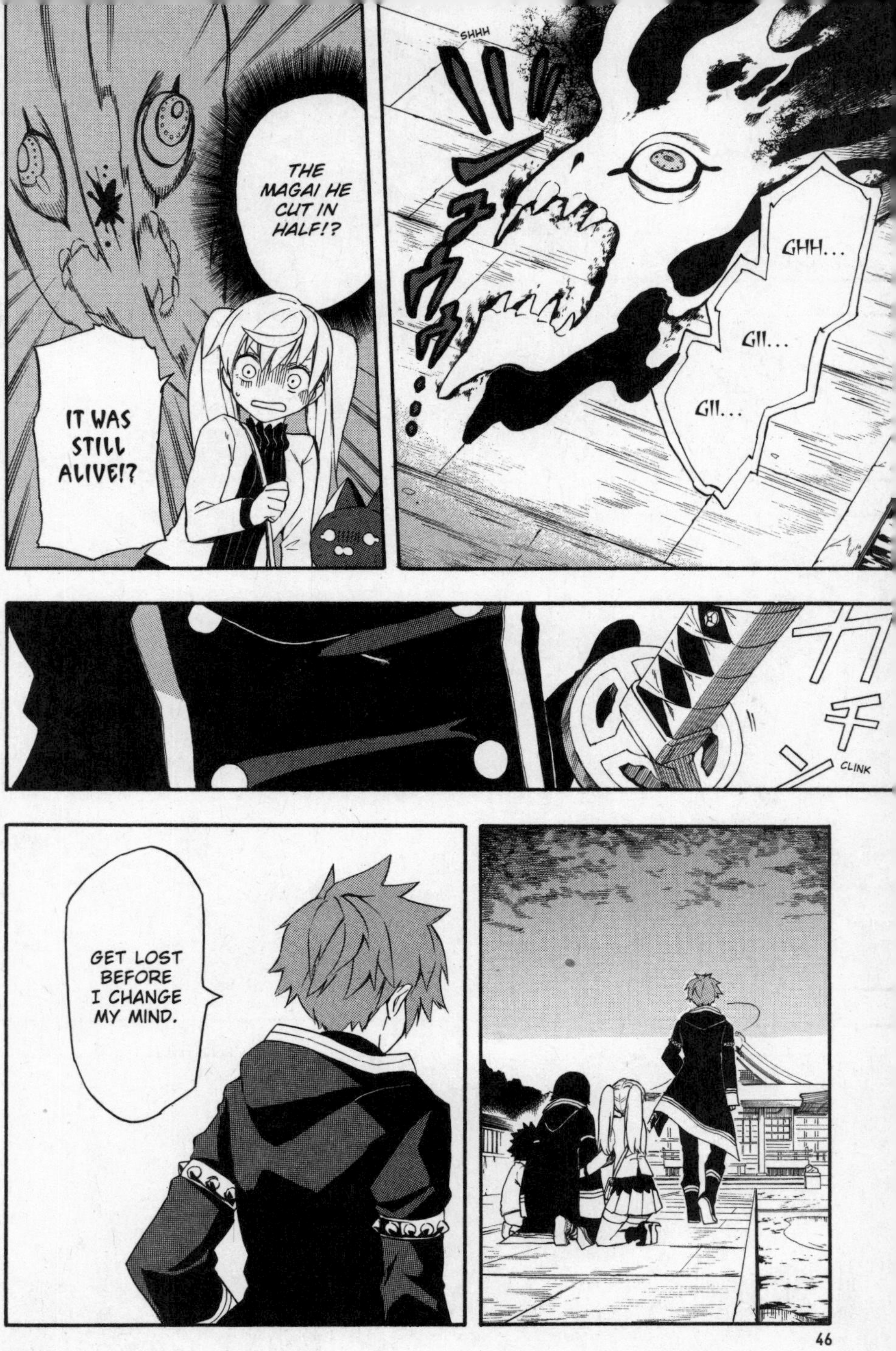
SHHH
GHH...
GII...
GII...
THE MAGAI HE CUT IN HALF!?
IT WAS STILL ALIVE!?
カチン
CLINK
GET LOST BEFORE I CHANGE MY MIND.

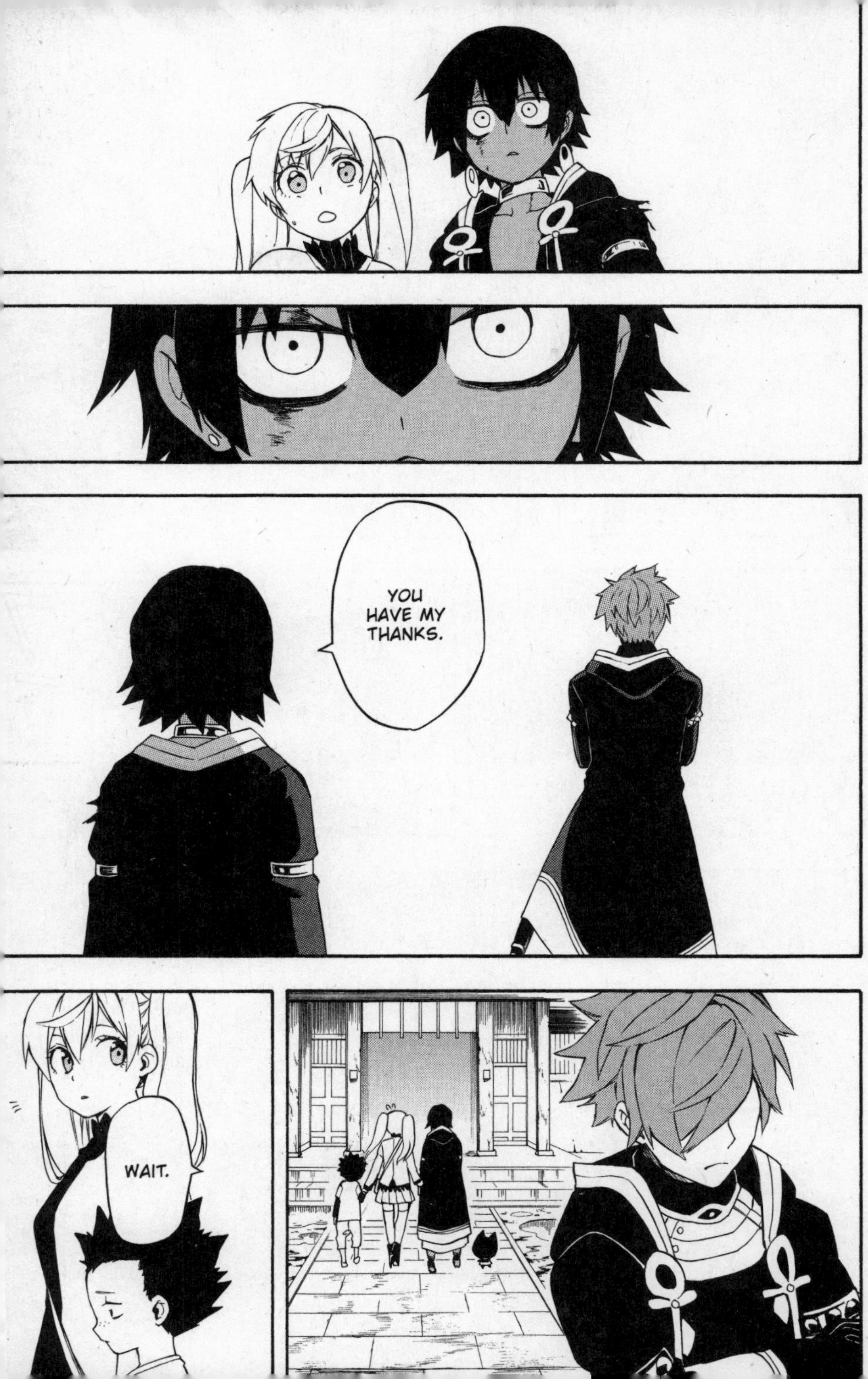
YOU HAVE MY THANKS.
WAIT.

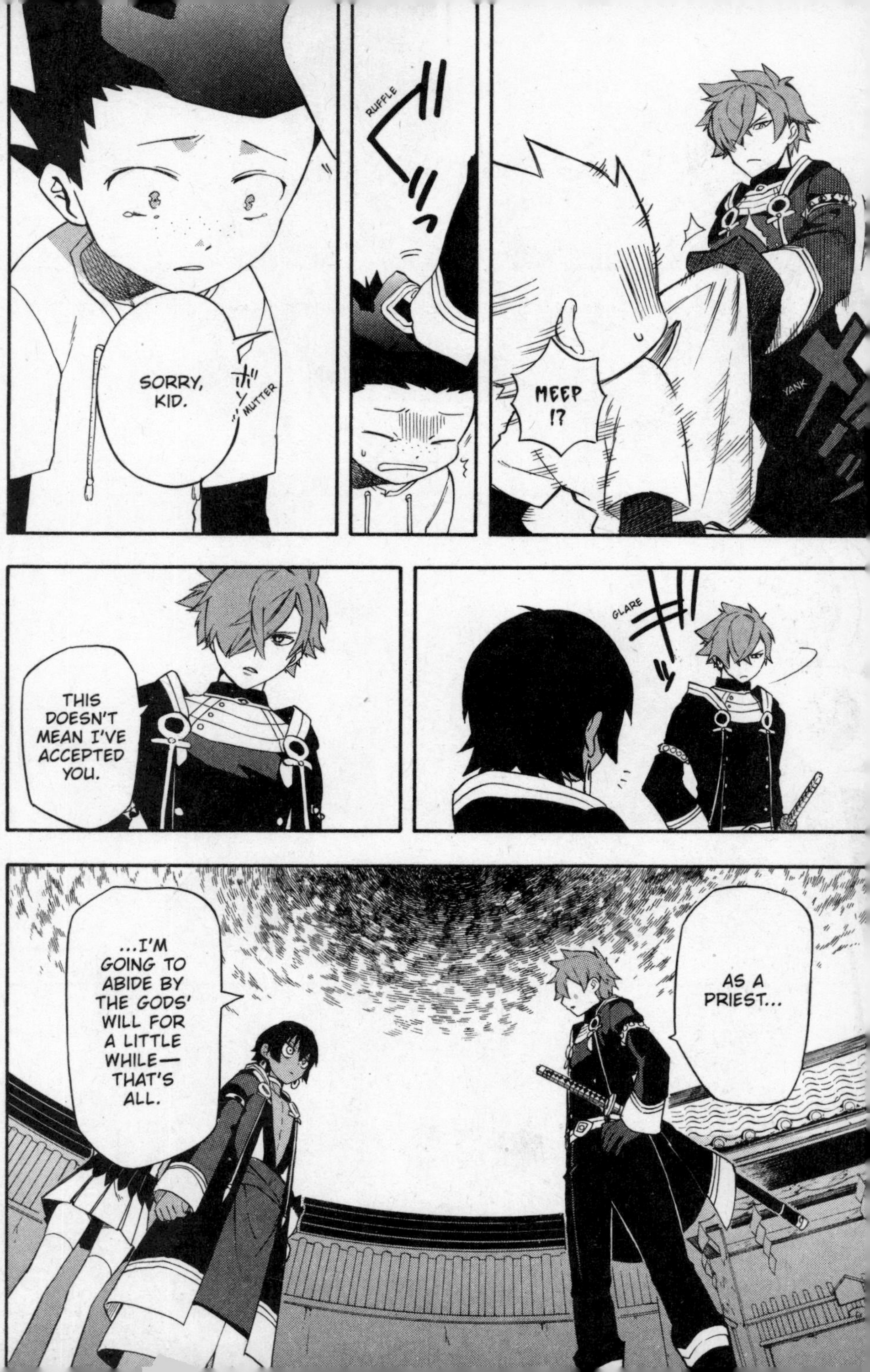
YANK
MEEP!?
RUFFLE
SORRY, KID.
MUTTER
GLARE
THIS DOESN'T MEAN I'VE ACCEPTED YOU.
AS A PRIEST...
...I'M GOING TO ABIDE BY THE GODS' WILL FOR A LITTLE WHILE—THAT'S ALL.

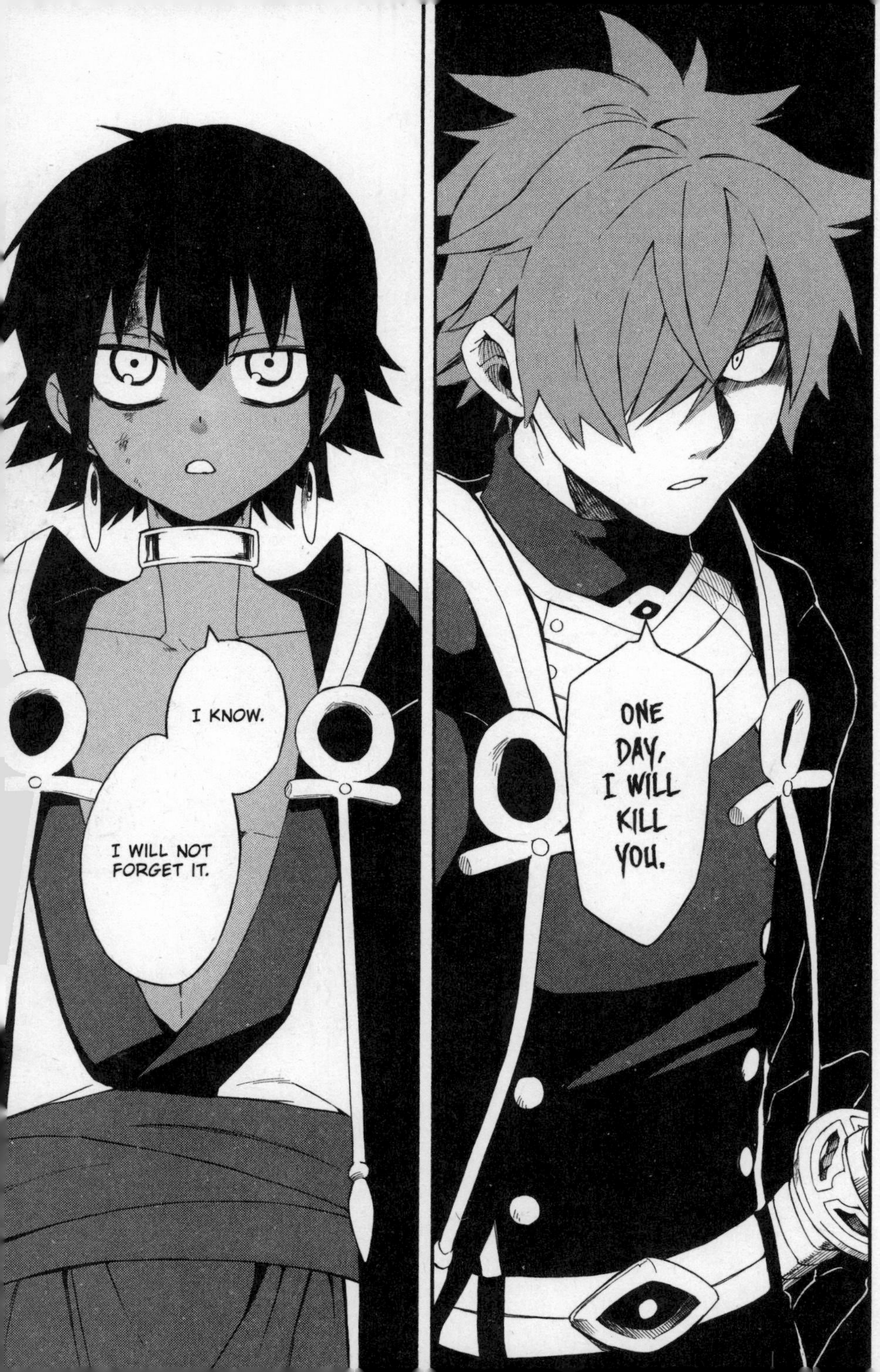
ONE DAY, I WILL KILL YOU.
I KNOW.
I WILL NOT FORGET IT.

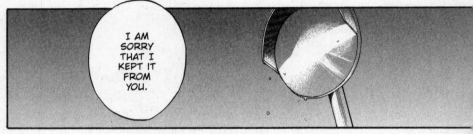

I AM SORRY THAT I KEPT IT FROM YOU.

YOU CALLED ME...

...YOUR FRIEND...

?

...HINOME.

OH, IT'S FINE. I'M OVER IT.

RIGHT?

RIGHT! ♪

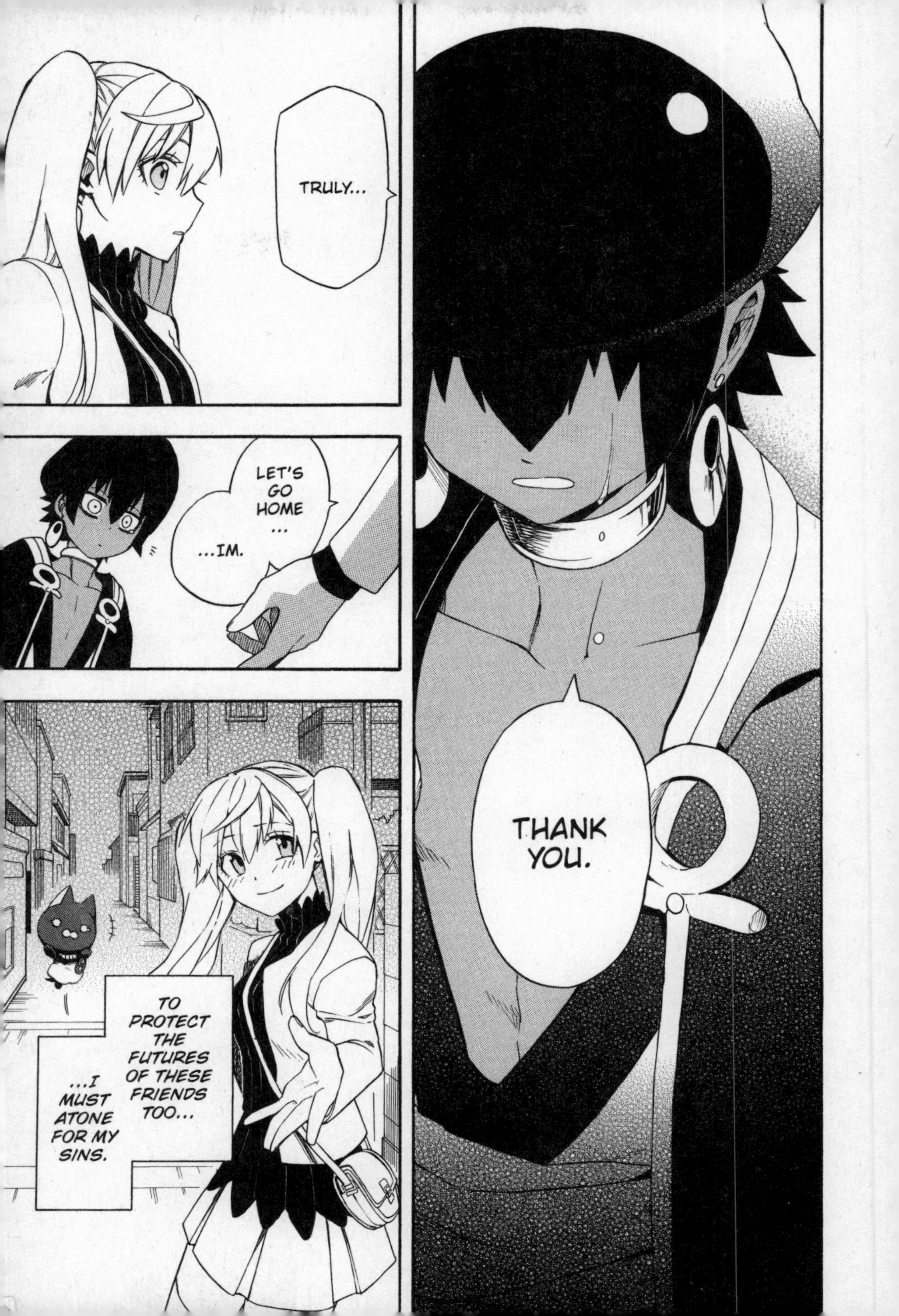
THANK YOU.
TRULY...
LET'S GO HOME ...
...IM.
TO PROTECT THE FUTURES OF THESE FRIENDS TOO...
...I MUST ATONE FOR MY SINS.

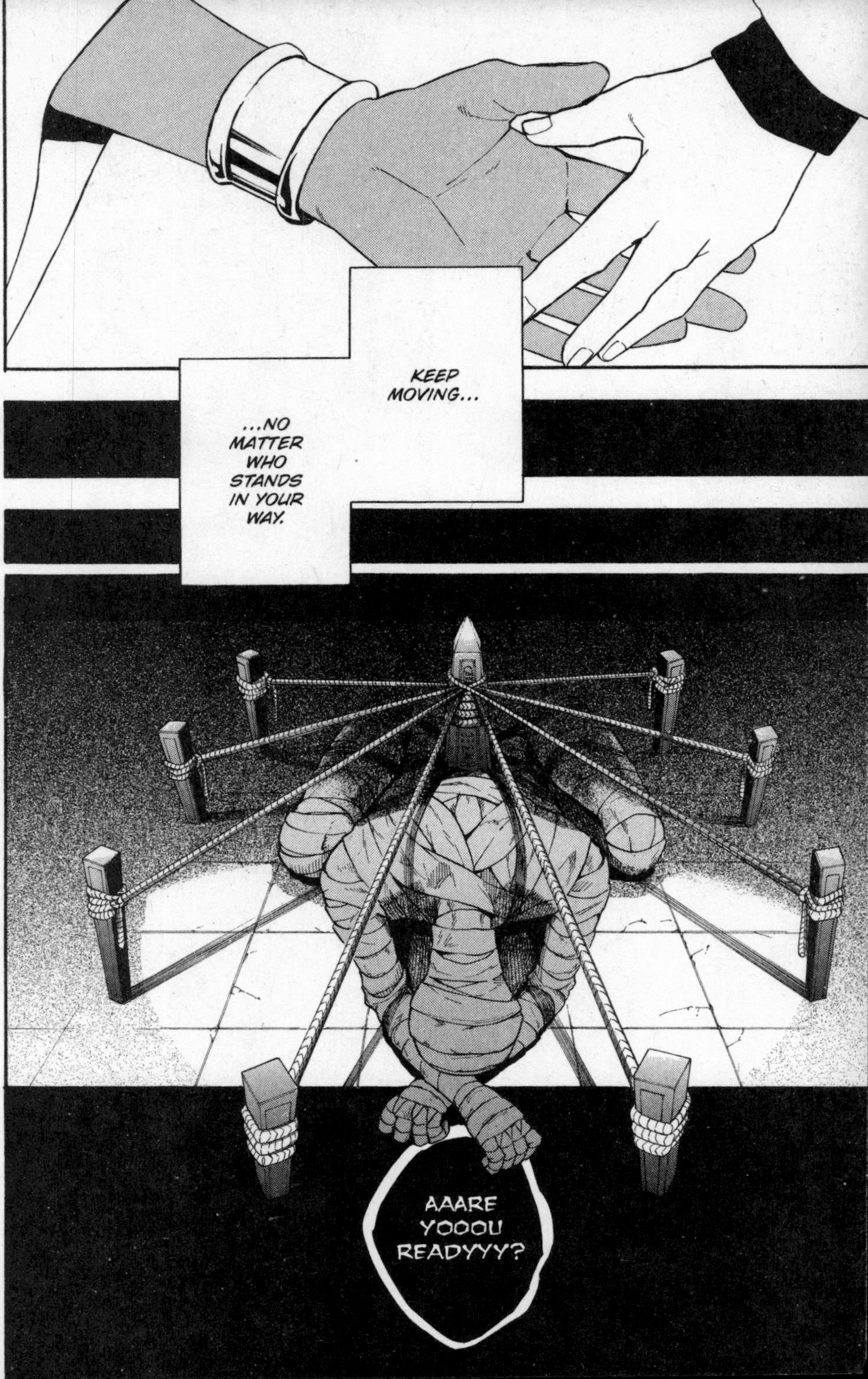
KEEP MOVING...
...NO MATTER WHO STANDS IN YOUR WAY.
AAARE YOOOU READYYY?

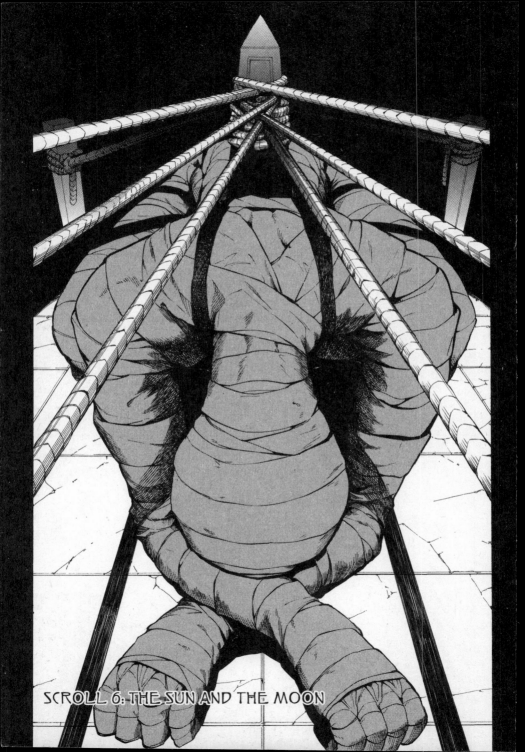

SCROLL 6: THE SUN AND THE MOON

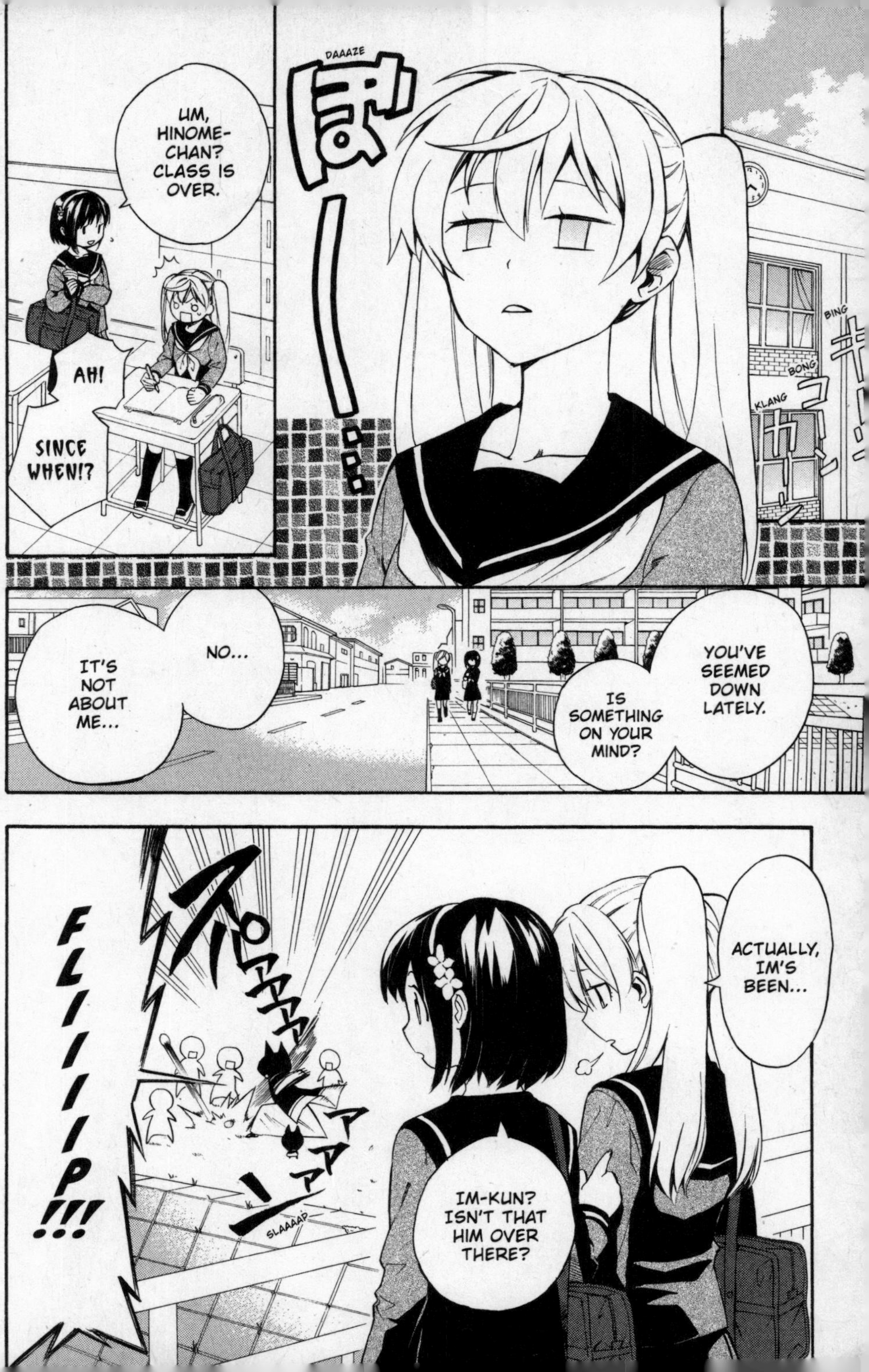
BING
BONG
KLANG
DAAAZE
UM, HINOME-CHAN? CLASS IS OVER.
AH!
SINCE WHEN!?
YOU'VE SEEMED DOWN LATELY.
IS SOMETHING ON YOUR MIND?
NO...
IT'S NOT ABOUT ME...
ACTUALLY, IM'S BEEN...
IM-KUN? ISN'T THAT HIM OVER THERE?
SLAAAAP
FLIIIIIP!!!

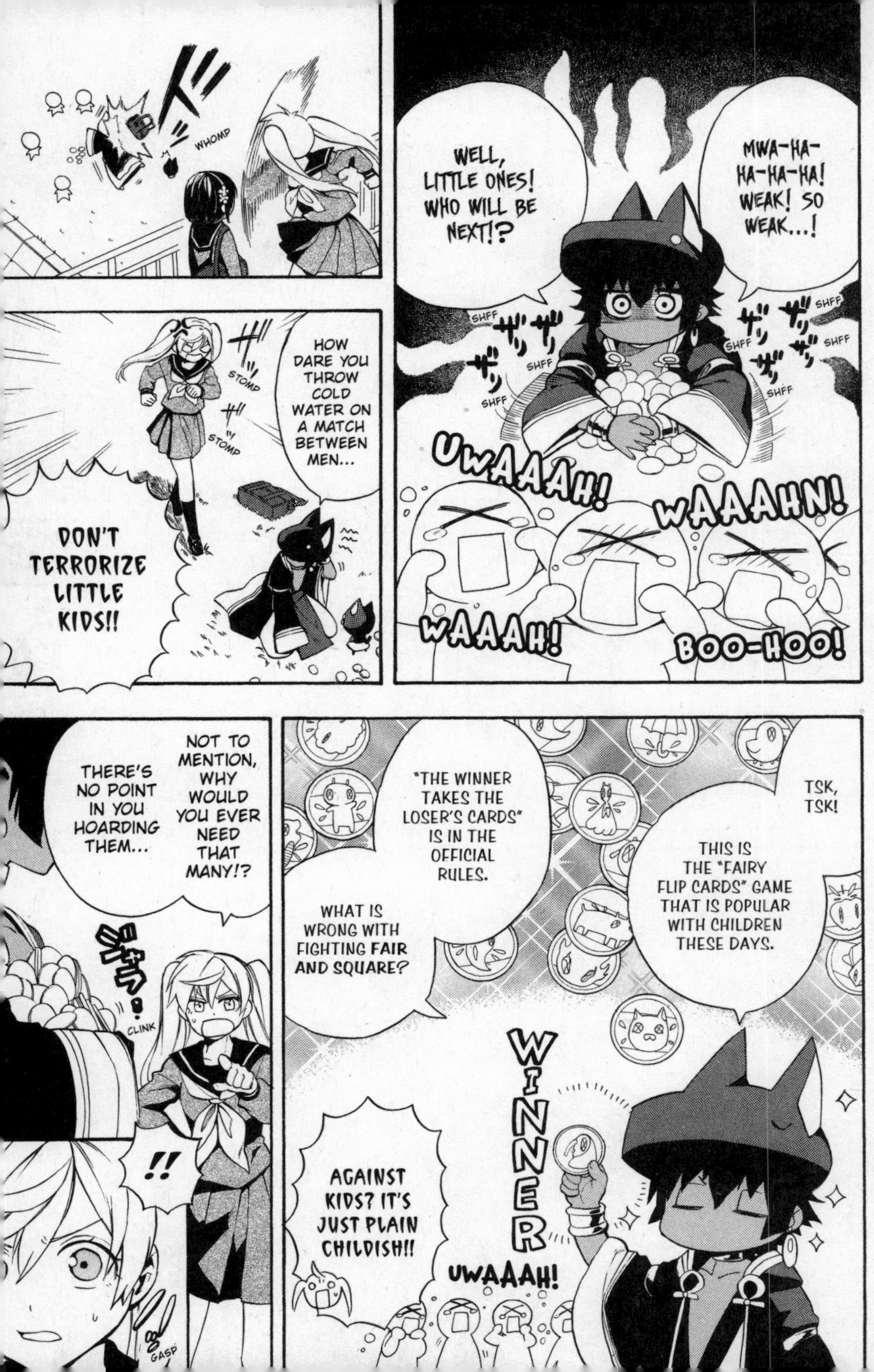
MWA-HA-HA-HA-HA! WEAK! SO WEAK...!
WELL, LITTLE ONES! WHO WILL BE NEXT!?
SHFF
SHFF
SHFF
SHFF
SHFF
SHFF
UWAAAAH!
WAAAAHN!
WAAAAH!
BOO-HOO!
WHOMP
HOW DARE YOU THROW COLD WATER ON A MATCH BETWEEN MEN...
STOMP
STOMP
DON'T TERRORIZE LITTLE KIDS!!
TSK, TSK!
THIS IS THE "FAIRY FLIP CARDS" GAME THAT IS POPULAR WITH CHILDREN THESE DAYS.
"THE WINNER TAKES THE LOSER'S CARDS" IS IN THE OFFICIAL RULES.
WHAT IS WRONG WITH FIGHTING FAIR AND SQUARE?
WINNER
AGAINST KIDS? IT'S JUST PLAIN CHILDISH!!
UWAAAH!
NOT TO MENTION, WHY WOULD YOU EVER NEED THAT MANY!?
THERE'S NO POINT IN YOU HOARDING THEM...
CLINK
!!
GASP

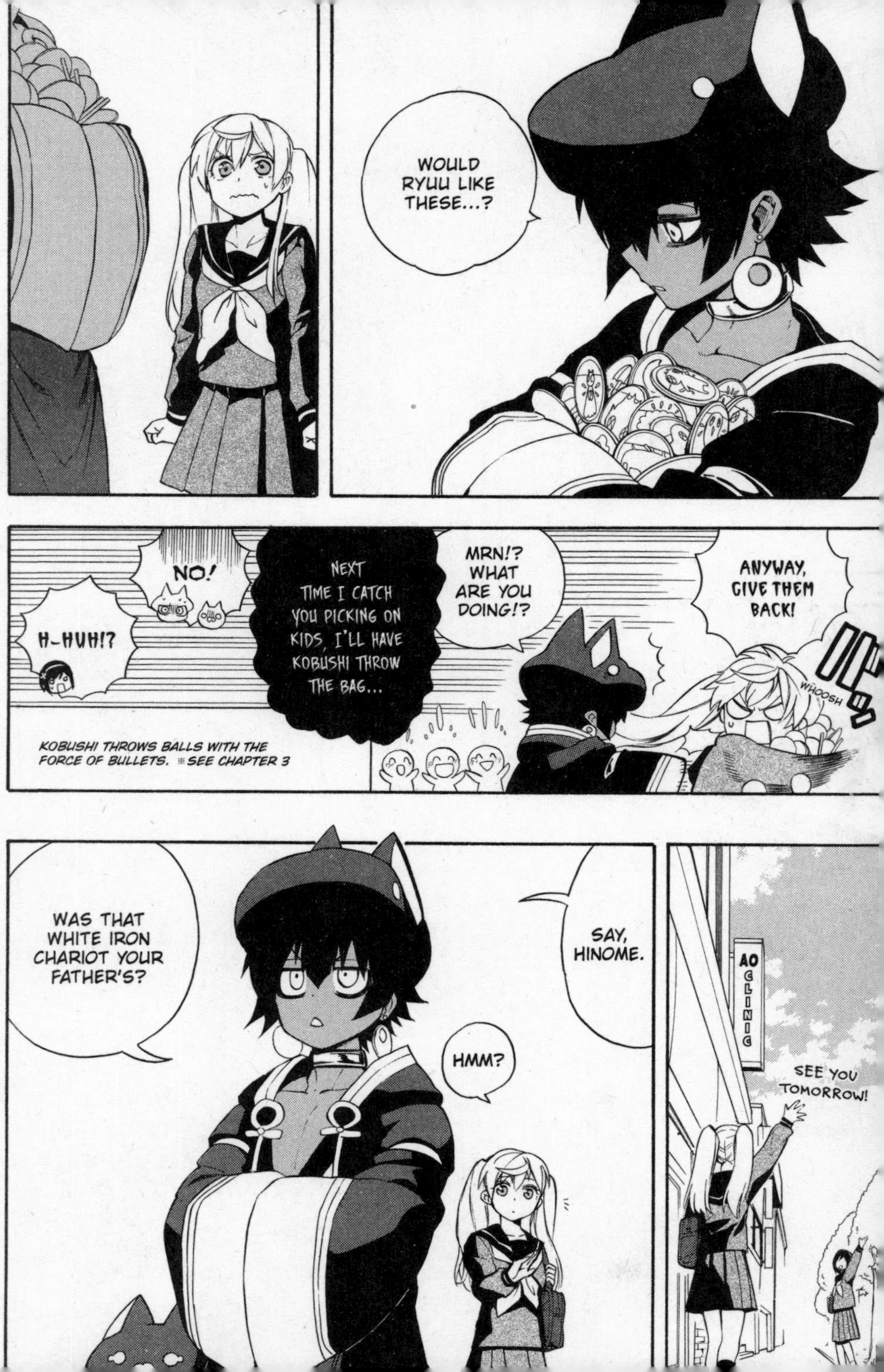
WOULD RYUU LIKE THESE...?
ANYWAY, GIVE THEM BACK!
WHOOSH
MRN!? WHAT ARE YOU DOING!?
NEXT TIME I CATCH YOU PICKING ON KIDS, I'LL HAVE KOBUSHI THROW THE BAG...
NO!
H-HUH!?
KOBUSHI THROWS BALLS WITH THE FORCE OF BULLETS. ※SEE CHAPTER 3
AO CLINIC
SEE YOU TOMORROW!
SAY, HINOME.
HMM?
WAS THAT WHITE IRON CHARIOT YOUR FATHER'S?

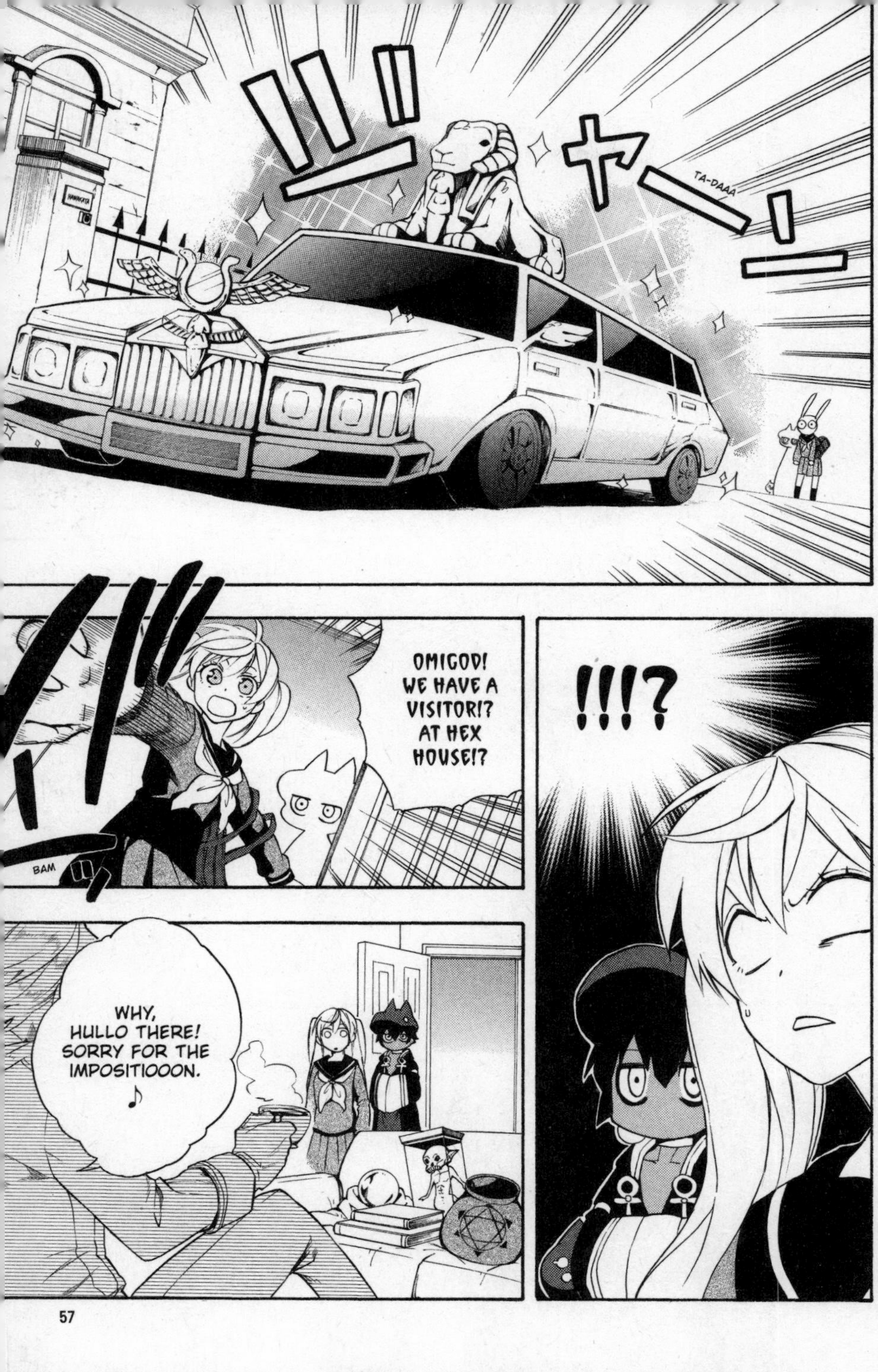
ジャーン
TA-DAAA
!!!?
OMIGOD! WE HAVE A VISITOR!? AT HEX HOUSE!?
BAM
WHY, HULLO THERE! SORRY FOR THE IMPOSITIOOON. ♪

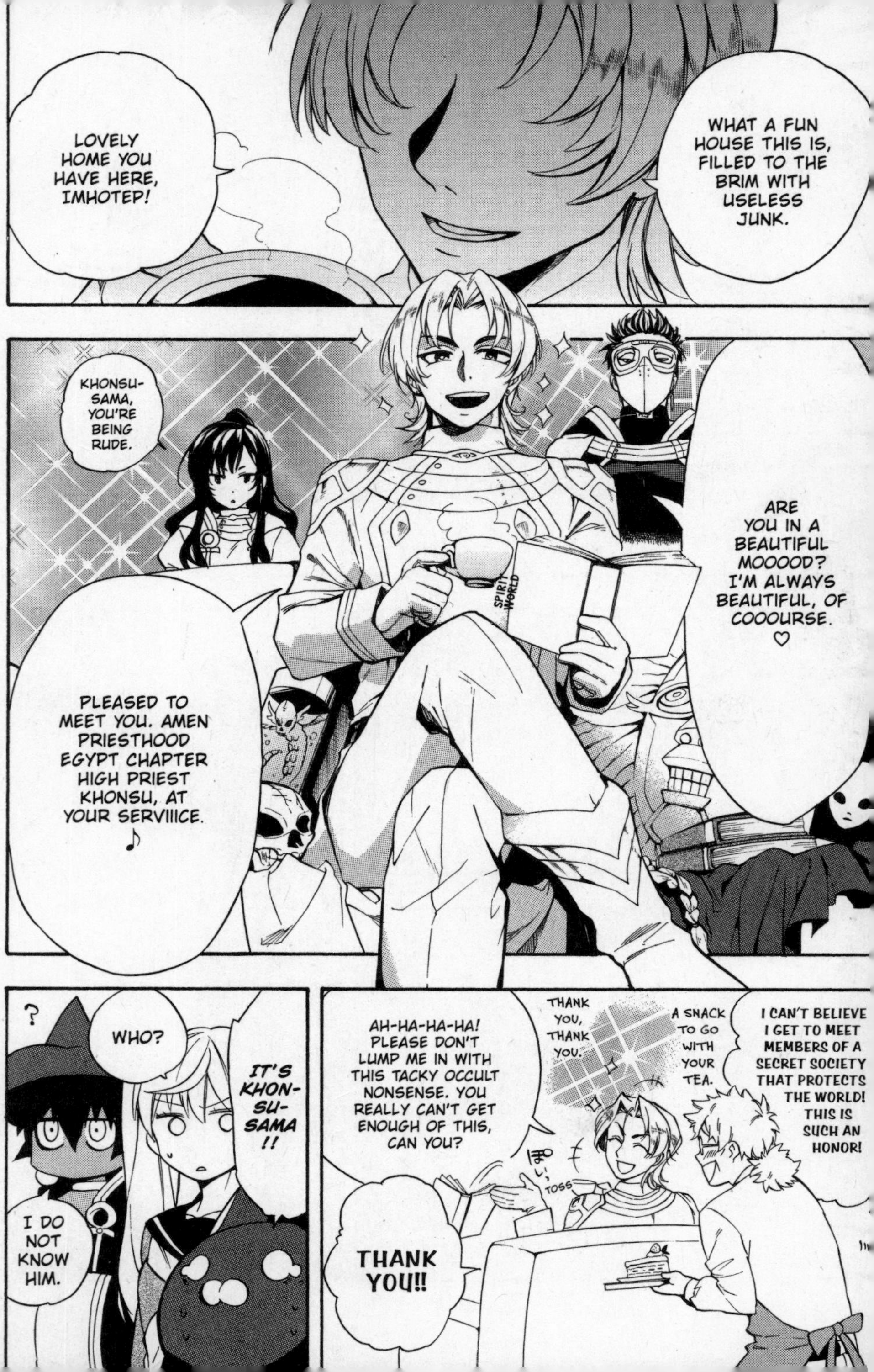
WHAT A FUN HOUSE THIS IS, FILLED TO THE BRIM WITH USELESS JUNK.
LOVELY HOME YOU HAVE HERE, IMHOTEP!
ARE YOU IN A BEAUTIFUL MOOOOD? I'M ALWAYS BEAUTIFUL, OF COOOURSE. ♡
KHONSU-SAMA, YOU'RE BEING RUDE.
SPIRIT WORLD
PLEASED TO MEET YOU. AMEN PRIESTHOOD EGYPT CHAPTER HIGH PRIEST KHONSU, AT YOUR SERVIIICE. ♪
I CAN'T BELIEVE I GET TO MEET MEMBERS OF A SECRET SOCIETY THAT PROTECTS THE WORLD! THIS IS SUCH AN HONOR!
A SNACK TO GO WITH YOUR TEA.
THANK YOU, THANK YOU.
AH-HA-HA-HA! PLEASE DON'T LUMP ME IN WITH THIS TACKY OCCULT NONSENSE. YOU REALLY CAN'T GET ENOUGH OF THIS, CAN YOU?
ぽい TOSS
THANK YOU!!
IT'S KHON-SU-SAMA!!
WHO?
?
I DO NOT KNOW HIM.

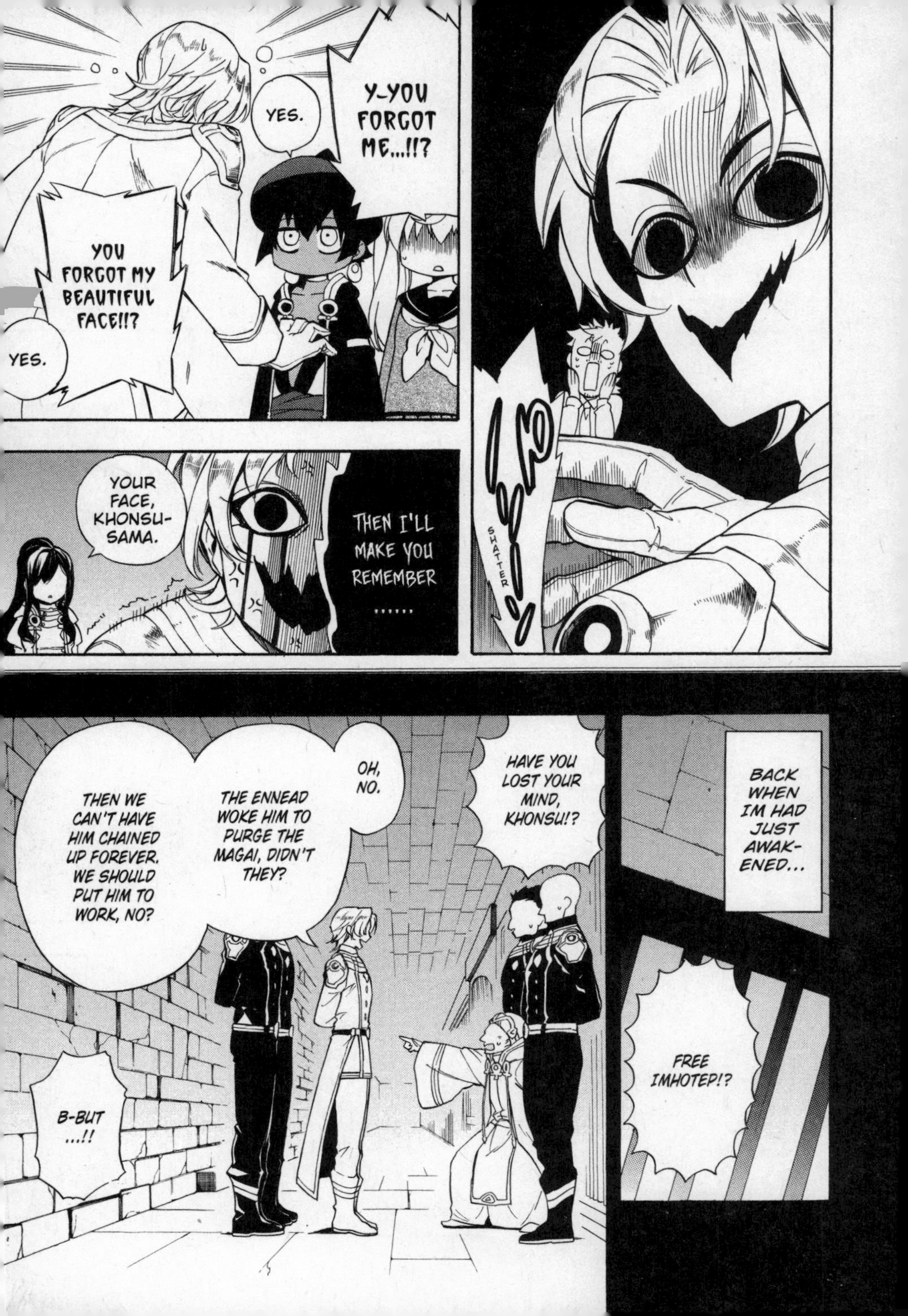
SHATTER
Y-YOU FORGOT ME...!!?
YES.
YOU FORGOT MY BEAUTIFUL FACE!!?
YES.
THEN I'LL MAKE YOU REMEMBER ......
YOUR FACE, KHONSU-SAMA.
BACK WHEN IM HAD JUST AWAK-ENED...
FREE IMHOTEP!?
HAVE YOU LOST YOUR MIND, KHONSU!?
OH, NO.
THE ENNEAD WOKE HIM TO PURGE THE MAGAI, DIDN'T THEY?
THEN WE CAN'T HAVE HIM CHAINED UP FOREVER. WE SHOULD PUT HIM TO WORK, NO?
B-BUT ...!!

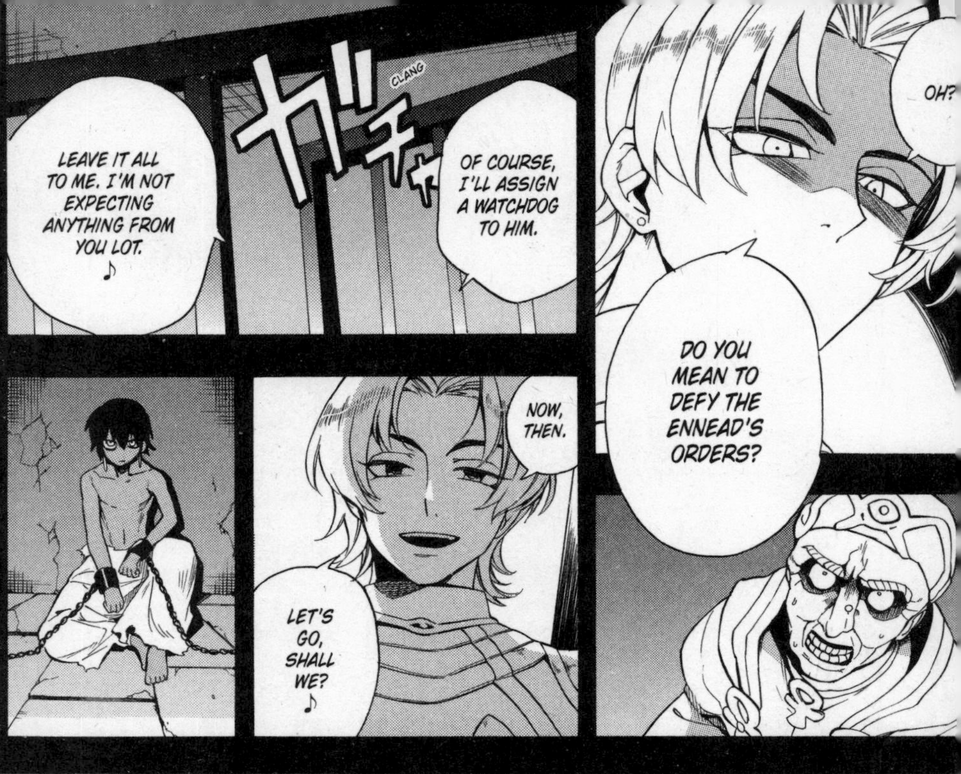
OH?
DO YOU MEAN TO DEFY THE ENNEAD'S ORDERS?
CLANG
OF COURSE, I'LL ASSIGN A WATCHDOG TO HIM.
LEAVE IT ALL TO ME. I'M NOT EXPECTING ANYTHING FROM YOU LOT. ♪
NOW, THEN.
LET'S GO, SHALL WE? ♪

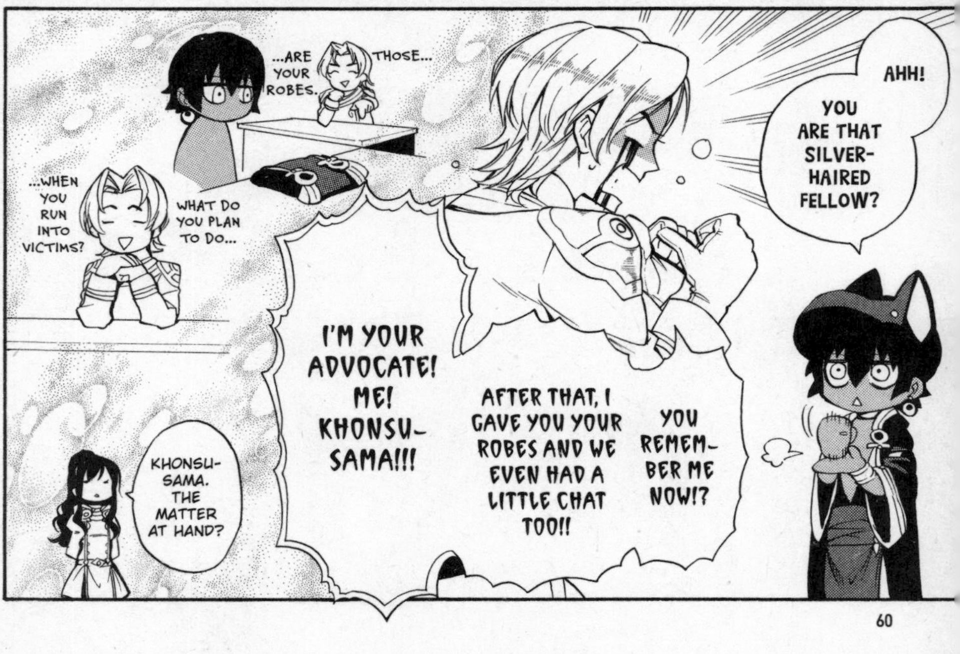
AHH! YOU ARE THAT SILVER-HAIRED FELLOW?
YOU REMEMBER ME NOW!?
AFTER THAT, I GAVE YOU YOUR ROBES AND WE EVEN HAD A LITTLE CHAT TOO!!
I'M YOUR ADVOCATE! ME! KHONSU-SAMA!!!
THOSE...
...ARE YOUR ROBES.
WHAT DO YOU PLAN TO DO...
...WHEN YOU RUN INTO VICTIMS?
KHONSU-SAMA. THE MATTER AT HAND?

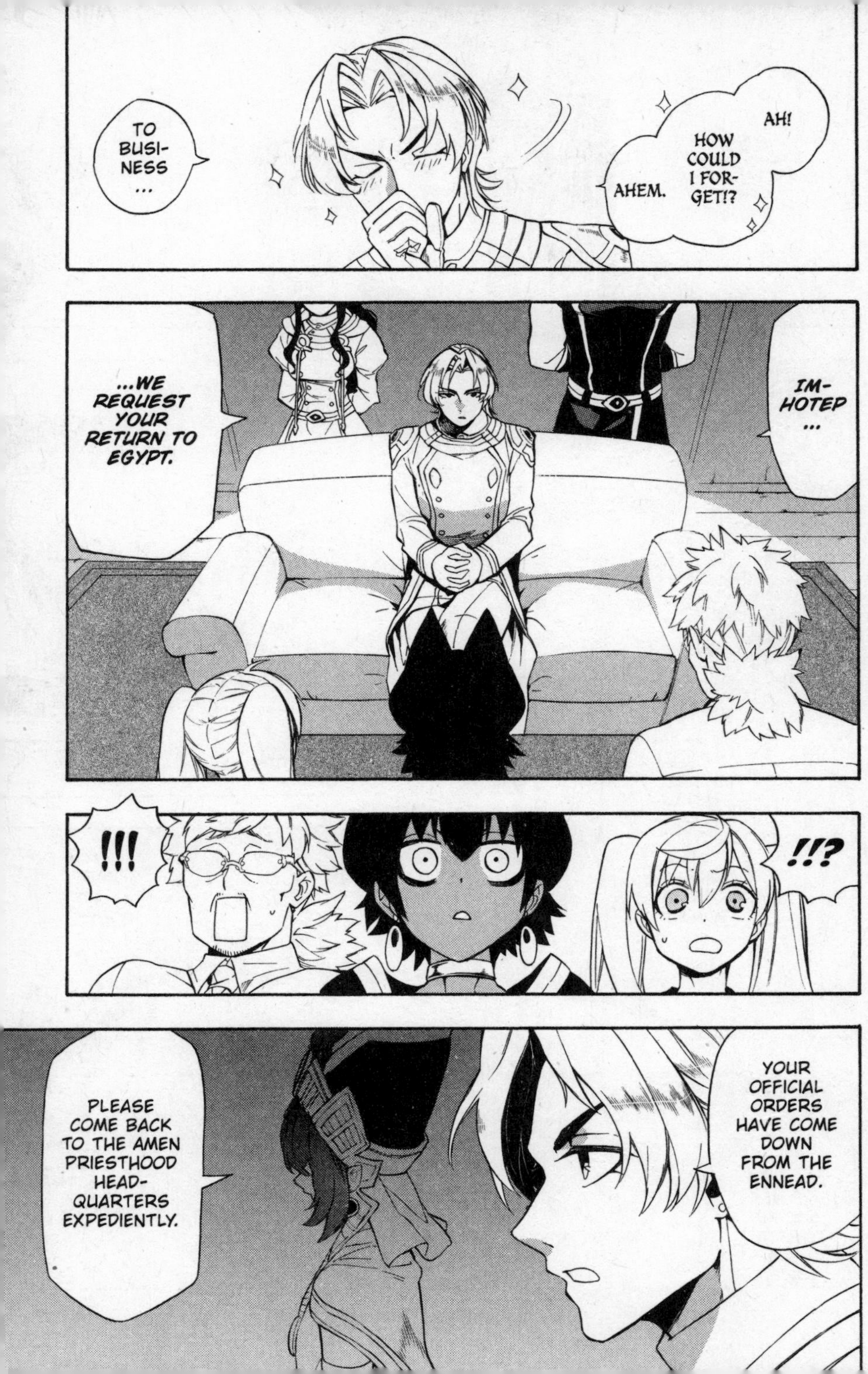
AH! HOW COULD I FORGET!? AHEM.
TO BUSINESS...
IMHOTEP...
...WE REQUEST YOUR RETURN TO EGYPT.
!!?
!!!
YOUR OFFICIAL ORDERS HAVE COME DOWN FROM THE ENNEAD.
PLEASE COME BACK TO THE AMEN PRIESTHOOD HEADQUARTERS EXPEDIENTLY.

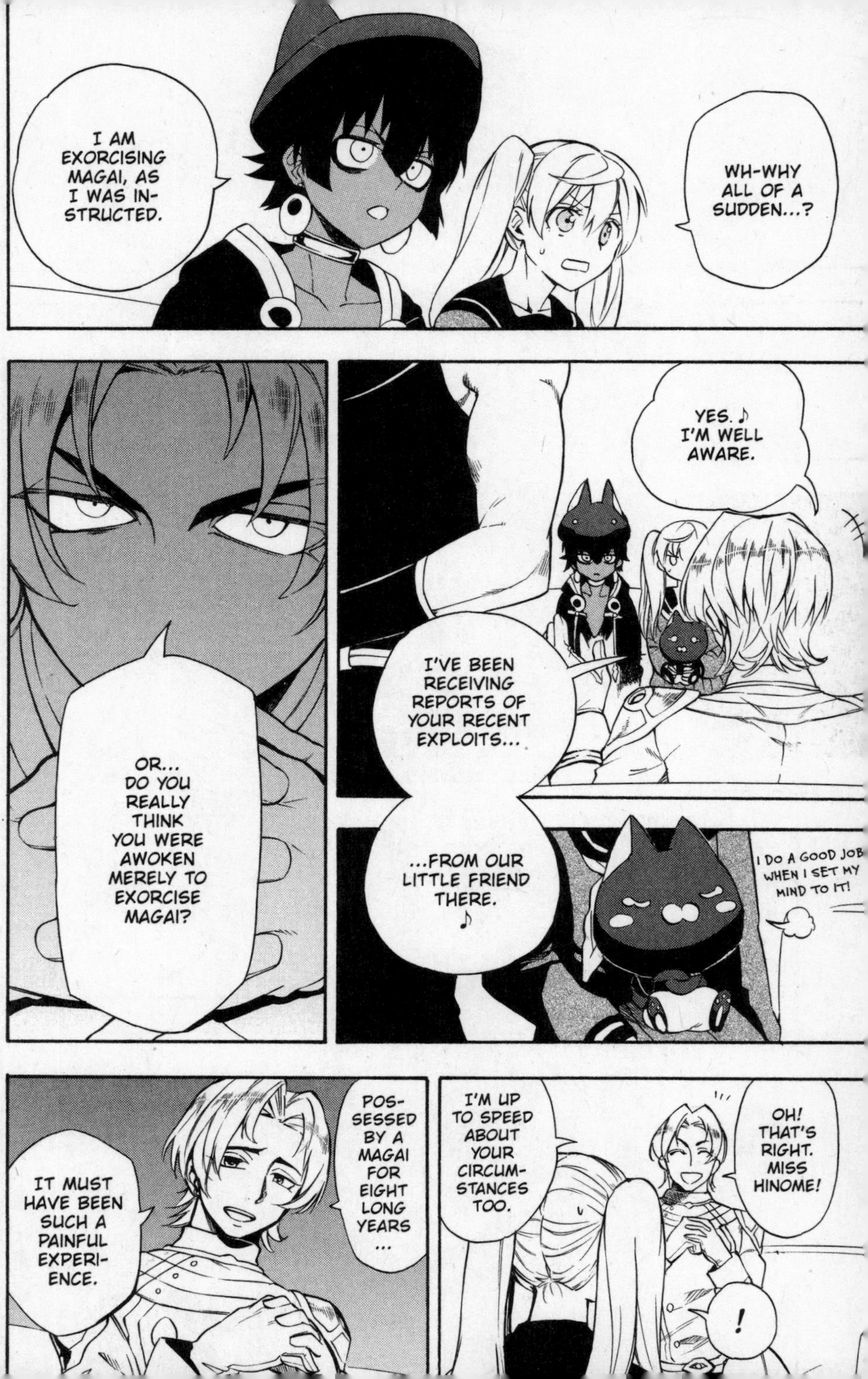
WH-WHY ALL OF A SUDDEN...?
I AM EXORCISING MAGAI, AS I WAS INSTRUCTED.
YES. ♪ I'M WELL AWARE.
I'VE BEEN RECEIVING REPORTS OF YOUR RECENT EXPLOITS...
...FROM OUR LITTLE FRIEND THERE. ♪
I DO A GOOD JOB WHEN I SET MY MIND TO IT!
OR... DO YOU REALLY THINK YOU WERE AWOKEN MERELY TO EXORCISE MAGAI?
OH! THAT'S RIGHT. MISS HINOME!
I'M UP TO SPEED ABOUT YOUR CIRCUMSTANCES TOO.
!
POSSESSED BY A MAGAI FOR EIGHT LONG YEARS...
IT MUST HAVE BEEN SUCH A PAINFUL EXPERIENCE.

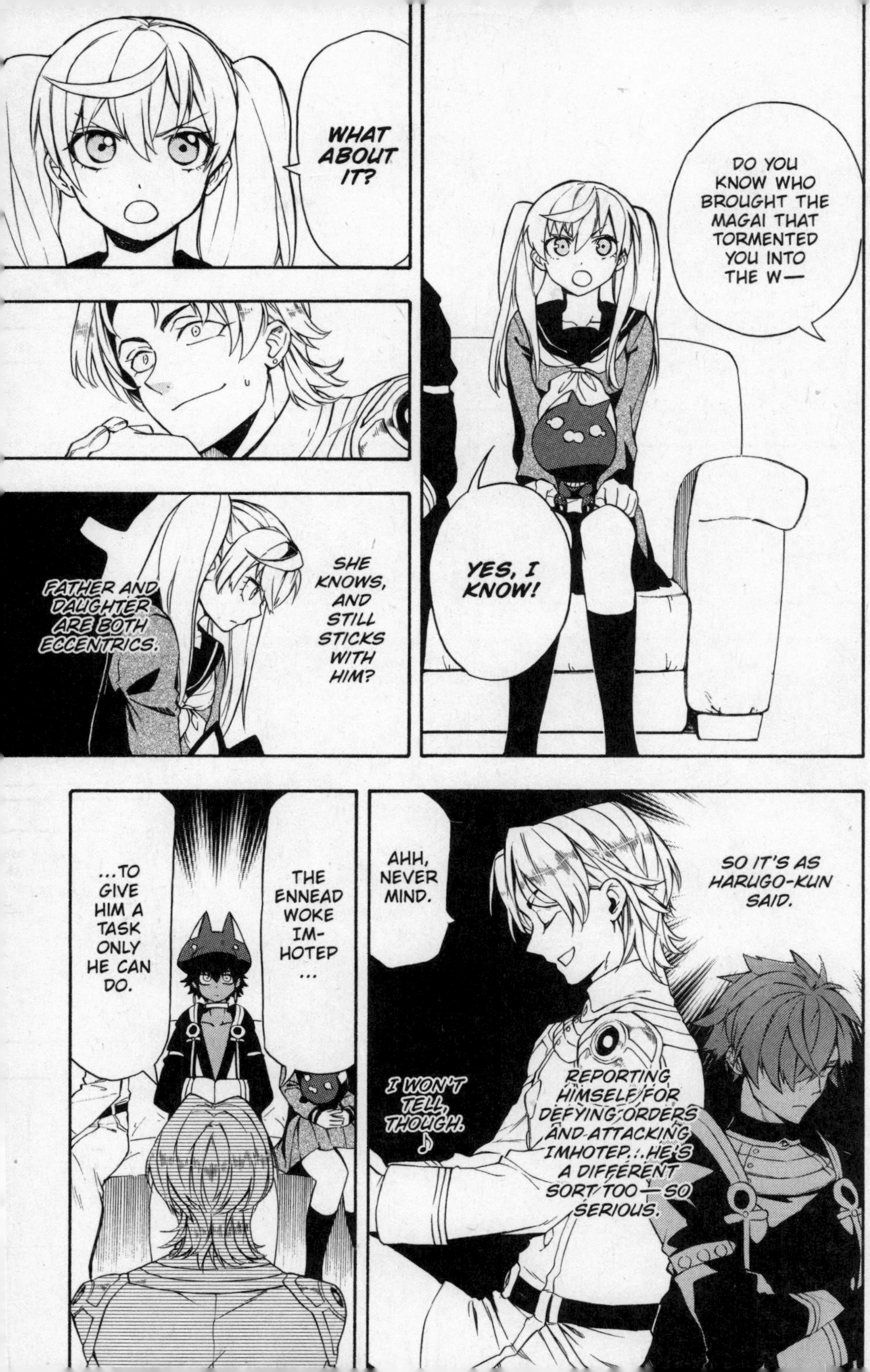
DO YOU KNOW WHO BROUGHT THE MAGAI THAT TORMENTED YOU INTO THE W—
YES, I KNOW!
WHAT ABOUT IT?
SHE KNOWS, AND STILL STICKS WITH HIM?
FATHER AND DAUGHTER ARE BOTH ECCENTRICS.
SO IT'S AS HARUGO-KUN SAID.
AHH, NEVER MIND.
REPORTING HIMSELF FOR DEFYING ORDERS AND ATTACKING IMHOTEP... HE'S A DIFFERENT SORT TOO— SO SERIOUS.
I WON'T TELL, THOUGH. ♪
THE ENNEAD WOKE IM-HOTEP...
...TO GIVE HIM A TASK ONLY HE CAN DO.

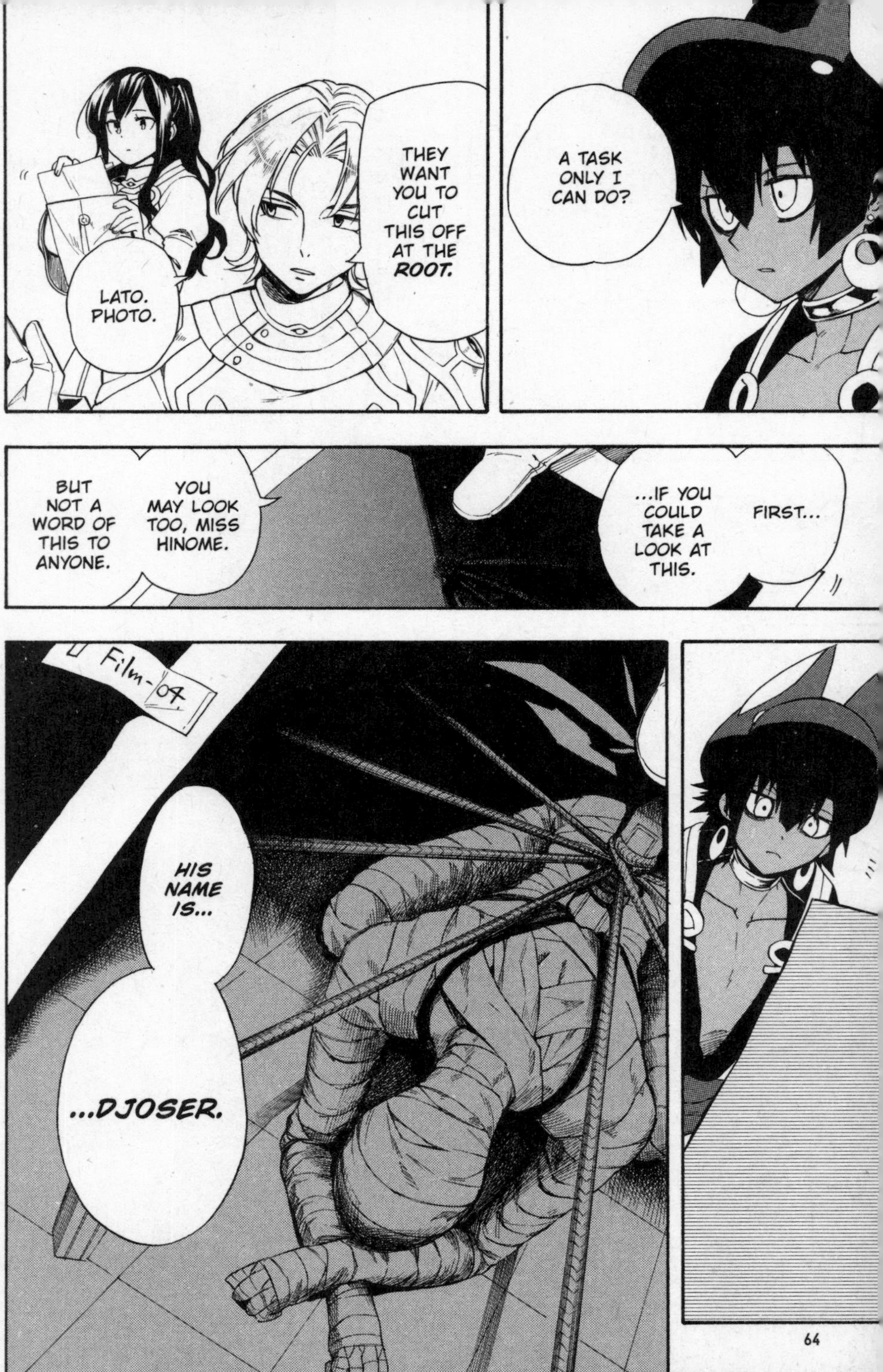
A TASK ONLY I CAN DO?
THEY WANT YOU TO CUT THIS OFF AT THE ROOT.
LATO. PHOTO.
FIRST...
...IF YOU COULD TAKE A LOOK AT THIS.
YOU MAY LOOK TOO, MISS HINOME.
BUT NOT A WORD OF THIS TO ANYONE.
Film-07
HIS NAME IS...
...DJOSER.

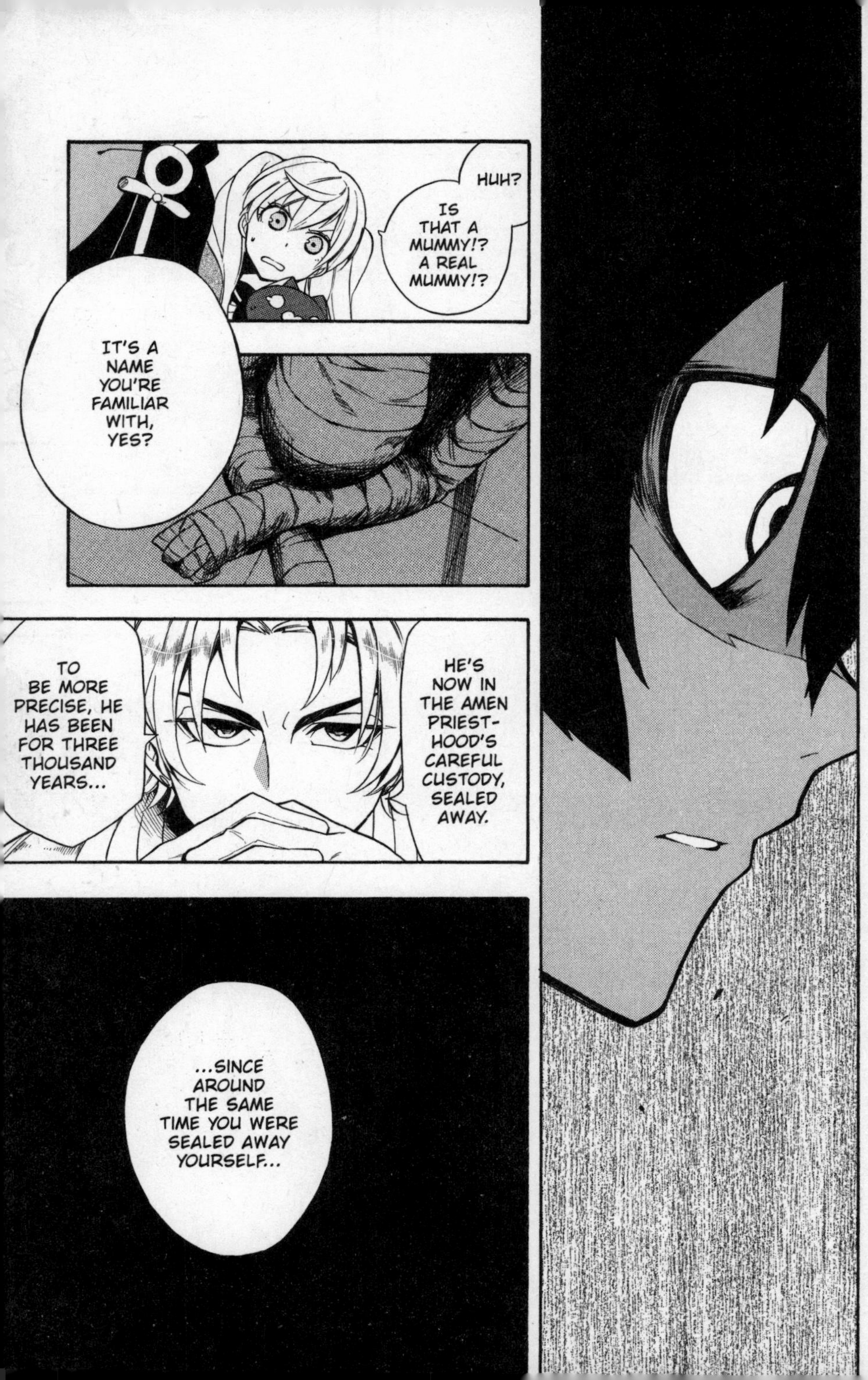
HUH?
IS THAT A MUMMY!? A REAL MUMMY!?
IT'S A NAME YOU'RE FAMILIAR WITH, YES?
HE'S NOW IN THE AMEN PRIEST-HOOD'S CAREFUL CUSTODY, SEALED AWAY.
TO BE MORE PRECISE, HE HAS BEEN FOR THREE THOUSAND YEARS...
...SINCE AROUND THE SAME TIME YOU WERE SEALED AWAY YOURSELF...

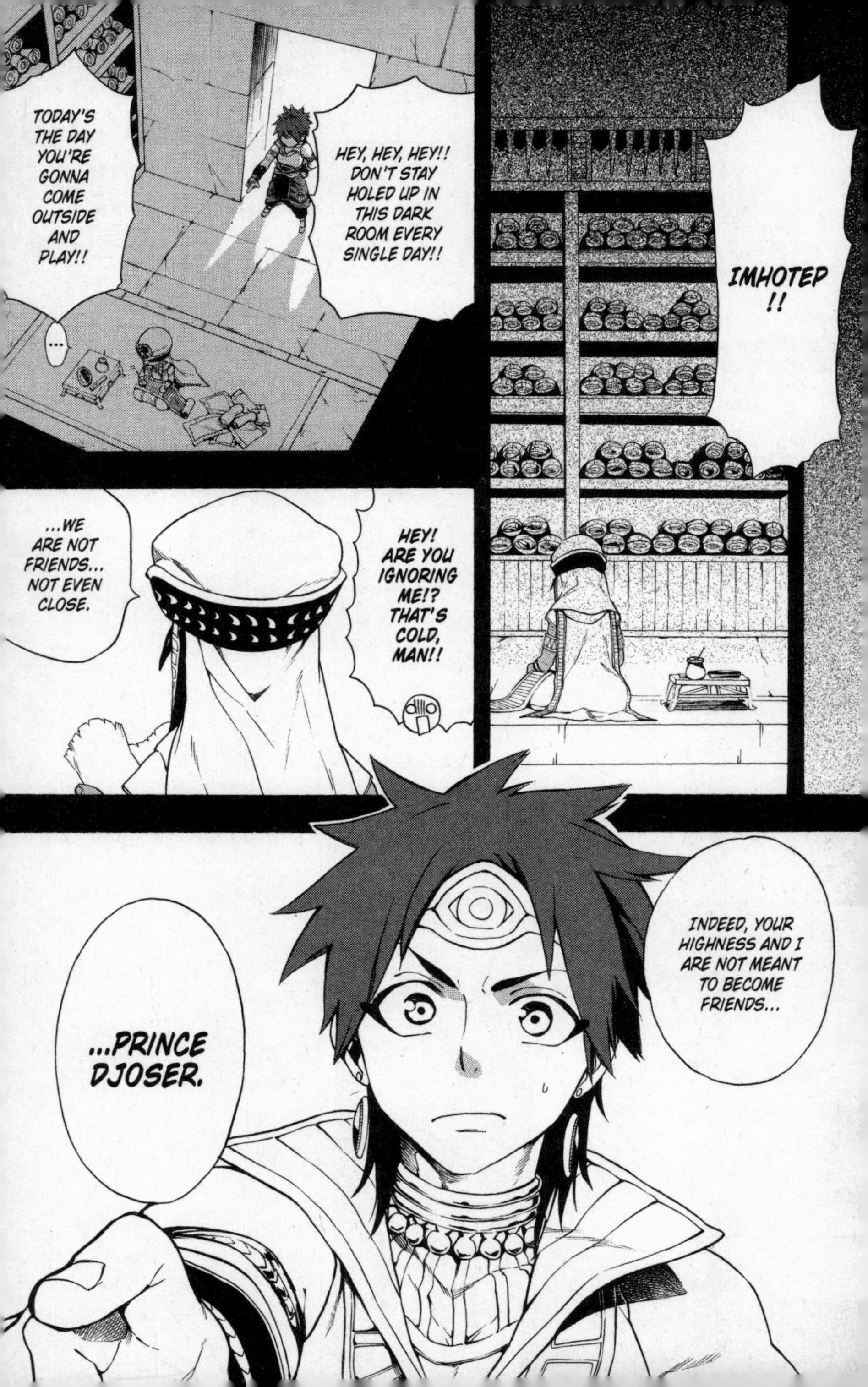
IMHOTEP !!
HEY, HEY, HEY!! DON'T STAY HOLED UP IN THIS DARK ROOM EVERY SINGLE DAY!!
TODAY'S THE DAY YOU'RE GONNA COME OUTSIDE AND PLAY!!
...
HEY! ARE YOU IGNORING ME!? THAT'S COLD, MAN!!
...WE ARE NOT FRIENDS... NOT EVEN CLOSE.
INDEED, YOUR HIGHNESS AND I ARE NOT MEANT TO BECOME FRIENDS...
...PRINCE DJOSER.

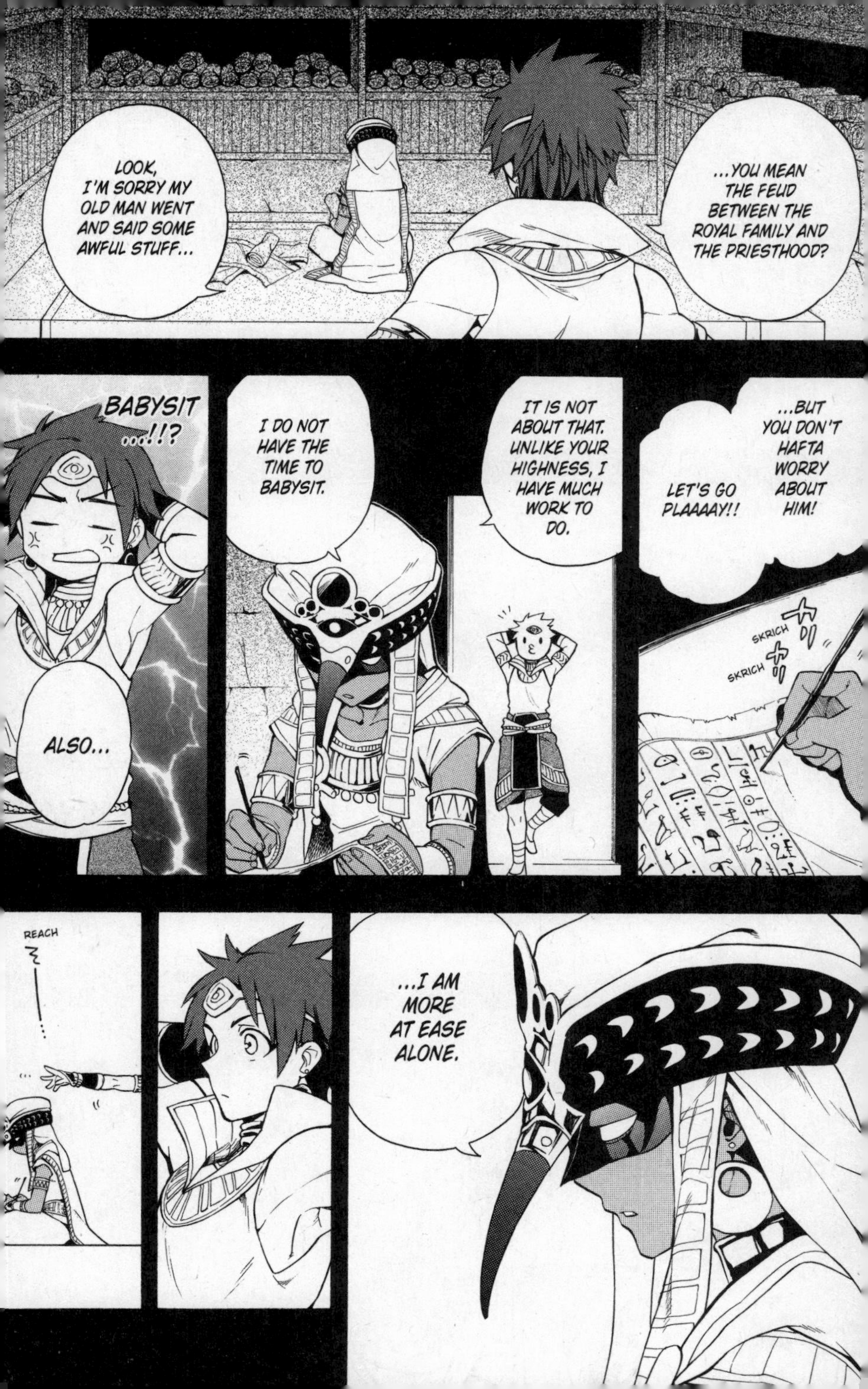
LOOK, I'M SORRY MY OLD MAN WENT AND SAID SOME AWFUL STUFF...
...YOU MEAN THE FEUD BETWEEN THE ROYAL FAMILY AND THE PRIESTHOOD?
...BUT YOU DON'T HAFTA WORRY ABOUT HIM!
LET'S GO PLAAAAY!!
SKRICH
SKRICH
IT IS NOT ABOUT THAT. UNLIKE YOUR HIGHNESS, I HAVE MUCH WORK TO DO.
I DO NOT HAVE THE TIME TO BABYSIT.
BABYSIT ...!!?
ALSO...
...I AM MORE AT EASE ALONE.
REACH

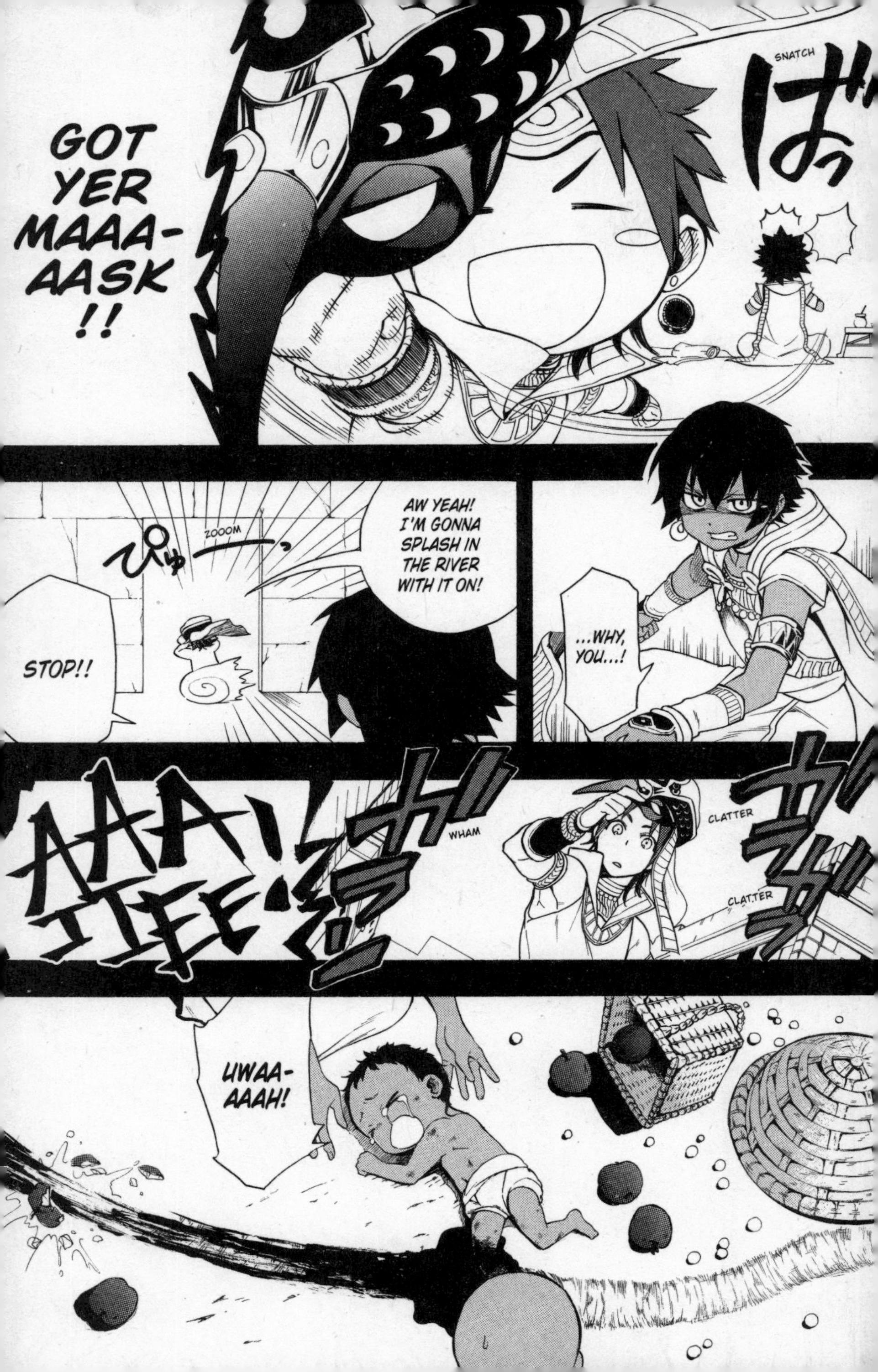
SNATCH
GOT YER MAAAA-AASK!!
...WHY, YOU...!
AW YEAH! I'M GONNA SPLASH IN THE RIVER WITH IT ON!
ZOOOM
STOP!!
CLATTER
CLATTER
WHAM
AAAIIEE
UWAA-AAAH!

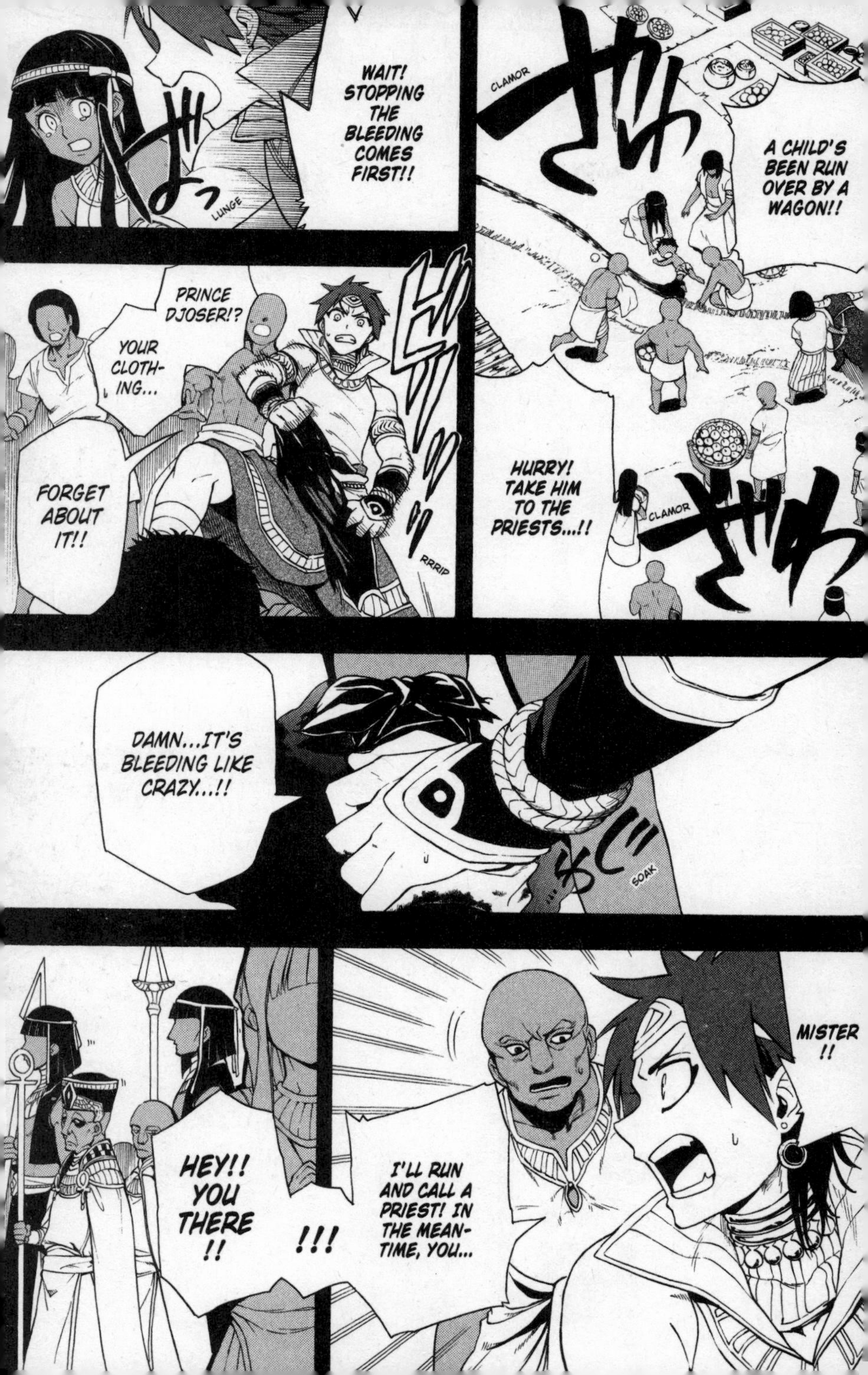
CLAMOR
A CHILD'S BEEN RUN OVER BY A WAGON!!
HURRY! TAKE HIM TO THE PRIESTS...!!
CLAMOR
WAIT! STOPPING THE BLEEDING COMES FIRST!!
LUNGE
PRINCE DJOSER!?
YOUR CLOTHING...
FORGET ABOUT IT!!
RRRIP
DAMN...IT'S BLEEDING LIKE CRAZY...!!
SOAK
MISTER!!
I'LL RUN AND CALL A PRIEST! IN THE MEANTIME, YOU...
!!!
HEY!! YOU THERE!!

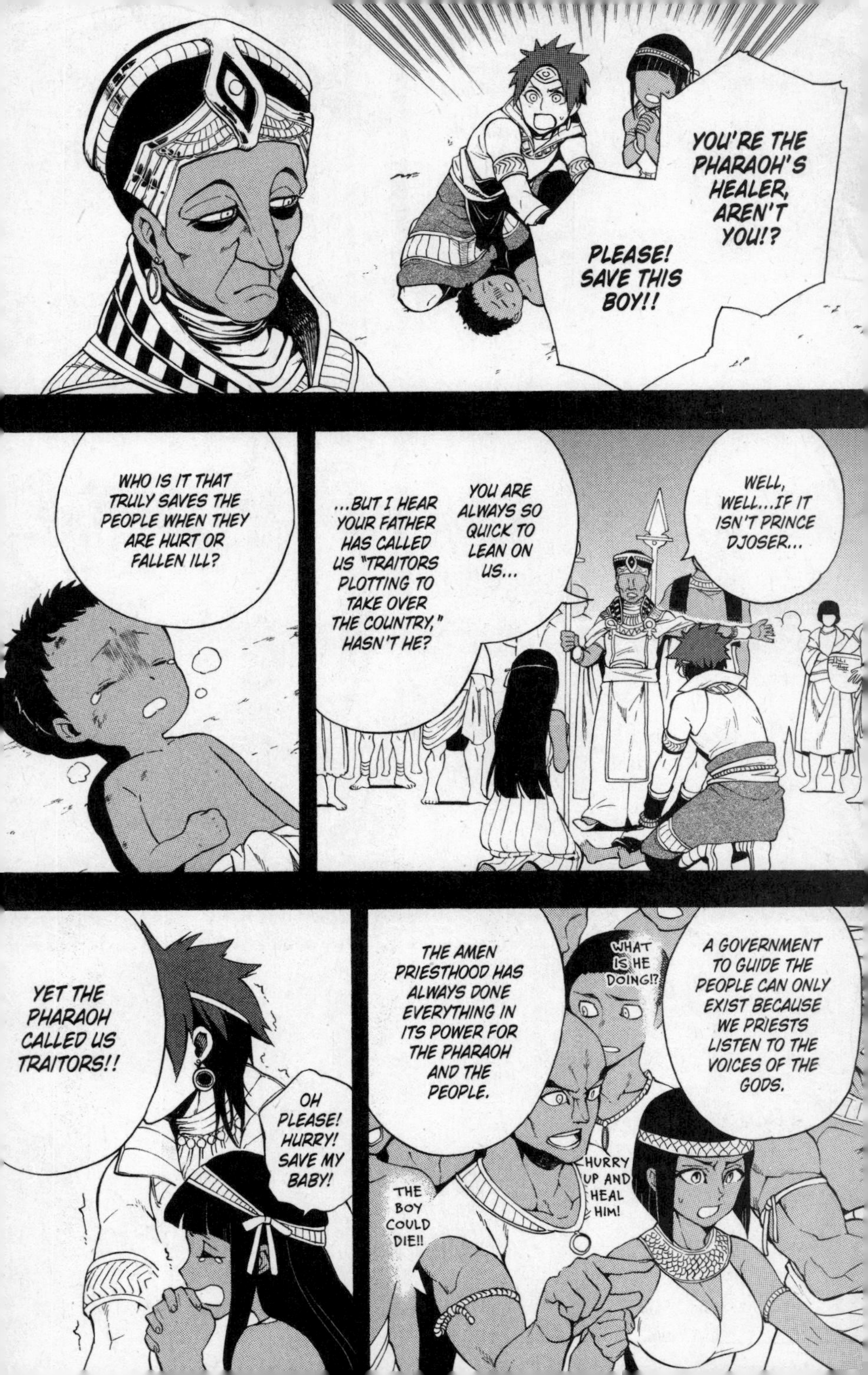
YOU'RE THE PHARAOH'S HEALER, AREN'T YOU!?
PLEASE! SAVE THIS BOY!!
WELL, WELL...IF IT ISN'T PRINCE DJOSER...
YOU ARE ALWAYS SO QUICK TO LEAN ON US...
...BUT I HEAR YOUR FATHER HAS CALLED US "TRAITORS PLOTTING TO TAKE OVER THE COUNTRY," HASN'T HE?
WHO IS IT THAT TRULY SAVES THE PEOPLE WHEN THEY ARE HURT OR FALLEN ILL?
A GOVERNMENT TO GUIDE THE PEOPLE CAN ONLY EXIST BECAUSE WE PRIESTS LISTEN TO THE VOICES OF THE GODS.
WHAT IS HE DOING!?
THE AMEN PRIESTHOOD HAS ALWAYS DONE EVERYTHING IN ITS POWER FOR THE PHARAOH AND THE PEOPLE.
HURRY UP AND HEAL HIM!
THE BOY COULD DIE!!
OH PLEASE! HURRY! SAVE MY BABY!
YET THE PHARAOH CALLED US TRAITORS!!

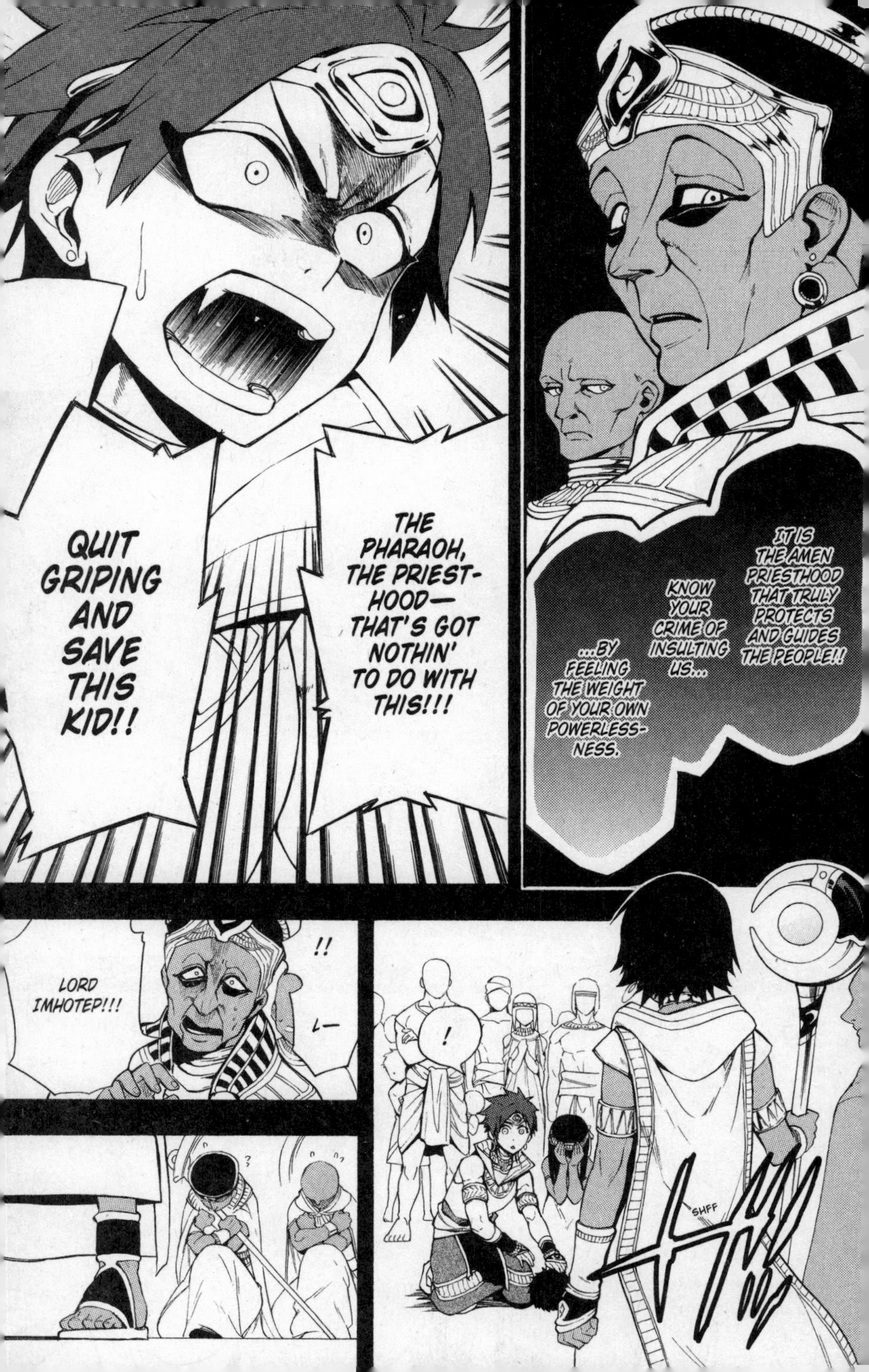
IT IS THE AMEN PRIESTHOOD THAT TRULY PROTECTS AND GUIDES THE PEOPLE!!
KNOW YOUR CRIME OF INSULTING US...
...BY FEELING THE WEIGHT OF YOUR OWN POWERLESS-NESS.
THE PHARAOH, THE PRIEST-HOOD—THAT'S GOT NOTHIN' TO DO WITH THIS!!!
QUIT GRIPING AND SAVE THIS KID!!
!
SHFF
!!
LORD IMHOTEP!!!

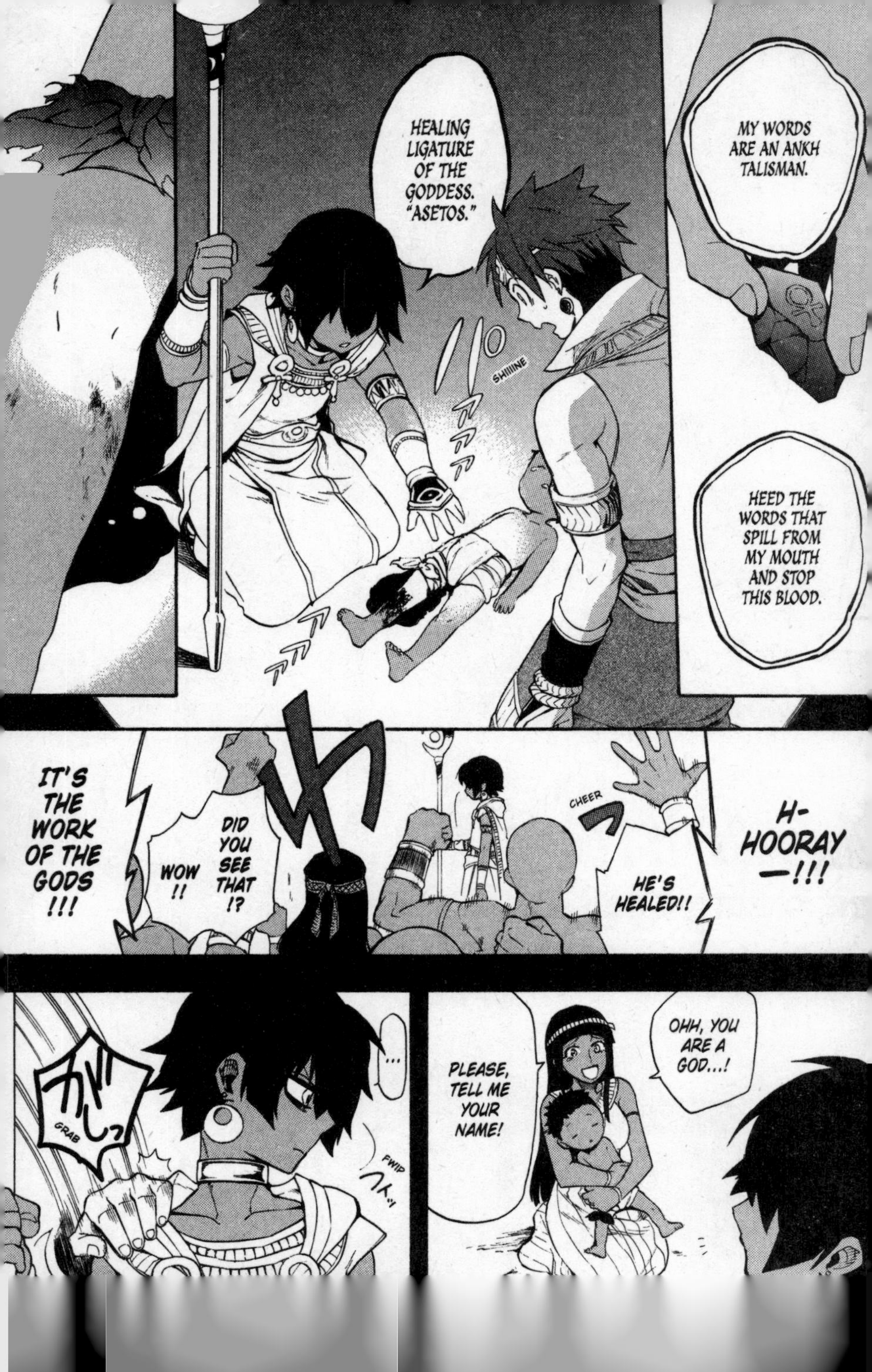
MY WORDS ARE AN ANKH TALISMAN.
HEED THE WORDS THAT SPILL FROM MY MOUTH AND STOP THIS BLOOD.
HEALING LIGATURE OF THE GODDESS. "ASETOS."
SHIIINE
H-HOORAY—!!!
HE'S HEALED!!
CHEER
DID YOU SEE THAT !?
WOW !!
IT'S THE WORK OF THE GODS !!!
OHH, YOU ARE A GOD...!
PLEASE, TELL ME YOUR NAME!
...
FWIP
GRAB

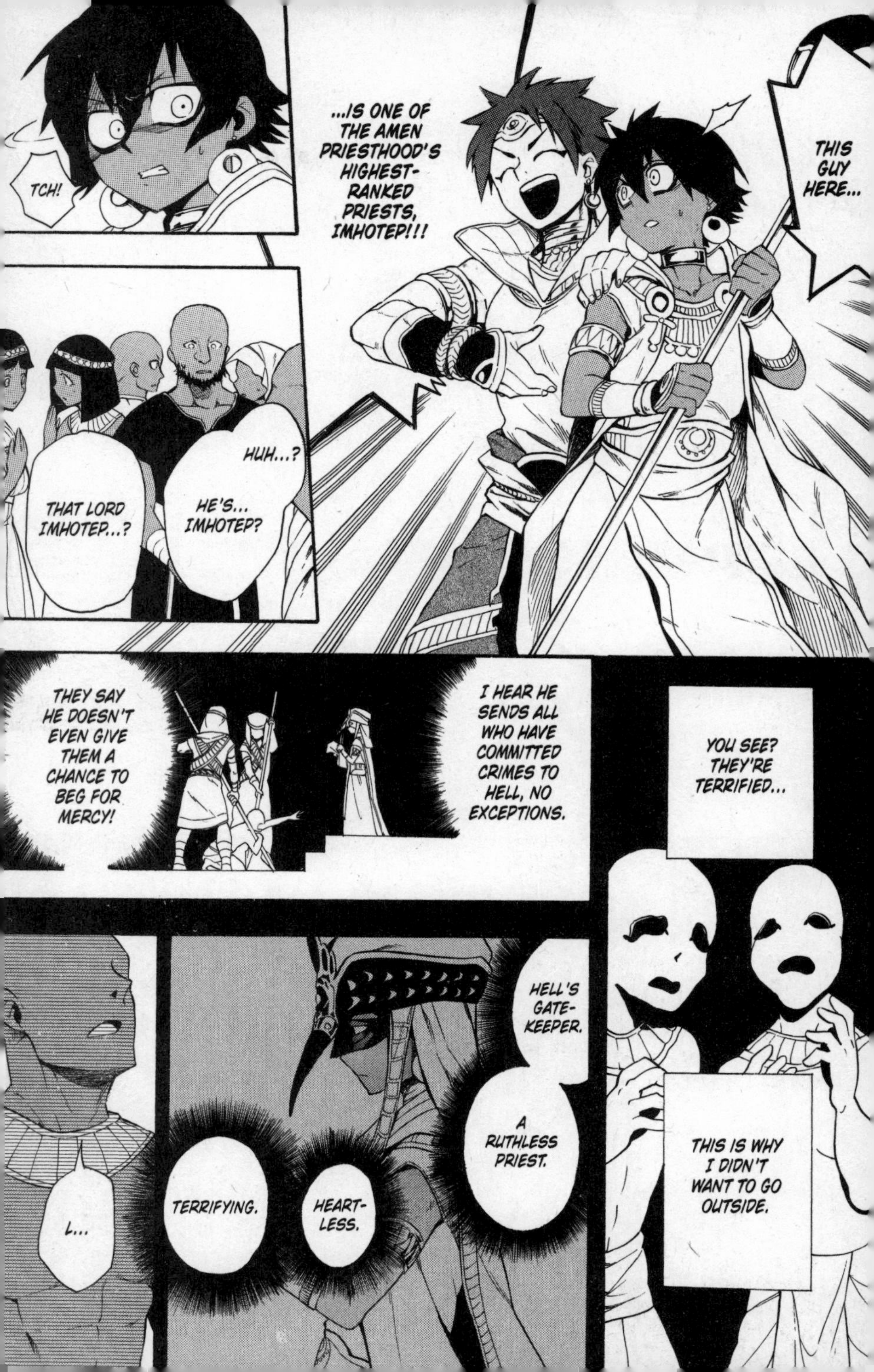

THIS GUY HERE...
...IS ONE OF THE AMEN PRIESTHOOD'S HIGHEST-RANKED PRIESTS, IMHOTEP!!!
TCH!
HUH...?
HE'S... IMHOTEP?
THAT LORD IMHOTEP...?
YOU SEE? THEY'RE TERRIFIED...
THIS IS WHY I DIDN'T WANT TO GO OUTSIDE.
I HEAR HE SENDS ALL WHO HAVE COMMITTED CRIMES TO HELL, NO EXCEPTIONS.
THEY SAY HE DOESN'T EVEN GIVE THEM A CHANCE TO BEG FOR MERCY!
HELL'S GATE-KEEPER.
A RUTHLESS PRIEST.
HEART-LESS.
TERRIFYING.
I...

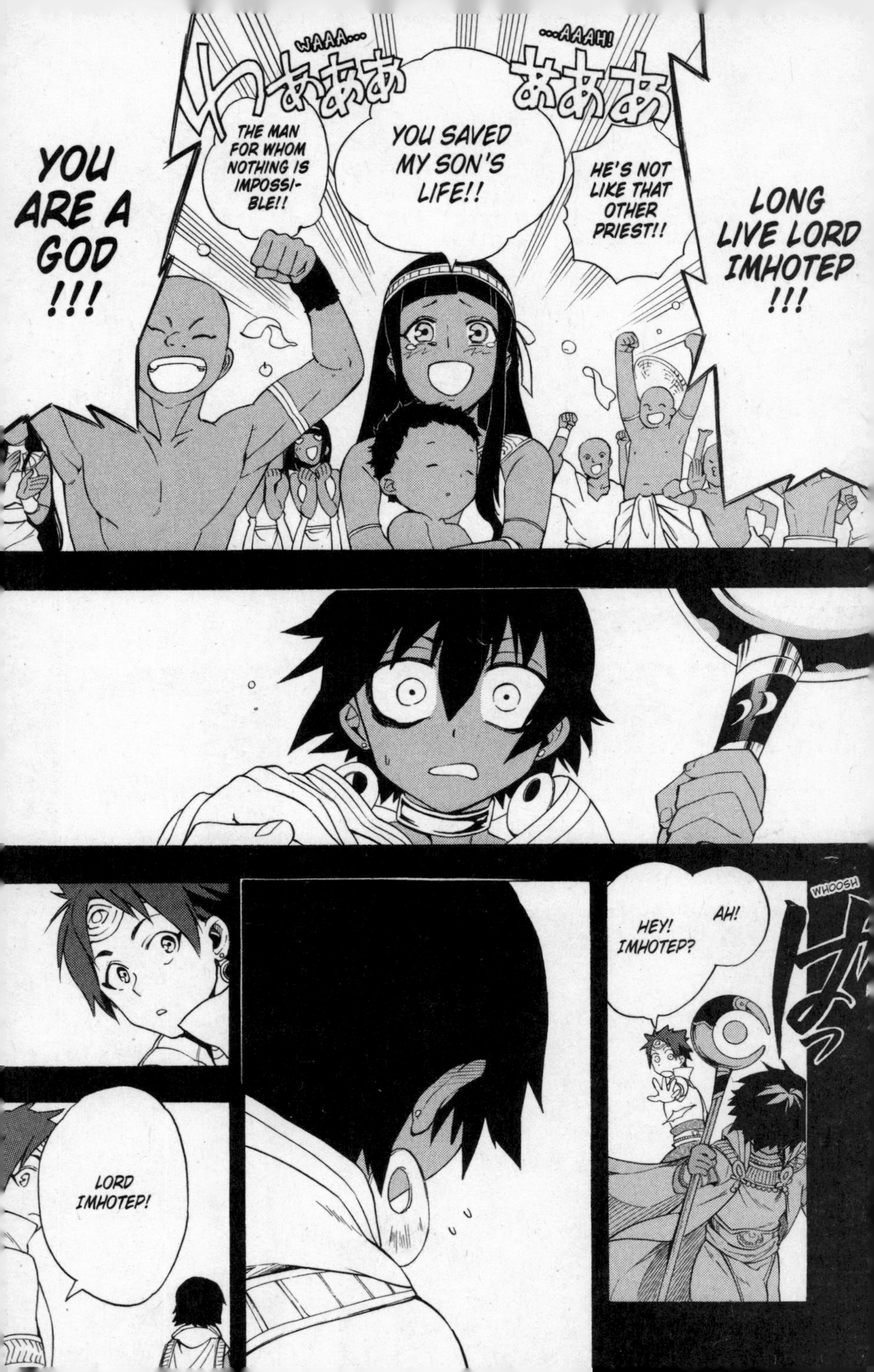
WAAA...
...AAAH!
LONG LIVE LORD IMHOTEP!!!
HE'S NOT LIKE THAT OTHER PRIEST!!
YOU SAVED MY SON'S LIFE!!
THE MAN FOR WHOM NOTHING IS IMPOSSI-BLE!!
YOU ARE A GOD!!!
WHOOSH
AH!
HEY! IMHOTEP?
LORD IMHOTEP!

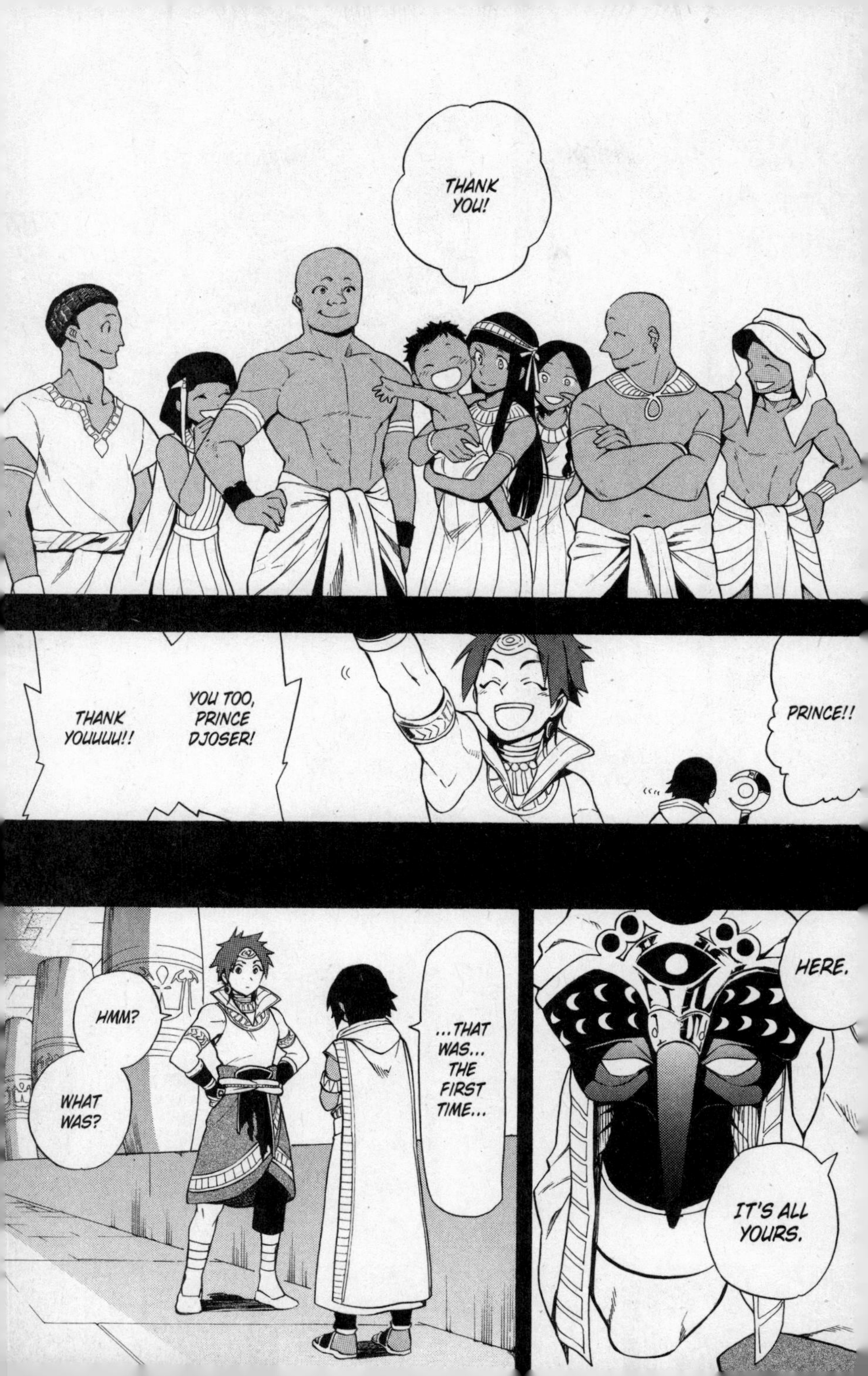
THANK YOU!
PRINCE!!
YOU TOO, PRINCE DJOSER!
THANK YOUUUU!!
HERE.
IT'S ALL YOURS.
...THAT WAS... THE FIRST TIME...
HMM?
WHAT WAS?

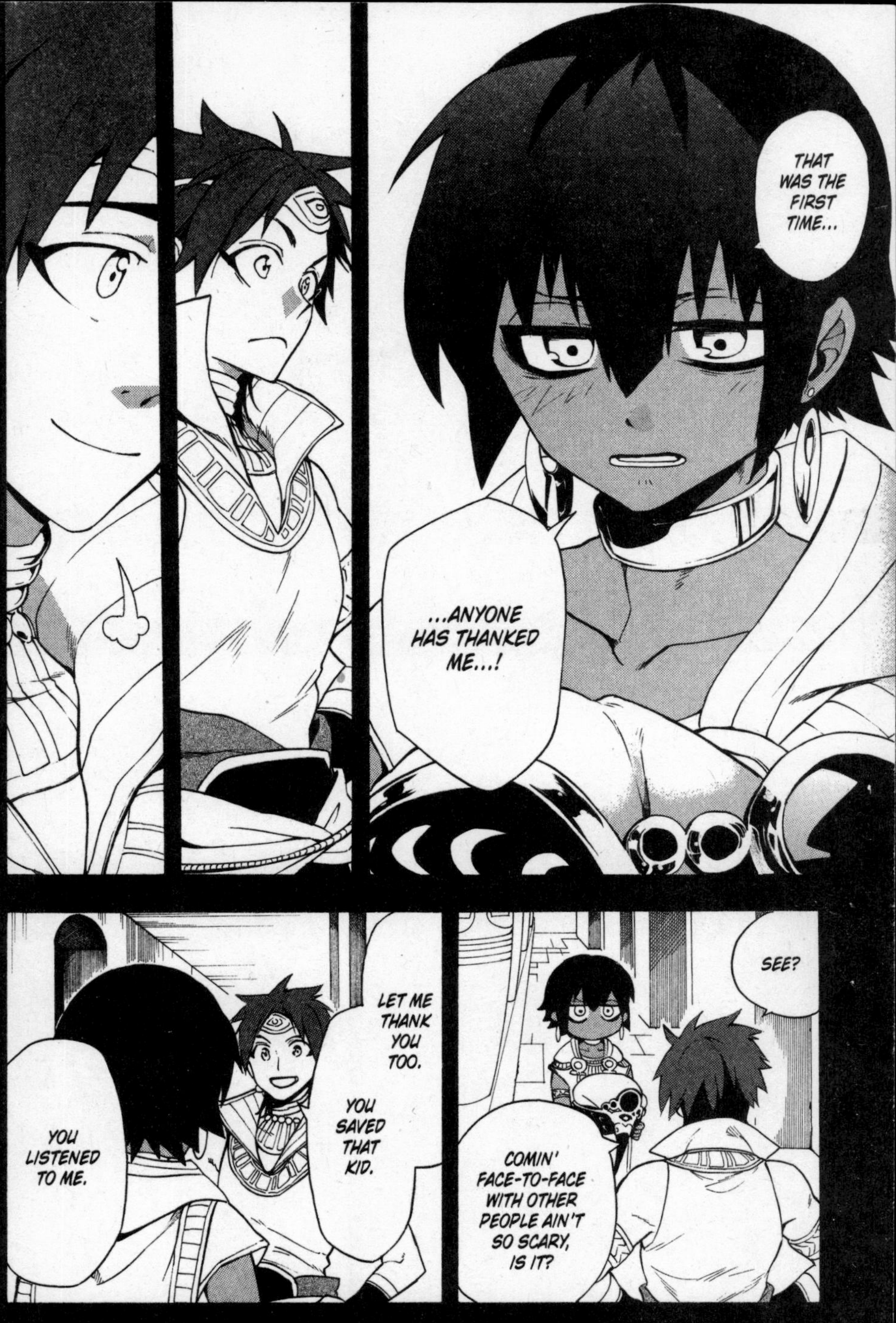
THAT WAS THE FIRST TIME...
...ANYONE HAS THANKED ME...!
SEE?
COMIN' FACE-TO-FACE WITH OTHER PEOPLE AIN'T SO SCARY, IS IT?
LET ME THANK YOU TOO.
YOU SAVED THAT KID.
YOU LISTENED TO ME.

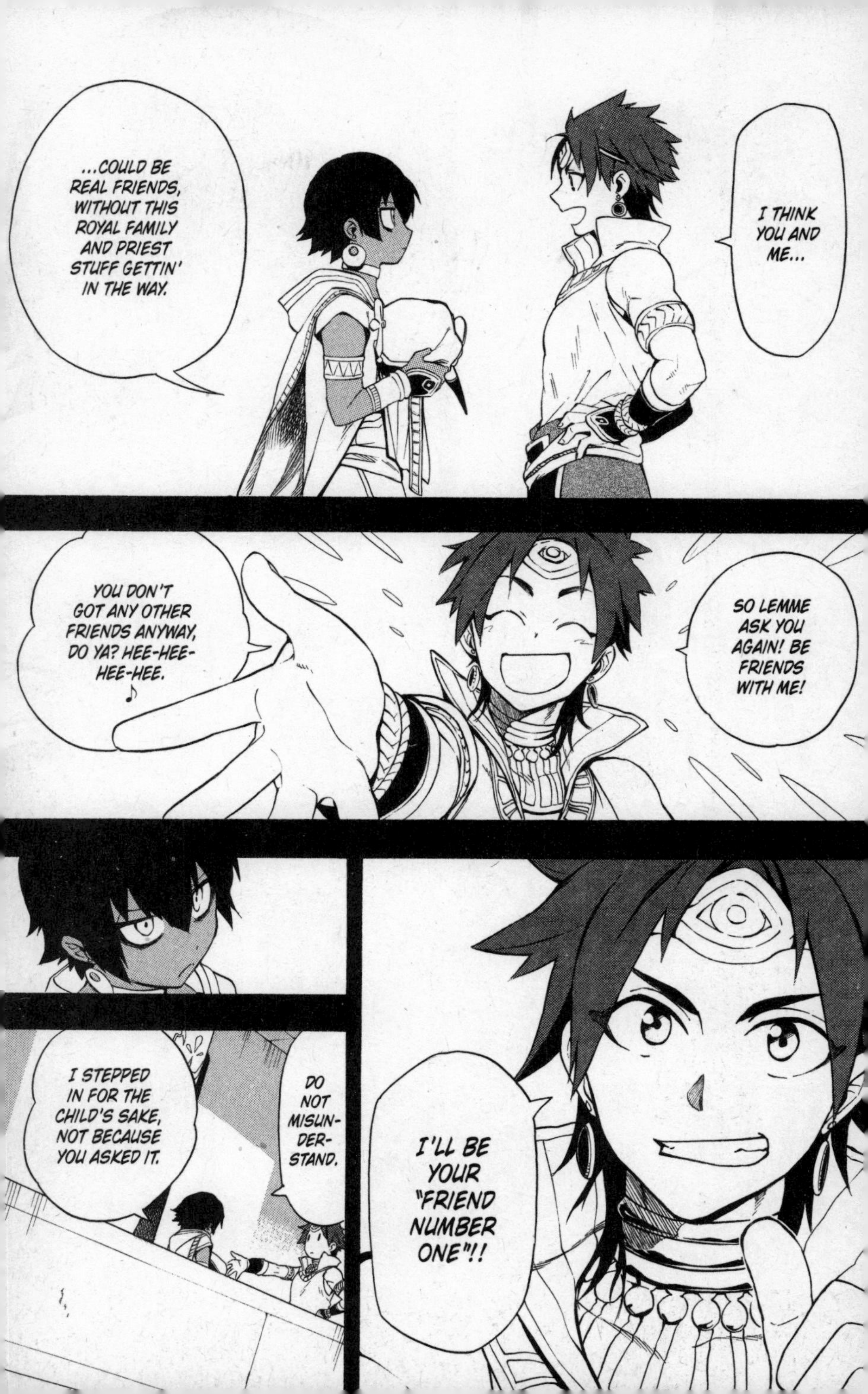
I THINK YOU AND ME...
...COULD BE REAL FRIENDS, WITHOUT THIS ROYAL FAMILY AND PRIEST STUFF GETTIN' IN THE WAY.
SO LEMME ASK YOU AGAIN! BE FRIENDS WITH ME!
YOU DON'T GOT ANY OTHER FRIENDS ANYWAY, DO YA? HEE-HEE-HEE-HEE. ♪
I'LL BE YOUR "FRIEND NUMBER ONE"!!
DO NOT MISUNDERSTAND.
I STEPPED IN FOR THE CHILD'S SAKE, NOT BECAUSE YOU ASKED IT.

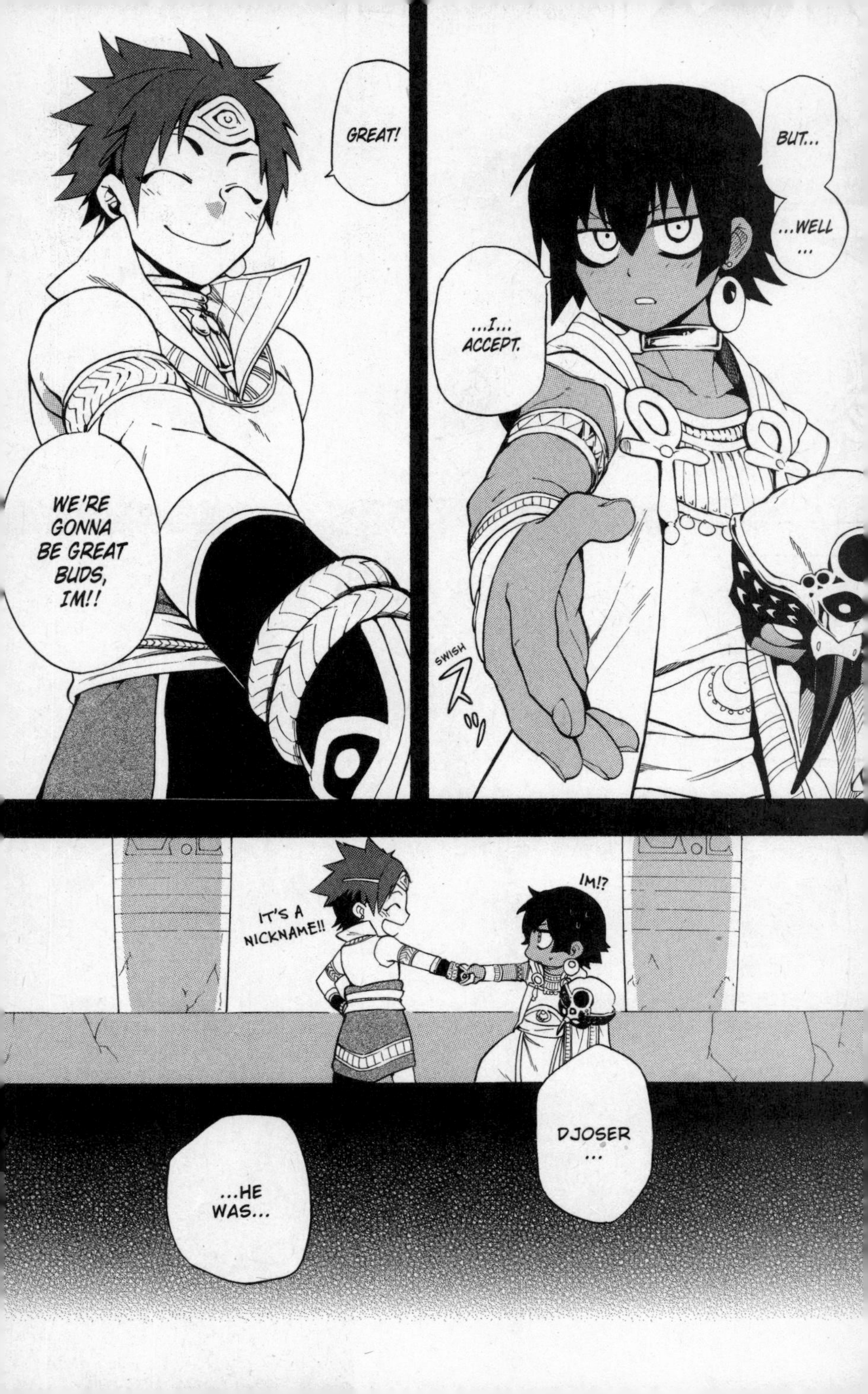
BUT...
...WELL ...
...I... ACCEPT.
SWISH
GREAT!
WE'RE GONNA BE GREAT BUDS, IM!!
IM!?
IT'S A NICKNAME!!
DJOSER ...
...HE WAS...

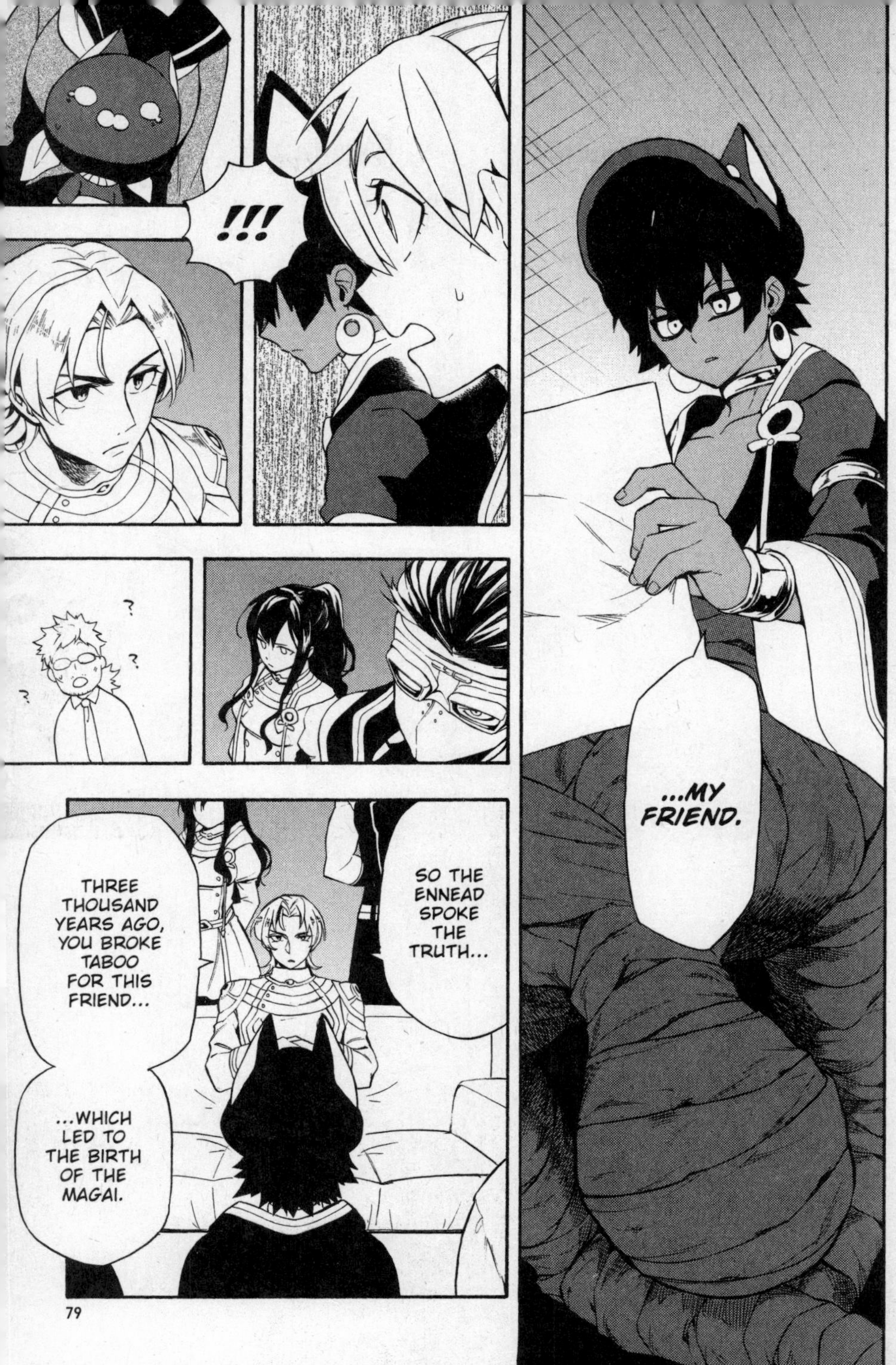
...MY FRIEND.
!!!
SO THE ENNEAD SPOKE THE TRUTH...
THREE THOUSAND YEARS AGO, YOU BROKE TABOO FOR THIS FRIEND...
...WHICH LED TO THE BIRTH OF THE MAGAI.

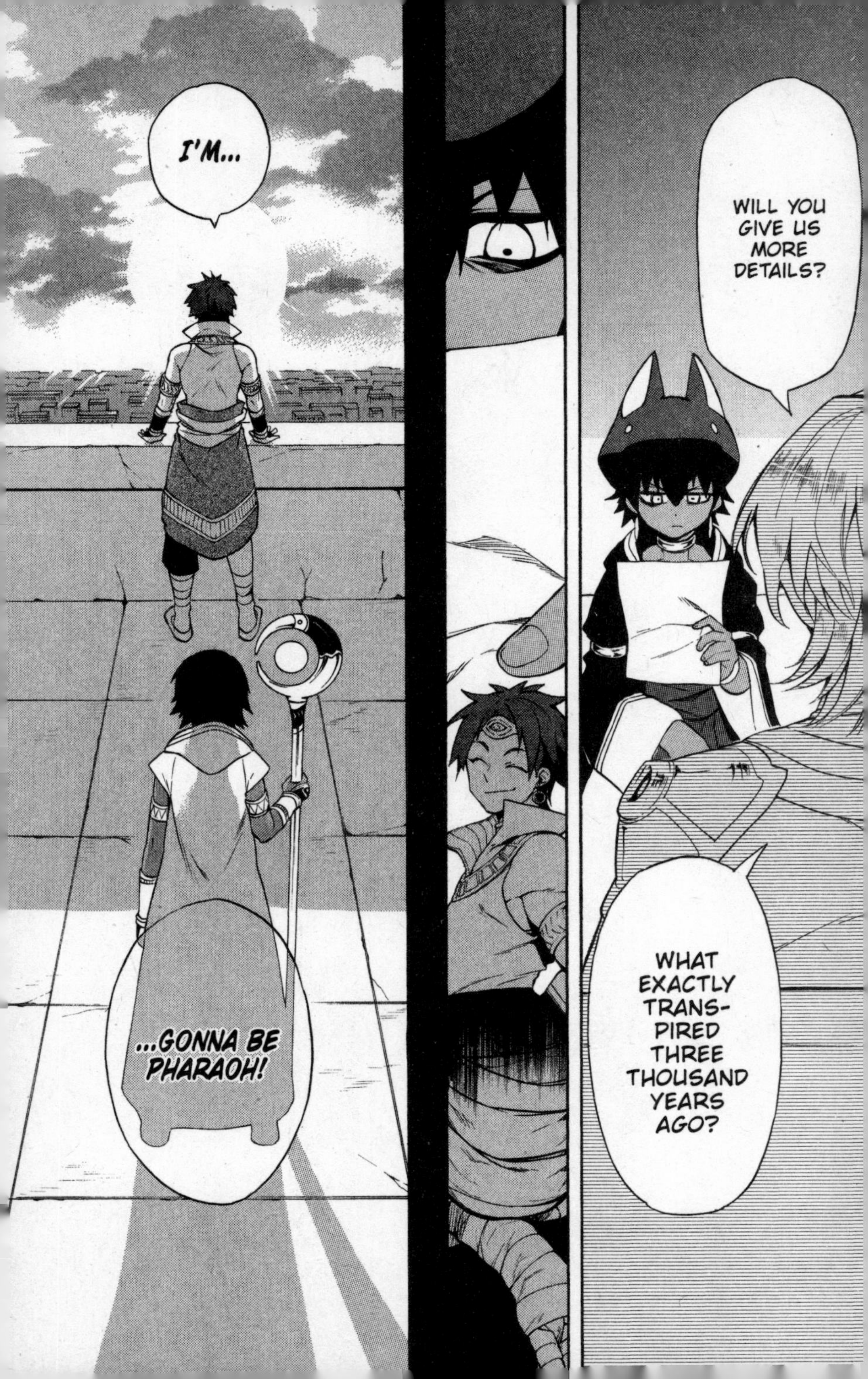
WILL YOU GIVE US MORE DETAILS?
WHAT EXACTLY TRANS-PIRED THREE THOUSAND YEARS AGO?
I'M...
...GONNA BE PHARAOH!

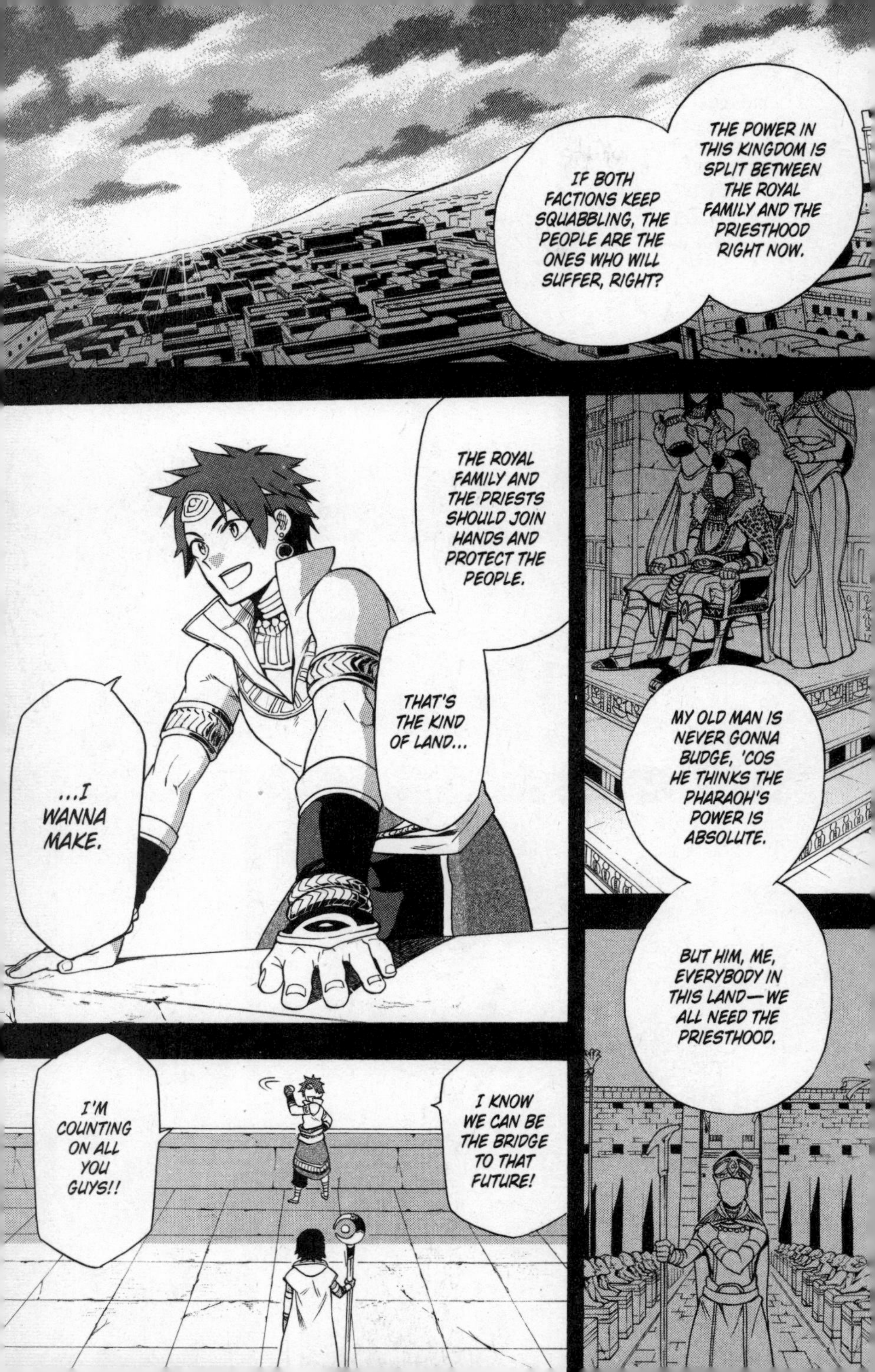
THE POWER IN THIS KINGDOM IS SPLIT BETWEEN THE ROYAL FAMILY AND THE PRIESTHOOD RIGHT NOW.
IF BOTH FACTIONS KEEP SQUABBLING, THE PEOPLE ARE THE ONES WHO WILL SUFFER, RIGHT?
MY OLD MAN IS NEVER GONNA BUDGE, 'COS HE THINKS THE PHARAOH'S POWER IS ABSOLUTE.
BUT HIM, ME, EVERYBODY IN THIS LAND—WE ALL NEED THE PRIESTHOOD.
THE ROYAL FAMILY AND THE PRIESTS SHOULD JOIN HANDS AND PROTECT THE PEOPLE.
THAT'S THE KIND OF LAND...
...I WANNA MAKE.
I KNOW WE CAN BE THE BRIDGE TO THAT FUTURE!
I'M COUNTING ON ALL YOU GUYS!!

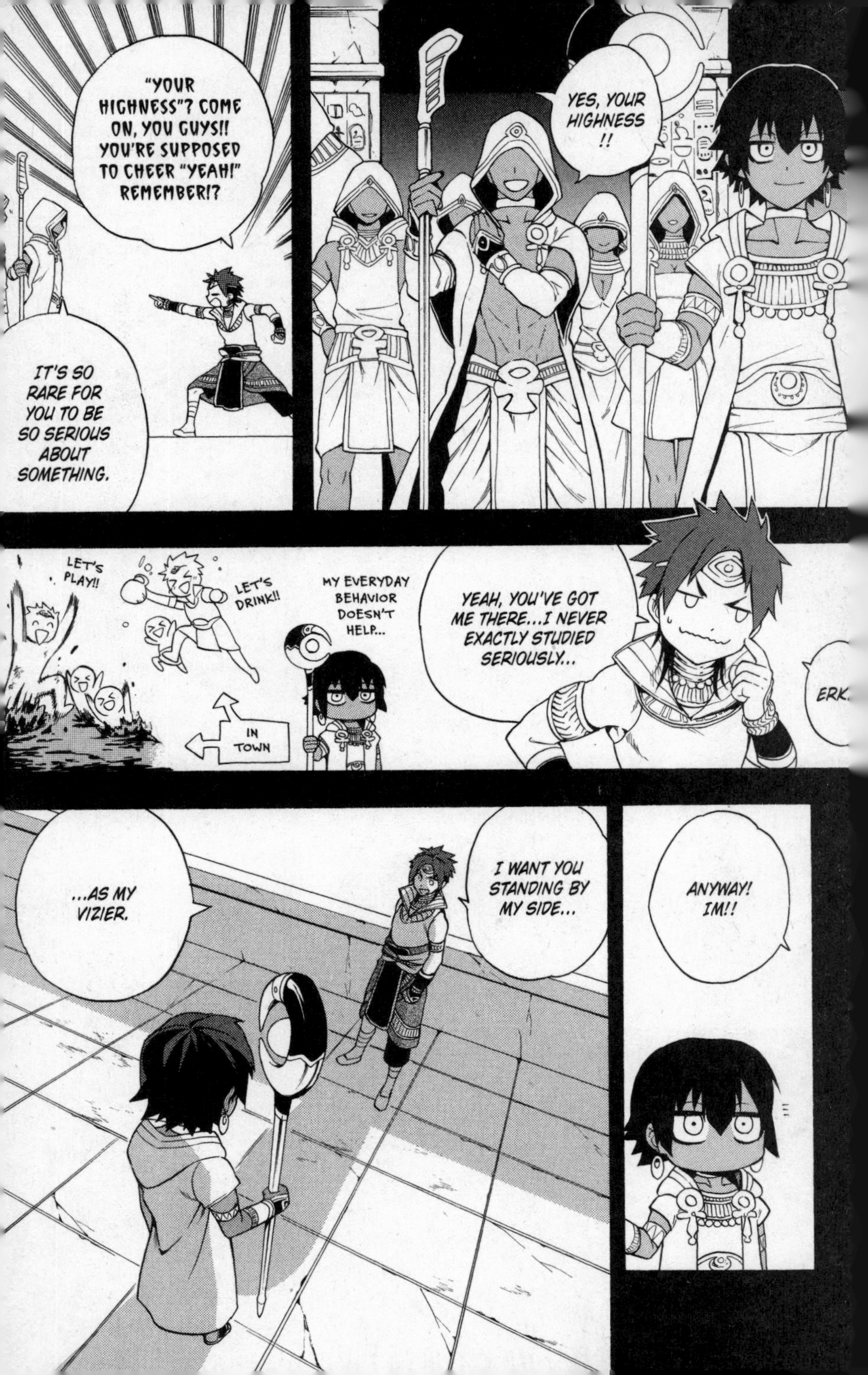
YES, YOUR HIGHNESS !!
"YOUR HIGHNESS"? COME ON, YOU GUYS!! YOU'RE SUPPOSED TO CHEER "YEAH!" REMEMBER!?
IT'S SO RARE FOR YOU TO BE SO SERIOUS ABOUT SOMETHING.
ERK.
YEAH, YOU'VE GOT ME THERE...I NEVER EXACTLY STUDIED SERIOUSLY...
MY EVERYDAY BEHAVIOR DOESN'T HELP...
LET'S DRINK!!
LET'S PLAY!!
IN TOWN
ANYWAY! IM!!
I WANT YOU STANDING BY MY SIDE...
...AS MY VIZIER.

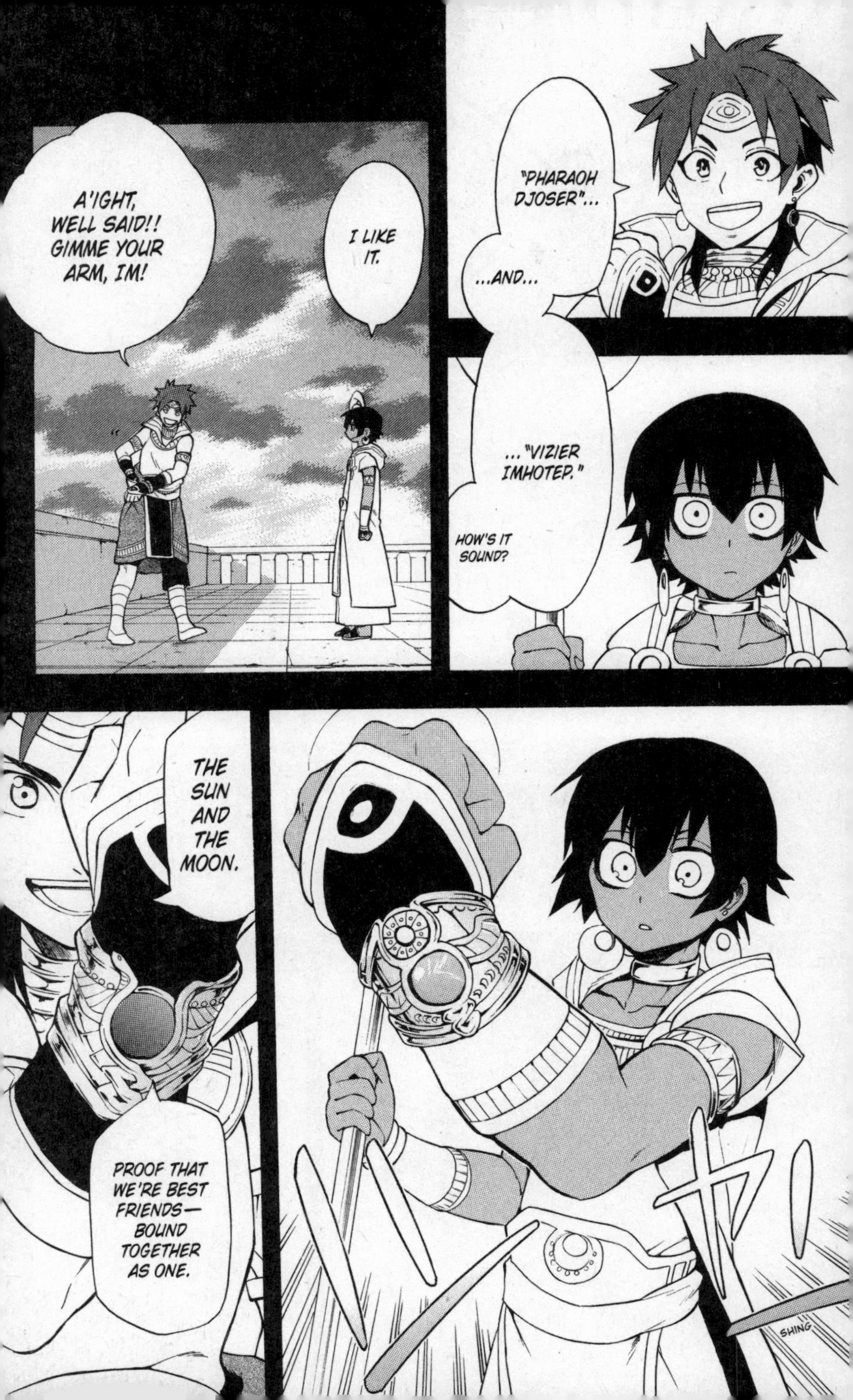
"PHARAOH DJOSER"...
...AND...
..."VIZIER IMHOTEP."
HOW'S IT SOUND?
I LIKE IT.
A'IGHT, WELL SAID!! GIMME YOUR ARM, IM!
SHING
THE SUN AND THE MOON.
PROOF THAT WE'RE BEST FRIENDS—BOUND TOGETHER AS ONE.

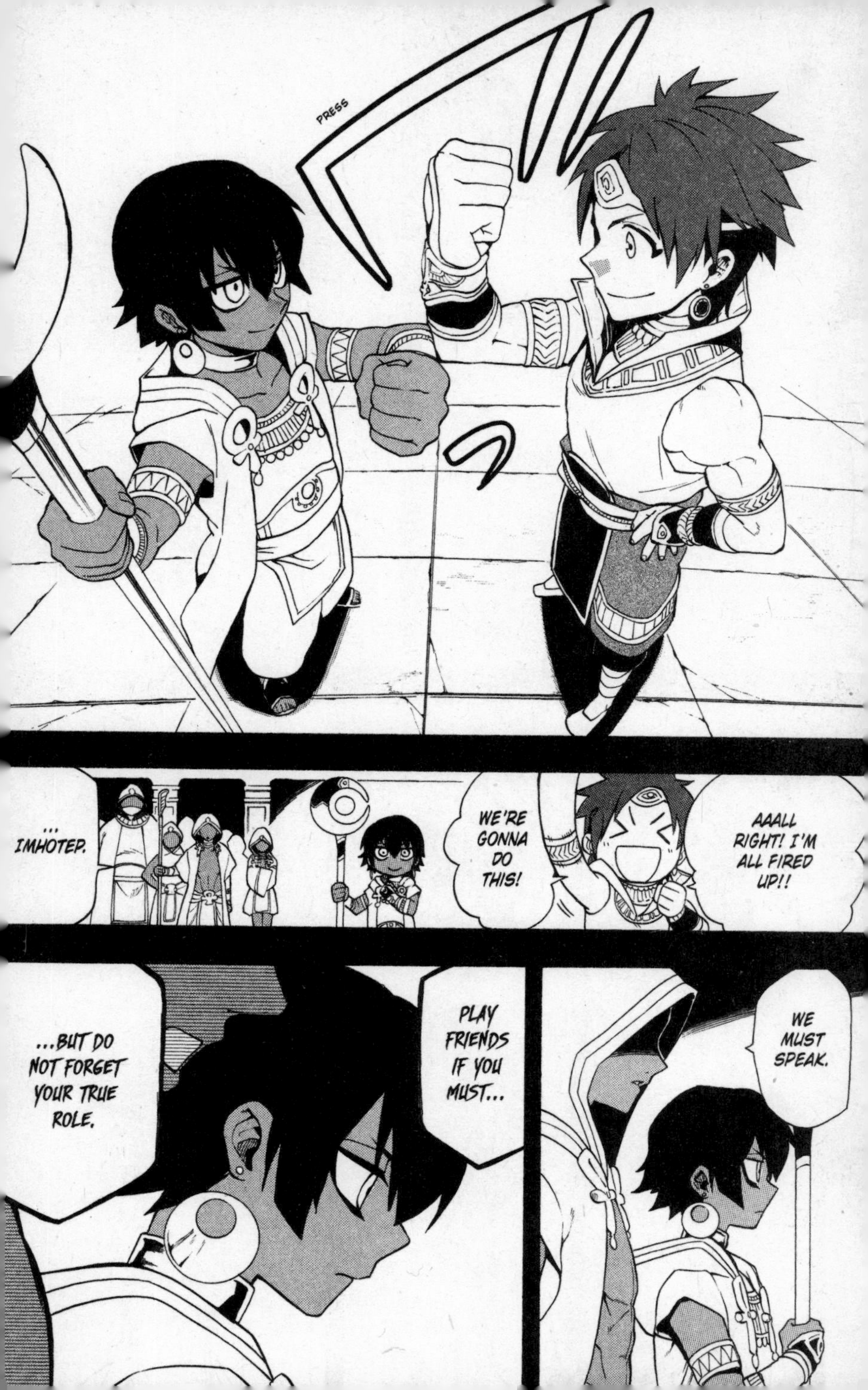
PRESS
AAALL RIGHT! I'M ALL FIRED UP!!
WE'RE GONNA DO THIS!
... IMHOTEP.
WE MUST SPEAK.
PLAY FRIENDS IF YOU MUST...
...BUT DO NOT FORGET YOUR TRUE ROLE.

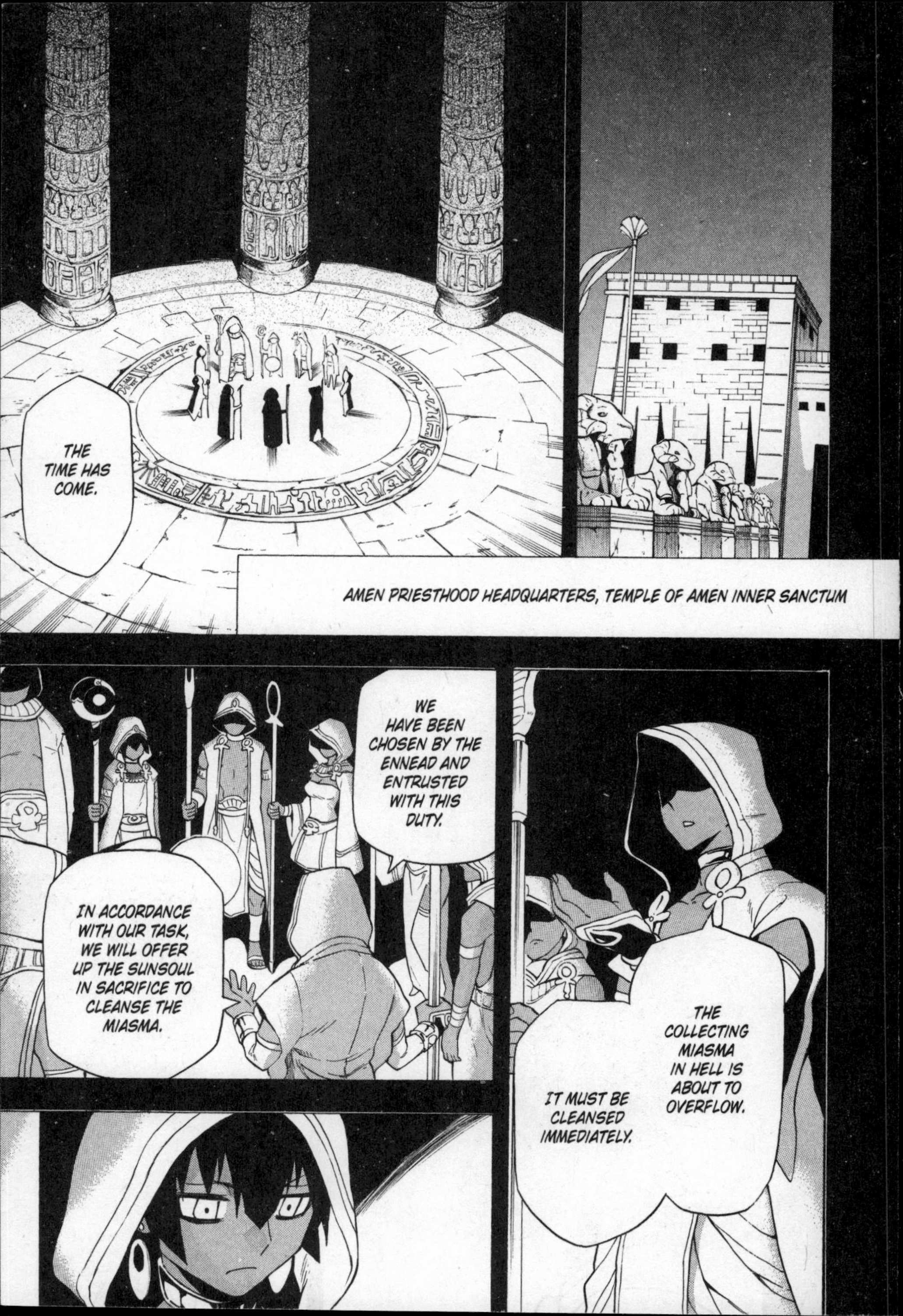
AMEN PRIESTHOOD HEADQUARTERS, TEMPLE OF AMEN INNER SANCTUM
THE TIME HAS COME.
THE COLLECTING MIASMA IN HELL IS ABOUT TO OVERFLOW.
IT MUST BE CLEANSED IMMEDIATELY.
WE HAVE BEEN CHOSEN BY THE ENNEAD AND ENTRUSTED WITH THIS DUTY.
IN ACCORDANCE WITH OUR TASK, WE WILL OFFER UP THE SUNSOUL IN SACRIFICE TO CLEANSE THE MIASMA.

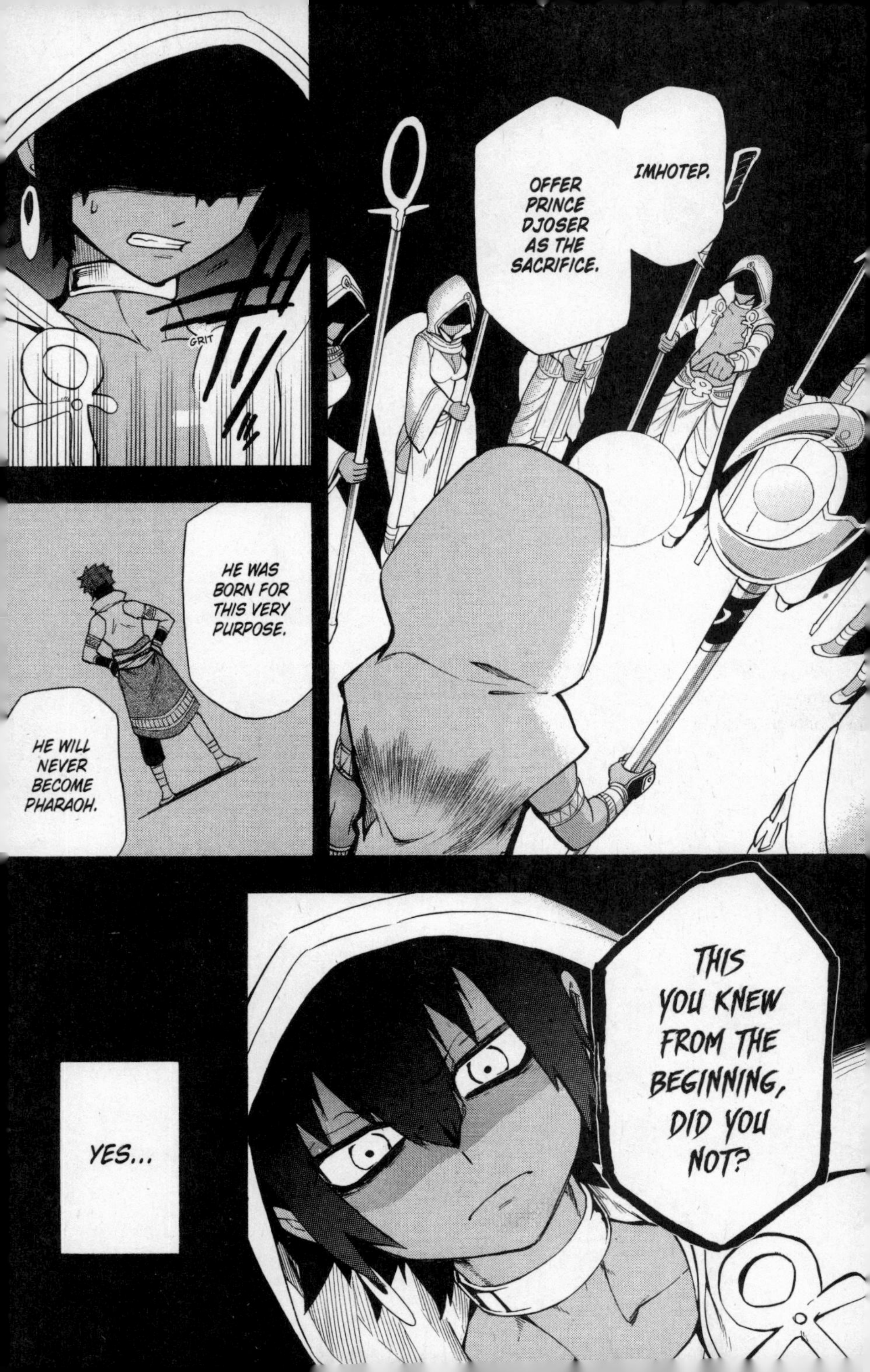
IMHOTEP.
OFFER PRINCE DJOSER AS THE SACRIFICE.
GRIT
HE WAS BORN FOR THIS VERY PURPOSE.
HE WILL NEVER BECOME PHARAOH.
THIS YOU KNEW FROM THE BEGINNING, DID YOU NOT?
YES...

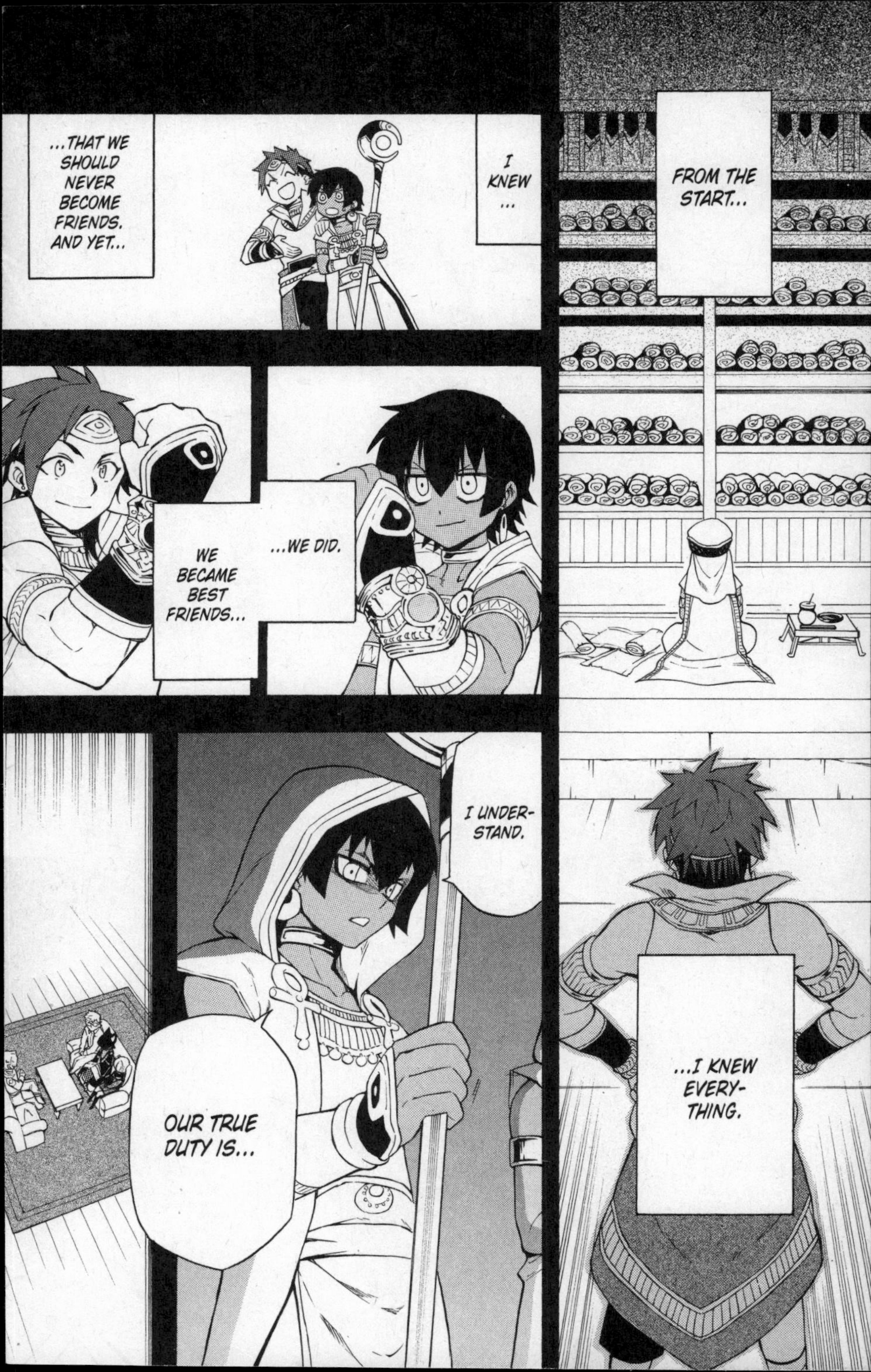
FROM THE START...
I KNEW...
...THAT WE SHOULD NEVER BECOME FRIENDS. AND YET...
...WE DID.
WE BECAME BEST FRIENDS...
...I KNEW EVERYTHING.
I UNDER-STAND.
OUR TRUE DUTY IS...

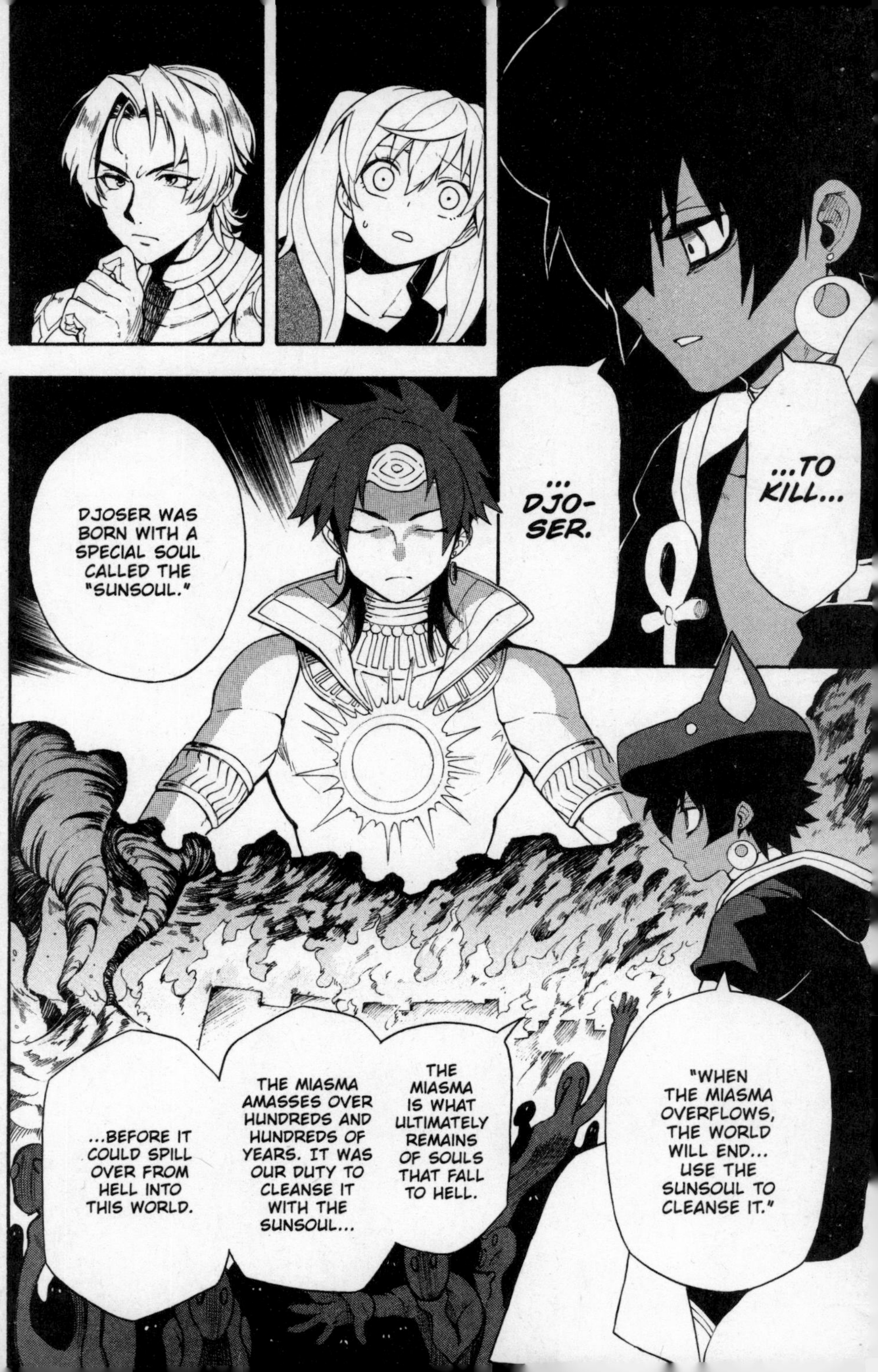
...TO KILL...
...DJOSER.
DJOSER WAS BORN WITH A SPECIAL SOUL CALLED THE "SUNSOUL."
"WHEN THE MIASMA OVERFLOWS, THE WORLD WILL END... USE THE SUNSOUL TO CLEANSE IT."
THE MIASMA IS WHAT ULTIMATELY REMAINS OF SOULS THAT FALL TO HELL.
THE MIASMA AMASSES OVER HUNDREDS AND HUNDREDS OF YEARS. IT WAS OUR DUTY TO CLEANSE IT WITH THE SUNSOUL...
...BEFORE IT COULD SPILL OVER FROM HELL INTO THIS WORLD.

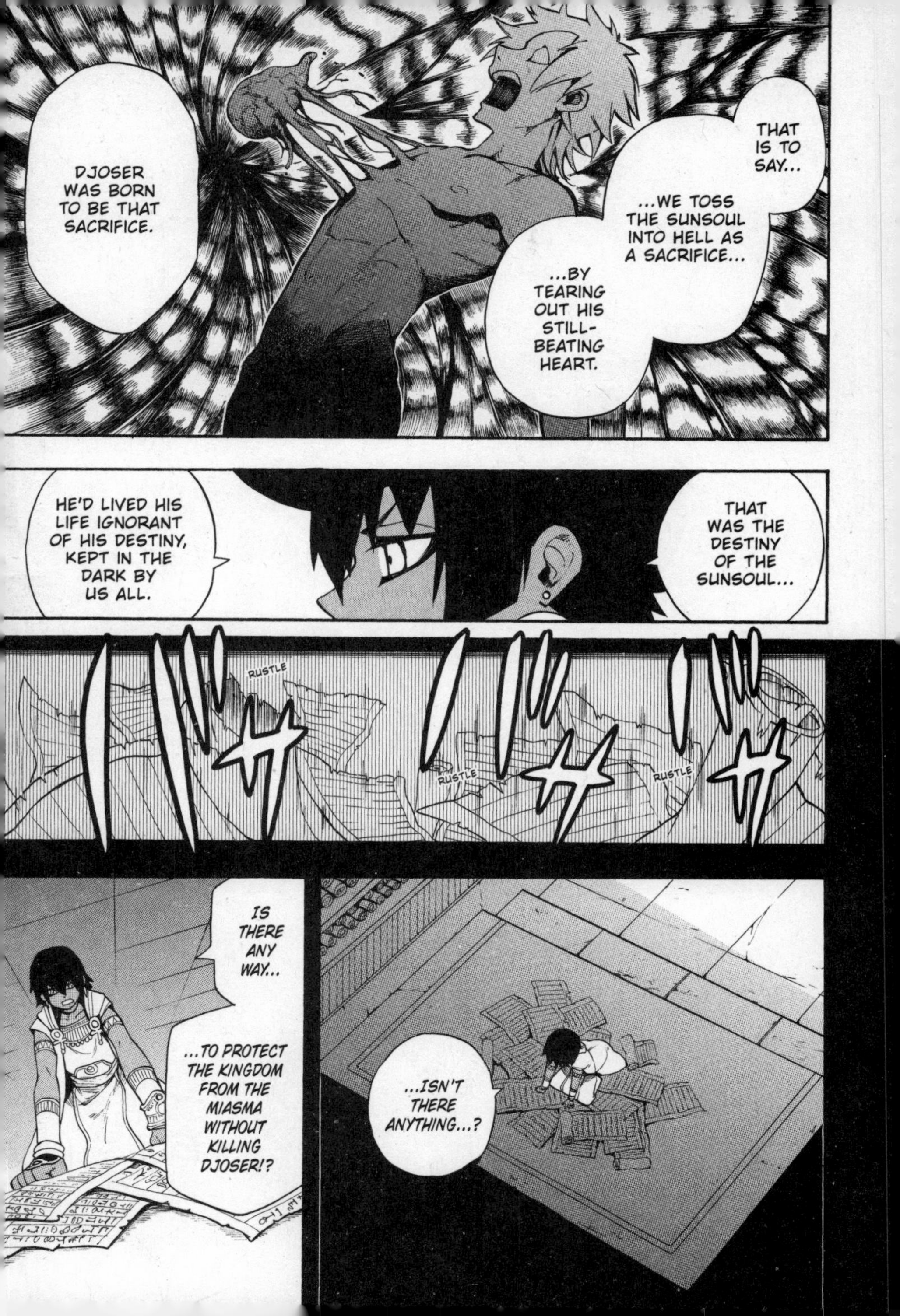
THAT IS TO SAY...
...WE TOSS THE SUNSOUL INTO HELL AS A SACRIFICE...
...BY TEARING OUT HIS STILL-BEATING HEART.
DJOSER WAS BORN TO BE THAT SACRIFICE.
THAT WAS THE DESTINY OF THE SUNSOUL...
HE'D LIVED HIS LIFE IGNORANT OF HIS DESTINY, KEPT IN THE DARK BY US ALL.
RUSTLE
RUSTLE
RUSTLE
...ISN'T THERE ANYTHING...?
IS THERE ANY WAY...
...TO PROTECT THE KINGDOM FROM THE MIASMA WITHOUT KILLING DJOSER!?

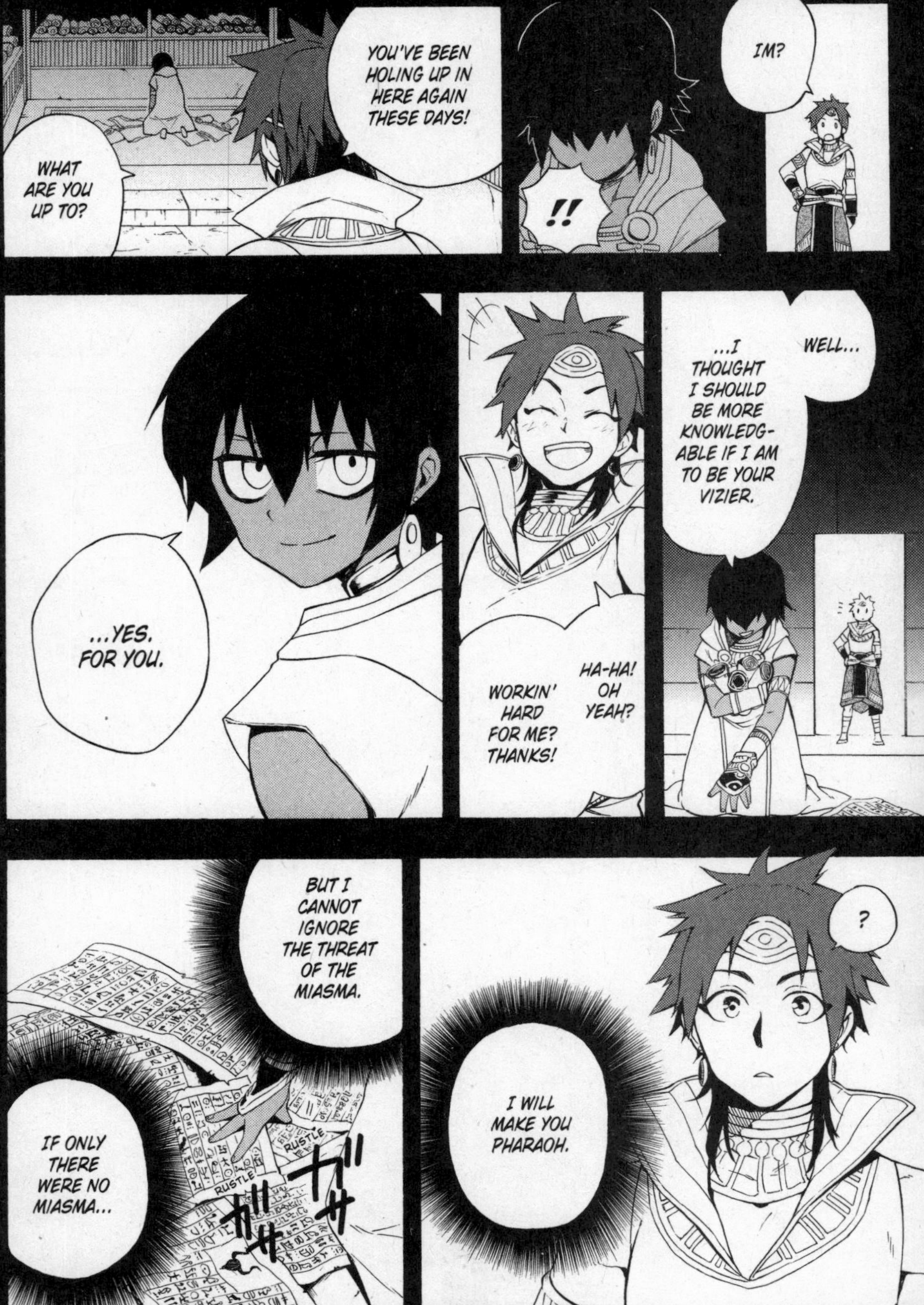
IM?
!!
YOU'VE BEEN HOLING UP IN HERE AGAIN THESE DAYS!
WHAT ARE YOU UP TO?
WELL...
...I THOUGHT I SHOULD BE MORE KNOWLEDG-ABLE IF I AM TO BE YOUR VIZIER.
HA-HA! OH YEAH?
WORKIN' HARD FOR ME? THANKS!
...YES. FOR YOU.
?
I WILL MAKE YOU PHARAOH.
BUT I CANNOT IGNORE THE THREAT OF THE MIASMA.
RUSTLE
RUSTLE
IF ONLY THERE WERE NO MIASMA...

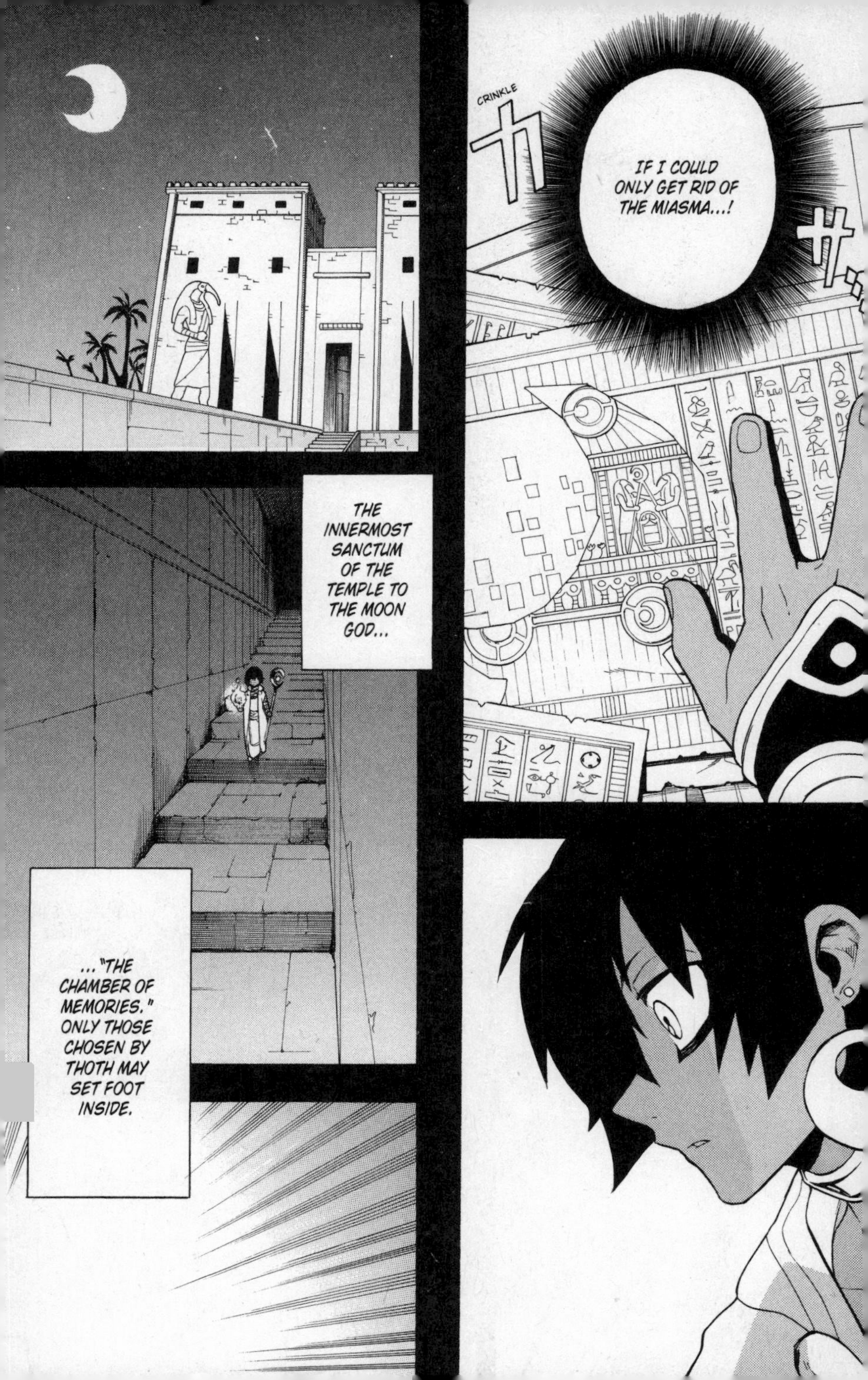
CRINKLE
IF I COULD ONLY GET RID OF THE MIASMA...!
THE INNERMOST SANCTUM OF THE TEMPLE TO THE MOON GOD...
..."THE CHAMBER OF MEMORIES." ONLY THOSE CHOSEN BY THOTH MAY SET FOOT INSIDE.

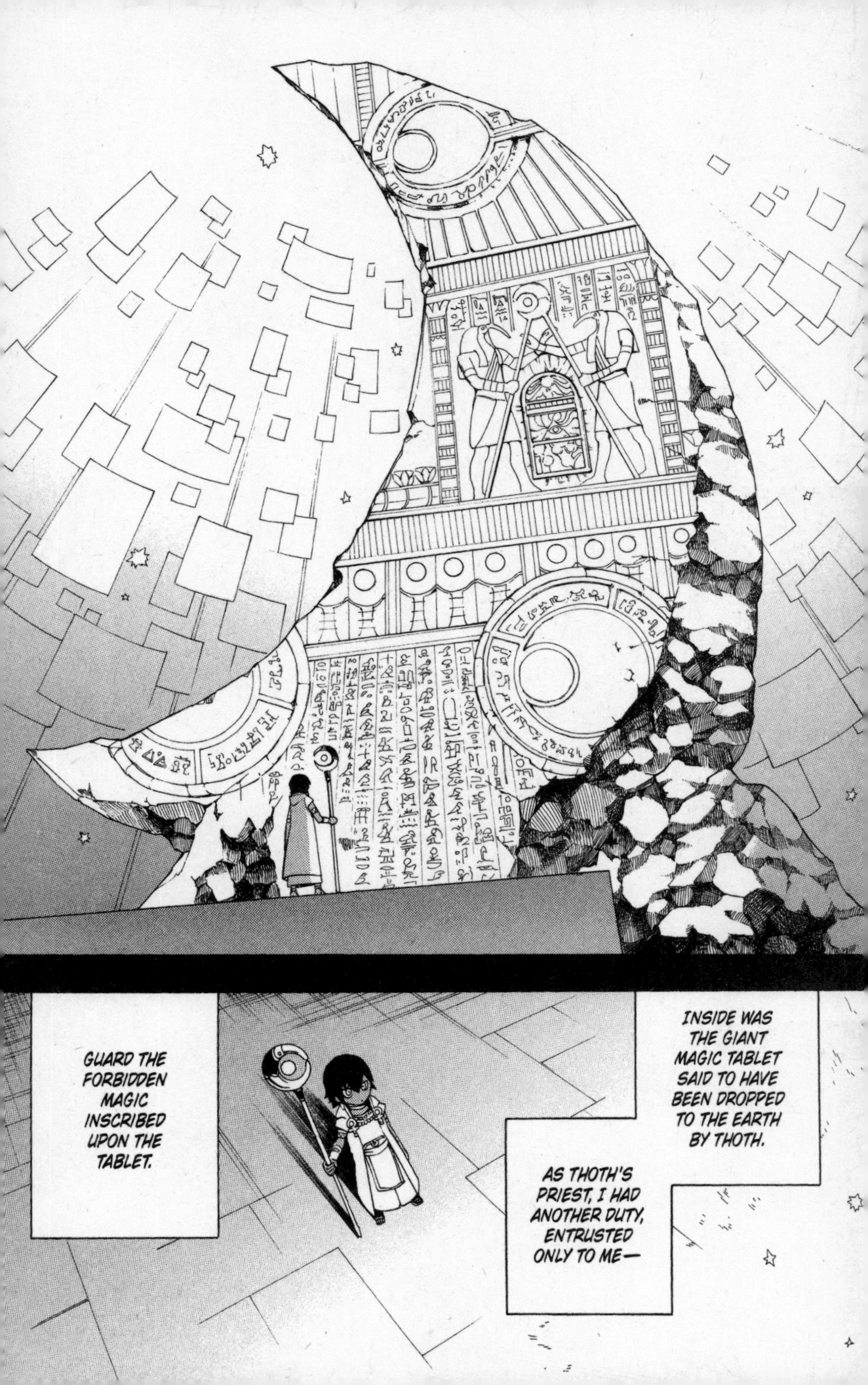
INSIDE WAS THE GIANT MAGIC TABLET SAID TO HAVE BEEN DROPPED TO THE EARTH BY THOTH.
AS THOTH'S PRIEST, I HAD ANOTHER DUTY, ENTRUSTED ONLY TO ME—
GUARD THE FORBIDDEN MAGIC INSCRIBED UPON THE TABLET.

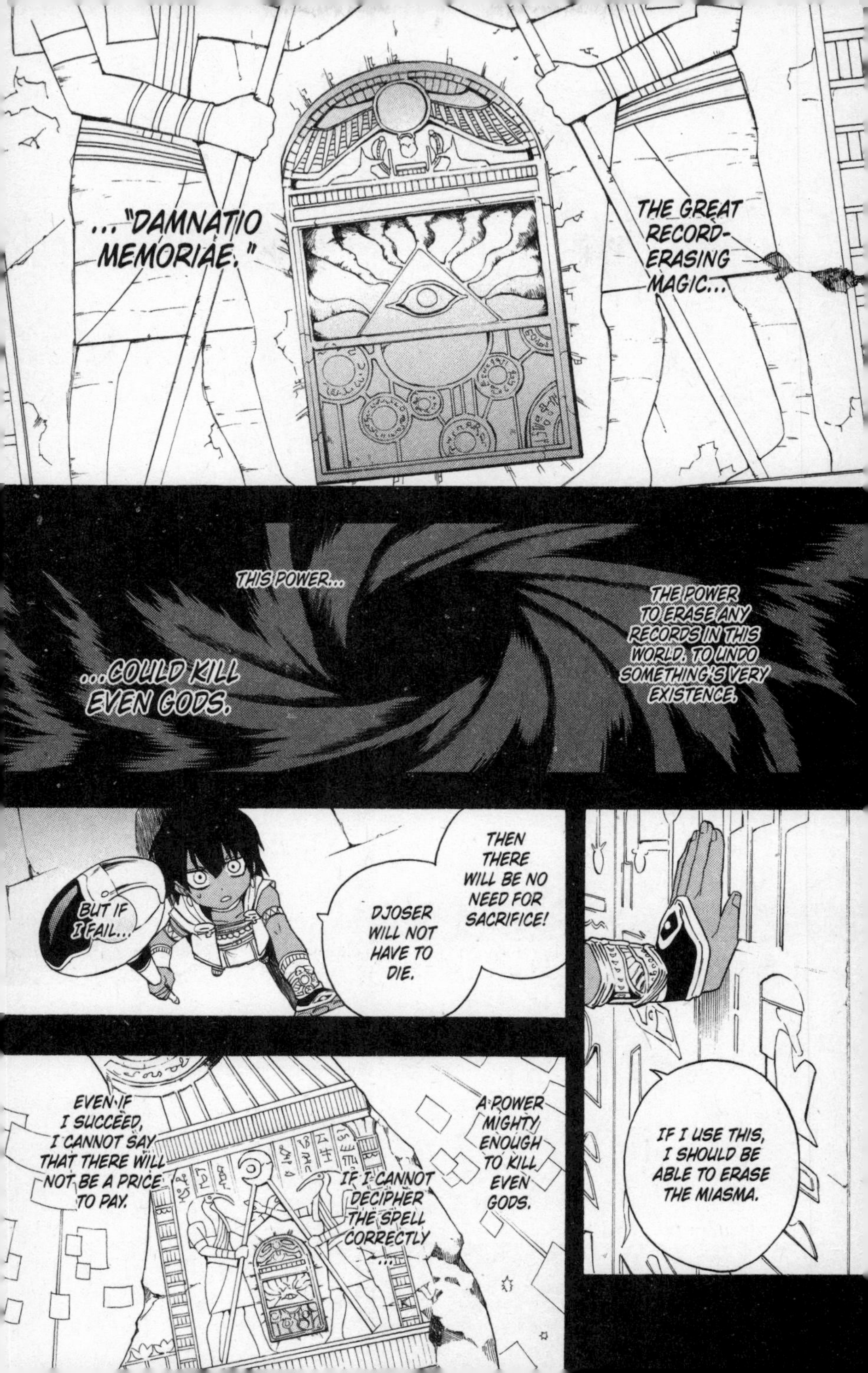
THE GREAT RECORD-ERASING MAGIC...
..."DAMNATIO MEMORIAE."
THE POWER TO ERASE ANY RECORDS IN THIS WORLD. TO UNDO SOMETHING'S VERY EXISTENCE.
THIS POWER...
...COULD KILL EVEN GODS.
IF I USE THIS, I SHOULD BE ABLE TO ERASE THE MIASMA.
THEN THERE WILL BE NO NEED FOR SACRIFICE!
DJOSER WILL NOT HAVE TO DIE.
BUT IF I FAIL...
A POWER MIGHTY ENOUGH TO KILL EVEN GODS.
IF I CANNOT DECIPHER THE SPELL CORRECTLY...
EVEN IF I SUCCEED, I CANNOT SAY THAT THERE WILL NOT BE A PRICE TO PAY.

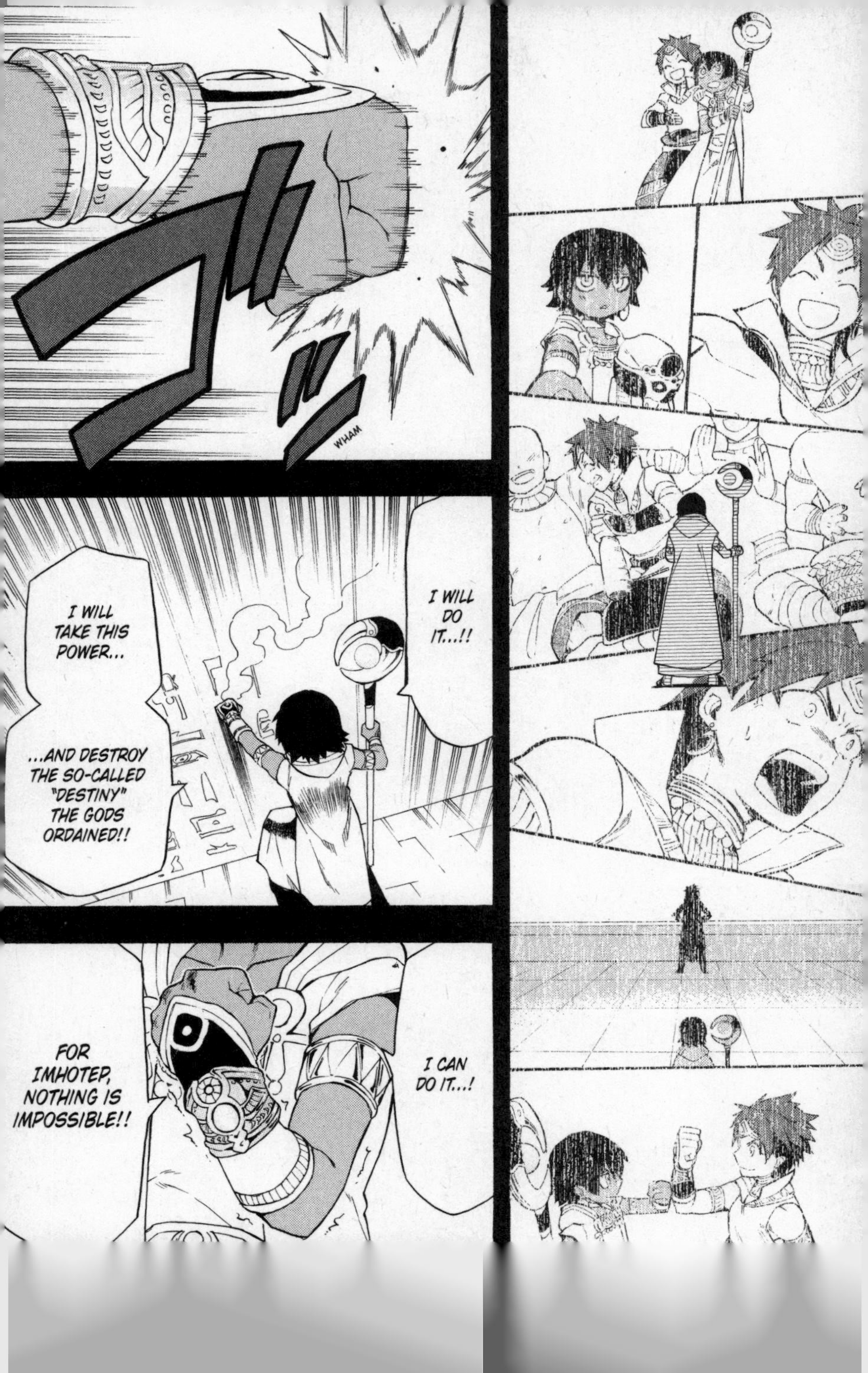
WHAM
I WILL DO IT...!!
I WILL TAKE THIS POWER...
...AND DESTROY THE SO-CALLED "DESTINY" THE GODS ORDAINED!!
I CAN DO IT...!
FOR IMHOTEP, NOTHING IS IMPOSSIBLE!!

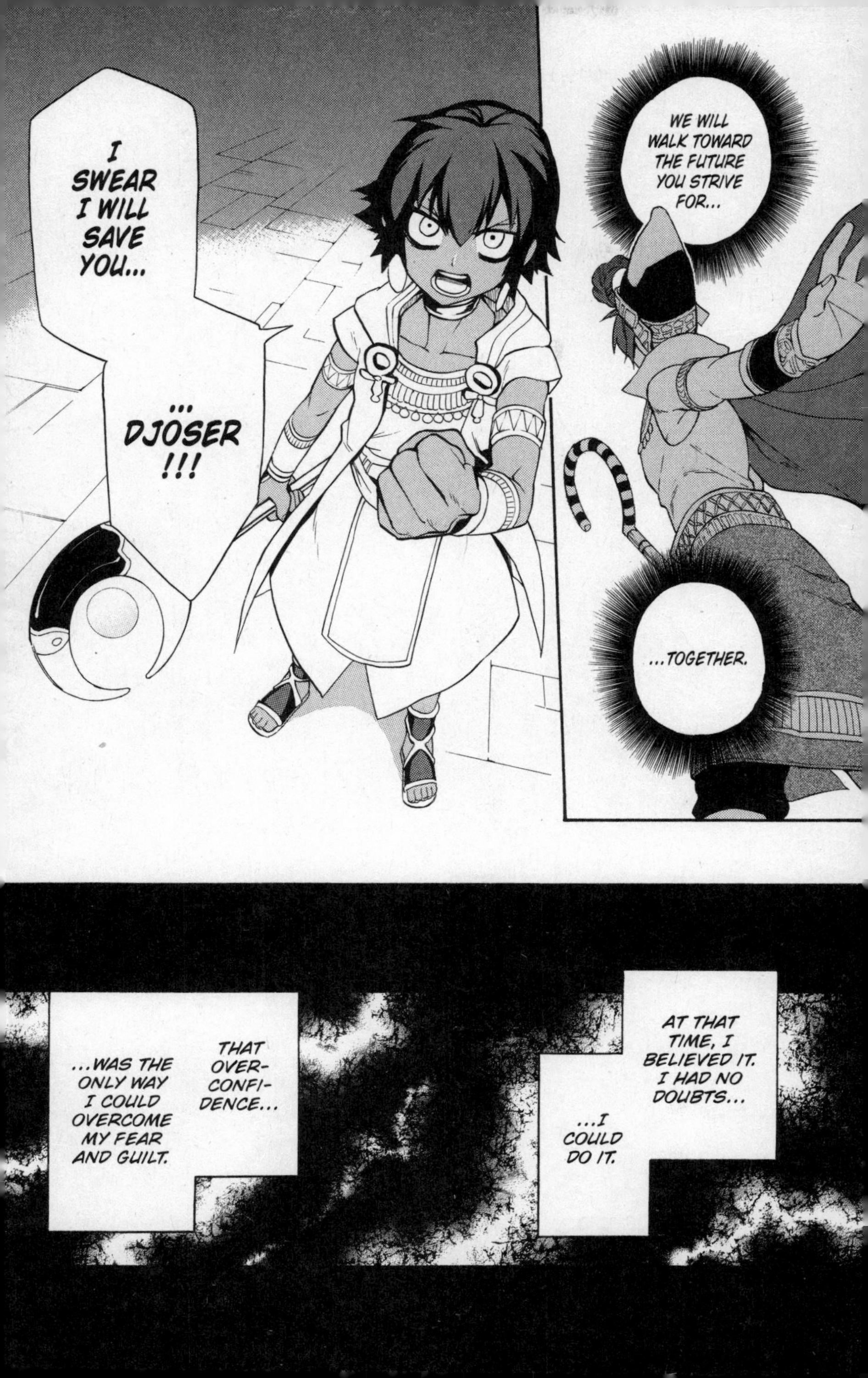
WE WILL WALK TOWARD THE FUTURE YOU STRIVE FOR...
...TOGETHER.
I SWEAR I WILL SAVE YOU...
...DJOSER!!!
AT THAT TIME, I BELIEVED IT. I HAD NO DOUBTS...
...I COULD DO IT.
THAT OVER-CONFI-DENCE...
...WAS THE ONLY WAY I COULD OVERCOME MY FEAR AND GUILT.

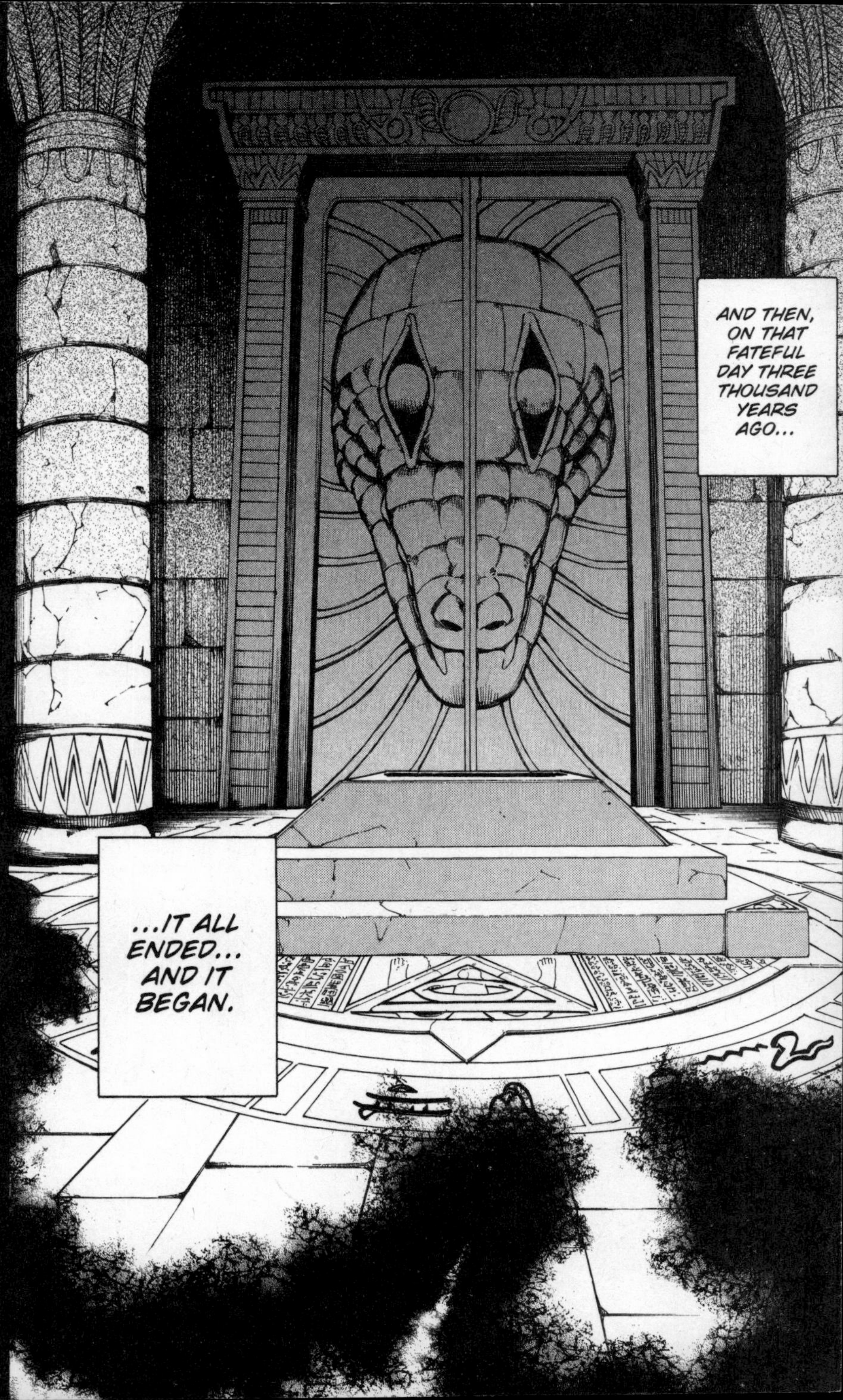
AND THEN, ON THAT FATEFUL DAY THREE THOUSAND YEARS AGO...
...IT ALL ENDED... AND IT BEGAN.

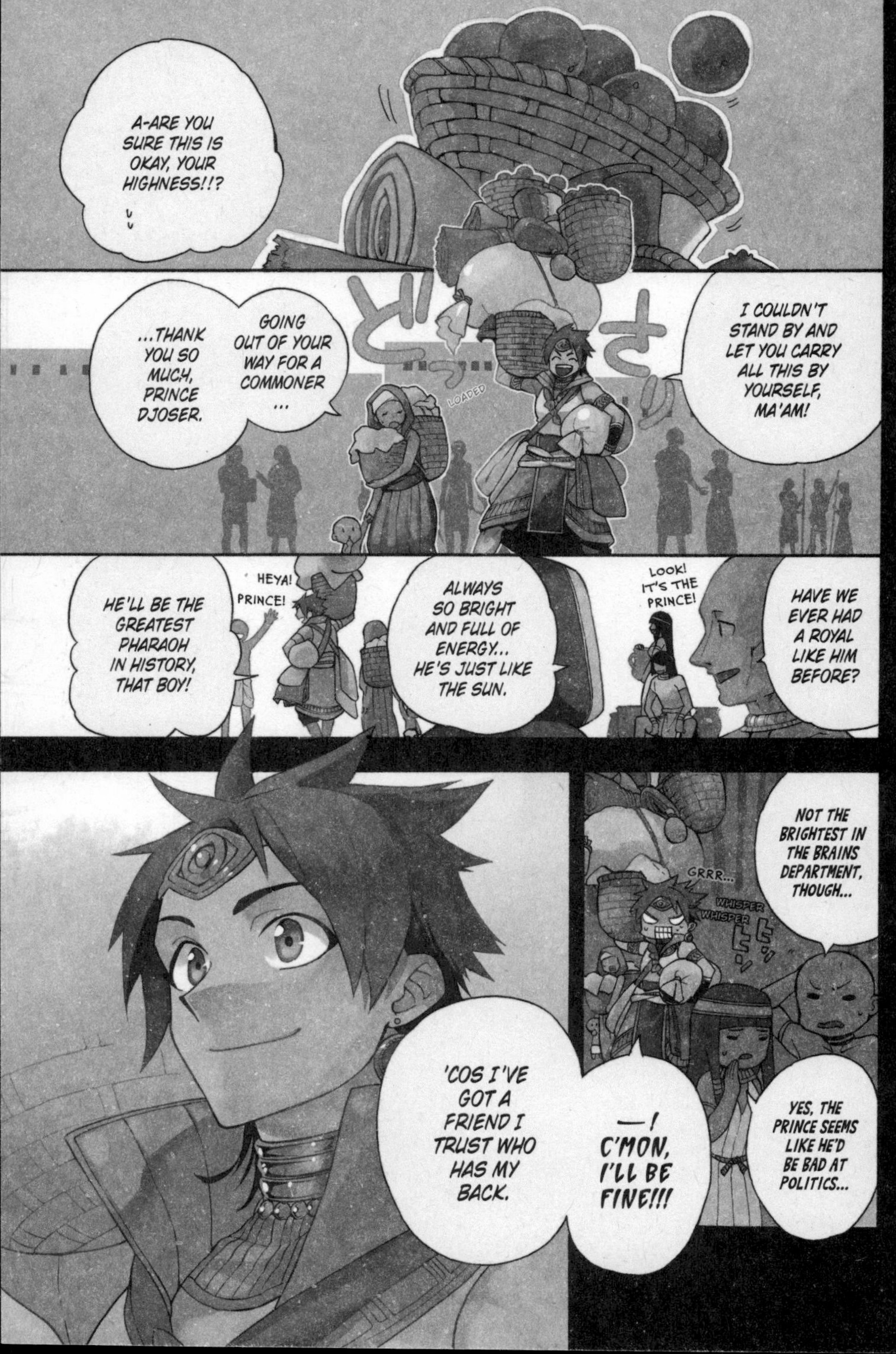
A-ARE YOU SURE THIS IS OKAY, YOUR HIGHNESS!!?
I COULDN'T STAND BY AND LET YOU CARRY ALL THIS BY YOURSELF, MA'AM!
LOADED
GOING OUT OF YOUR WAY FOR A COMMONER...
...THANK YOU SO MUCH, PRINCE DJOSER.
HAVE WE EVER HAD A ROYAL LIKE HIM BEFORE?
LOOK! IT'S THE PRINCE!
ALWAYS SO BRIGHT AND FULL OF ENERGY... HE'S JUST LIKE THE SUN.
HEYA! PRINCE!
HE'LL BE THE GREATEST PHARAOH IN HISTORY, THAT BOY!
NOT THE BRIGHTEST IN THE BRAINS DEPARTMENT, THOUGH...
GRRR...
WHISPER WHISPER
YES, THE PRINCE SEEMS LIKE HE'D BE BAD AT POLITICS...
—! C'MON, I'LL BE FINE!!!
'COS I'VE GOT A FRIEND I TRUST WHO HAS MY BACK.

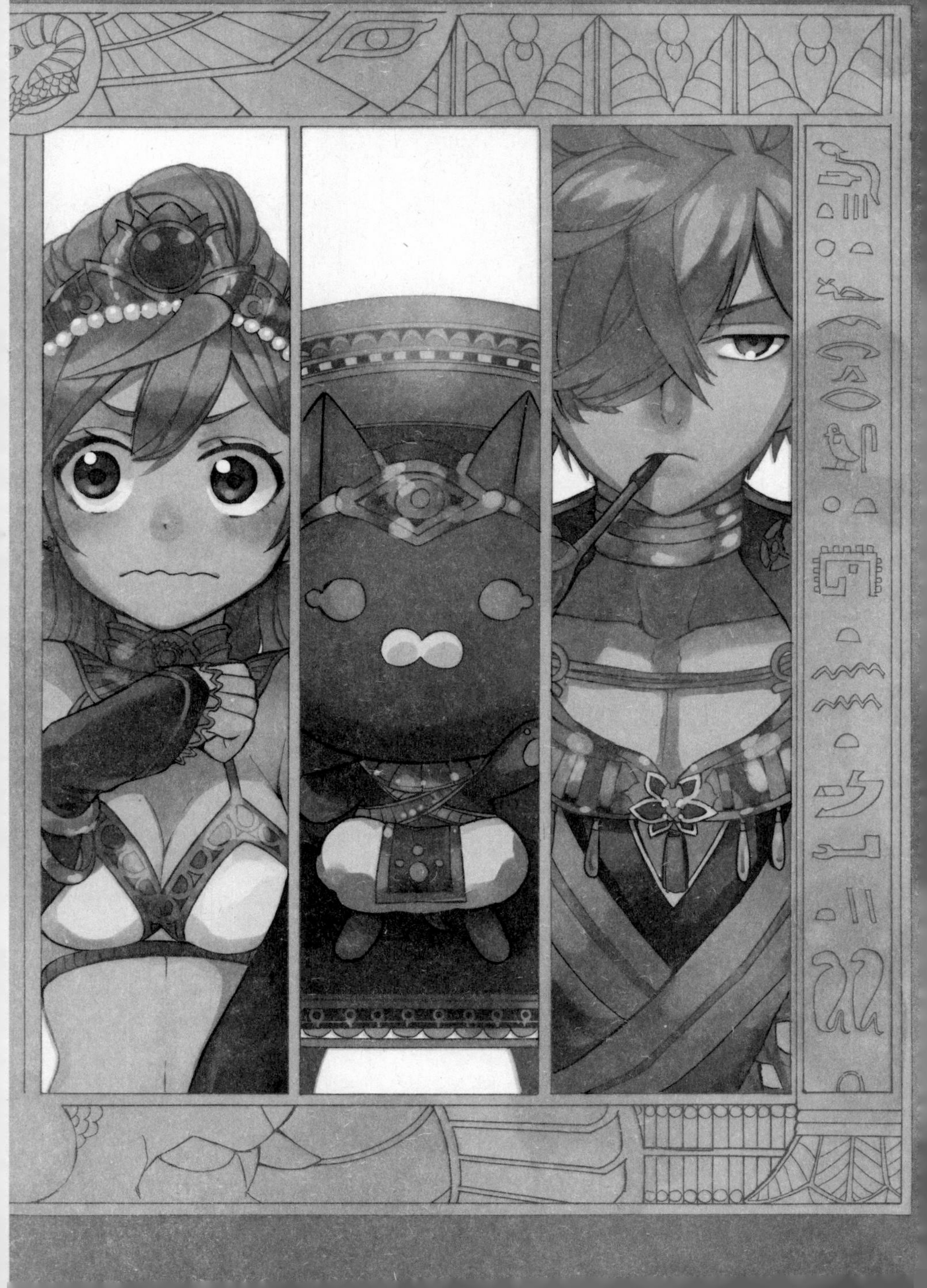

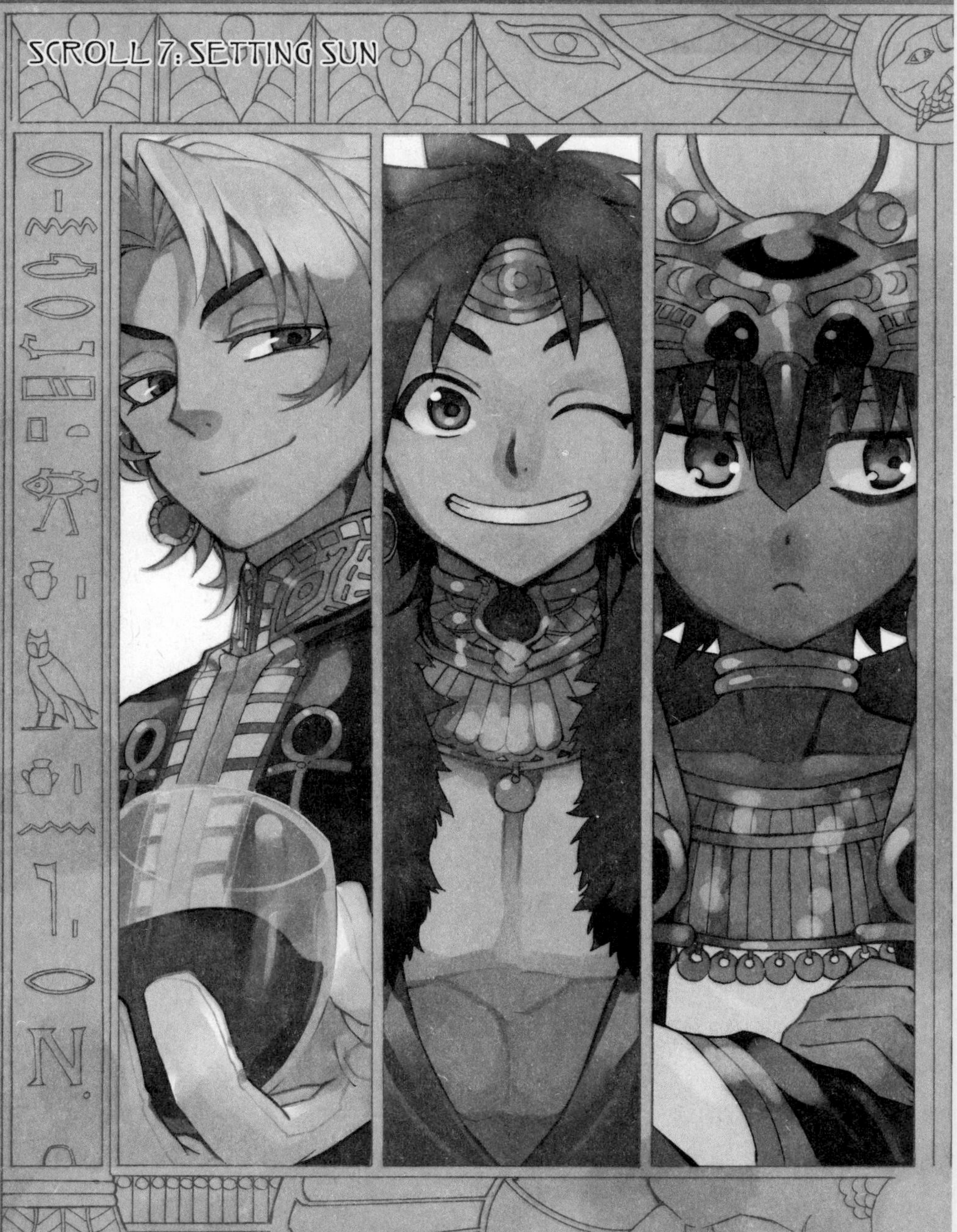
SCROLL 7: SETTING SUN

Great Priest Imhotep

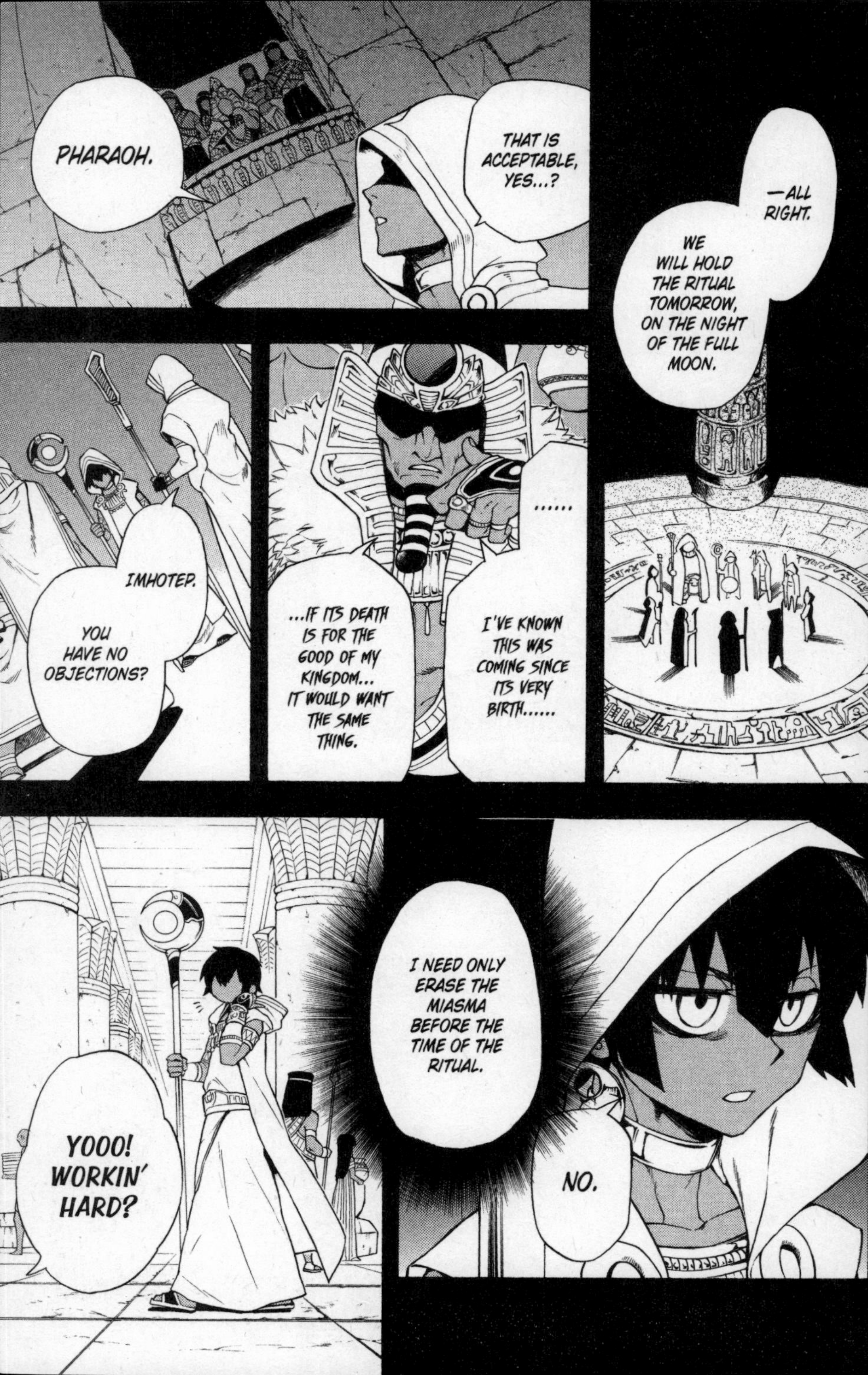
—ALL RIGHT.
WE WILL HOLD THE RITUAL TOMORROW, ON THE NIGHT OF THE FULL MOON.
THAT IS ACCEPTABLE, YES...?
PHARAOH.
......
I'VE KNOWN THIS WAS COMING SINCE ITS VERY BIRTH......
...IF ITS DEATH IS FOR THE GOOD OF MY KINGDOM... IT WOULD WANT THE SAME THING.
IMHOTEP.
YOU HAVE NO OBJECTIONS?
I NEED ONLY ERASE THE MIASMA BEFORE THE TIME OF THE RITUAL.
NO.
YOOO! WORKIN' HARD?

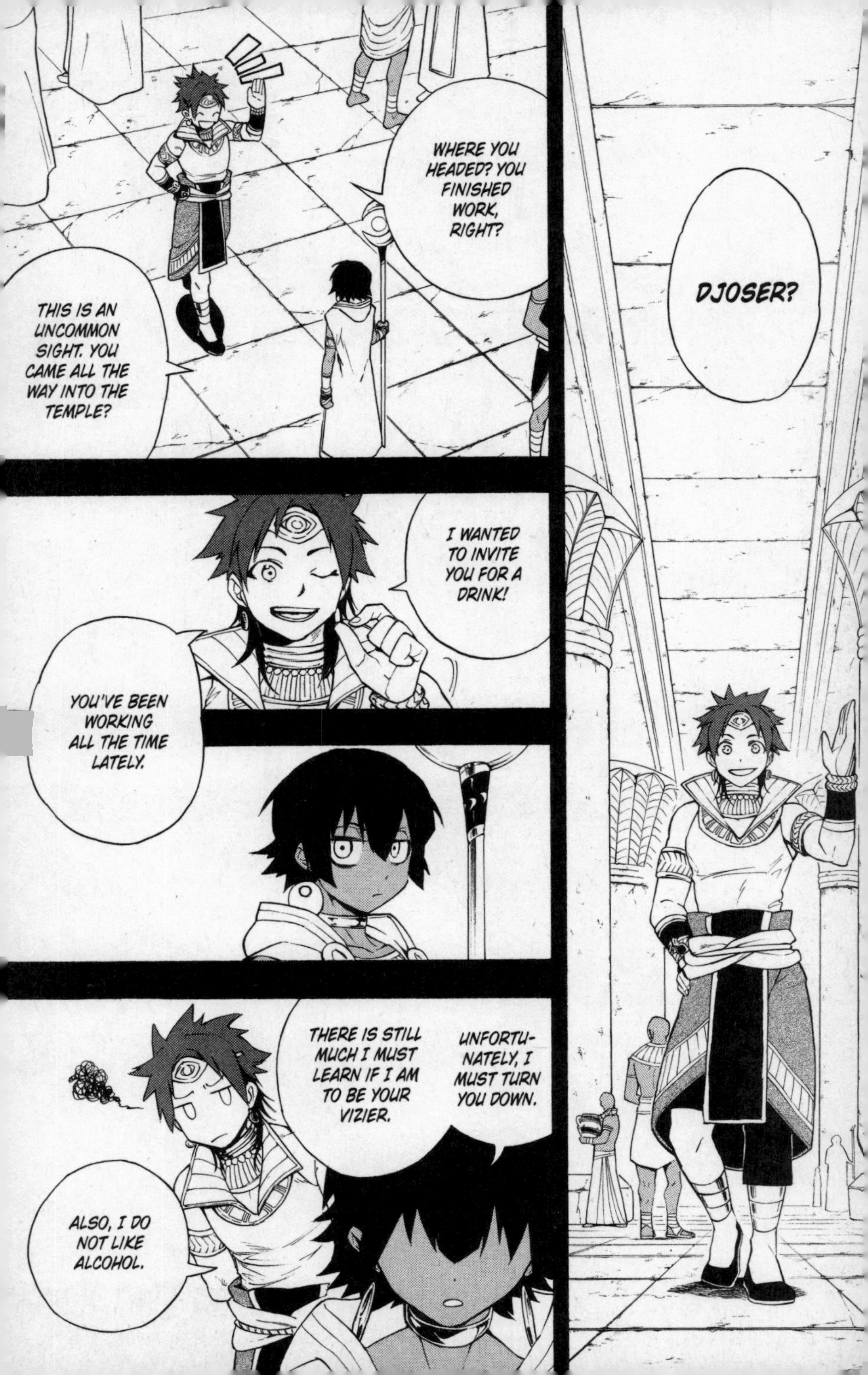
DJOSER?
WHERE YOU HEADED? YOU FINISHED WORK, RIGHT?
THIS IS AN UNCOMMON SIGHT. YOU CAME ALL THE WAY INTO THE TEMPLE?
I WANTED TO INVITE YOU FOR A DRINK!
YOU'VE BEEN WORKING ALL THE TIME LATELY.
UNFORTU-NATELY, I MUST TURN YOU DOWN.
THERE IS STILL MUCH I MUST LEARN IF I AM TO BE YOUR VIZIER.
ALSO, I DO NOT LIKE ALCOHOL.

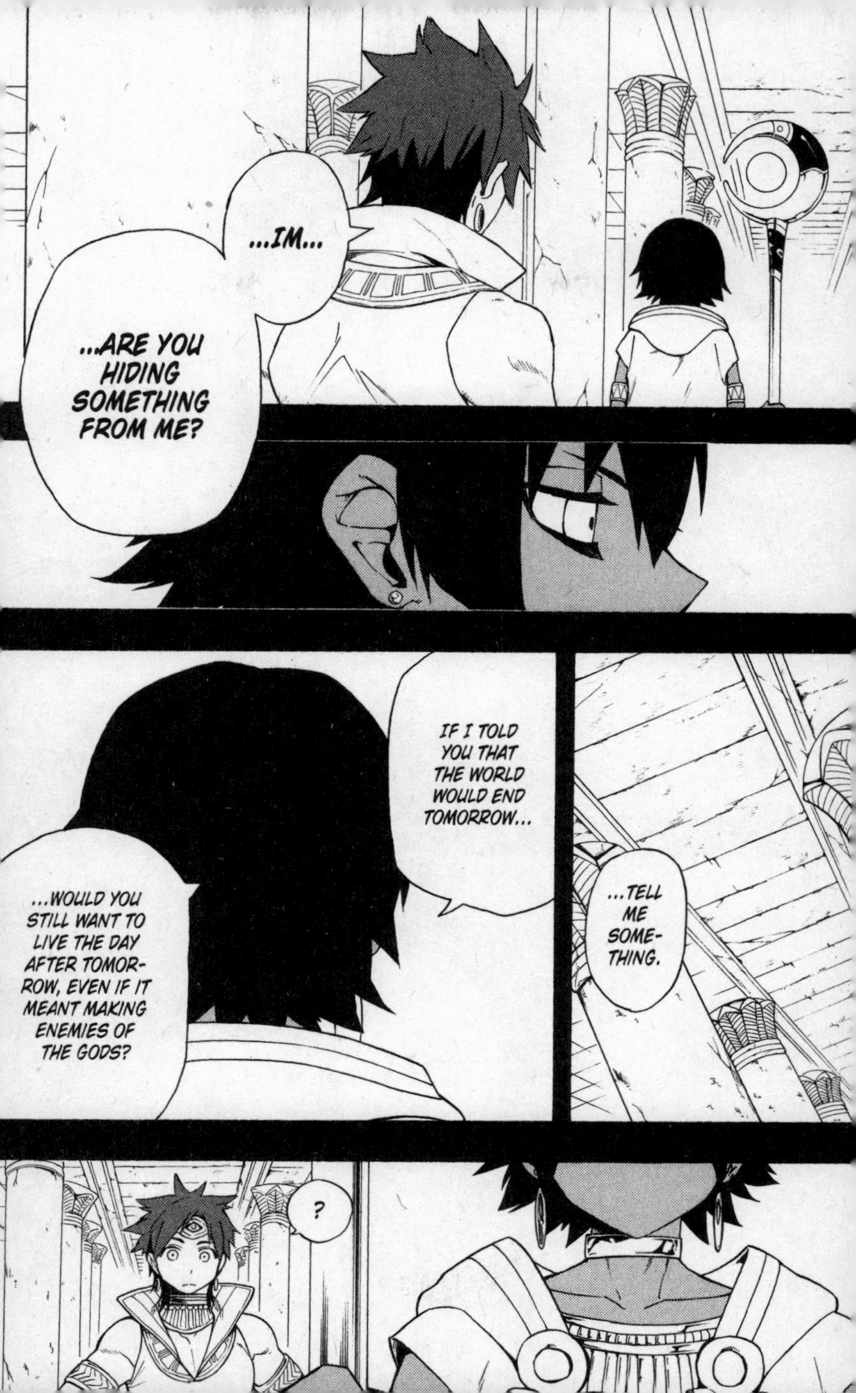
...IM...
...ARE YOU HIDING SOMETHING FROM ME?
...TELL ME SOME-THING.
IF I TOLD YOU THAT THE WORLD WOULD END TOMORROW...
...WOULD YOU STILL WANT TO LIVE THE DAY AFTER TOMOR-ROW, EVEN IF IT MEANT MAKING ENEMIES OF THE GODS?
?

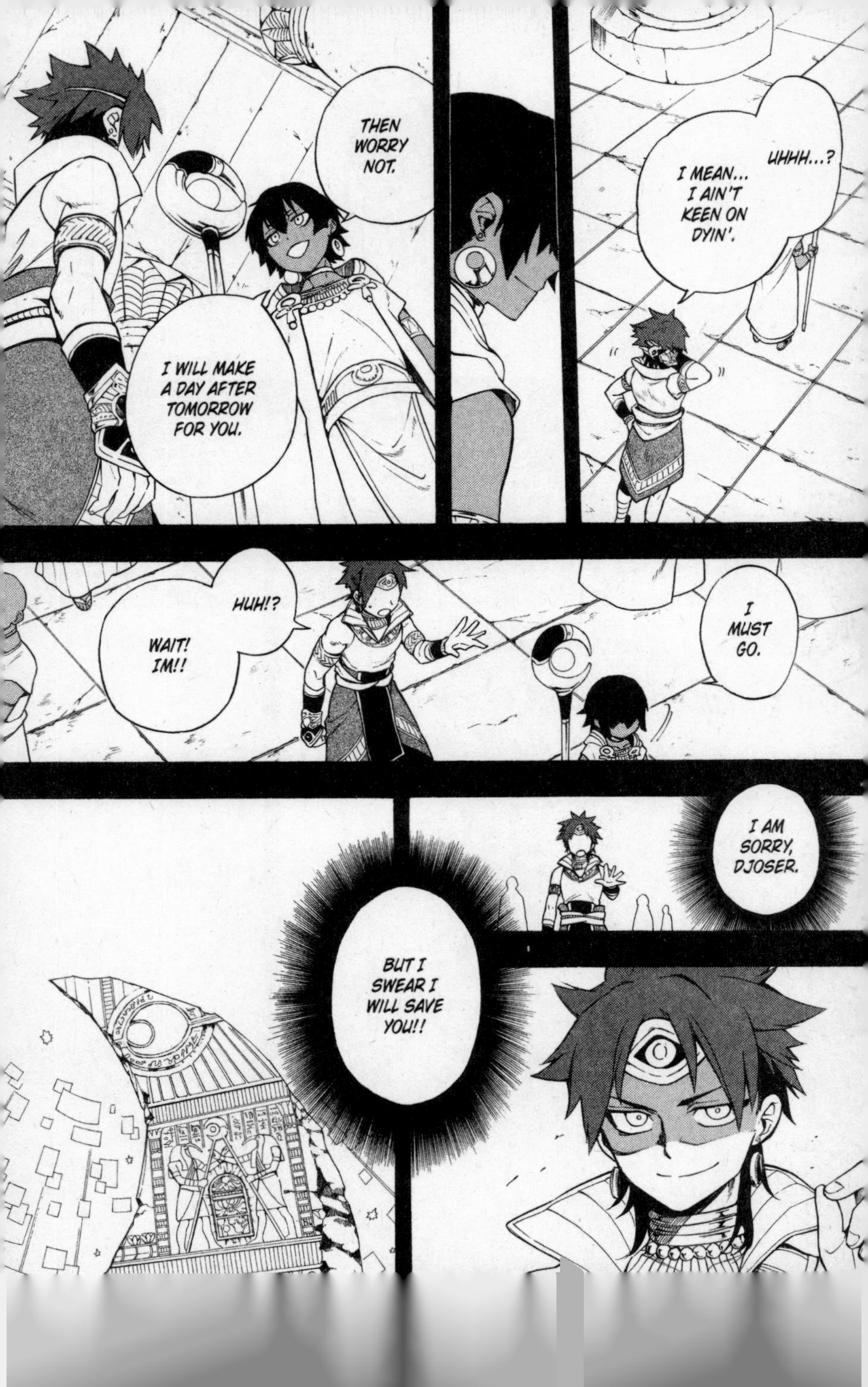
UHHH...?
I MEAN... I AIN'T KEEN ON DYIN'.
THEN WORRY NOT.
I WILL MAKE A DAY AFTER TOMORROW FOR YOU.
I MUST GO.
HUH!?
WAIT! IM!!
I AM SORRY, DJOSER.
BUT I SWEAR I WILL SAVE YOU!!

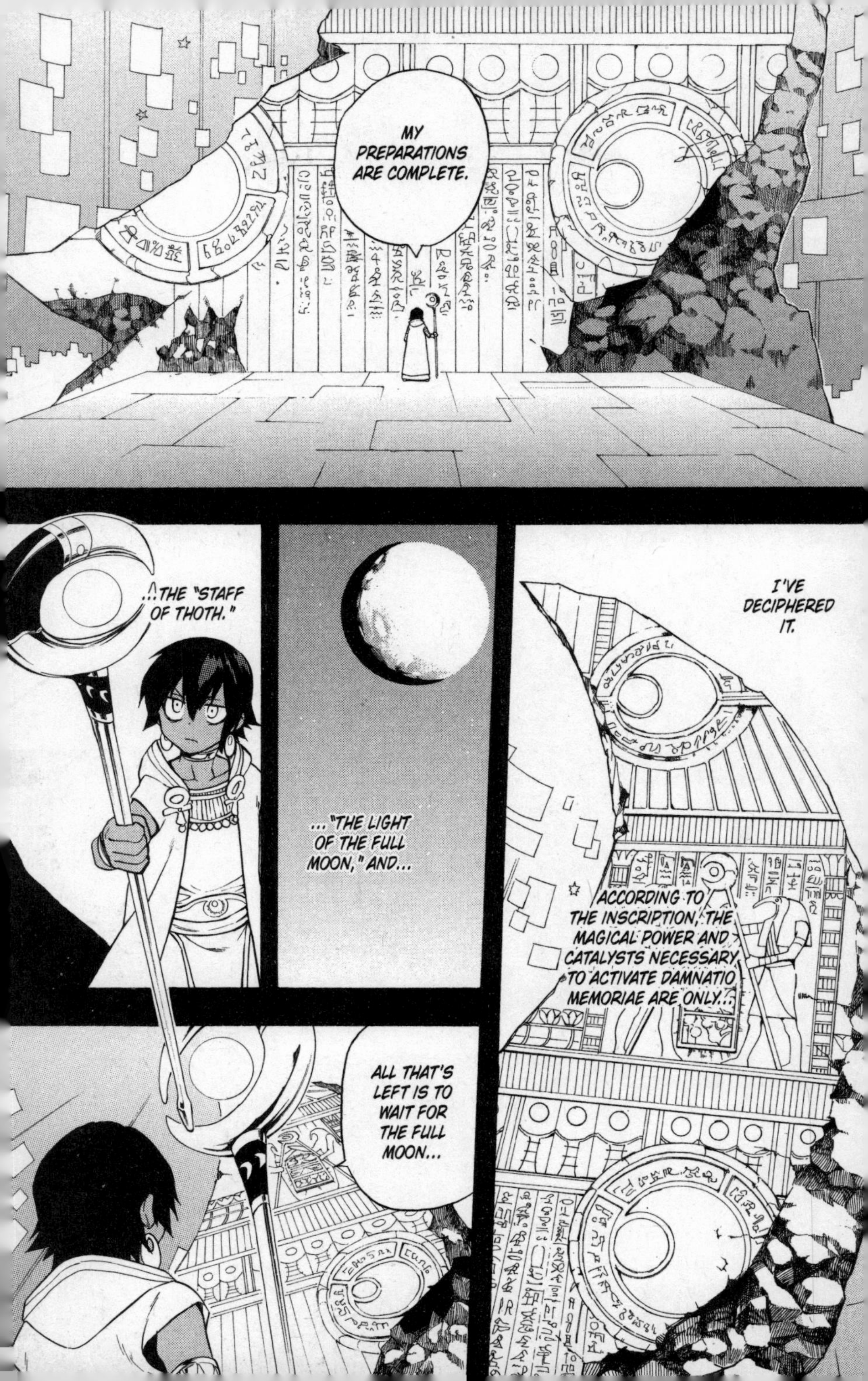
MY PREPARATIONS ARE COMPLETE.
I'VE DECIPHERED IT.
ACCORDING TO THE INSCRIPTION, THE MAGICAL POWER AND CATALYSTS NECESSARY TO ACTIVATE DAMNATIO MEMORIAE ARE ONLY...
..."THE LIGHT OF THE FULL MOON," AND...
...THE "STAFF OF THOTH."
ALL THAT'S LEFT IS TO WAIT FOR THE FULL MOON...

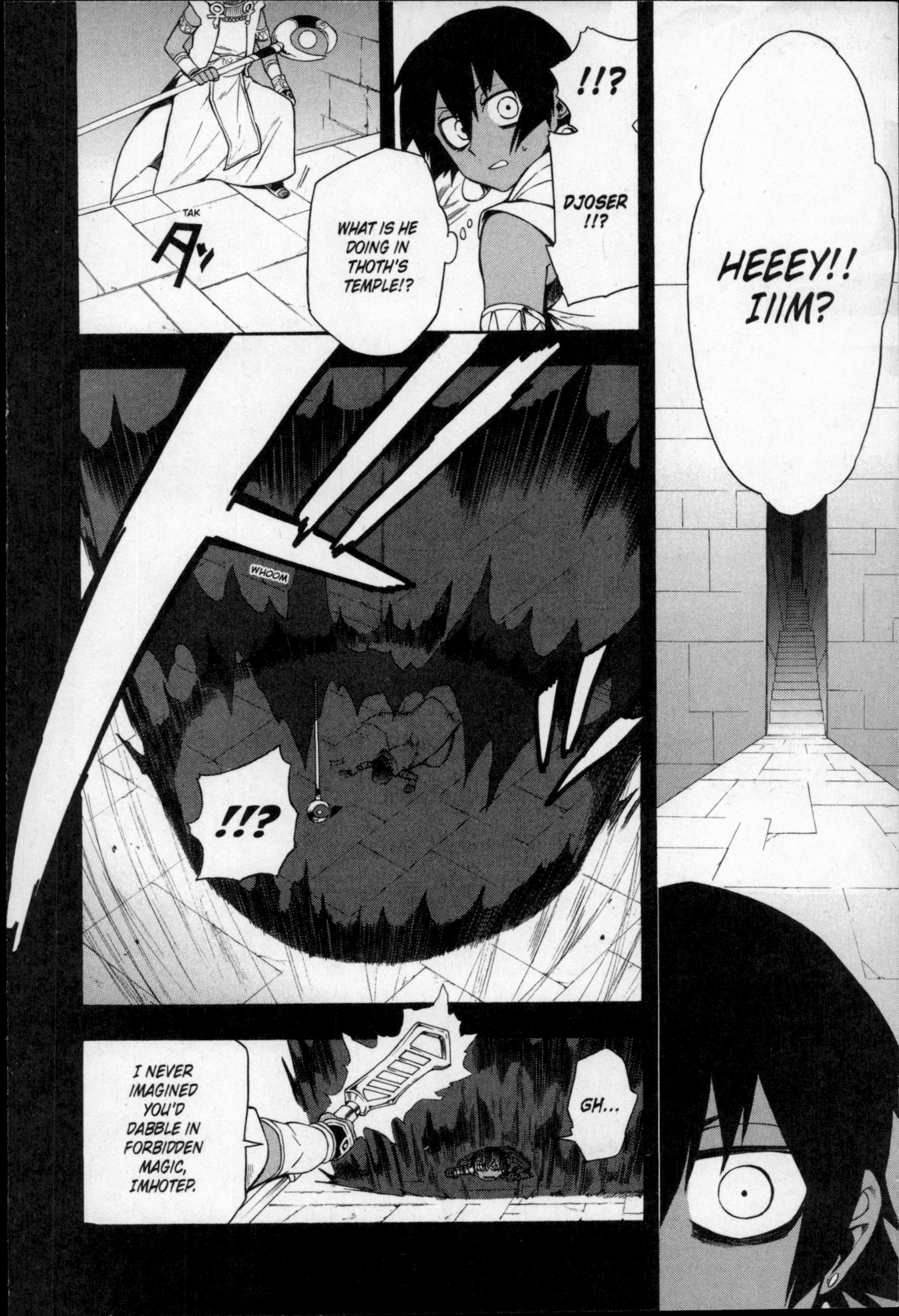
HEEEY!! IIIM?
!!?
DJOSER !!?
WHAT IS HE DOING IN THOTH'S TEMPLE!?
TAK
WHOOM
!!?
I NEVER IMAGINED YOU'D DABBLE IN FORBIDDEN MAGIC, IMHOTEP.
GH...

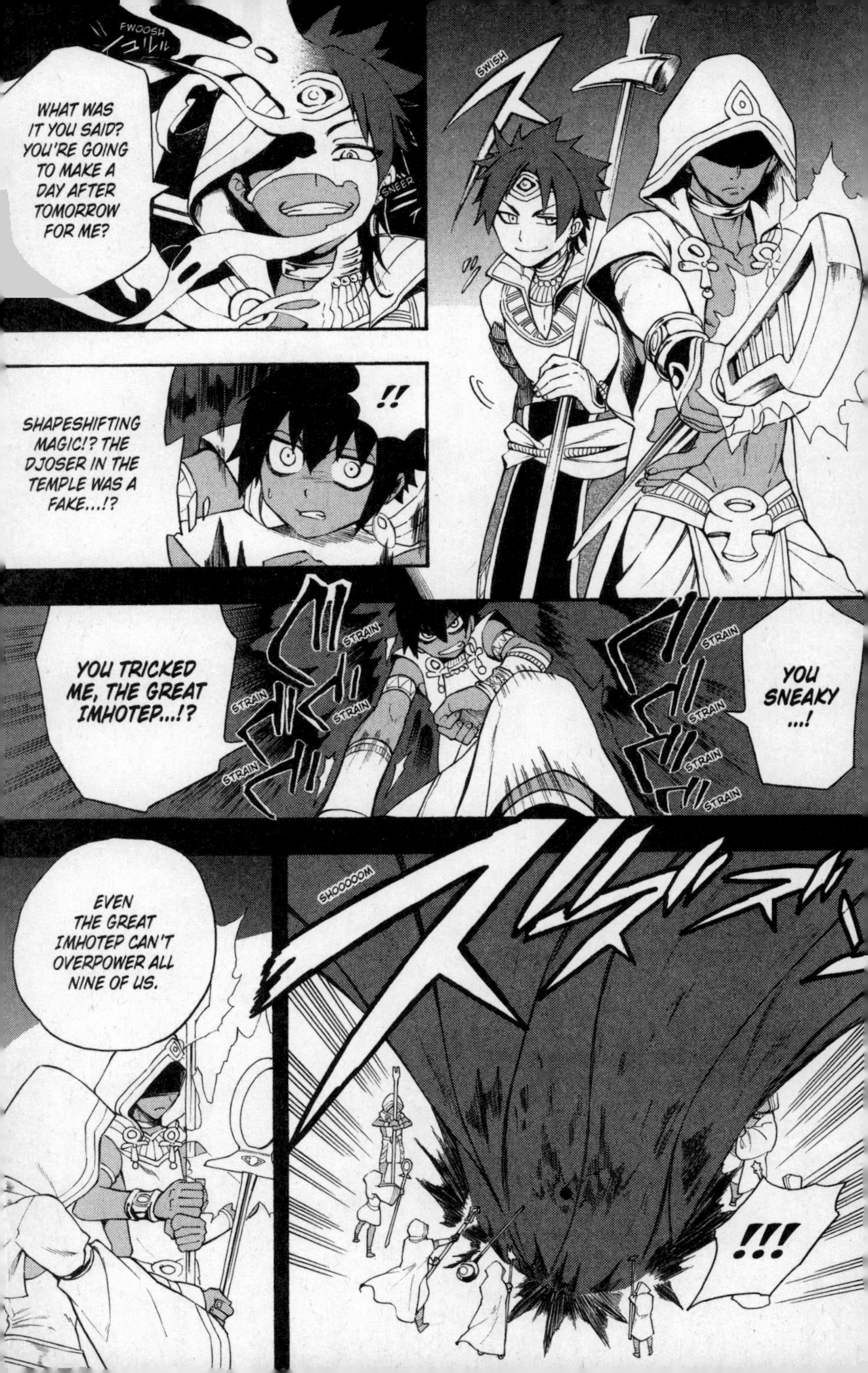

SWISH
FWOOSH
WHAT WAS IT YOU SAID? YOU'RE GOING TO MAKE A DAY AFTER TOMORROW FOR ME?
SNEER
!!
SHAPESHIFTING MAGIC!? THE DJOSER IN THE TEMPLE WAS A FAKE...!?
YOU SNEAKY ...!
STRAIN STRAIN STRAIN STRAIN
STRAIN STRAIN STRAIN STRAIN
YOU TRICKED ME, THE GREAT IMHOTEP...!?
SHOOOOOM
!!!
EVEN THE GREAT IMHOTEP CAN'T OVERPOWER ALL NINE OF US.

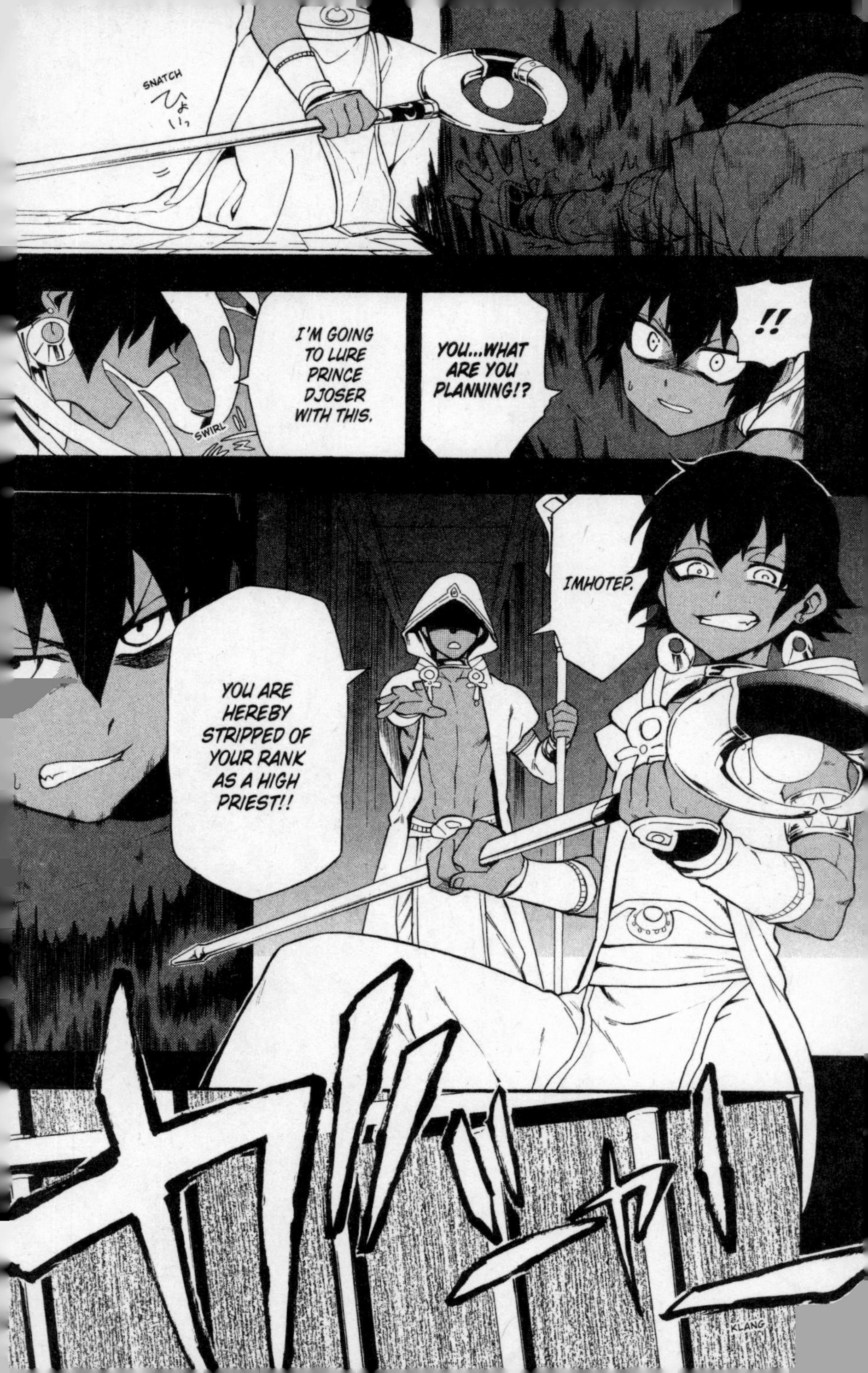
SNATCH
ひょいっ
!!
YOU...WHAT ARE YOU PLANNING!?
I'M GOING TO LURE PRINCE DJOSER WITH THIS.
SWIRL
IMHOTEP.
YOU ARE HEREBY STRIPPED OF YOUR RANK AS A HIGH PRIEST!!
KLANG

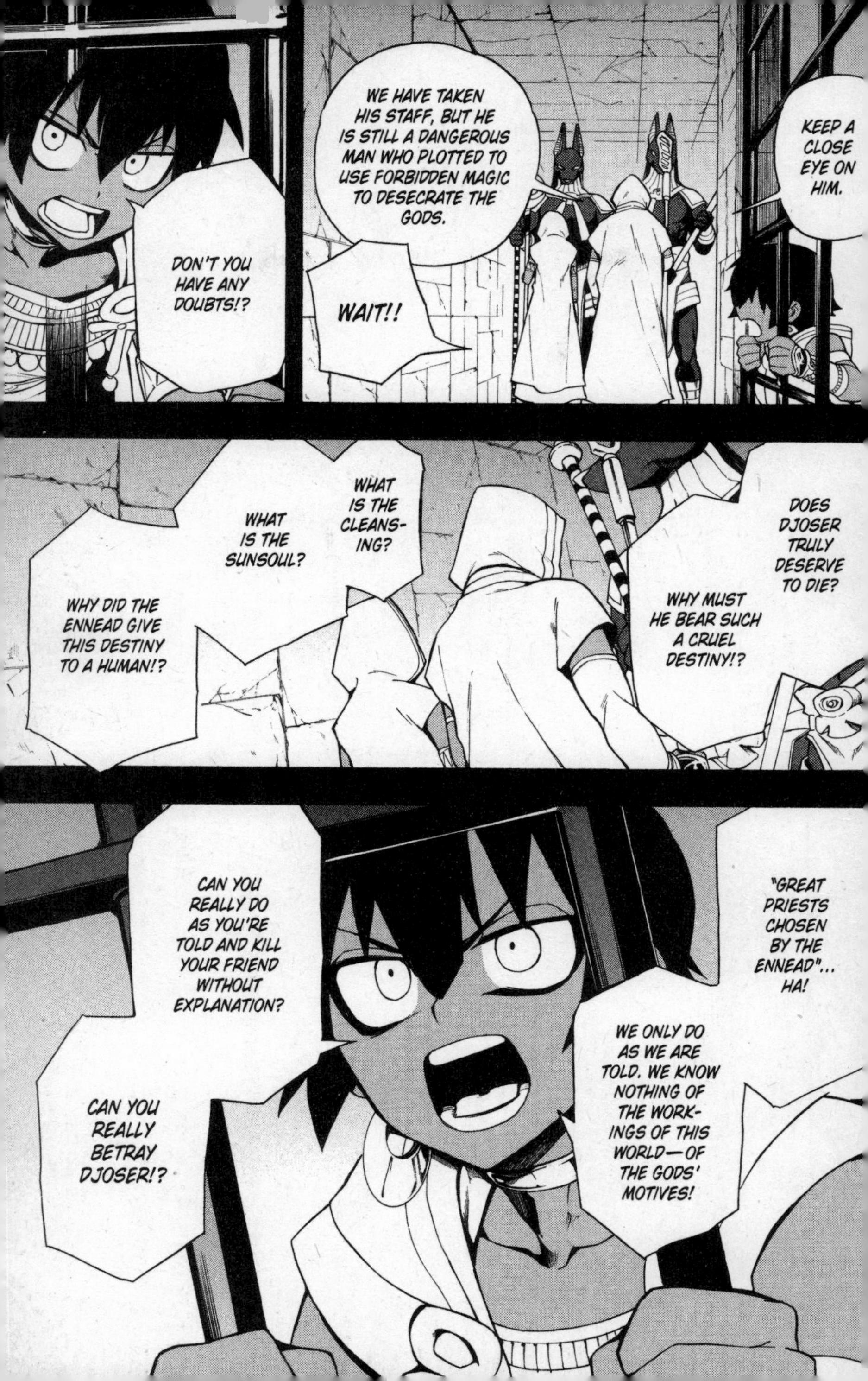
KEEP A CLOSE EYE ON HIM.
WE HAVE TAKEN HIS STAFF, BUT HE IS STILL A DANGEROUS MAN WHO PLOTTED TO USE FORBIDDEN MAGIC TO DESECRATE THE GODS.
WAIT!!
DON'T YOU HAVE ANY DOUBTS!?
DOES DJOSER TRULY DESERVE TO DIE?
WHY MUST HE BEAR SUCH A CRUEL DESTINY!?
WHAT IS THE CLEANS-ING?
WHAT IS THE SUNSOUL?
WHY DID THE ENNEAD GIVE THIS DESTINY TO A HUMAN!?
"GREAT PRIESTS CHOSEN BY THE ENNEAD"... HA!
WE ONLY DO AS WE ARE TOLD. WE KNOW NOTHING OF THE WORK-INGS OF THIS WORLD—OF THE GODS' MOTIVES!
CAN YOU REALLY DO AS YOU'RE TOLD AND KILL YOUR FRIEND WITHOUT EXPLANATION?
CAN YOU REALLY BETRAY DJOSER!?

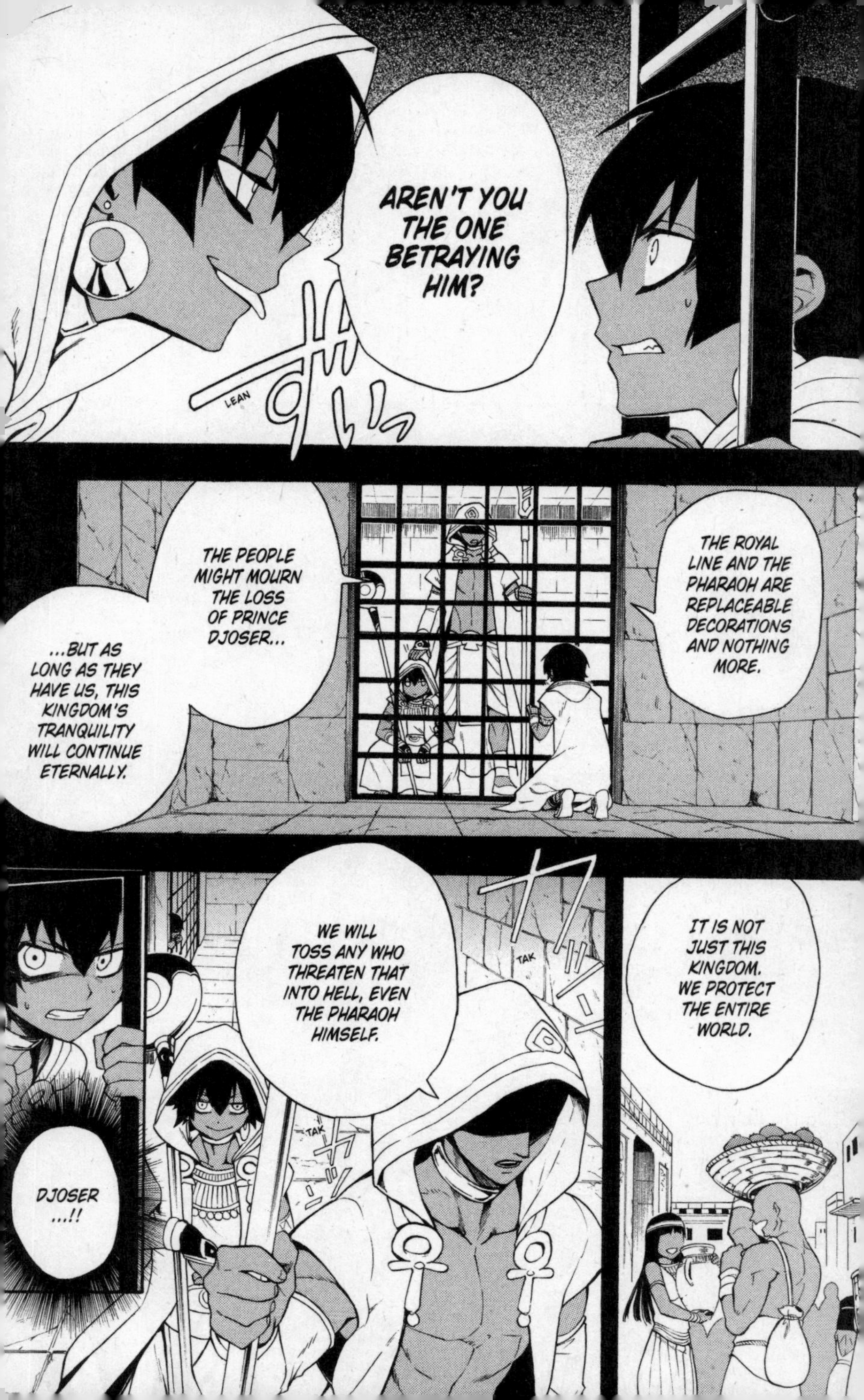
AREN'T YOU THE ONE BETRAYING HIM?
LEAN
THE ROYAL LINE AND THE PHARAOH ARE REPLACEABLE DECORATIONS AND NOTHING MORE.
THE PEOPLE MIGHT MOURN THE LOSS OF PRINCE DJOSER...
...BUT AS LONG AS THEY HAVE US, THIS KINGDOM'S TRANQUILITY WILL CONTINUE ETERNALLY.
IT IS NOT JUST THIS KINGDOM. WE PROTECT THE ENTIRE WORLD.
TAK
WE WILL TOSS ANY WHO THREATEN THAT INTO HELL, EVEN THE PHARAOH HIMSELF.
TAK
DJOSER ...!!

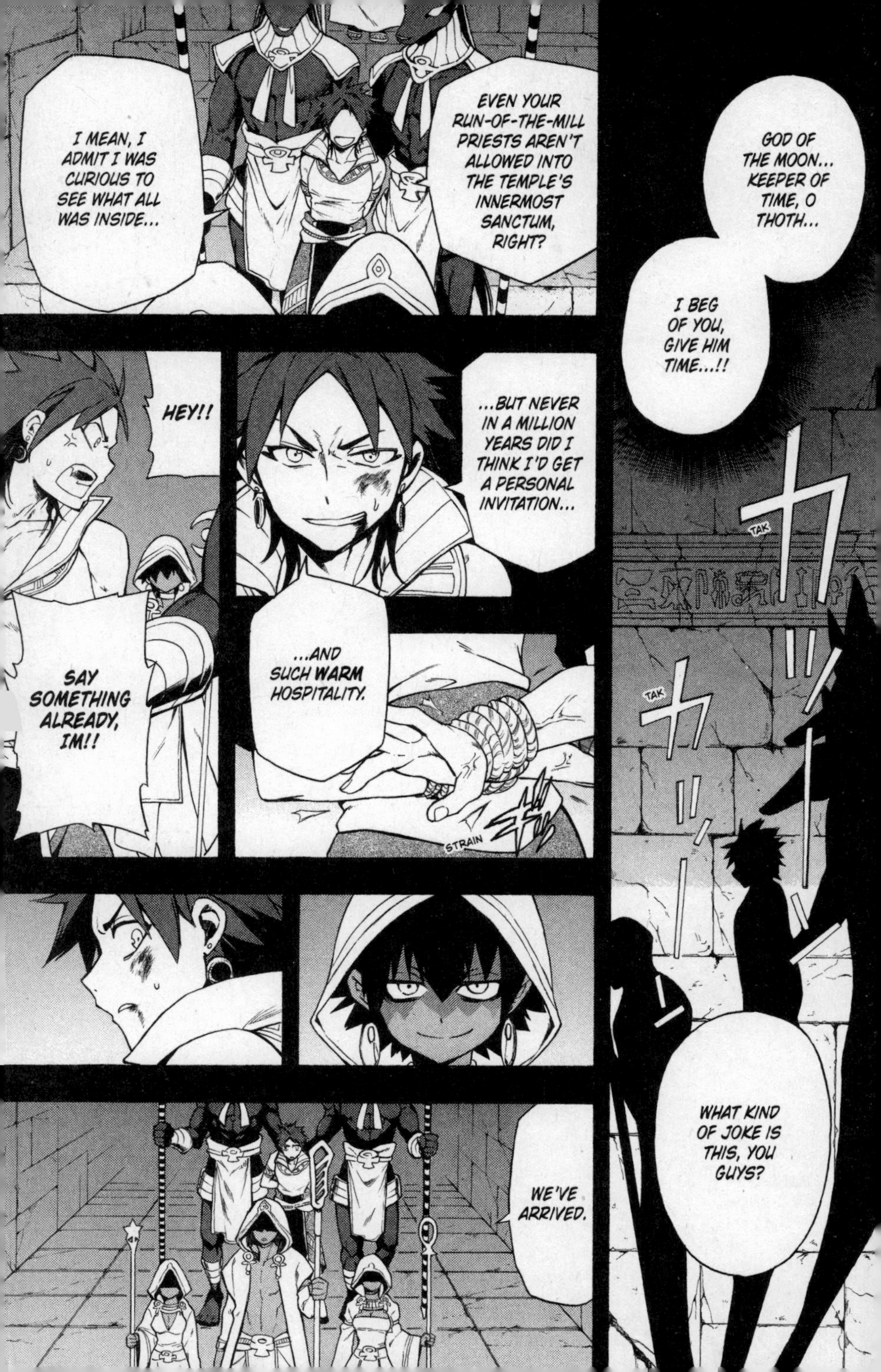
GOD OF THE MOON... KEEPER OF TIME, O THOTH...
I BEG OF YOU, GIVE HIM TIME...!!
TAK
TAK
WHAT KIND OF JOKE IS THIS, YOU GUYS?
EVEN YOUR RUN-OF-THE-MILL PRIESTS AREN'T ALLOWED INTO THE TEMPLE'S INNERMOST SANCTUM, RIGHT?
I MEAN, I ADMIT I WAS CURIOUS TO SEE WHAT ALL WAS INSIDE...
...BUT NEVER IN A MILLION YEARS DID I THINK I'D GET A PERSONAL INVITATION...
...AND SUCH WARM HOSPITALITY.
STRAIN
HEY!!
SAY SOMETHING ALREADY, IM!!
WE'VE ARRIVED.

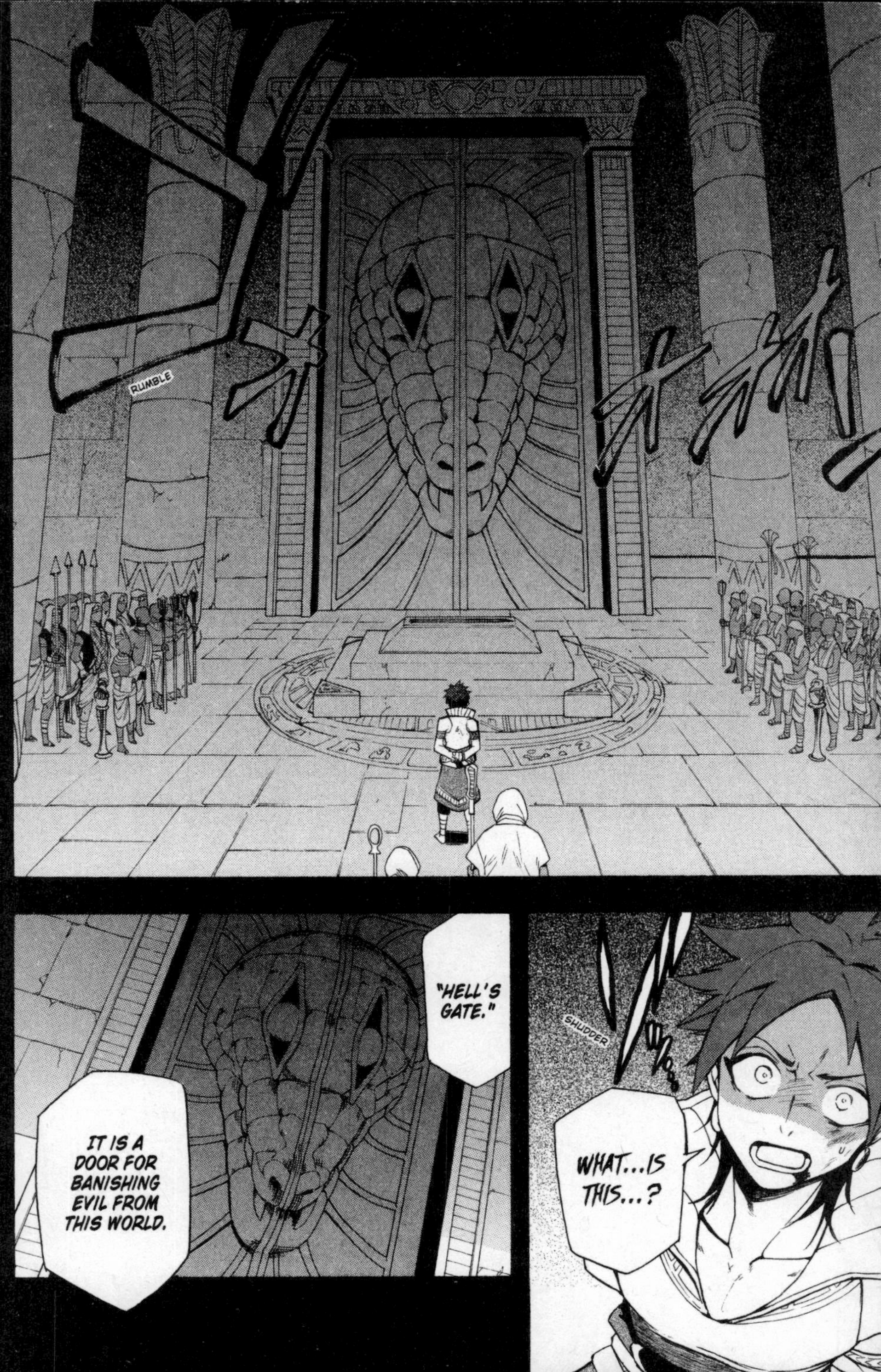
RUMBLE
SHUDDER
WHAT...IS THIS...?
"HELL'S GATE."
IT IS A DOOR FOR BANISHING EVIL FROM THIS WORLD.

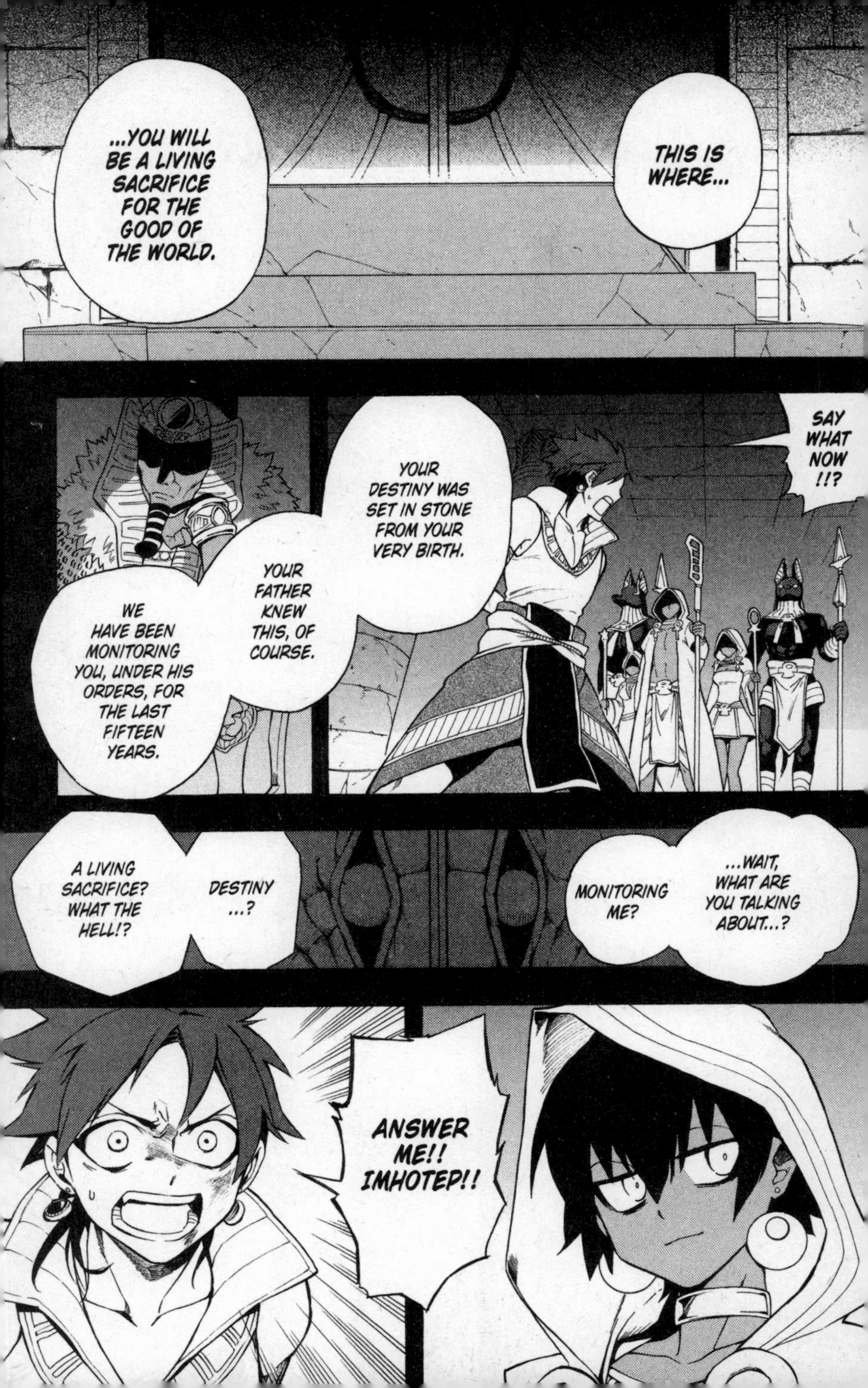
THIS IS WHERE...
...YOU WILL BE A LIVING SACRIFICE FOR THE GOOD OF THE WORLD.
SAY WHAT NOW!!?
YOUR DESTINY WAS SET IN STONE FROM YOUR VERY BIRTH.
YOUR FATHER KNEW THIS, OF COURSE.
WE HAVE BEEN MONITORING YOU, UNDER HIS ORDERS, FOR THE LAST FIFTEEN YEARS.
...WAIT, WHAT ARE YOU TALKING ABOUT...?
MONITORING ME?
DESTINY...?
A LIVING SACRIFICE? WHAT THE HELL!?
ANSWER ME!! IMHOTEP!!

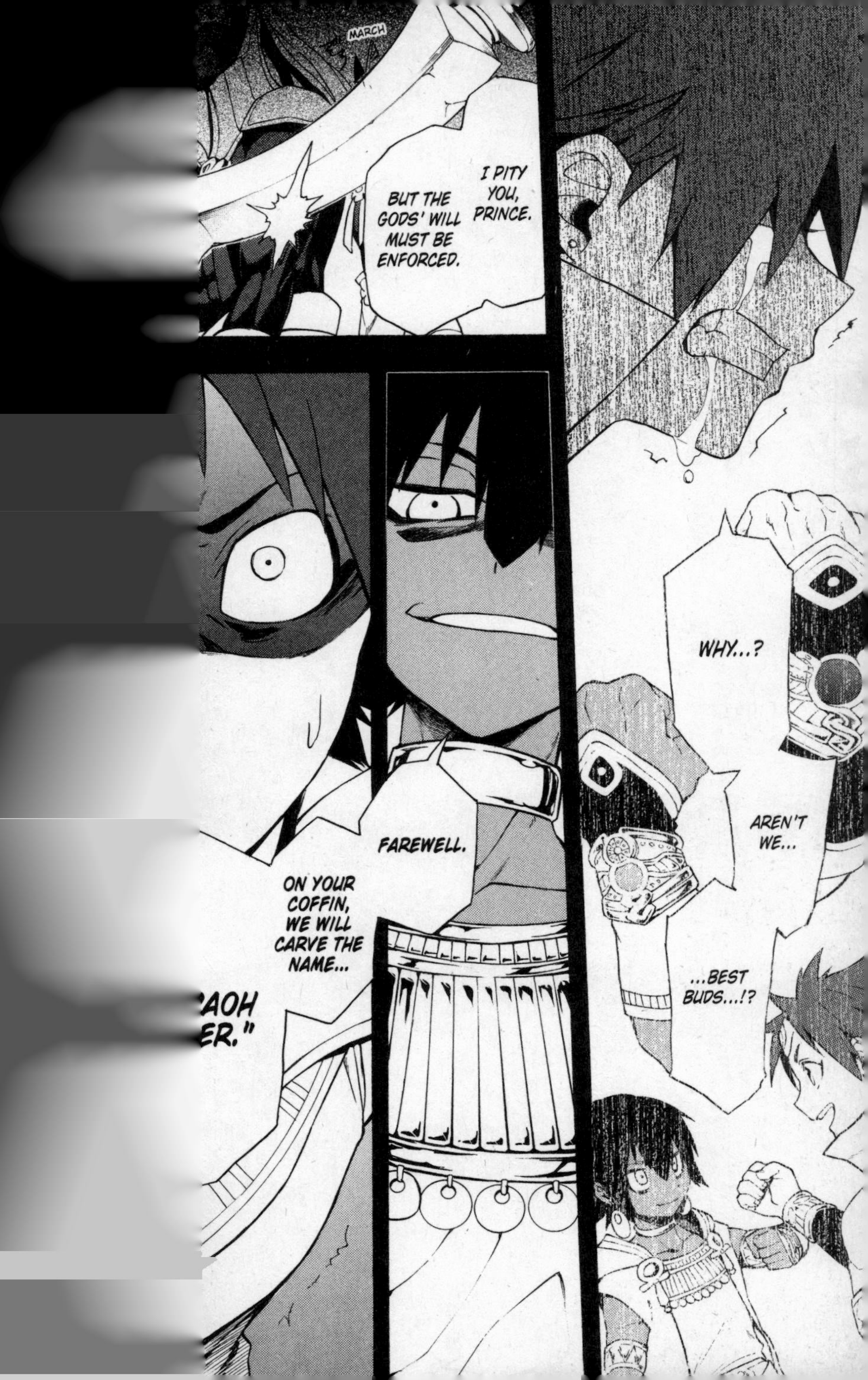
MARCH
I PITY YOU, PRINCE.
BUT THE GODS' WILL MUST BE ENFORCED.
WHY...?
AREN'T WE...
...BEST BUDS...!?
FAREWELL.
ON YOUR COFFIN, WE WILL CARVE THE NAME...

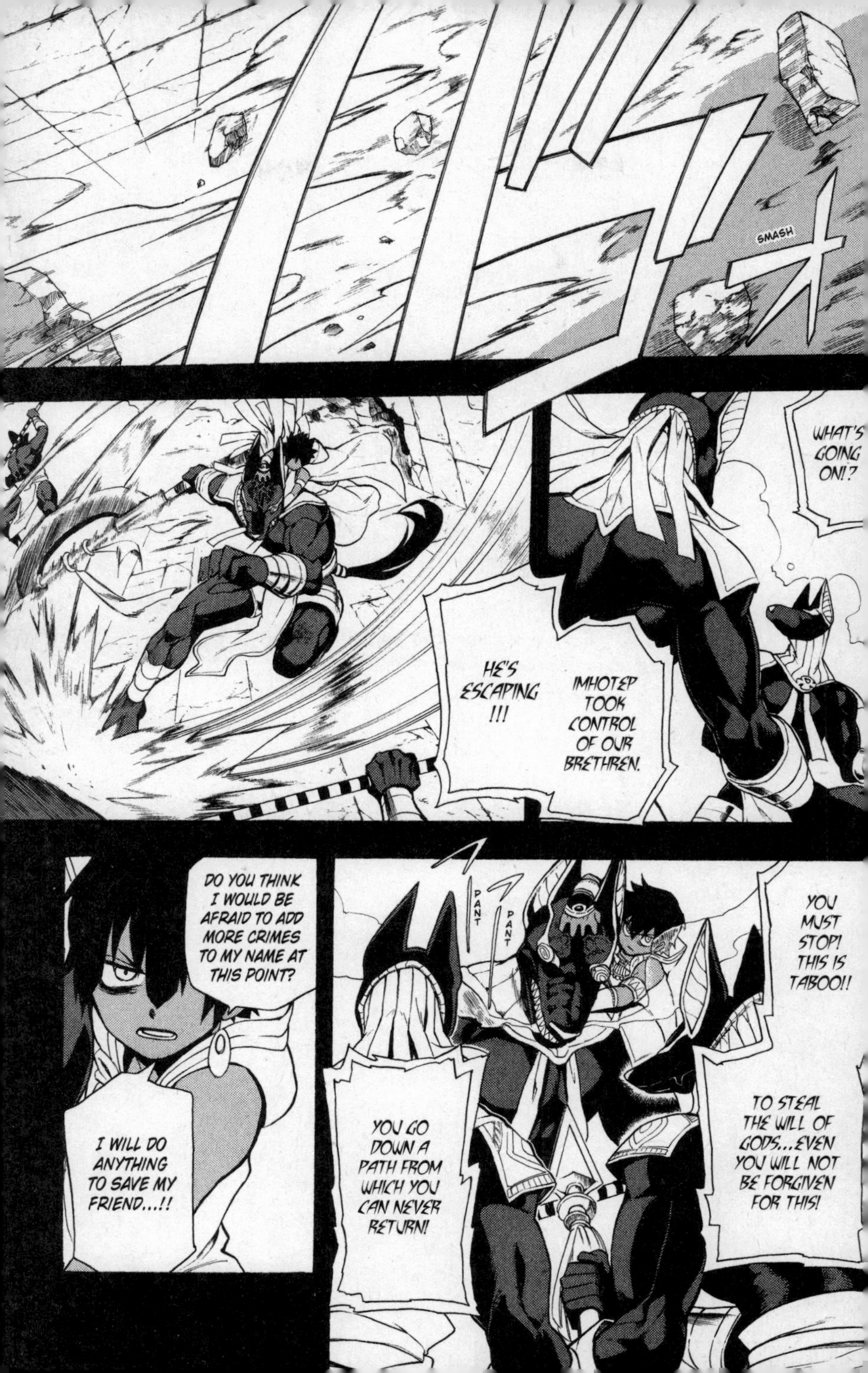
SMASH
WHAT'S GOING ON!?
IMHOTEP TOOK CONTROL OF OUR BRETHREN.
HE'S ESCAPING!!!
YOU MUST STOP! THIS IS TABOO!!
PANT
PANT
TO STEAL THE WILL OF GODS...EVEN YOU WILL NOT BE FORGIVEN FOR THIS!
YOU GO DOWN A PATH FROM WHICH YOU CAN NEVER RETURN!
DO YOU THINK I WOULD BE AFRAID TO ADD MORE CRIMES TO MY NAME AT THIS POINT?
I WILL DO ANYTHING TO SAVE MY FRIEND...!!

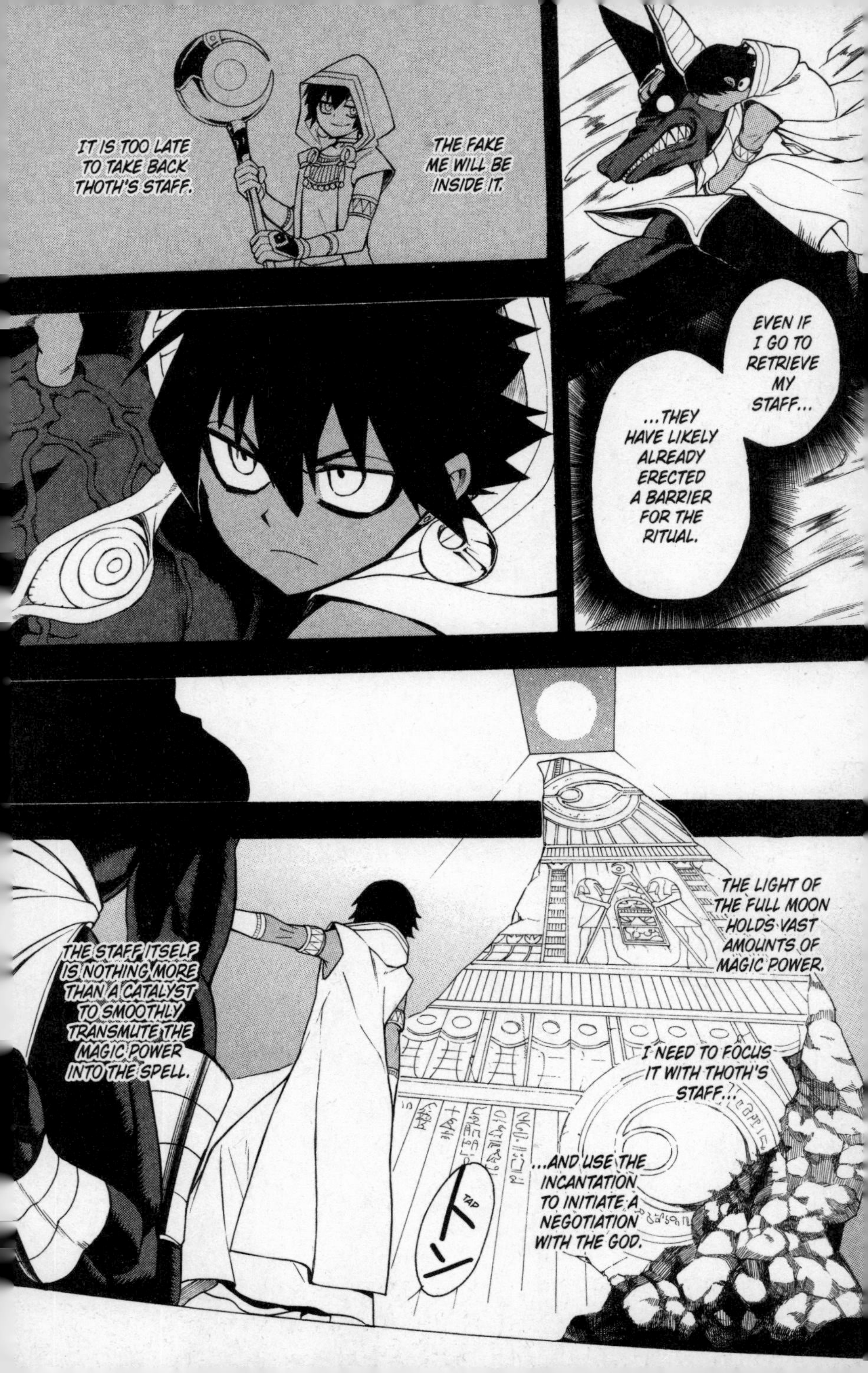
EVEN IF I GO TO RETRIEVE MY STAFF...
...THEY HAVE LIKELY ALREADY ERECTED A BARRIER FOR THE RITUAL.
THE FAKE ME WILL BE INSIDE IT.
IT IS TOO LATE TO TAKE BACK THOTH'S STAFF.
THE LIGHT OF THE FULL MOON HOLDS VAST AMOUNTS OF MAGIC POWER.
THE STAFF ITSELF IS NOTHING MORE THAN A CATALYST TO SMOOTHLY TRANSMUTE THE MAGIC POWER INTO THE SPELL.
I NEED TO FOCUS IT WITH THOTH'S STAFF...
...AND USE THE INCANTATION TO INITIATE A NEGOTIATION WITH THE GOD.
TAP

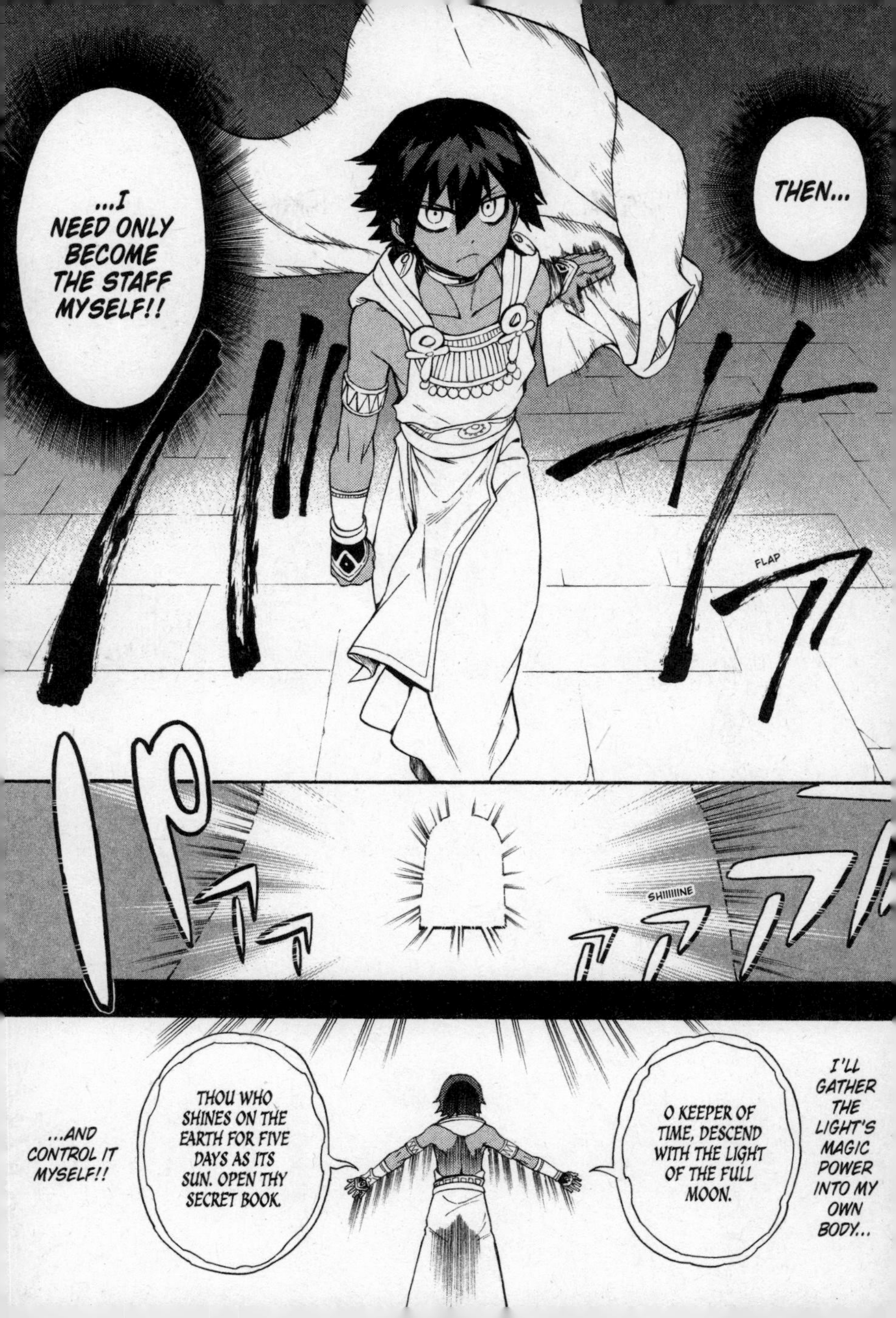
THEN...
...I NEED ONLY BECOME THE STAFF MYSELF!!
FLAP
SHIIIIIINE
I'LL GATHER THE LIGHT'S MAGIC POWER INTO MY OWN BODY...
O KEEPER OF TIME, DESCEND WITH THE LIGHT OF THE FULL MOON.
THOU WHO SHINES ON THE EARTH FOR FIVE DAYS AS ITS SUN. OPEN THY SECRET BOOK.
...AND CONTROL IT MYSELF!!

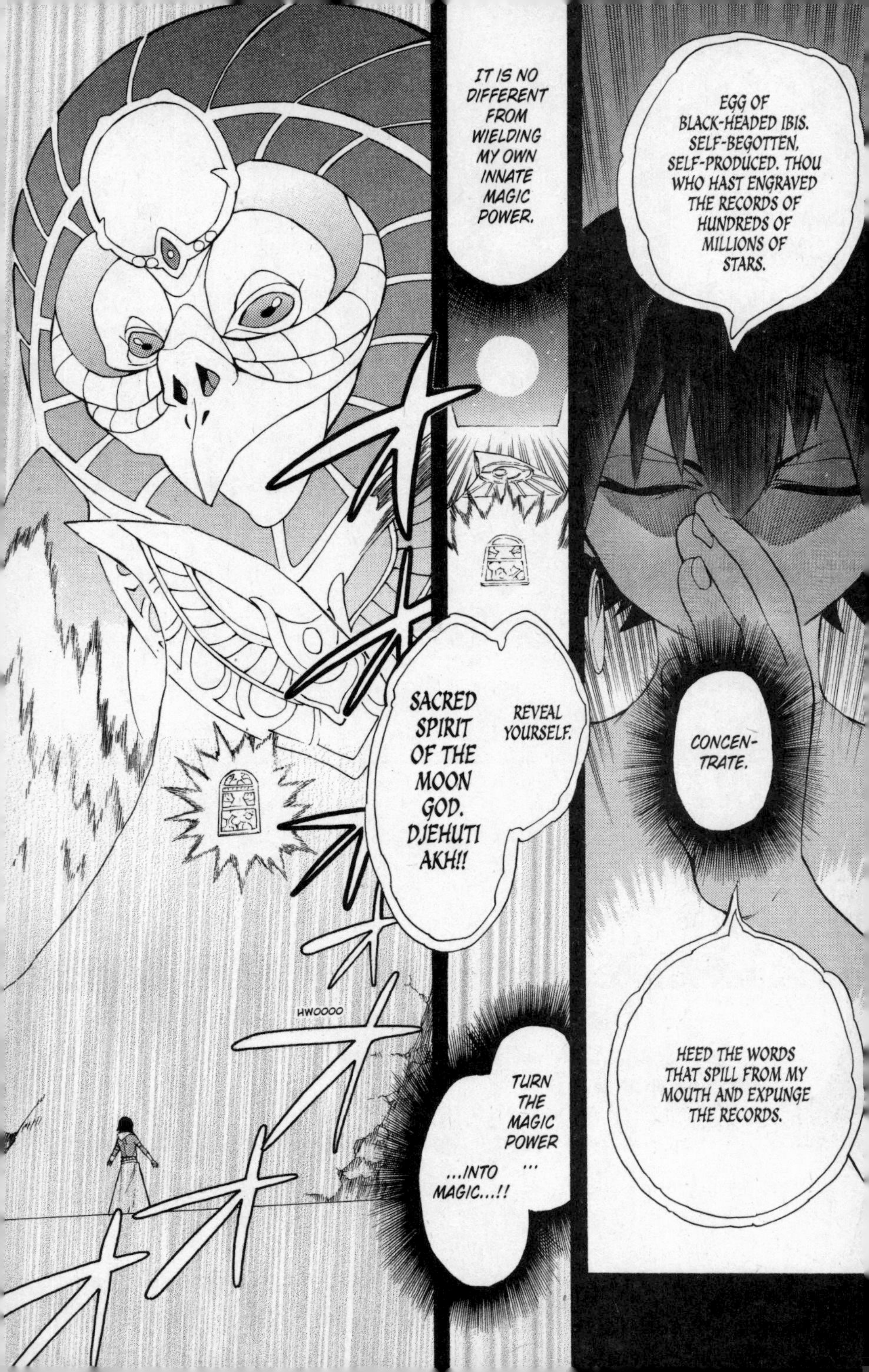
EGG OF BLACK-HEADED IBIS. SELF-BEGOTTEN, SELF-PRODUCED. THOU WHO HAST ENGRAVED THE RECORDS OF HUNDREDS OF MILLIONS OF STARS.
CONCEN-TRATE.
HEED THE WORDS THAT SPILL FROM MY MOUTH AND EXPUNGE THE RECORDS.
IT IS NO DIFFERENT FROM WIELDING MY OWN INNATE MAGIC POWER.
TURN THE MAGIC POWER ...
...INTO MAGIC...!!
REVEAL YOURSELF.
SACRED SPIRIT OF THE MOON GOD. DJEHUTI AKH!!
HWOOOO

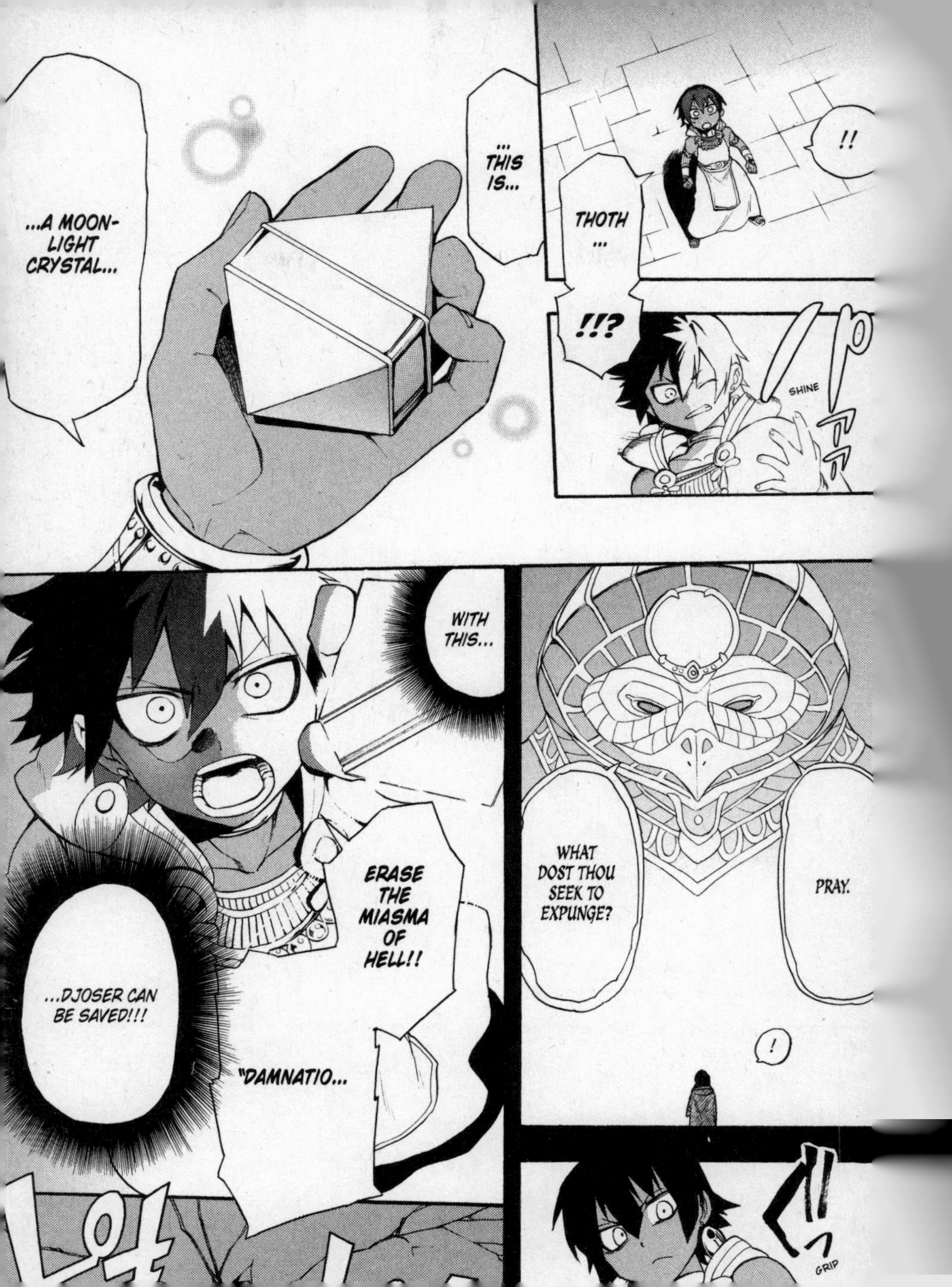
!!
THOTH ...
!!?
SHINE
... THIS IS...
...A MOON-LIGHT CRYSTAL...
PRAY.
WHAT DOST THOU SEEK TO EXPUNGE?
!
GRIP
WITH THIS...
...DJOSER CAN BE SAVED!!!
ERASE THE MIASMA OF HELL!!
"DAMNATIO...

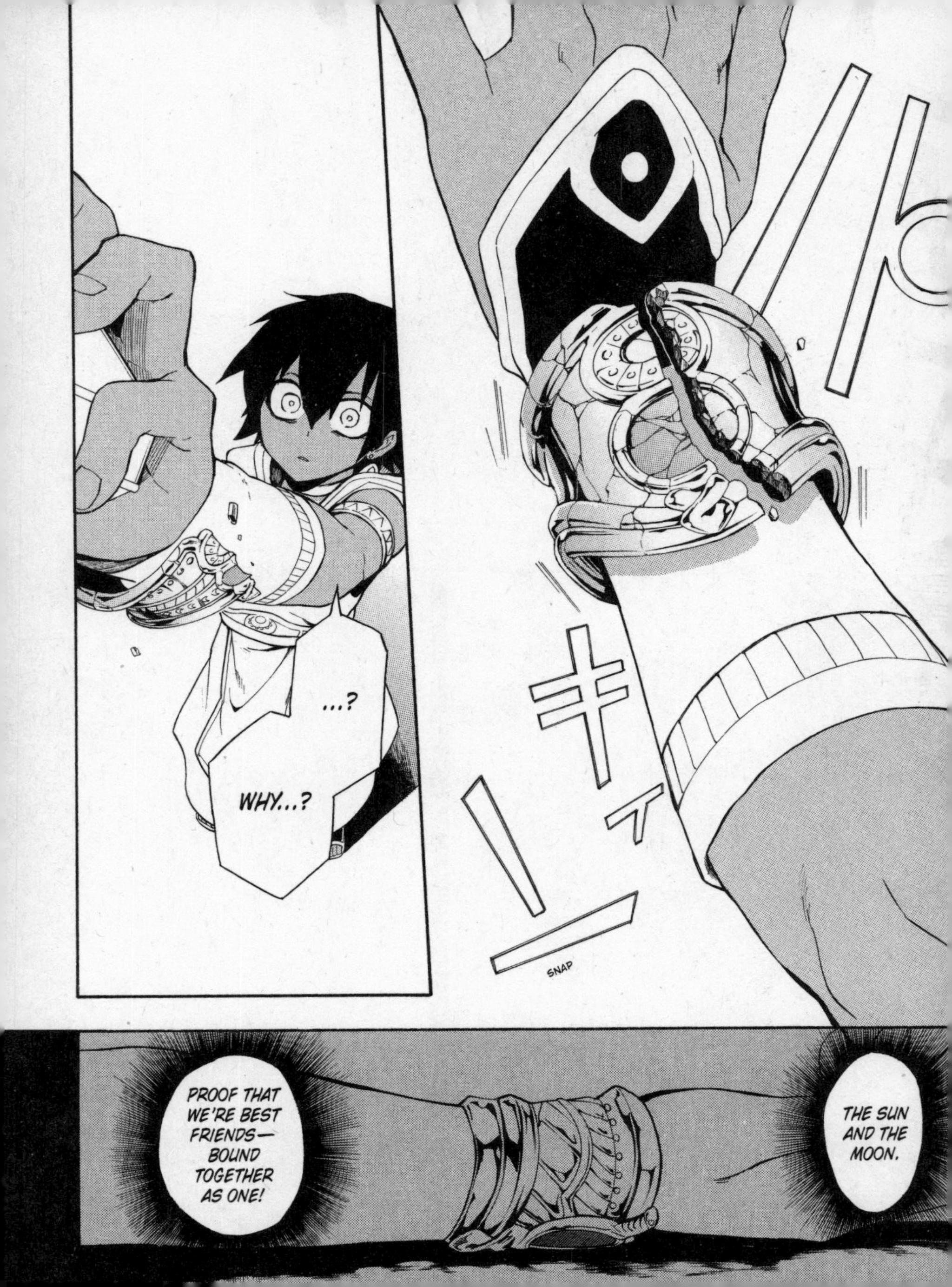
SNAP
...?
WHY...?
THE SUN AND THE MOON.
PROOF THAT WE'RE BEST FRIENDS—BOUND TOGETHER AS ONE!

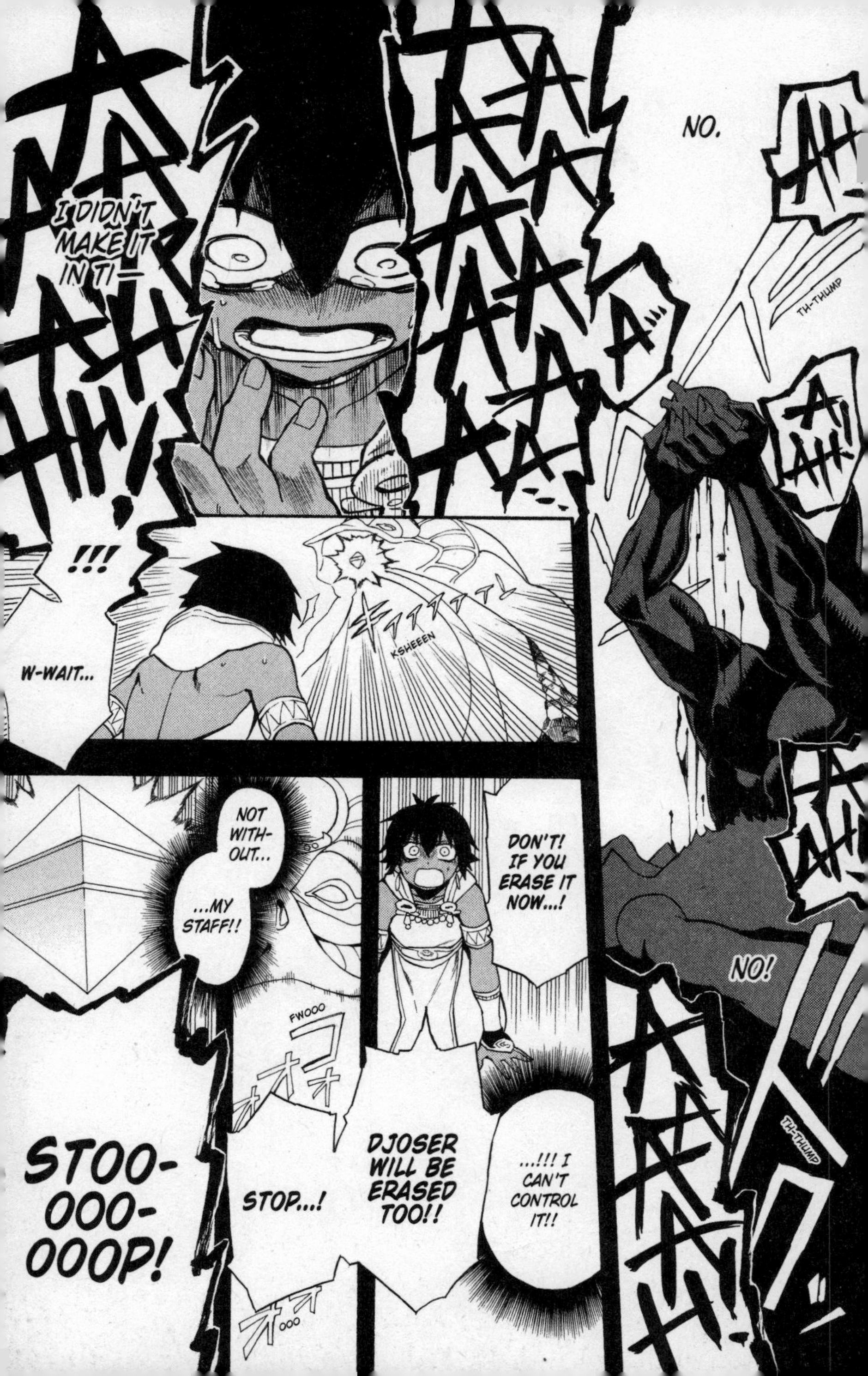
NO.
TH-THUMP
NO!
TH-THUMP
I DIDN'T MAKE IT IN TI—
!!!
KSHEEEN
W-WAIT...
DON'T! IF YOU ERASE IT NOW...!
NOT WITHOUT...
...MY STAFF!!
FWOOO
...!!! I CAN'T CONTROL IT!!
DJOSER WILL BE ERASED TOO!!
STOP...!
STOO-OOO-OOOP!

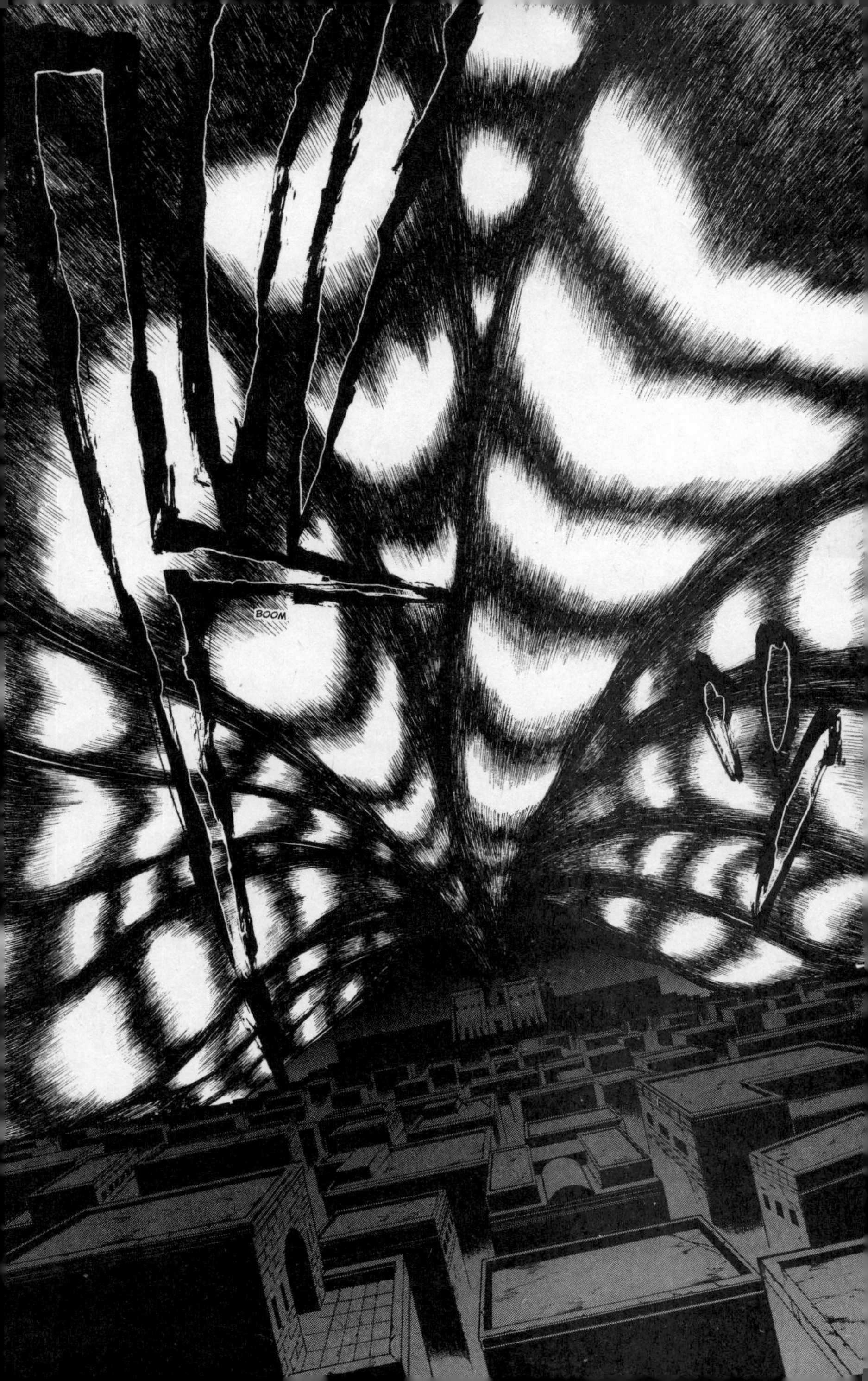
BOOM

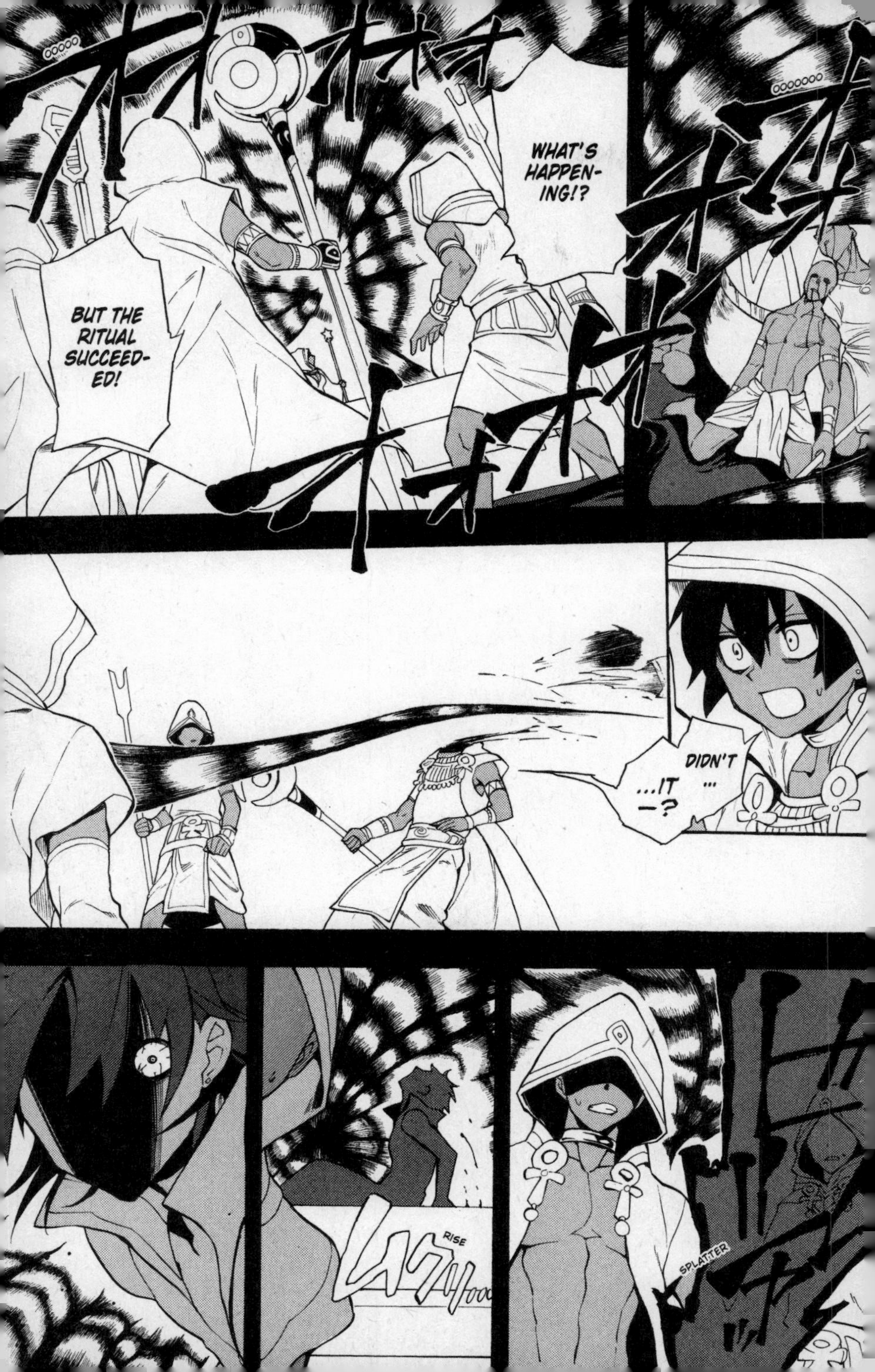

OOOOOOO
WHAT'S HAPPEN-ING!?
BUT THE RITUAL SUCCEED-ED!
OOOOO
DIDN'T ... ...IT —?
SPLATTER
RISE

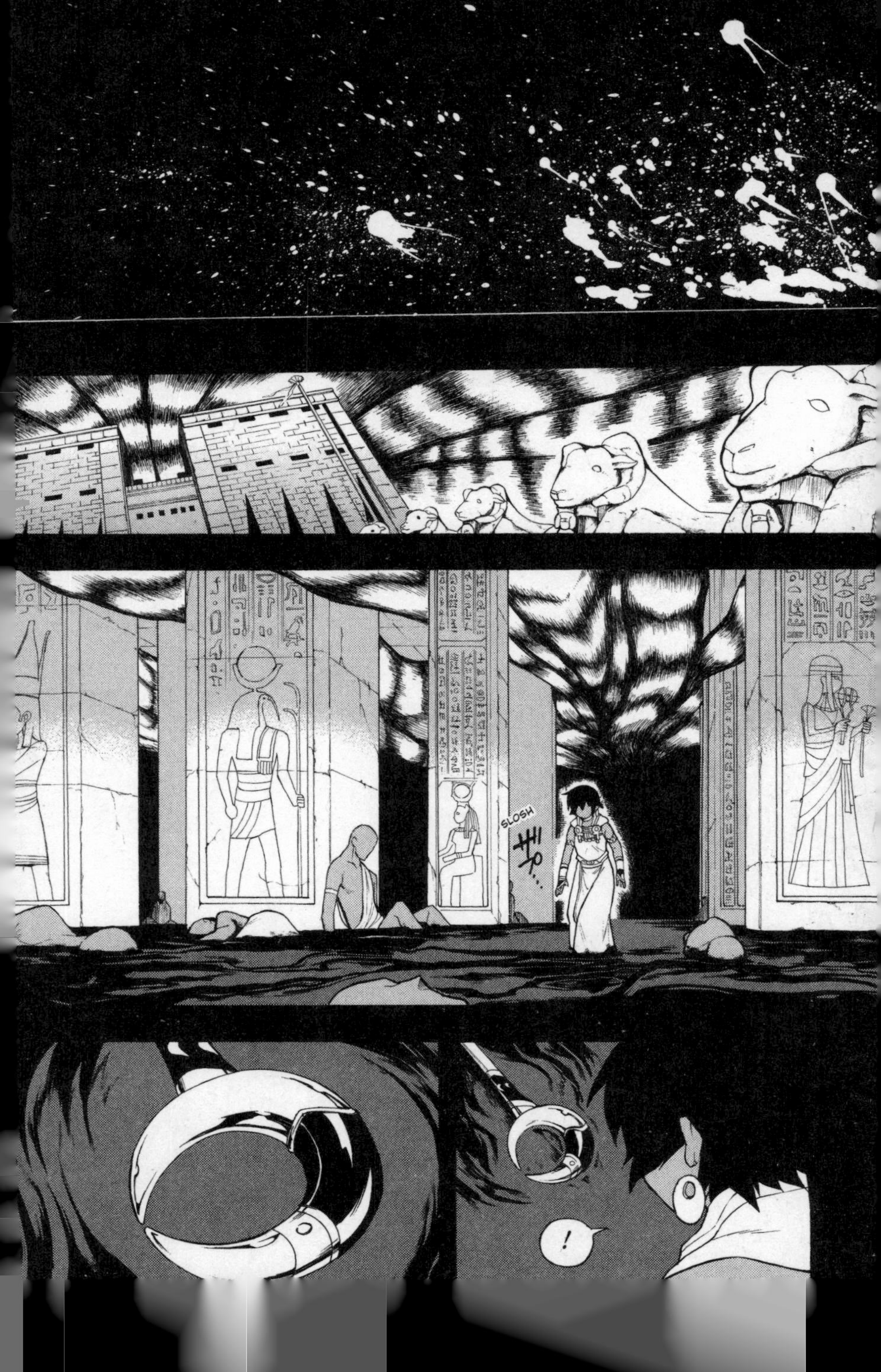
SLOSH
!

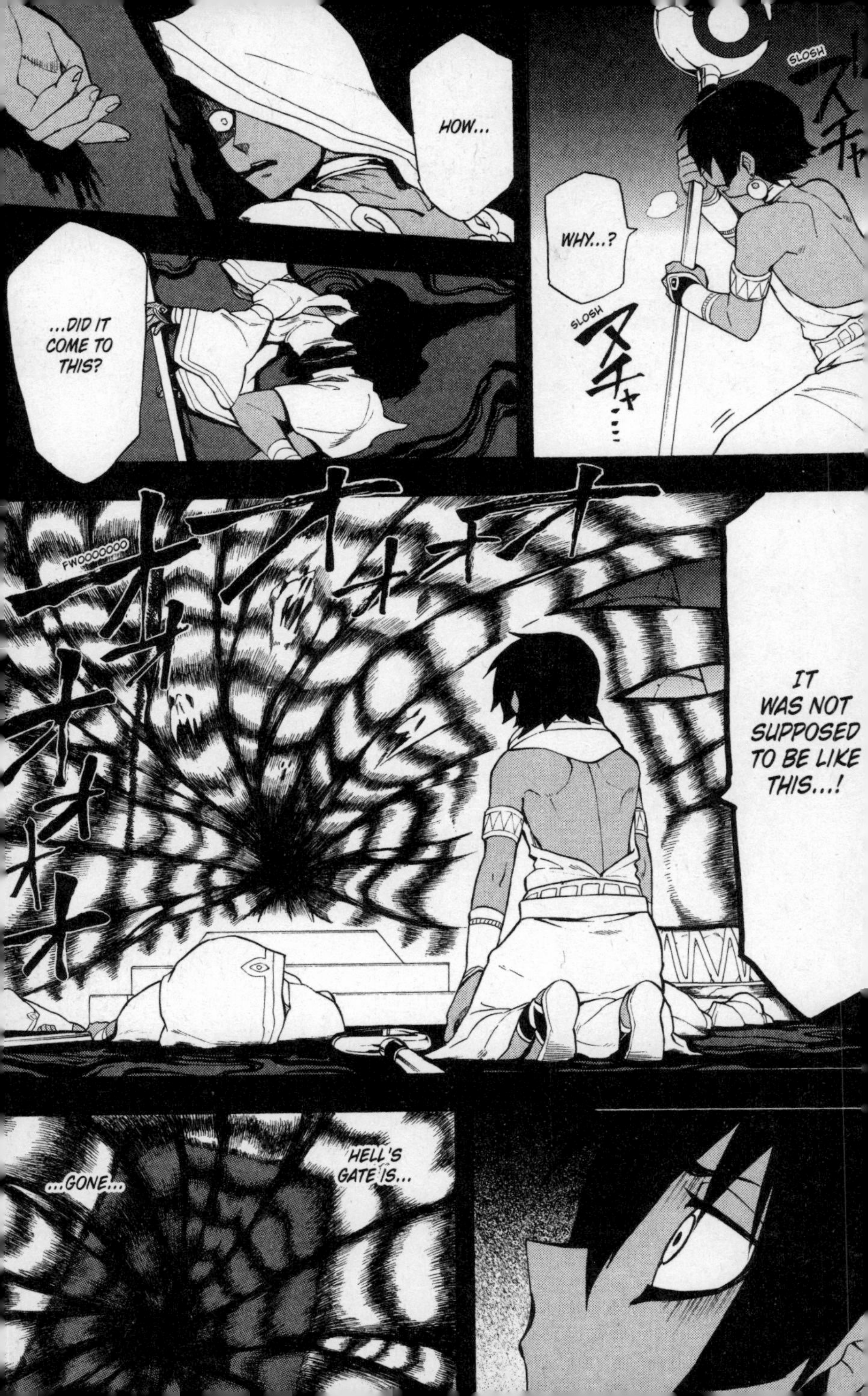
SLOSH
WHY...?
SLOSH
HOW...
...DID IT COME TO THIS?
FWOOOOOOO
IT WAS NOT SUPPOSED TO BE LIKE THIS...!
HELL'S GATE IS...
...GONE...

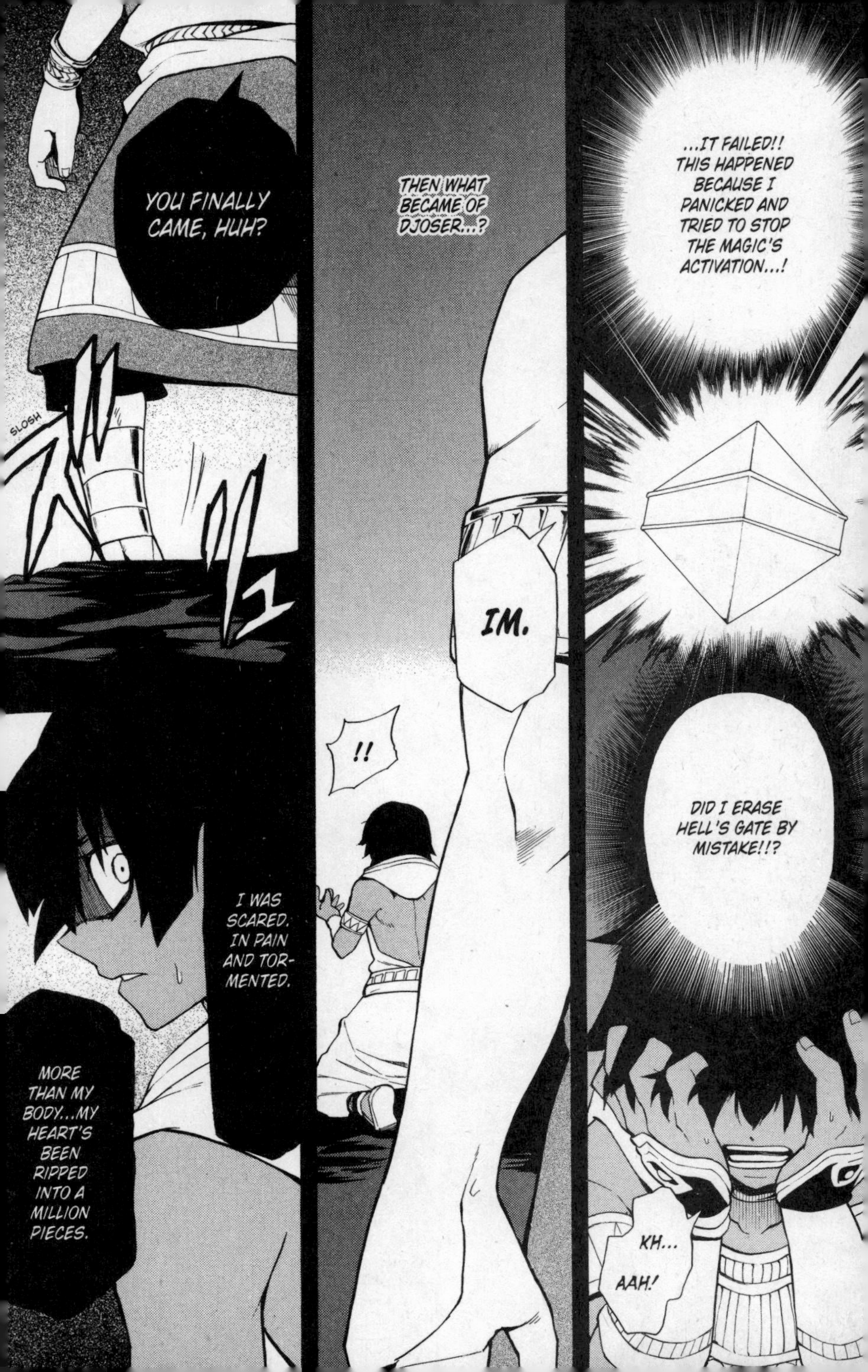
...IT FAILED!! THIS HAPPENED BECAUSE I PANICKED AND TRIED TO STOP THE MAGIC'S ACTIVATION...!
DID I ERASE HELL'S GATE BY MISTAKE!!?
KH...
AAH!
THEN WHAT BECAME OF DJOSER...?
IM.
!!
YOU FINALLY CAME, HUH?
SLOSH
I WAS SCARED. IN PAIN AND TOR-MENTED.
MORE THAN MY BODY...MY HEART'S BEEN RIPPED INTO A MILLION PIECES.

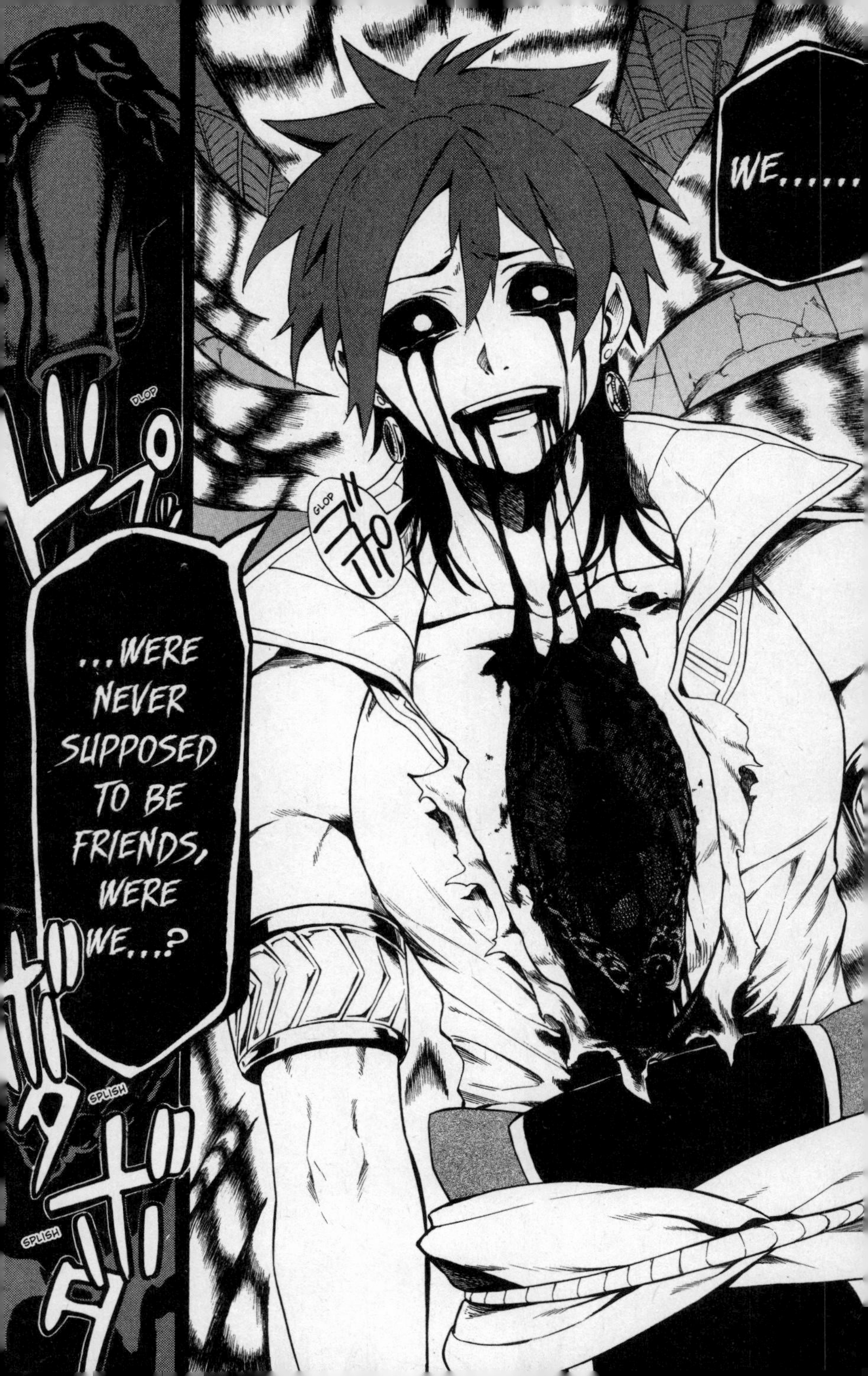
WE......
GLOP
DLOP
...WERE NEVER SUPPOSED TO BE FRIENDS, WERE WE...?
SPLISH
SPLISH

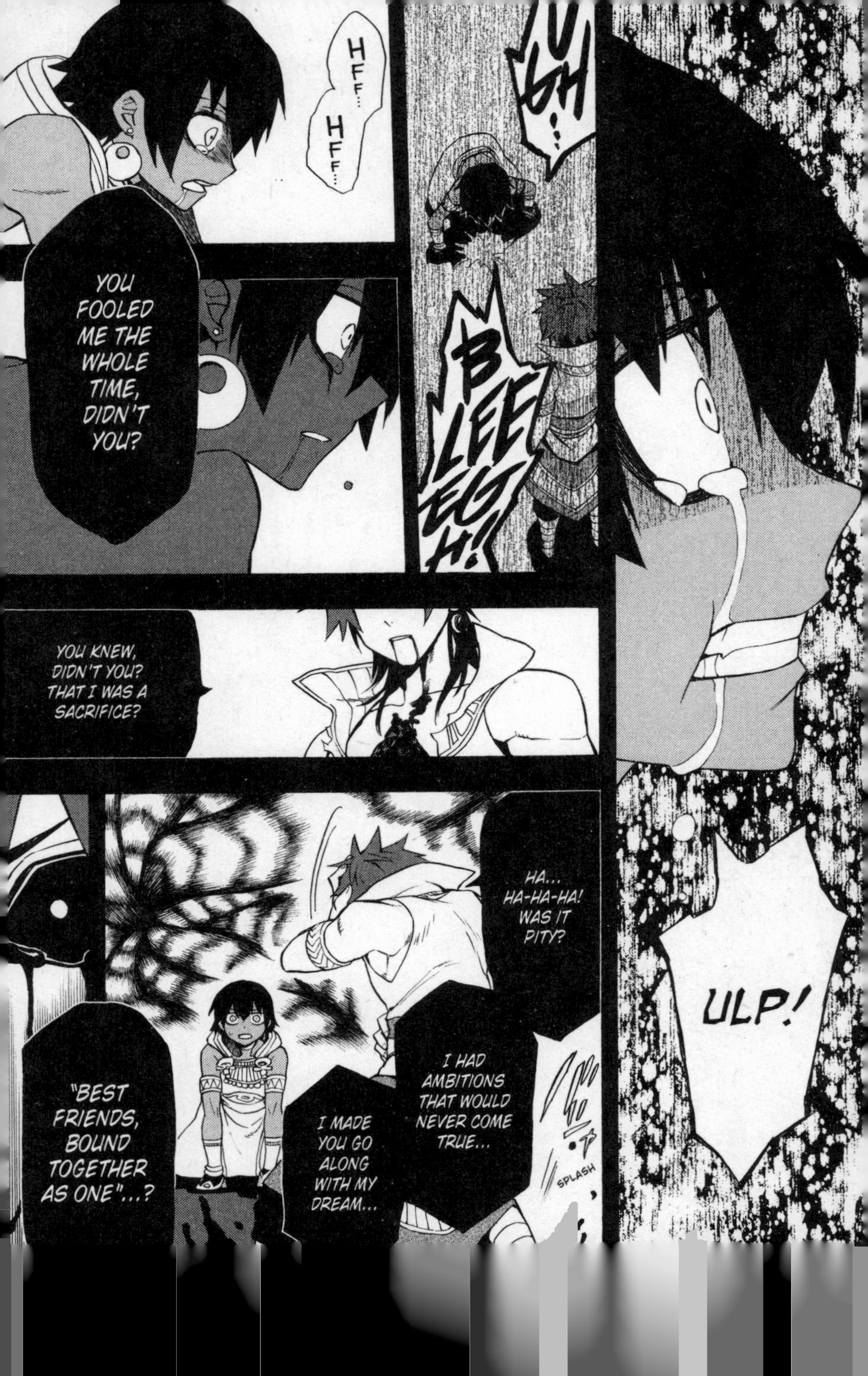
ULP!
UGH...!
BLEEEGH!
HFF... HFF...
YOU FOOLED ME THE WHOLE TIME, DIDN'T YOU?
YOU KNEW, DIDN'T YOU? THAT I WAS A SACRIFICE?
HA... HA-HA-HA! WAS IT PITY?
SPLASH
I HAD AMBITIONS THAT WOULD NEVER COME TRUE...
I MADE YOU GO ALONG WITH MY DREAM...
"BEST FRIENDS, BOUND TOGETHER AS ONE"...?

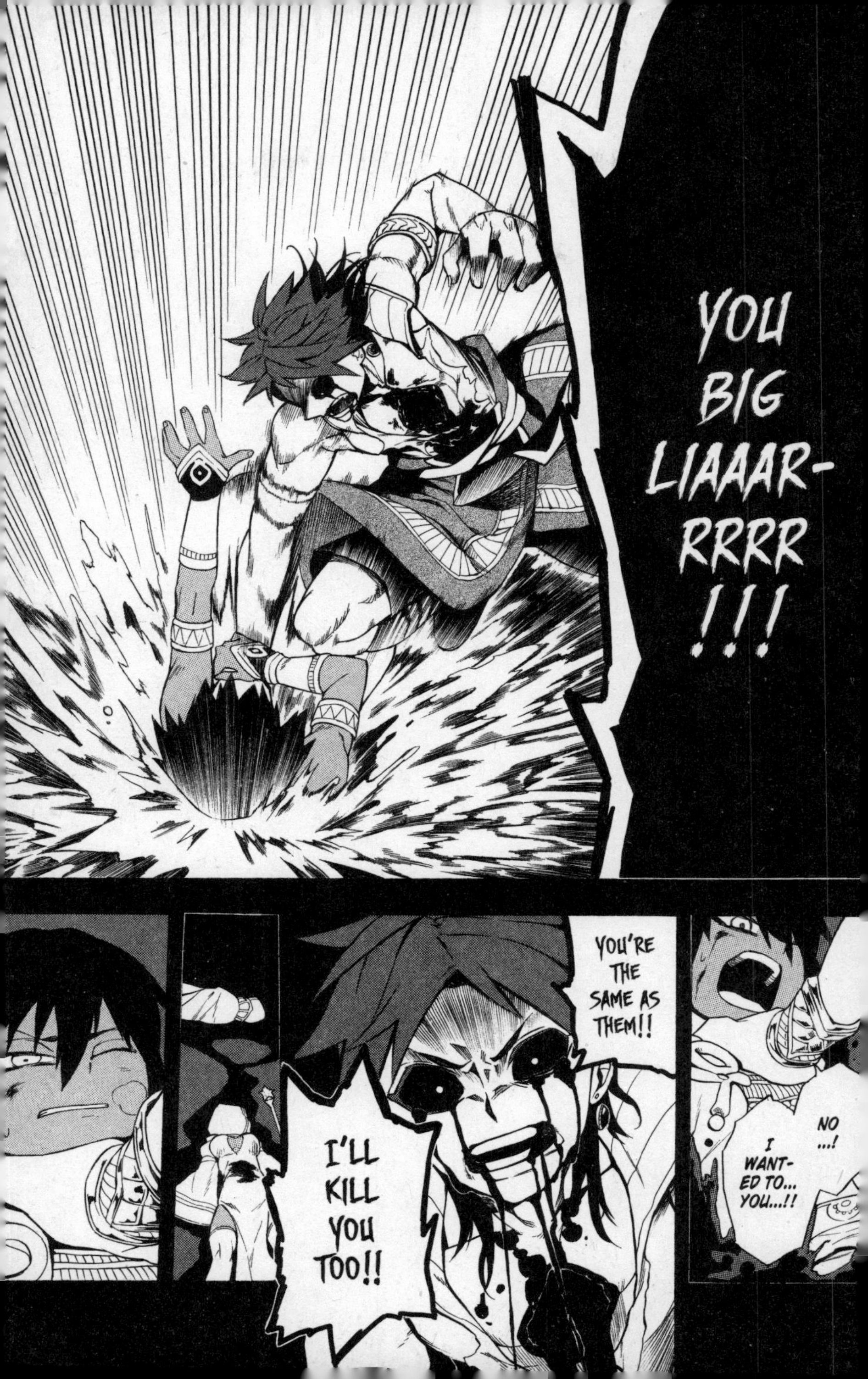
YOU BIG LIAAAR-RRRR!!!
NO ...!
I WANT-ED TO... YOU...!!
YOU'RE THE SAME AS THEM!!
I'LL KILL YOU TOO!!

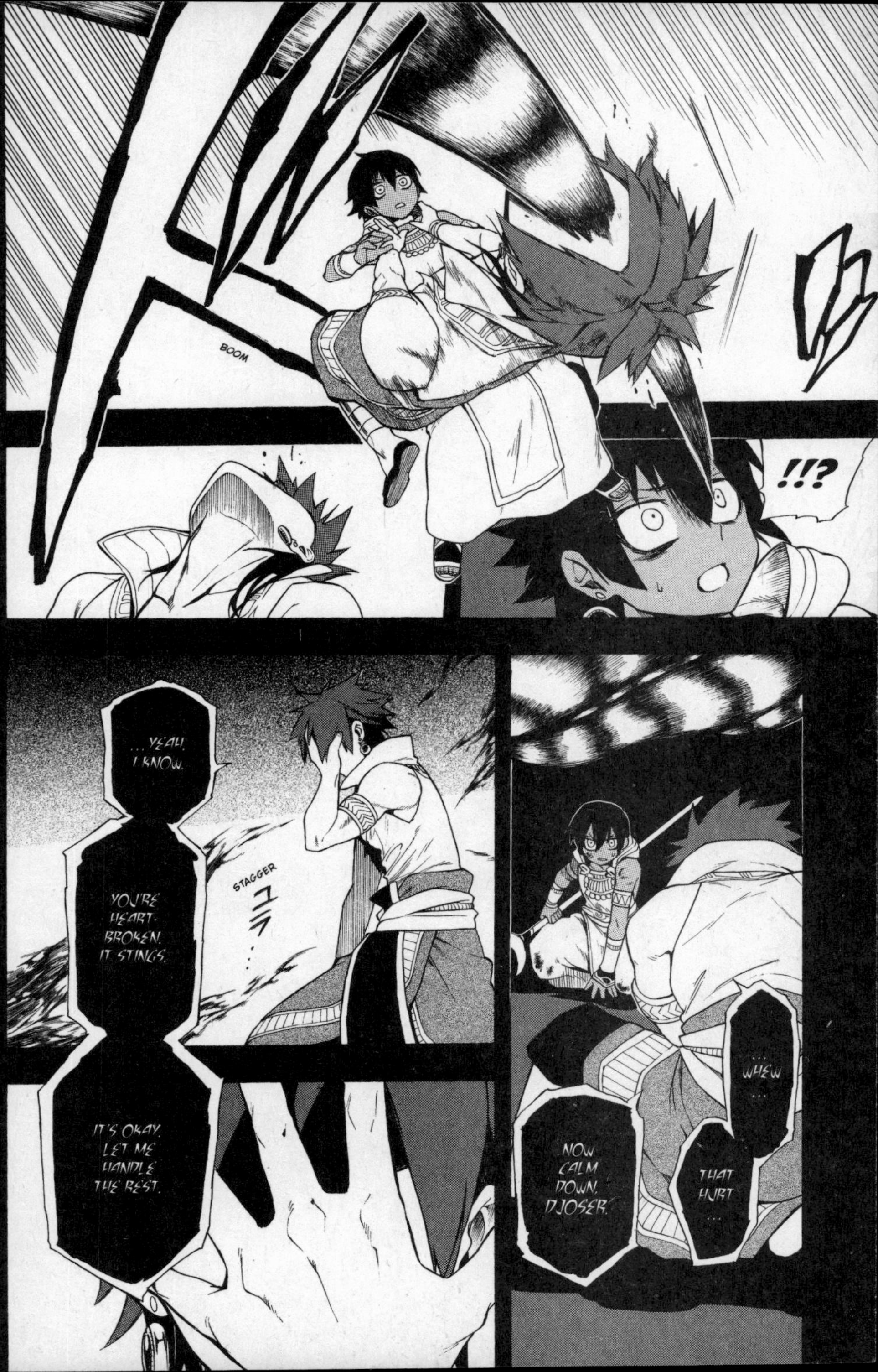
BOOM
!!?
...WHEW...
THAT HURT...
NOW CALM DOWN, DJOSER.
...YEAH, I KNOW.
STAGGER
YOU'RE HEART-BROKEN. IT STINGS.
IT'S OKAY. LET ME HANDLE THE REST.

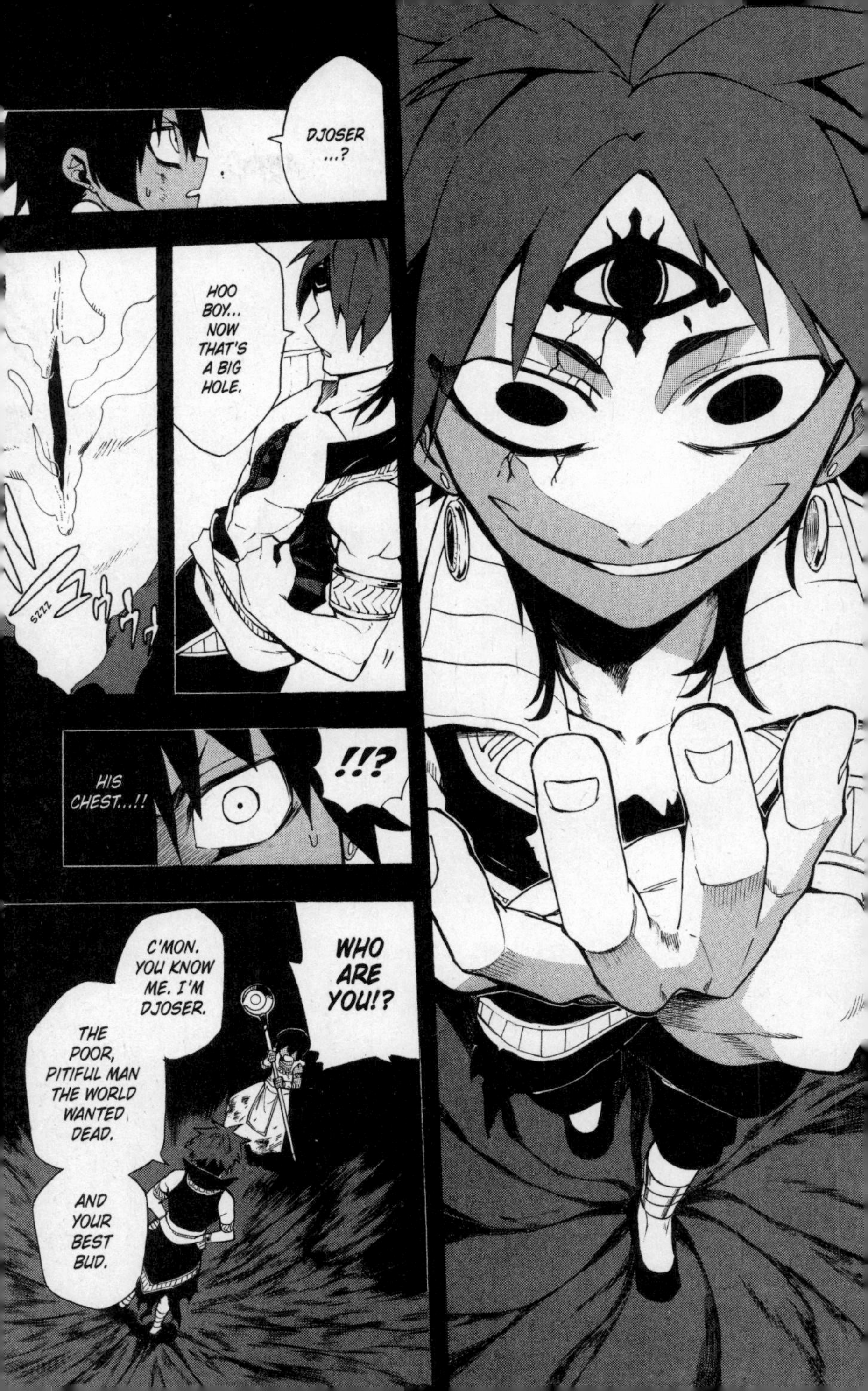
DJOSER ...?
HOO BOY... NOW THAT'S A BIG HOLE.
SZZZ
!!?
HIS CHEST...!!
WHO ARE YOU!?
C'MON. YOU KNOW ME. I'M DJOSER.
THE POOR, PITIFUL MAN THE WORLD WANTED DEAD.
AND YOUR BEST BUD.

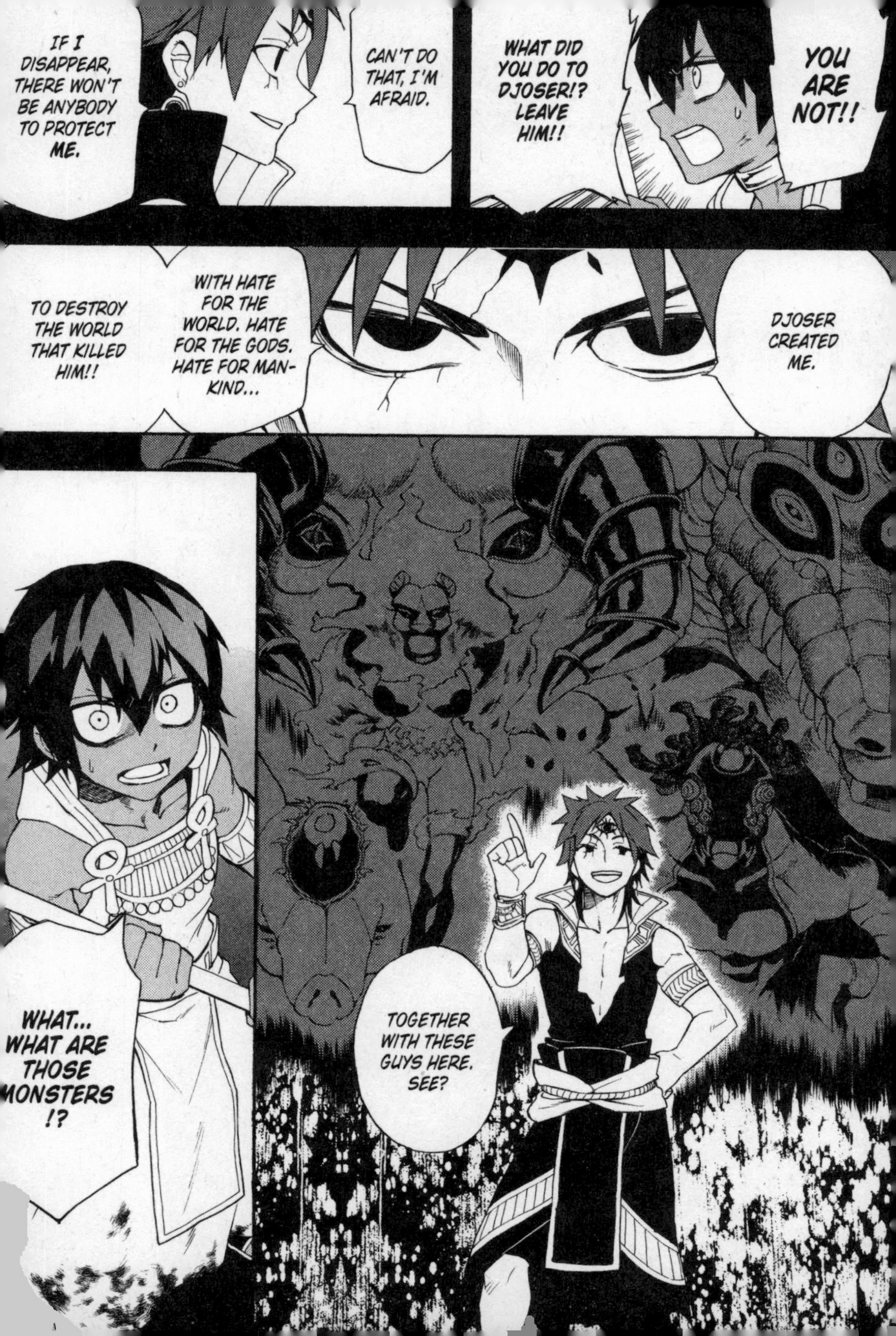
YOU ARE NOT!!
WHAT DID YOU DO TO DJOSER!? LEAVE HIM!!
CAN'T DO THAT, I'M AFRAID.
IF I DISAPPEAR, THERE WON'T BE ANYBODY TO PROTECT ME.
DJOSER CREATED ME.
WITH HATE FOR THE WORLD. HATE FOR THE GODS. HATE FOR MAN-KIND...
TO DESTROY THE WORLD THAT KILLED HIM!!
TOGETHER WITH THESE GUYS HERE. SEE?
WHAT... WHAT ARE THOSE MONSTERS !?

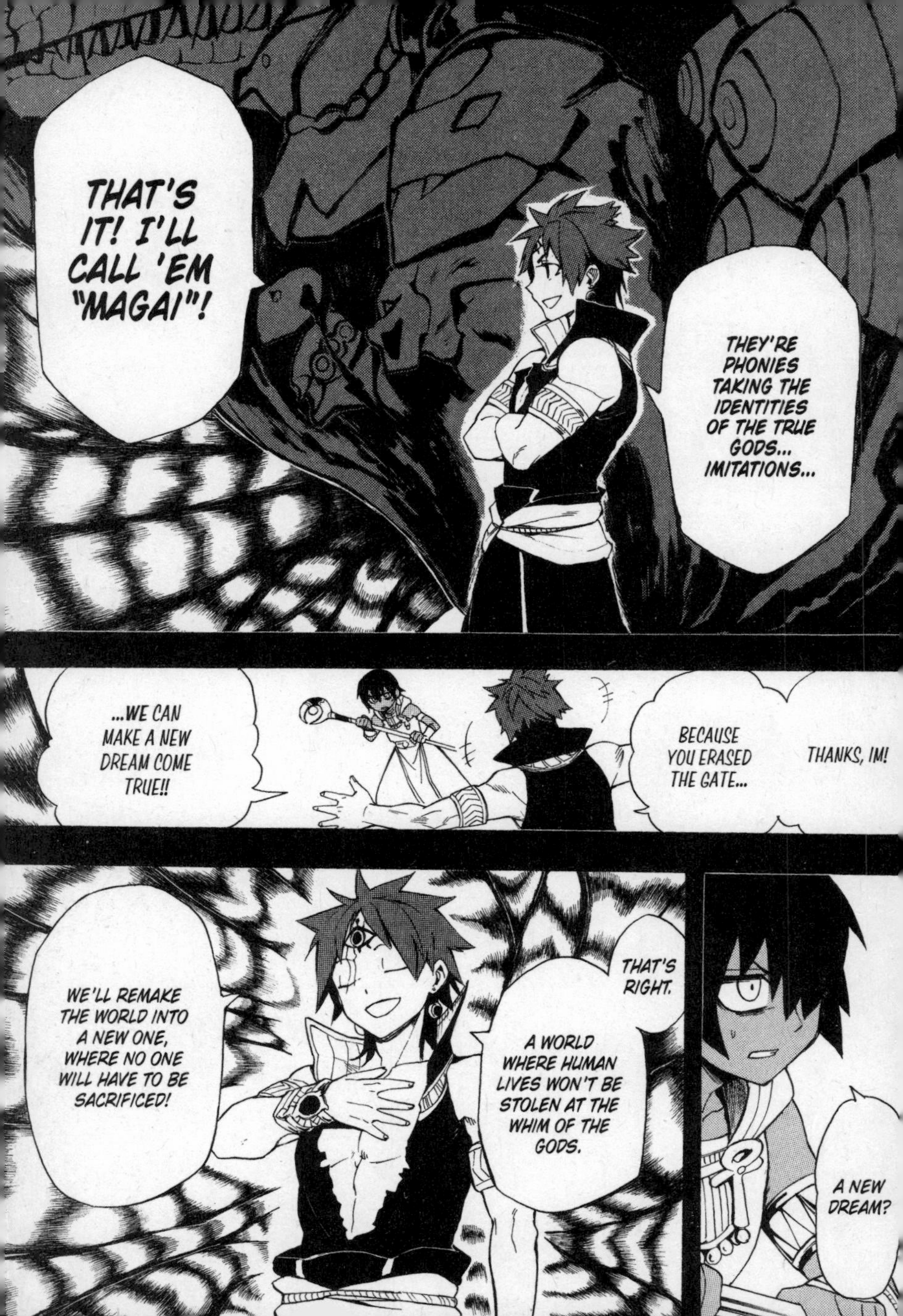
THEY'RE PHONIES TAKING THE IDENTITIES OF THE TRUE GODS... IMITATIONS...
THAT'S IT! I'LL CALL 'EM "MAGAI"!
THANKS, IM!
BECAUSE YOU ERASED THE GATE...
...WE CAN MAKE A NEW DREAM COME TRUE!!
A NEW DREAM?
THAT'S RIGHT.
A WORLD WHERE HUMAN LIVES WON'T BE STOLEN AT THE WHIM OF THE GODS.
WE'LL REMAKE THE WORLD INTO A NEW ONE, WHERE NO ONE WILL HAVE TO BE SACRIFICED!

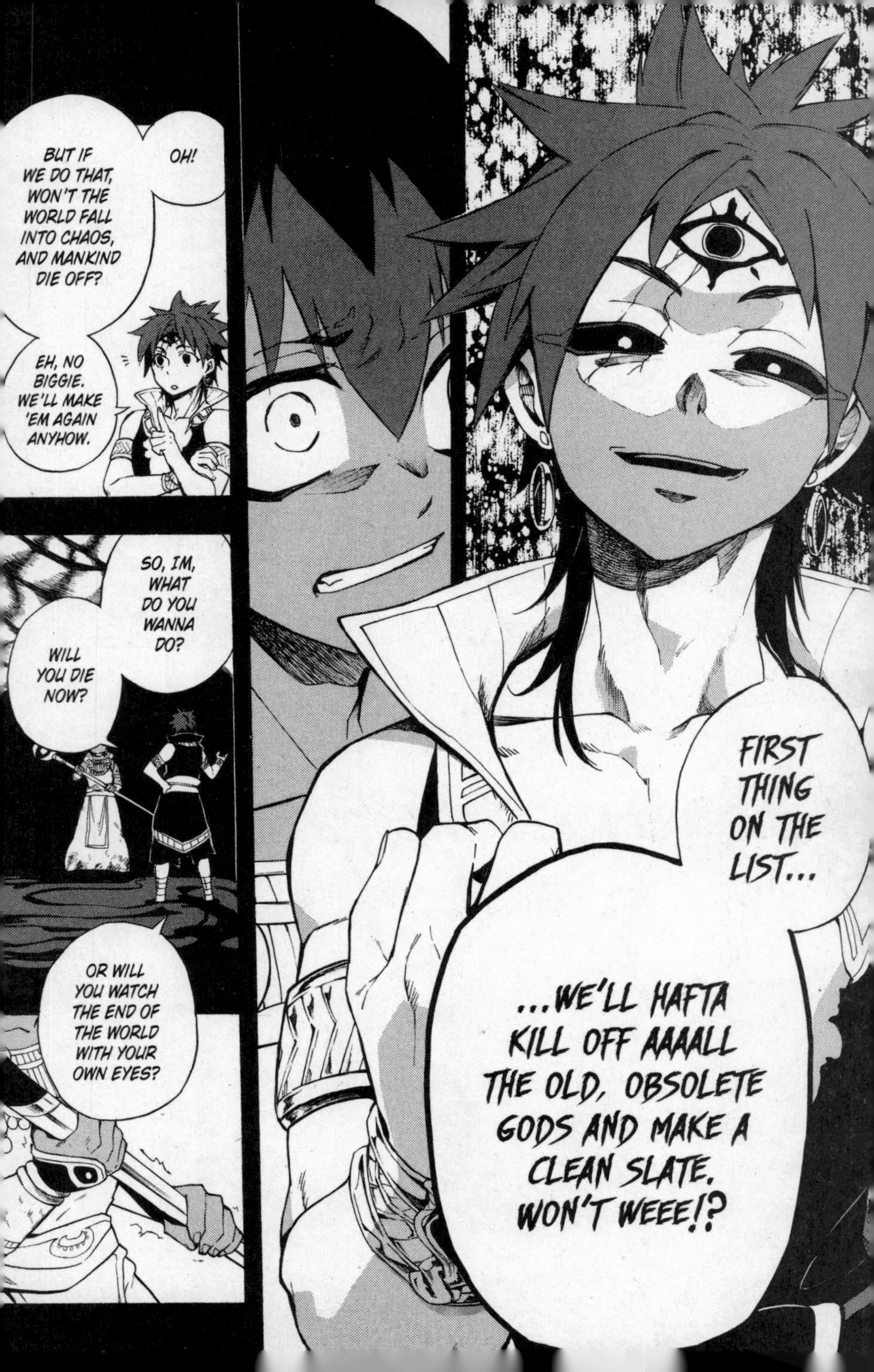
FIRST THING ON THE LIST...
...WE'LL HAFTA KILL OFF AAAALL THE OLD, OBSOLETE GODS AND MAKE A CLEAN SLATE, WON'T WEEE!?
OH!
BUT IF WE DO THAT, WON'T THE WORLD FALL INTO CHAOS, AND MANKIND DIE OFF?
EH, NO BIGGIE. WE'LL MAKE 'EM AGAIN ANYHOW.
SO, IM, WHAT DO YOU WANNA DO?
WILL YOU DIE NOW?
OR WILL YOU WATCH THE END OF THE WORLD WITH YOUR OWN EYES?

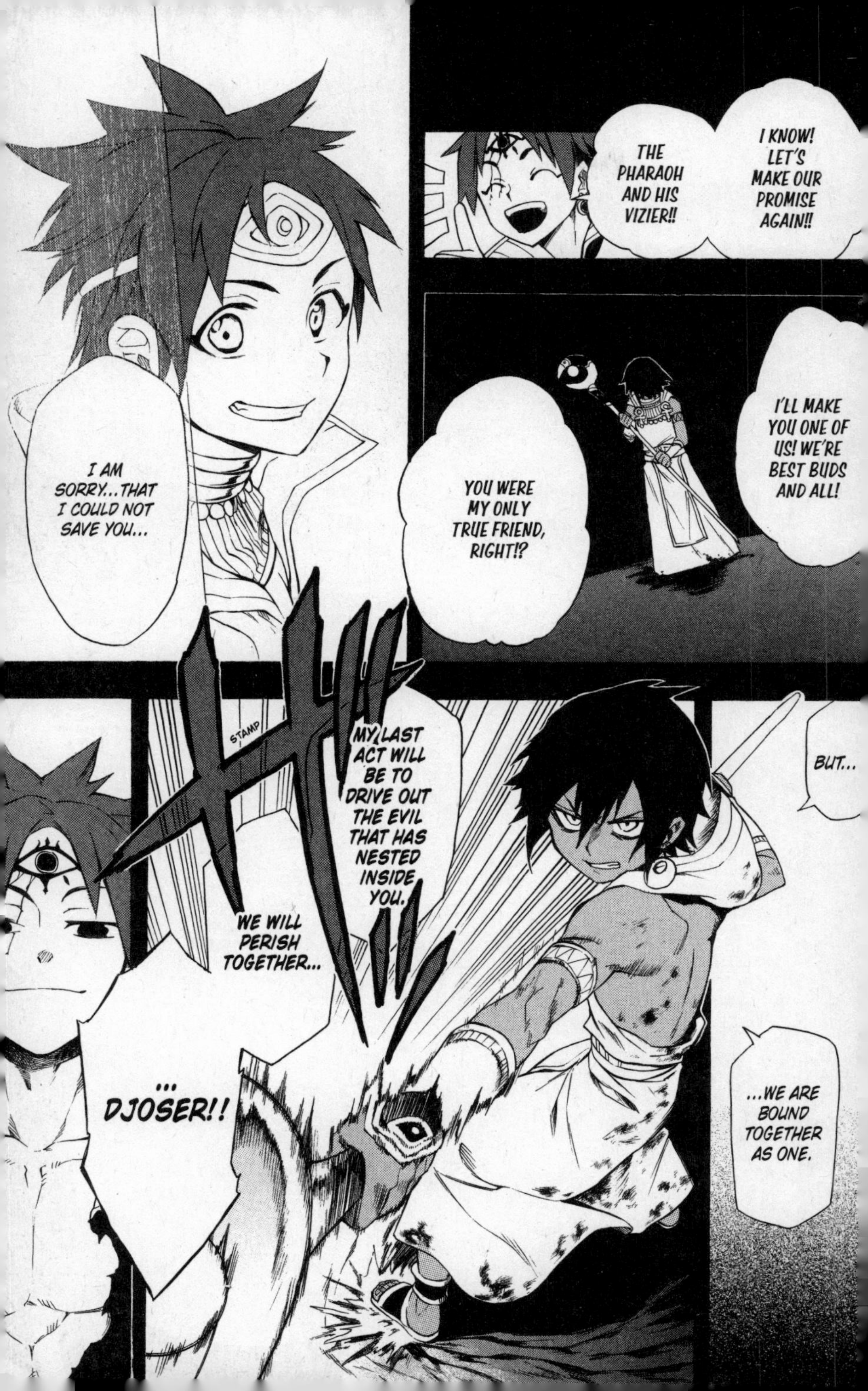
I KNOW! LET'S MAKE OUR PROMISE AGAIN!!
THE PHARAOH AND HIS VIZIER!!
I'LL MAKE YOU ONE OF US! WE'RE BEST BUDS AND ALL!
YOU WERE MY ONLY TRUE FRIEND, RIGHT!?
I AM SORRY...THAT I COULD NOT SAVE YOU...
BUT...
MY LAST ACT WILL BE TO DRIVE OUT THE EVIL THAT HAS NESTED INSIDE YOU.
STAMP
WE WILL PERISH TOGETHER...
...WE ARE BOUND TOGETHER AS ONE.
... DJOSER!!

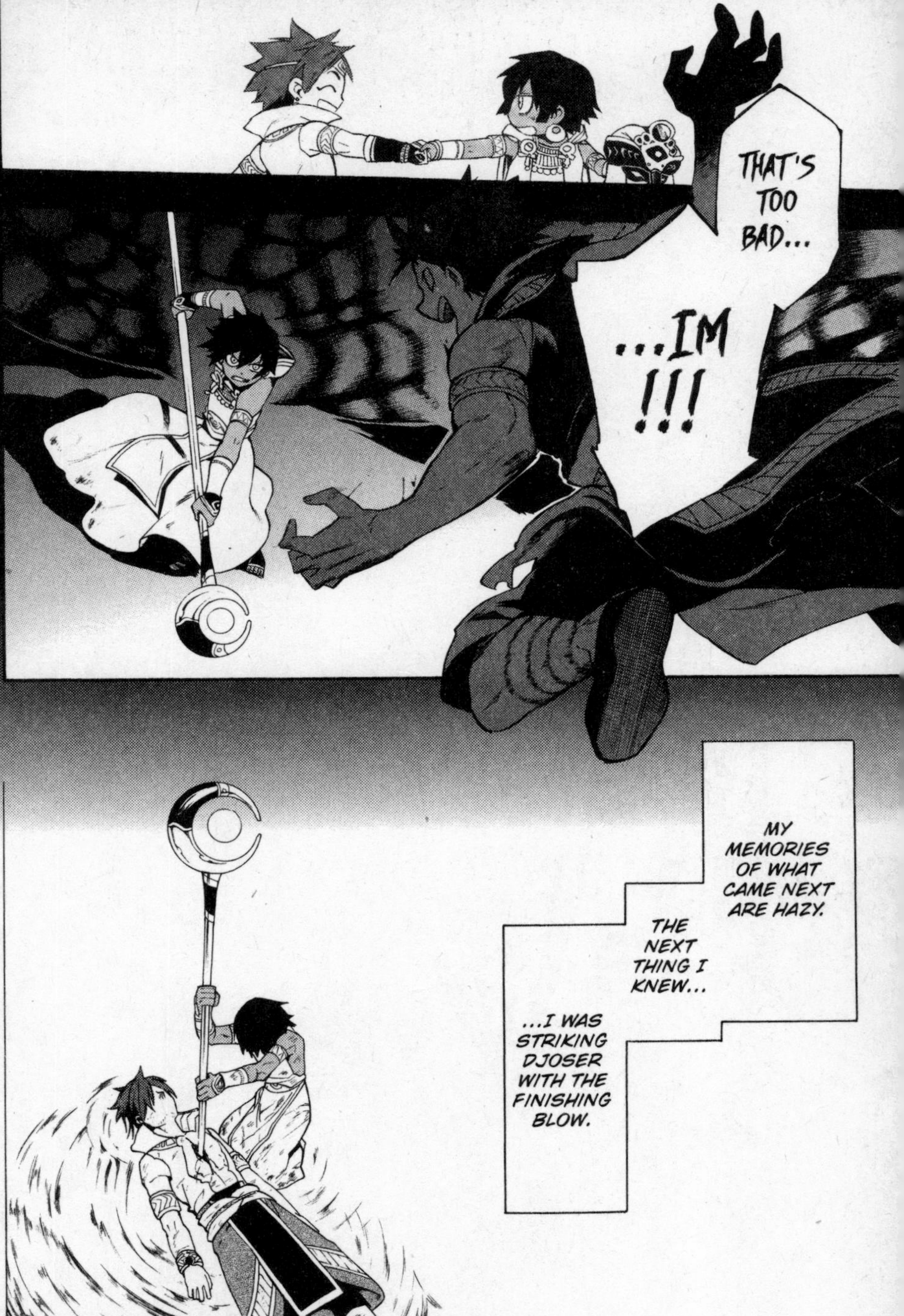
THAT'S TOO BAD...
...IM !!!
MY MEMORIES OF WHAT CAME NEXT ARE HAZY.
THE NEXT THING I KNEW...
...I WAS STRIKING DJOSER WITH THE FINISHING BLOW.

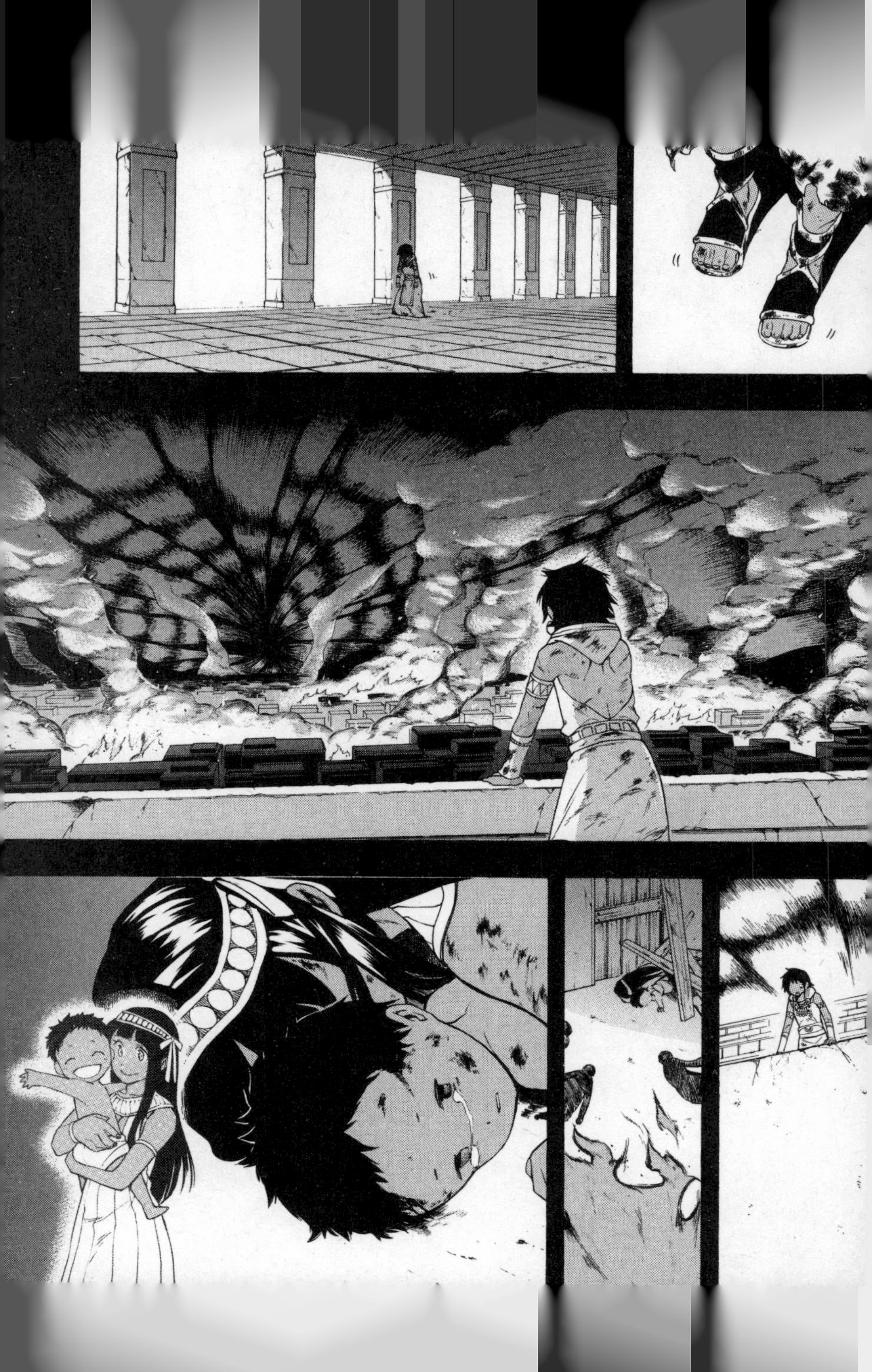

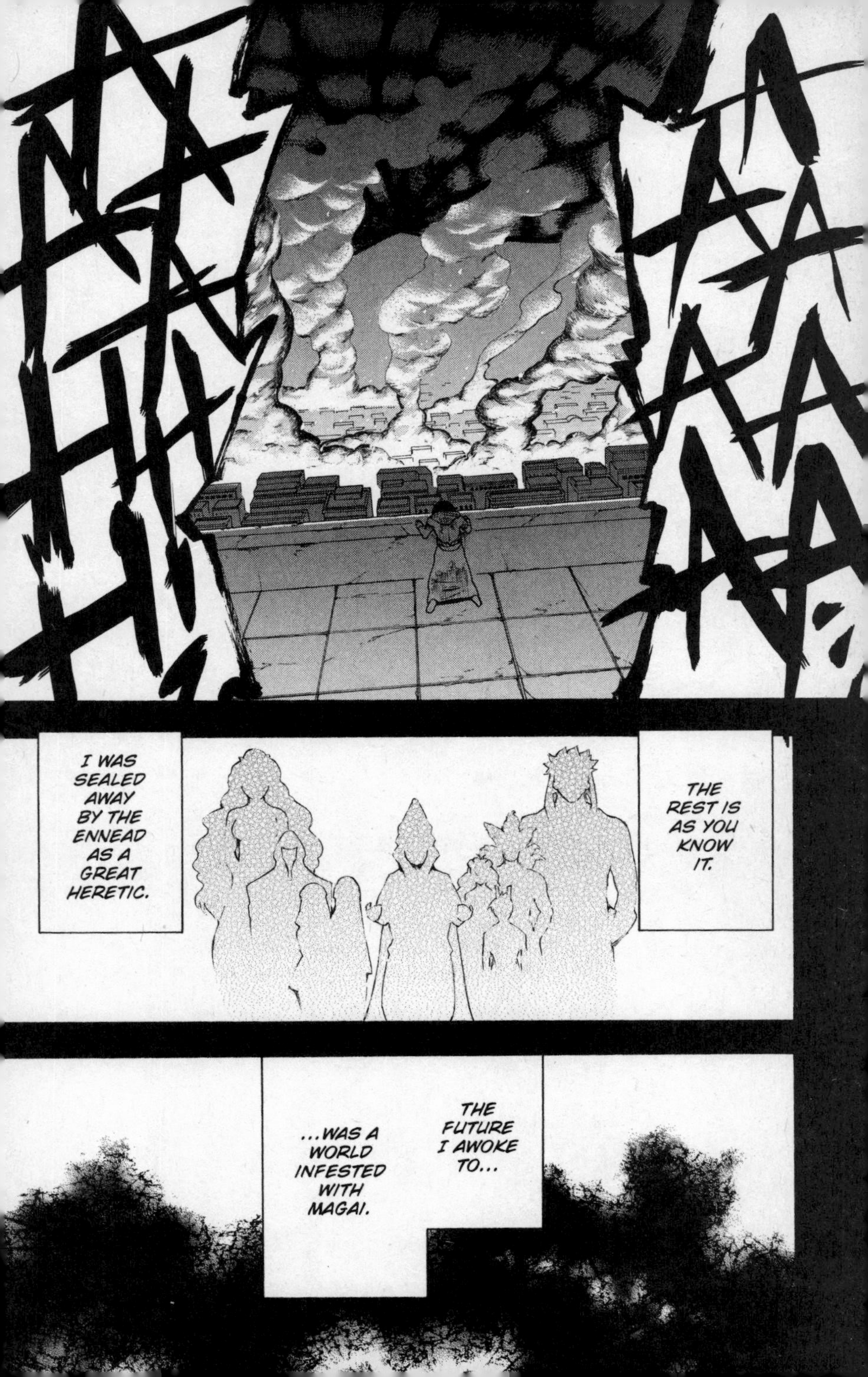
THE REST IS AS YOU KNOW IT.
I WAS SEALED AWAY BY THE ENNEAD AS A GREAT HERETIC.
THE FUTURE I AWOKE TO...
...WAS A WORLD INFESTED WITH MAGAI.

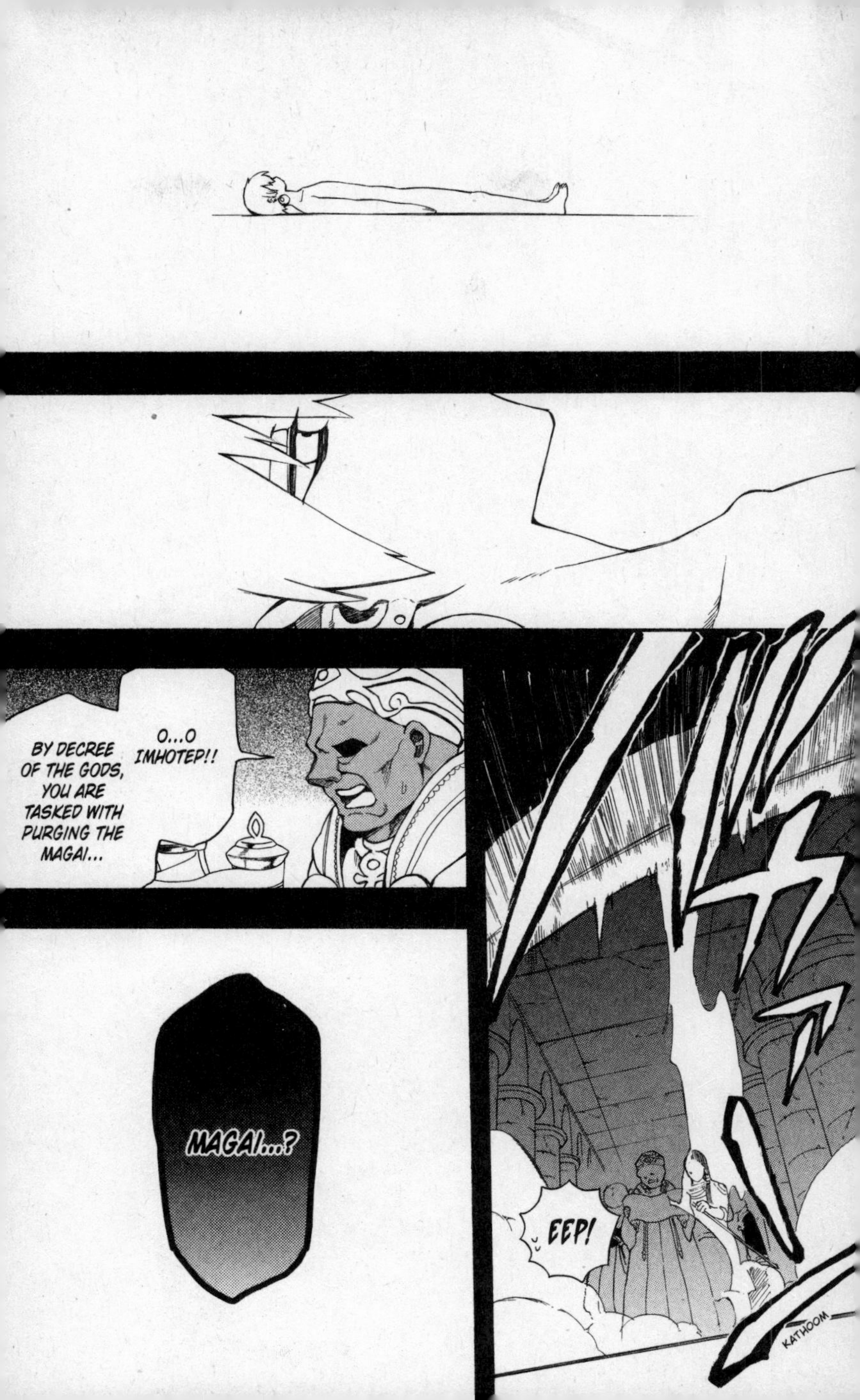
EEP!
KATHOOM
O...O IMHOTEP!!
BY DECREE OF THE GODS, YOU ARE TASKED WITH PURGING THE MAGAI...
MAGAI...?

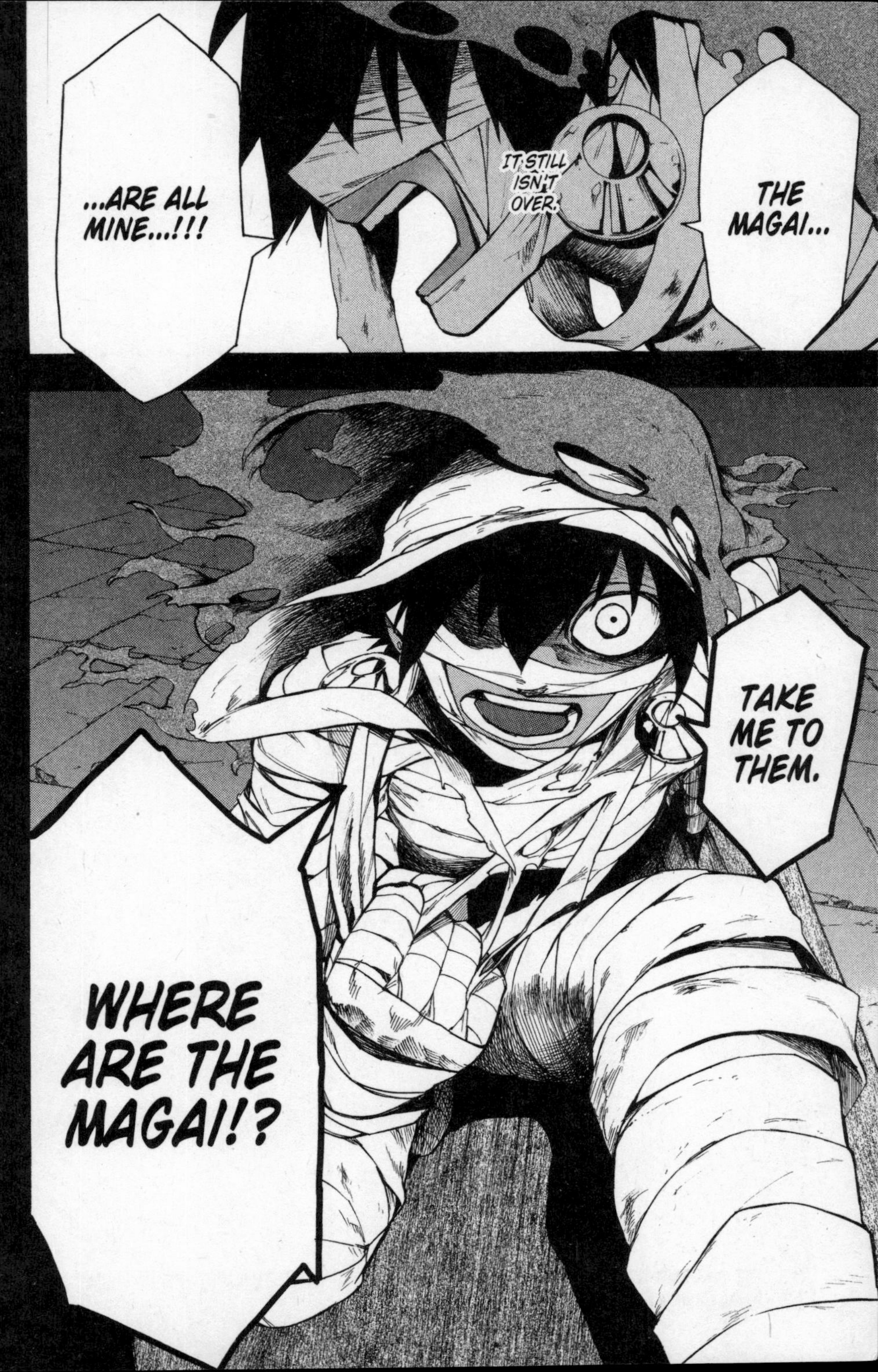
THE MAGAI...
IT STILL ISN'T OVER.
...ARE ALL MINE...!!!
TAKE ME TO THEM.
WHERE ARE THE MAGAI!?

Great Priest Imhotep

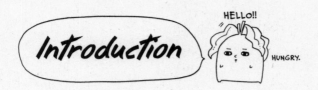

Introduction

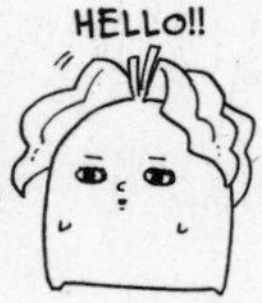
HELLO!!
HUNGRY.

The following pages are the one-shot pilot chapter of *Im* that ran in the February 2013 issue of *Shounen Gangan*. There's actually a second version that had major changes to the setting and plot. The one-shot chapter included in this volume is the one that became *Im* as we know it. Rereading this for the first time in a long time, my impressions are..."Huh? Im's actually cool?" "Come on, heroine, smile more!!!" Etc., etc. I really feel a gap between the Im and friends of old and the characters as we know them now. I also really got that "Oh yeah...this is where it all started" feeling. With this chapter, I was finally published at a time when I was anguishing over whether I should pursue my dreams of a career as a manga artist, so to me, it's quite the treasure.

As a digression, my debut work was in the February 2011 issue.
This one-shot was in the February 2013 issue.
And the serialization started in the February 2015 issue.
...What's waiting in February 2017...!?
Actually, will this manga still be going then...!?

Let's not think about scary things like that.
Anyway, enjoy!!!

MAKOTO MORISHITA

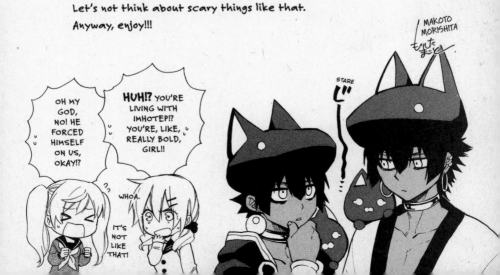

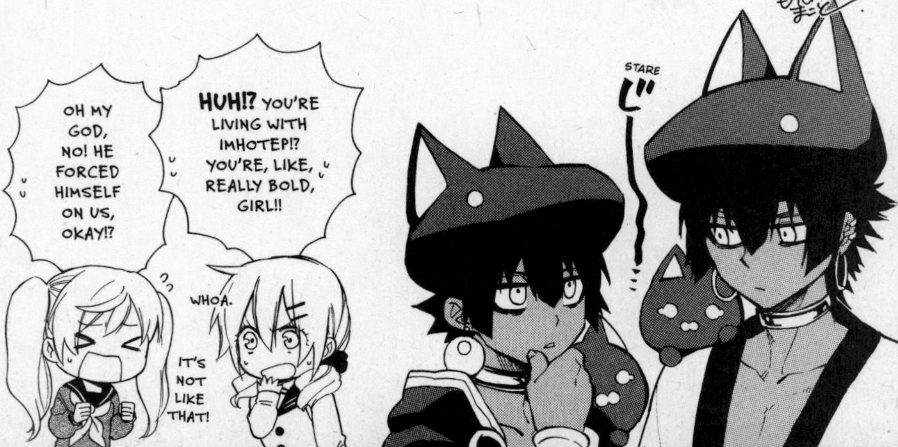
STARE
HUH!? YOU'RE LIVING WITH IMHOTEP!? YOU'RE, LIKE, REALLY BOLD, GIRL!!
OH MY GOD, NO! HE FORCED HIMSELF ON US, OKAY!?
WHOA.
IT'S NOT LIKE THAT!

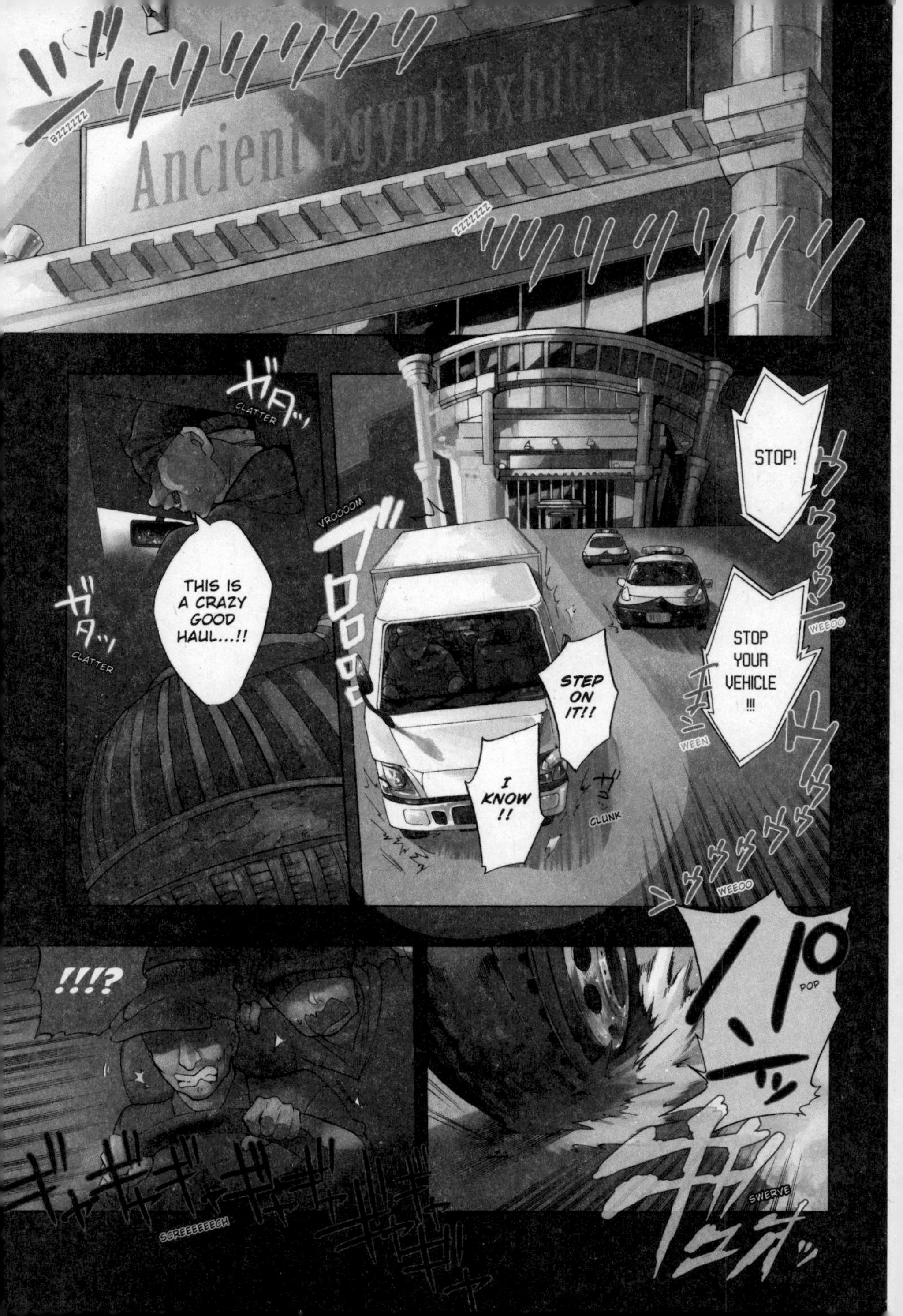
Ancient Egypt Exh
BZZZZZZ
ZZZZZZZ
STOP!
WEEOO
STOP YOUR VEHICLE !!!
WEEN
WEEOO
VROOOOM
STEP ON IT!!
I KNOW !!
CLUNK
CLATTER
THIS IS A CRAZY GOOD HAUL...!!
CLATTER
POP
SWERVE
!!!?
SCREEEEEECH

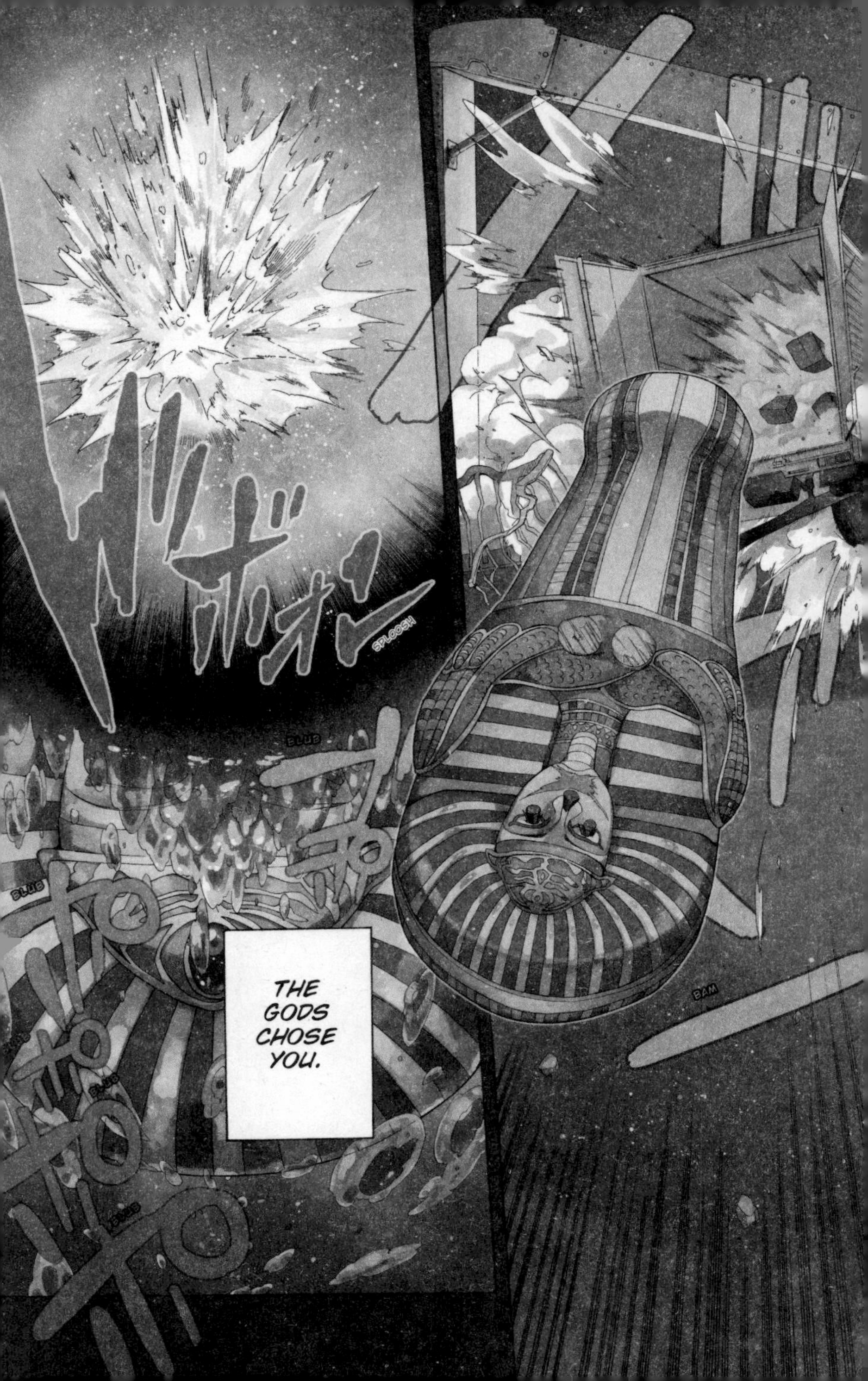
SPLOOSH
BLUB
BLUB
BLUB
BLUB
BLUB
THE GODS CHOSE YOU.
BAM

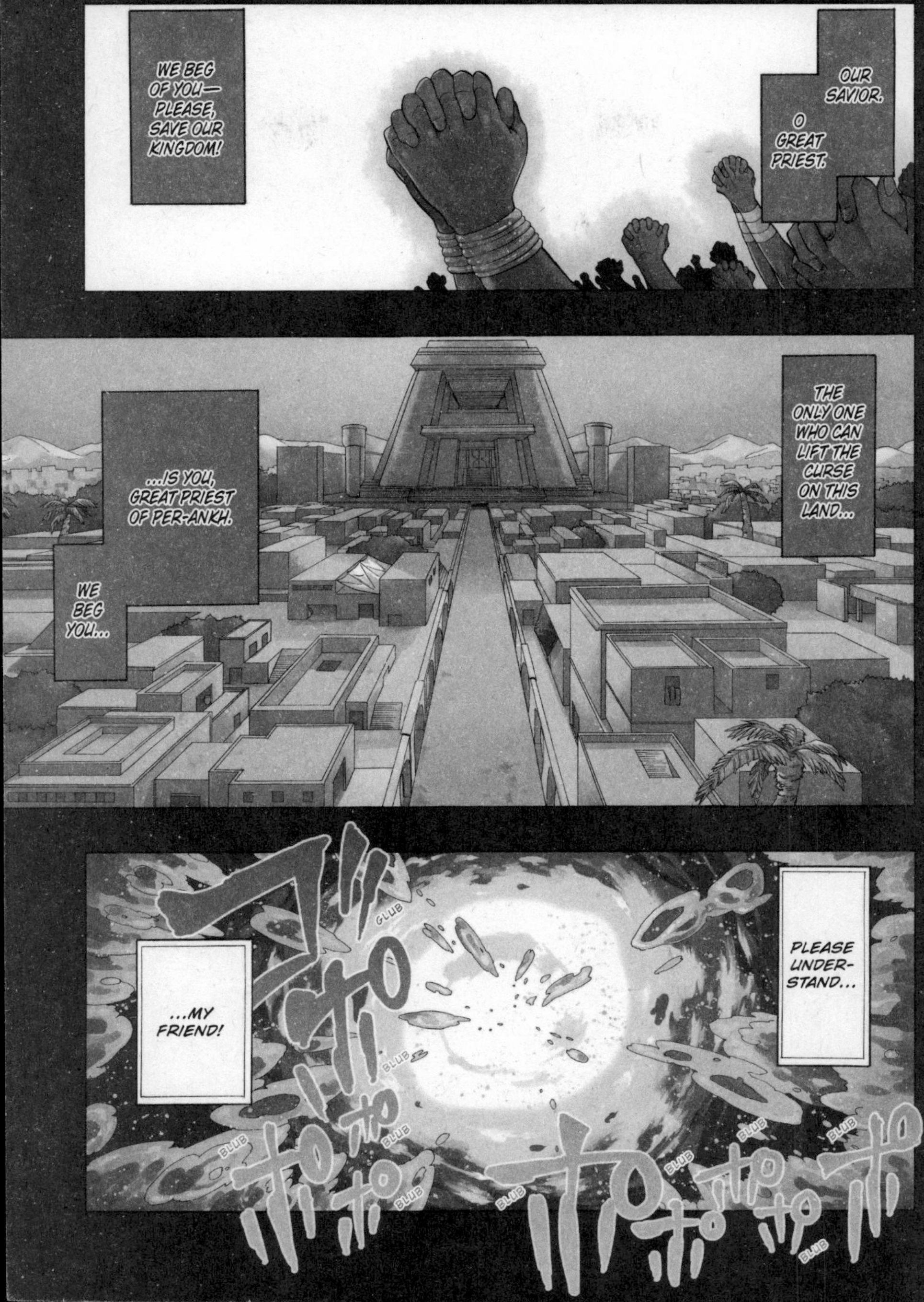
OUR SAVIOR.
O GREAT PRIEST.
WE BEG OF YOU—PLEASE, SAVE OUR KINGDOM!
THE ONLY ONE WHO CAN LIFT THE CURSE ON THIS LAND...
...IS YOU, GREAT PRIEST OF PER-ANKH.
WE BEG YOU...
PLEASE UNDER-STAND...
GLUB
...MY FRIEND!
BLUB
BLUB
BLUB
BLUB
BLUB
BLUB
BLUB
BLUB
BLUB
BLUB

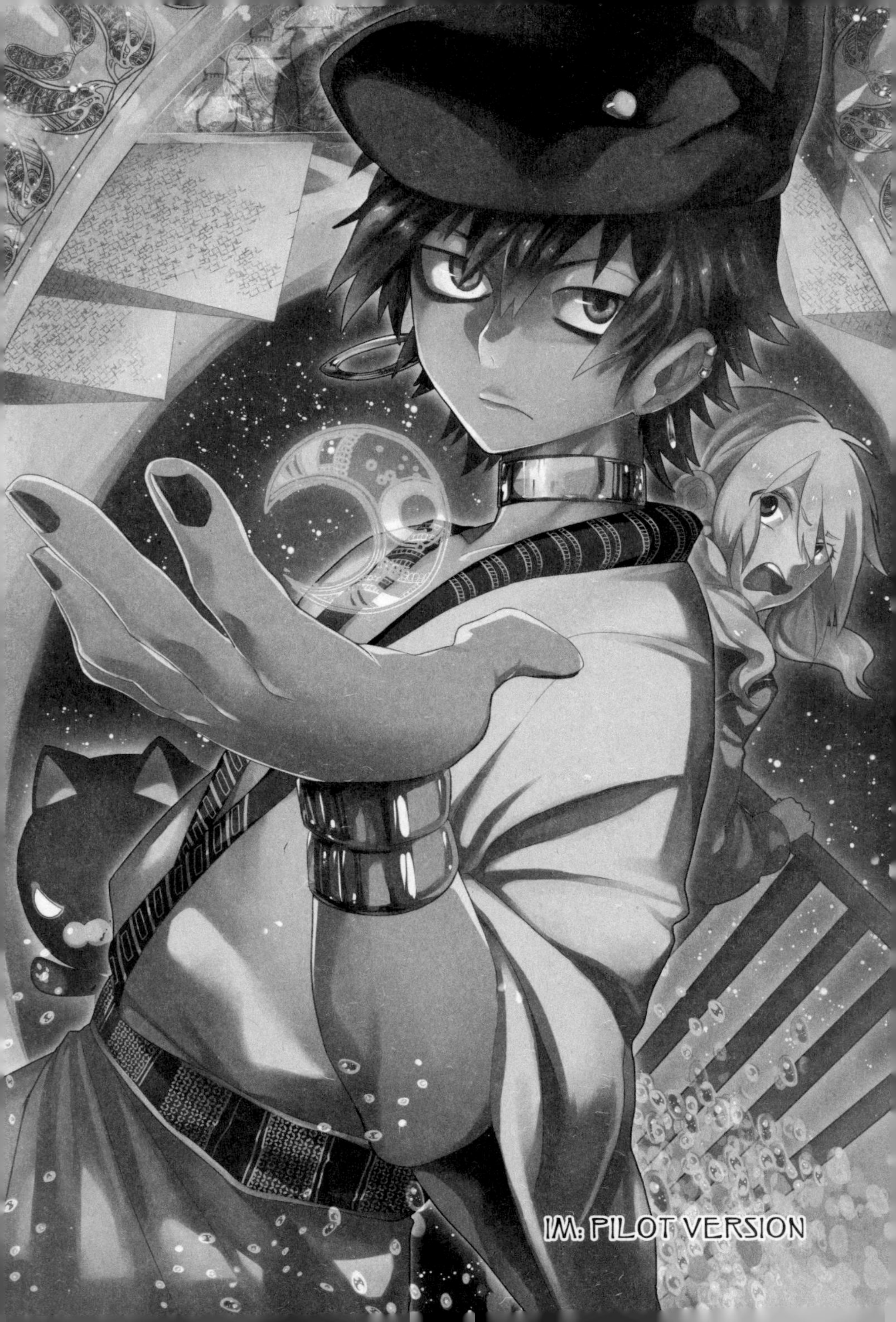
IM: PILOT VERSION

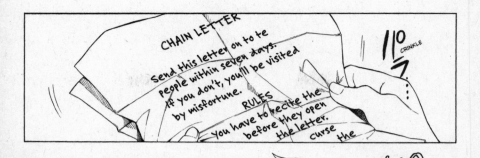

CHAIN LETTER

Send this letter on to te people within seven days. If you don't, you'll be visited by misfortune.

RULES
You have to recite the curse before they open the letter. the

CRINKLE

THERE'S ALWAYS A NEW RUMOR. AMUSING, RIGHT?

LOOK, IT'S HER!

HAVE YOU HEARD ABOUT HER HOUSE?

CUT IT OUT, YOU'LL GET US CURSED!

CRINKLE

CRINKLE

A CURSE? SPARE ME.

THERE'S NO SUCH THING AS CURSES.

DIVE

FLOAT

WHAT A JOKE.

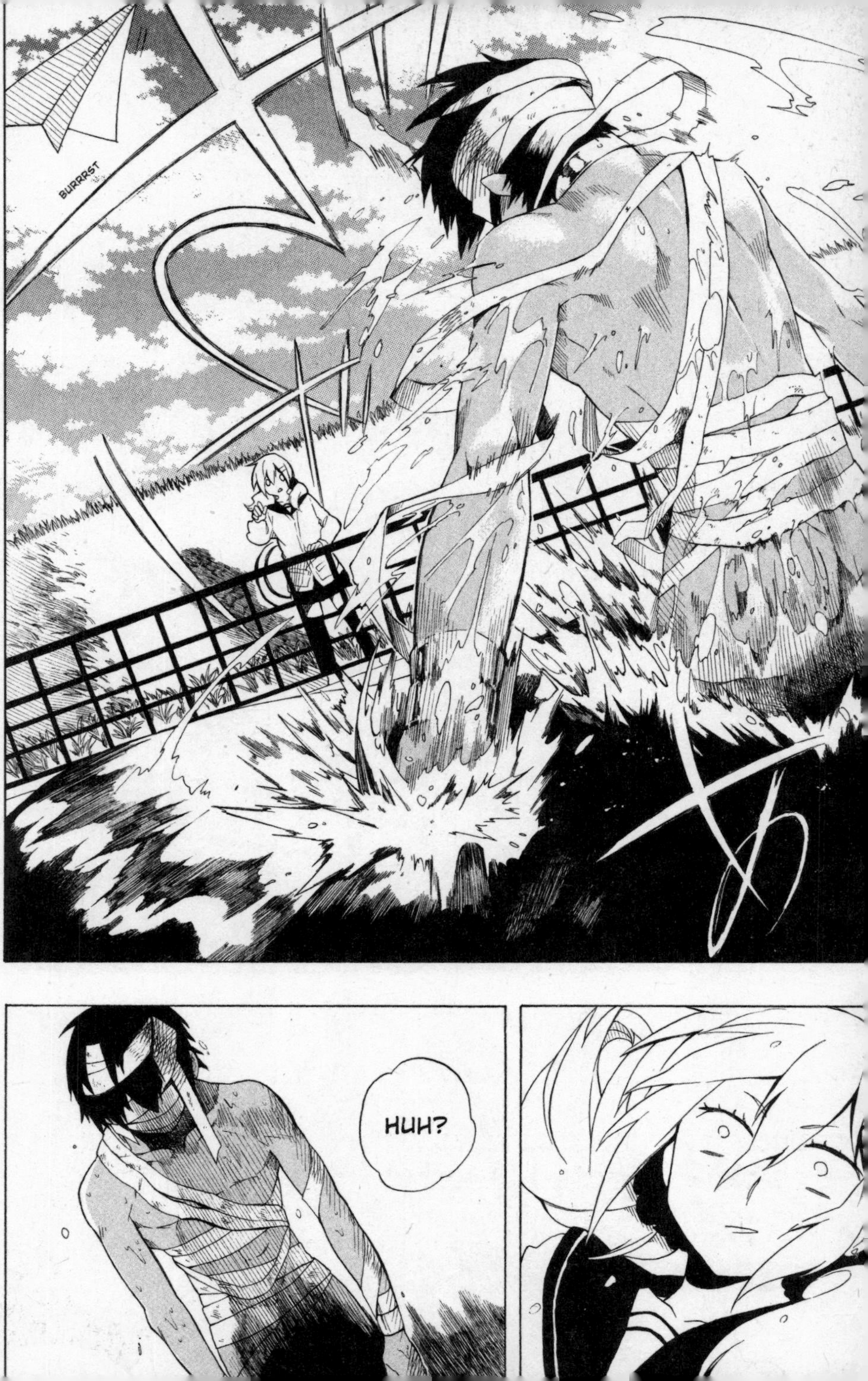
BURRRST
HUH?

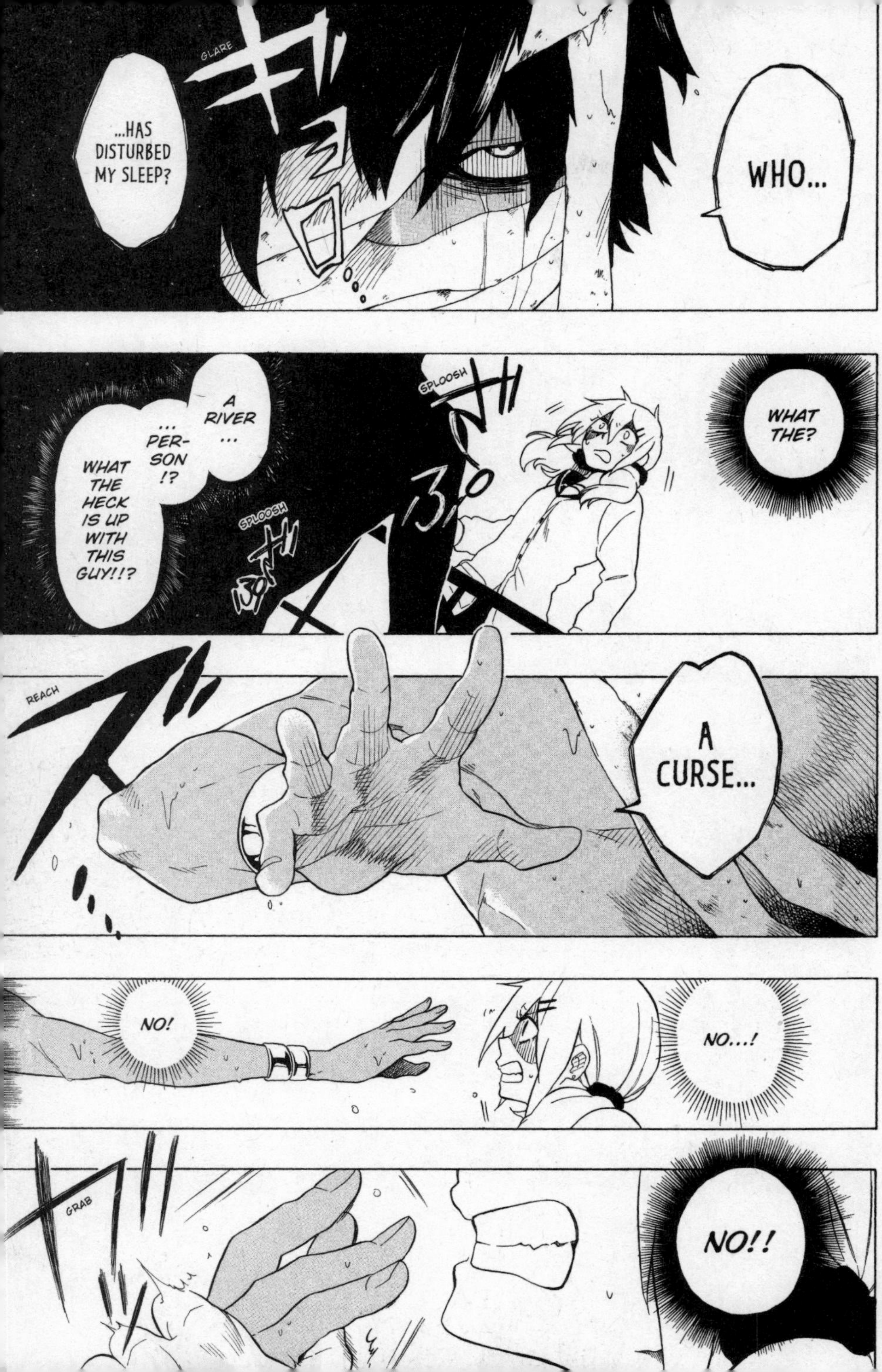
GLARE
WHO...
...HAS DISTURBED MY SLEEP?
WHAT THE?
SPLOOSH
A RIVER...
...PERSON!?
WHAT THE HECK IS UP WITH THIS GUY!!?
SPLOOSH
A CURSE...
REACH
NO...!
NO!
NO!!
GRAB

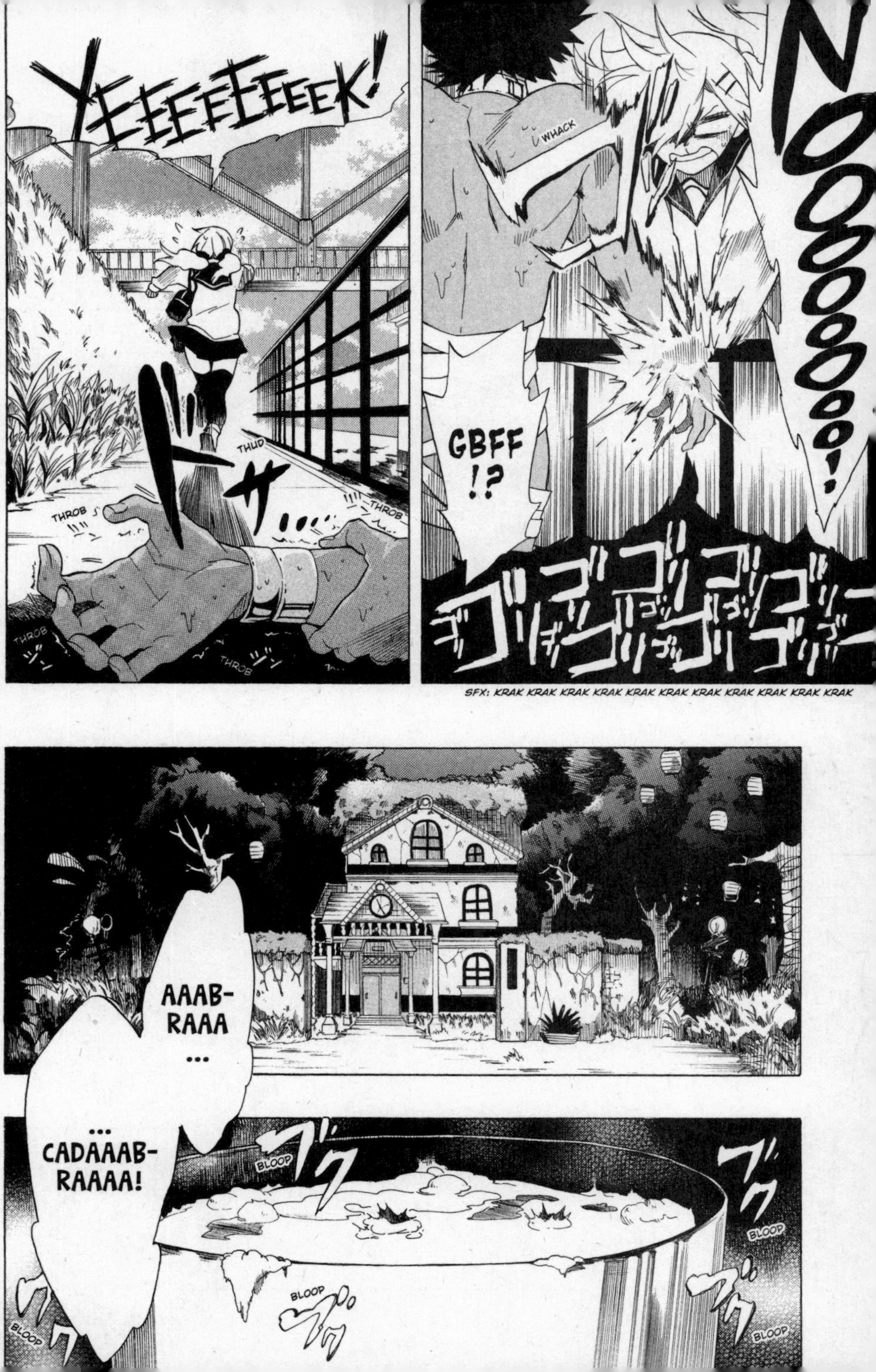
NOOOOOOOOOO!
WHACK
GBFF !?
SFX: KRAK KRAK KRAK KRAK KRAK KRAK KRAK KRAK KRAK KRAK KRAK
YEEEEEEEEK!
THUD
THROB
THROB
THROB
THROB
AAAB-RAAA ...
... CADÁAAB-RAAAA!
BLOOP
BLOOP
BLOOP
BLOOP
BLOOP

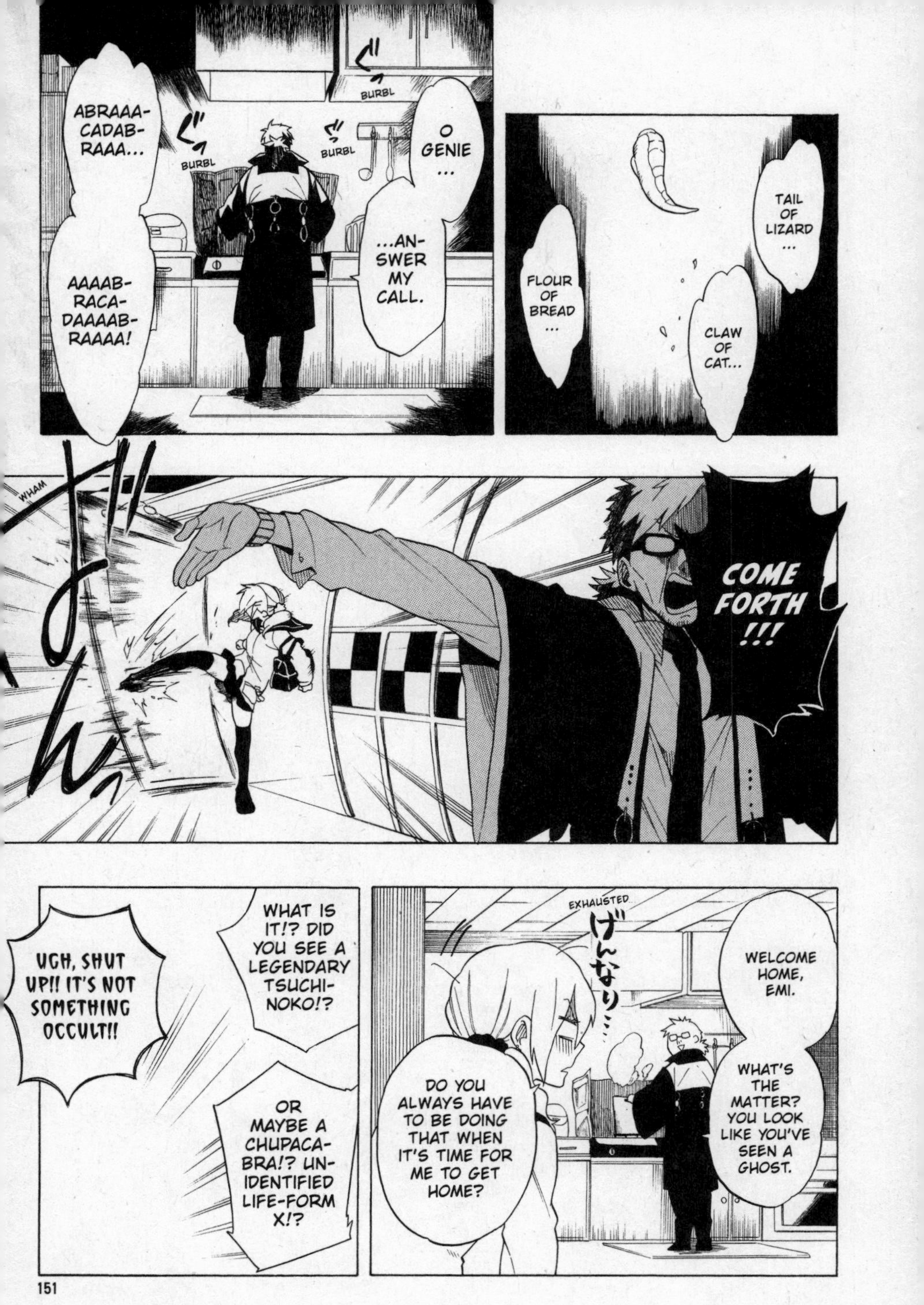
TAIL OF LIZARD...
CLAW OF CAT...
FLOUR OF BREAD...
BURBL
O GENIE...
...ANSWER MY CALL.
BURBL
BURBL
ABRAAA-CADABRAAA...
AAAAB-RACA-DAAAAB-RAAAA!
COME FORTH!!!
WHAM
EXHAUSTED
げんなり
WELCOME HOME, EMI.
WHAT'S THE MATTER? YOU LOOK LIKE YOU'VE SEEN A GHOST.
DO YOU ALWAYS HAVE TO BE DOING THAT WHEN IT'S TIME FOR ME TO GET HOME?
WHAT IS IT!? DID YOU SEE A LEGENDARY TSUCHI-NOKO!?
UGH, SHUT UP!! IT'S NOT SOMETHING OCCULT!!
OR MAYBE A CHUPACA-BRA!? UN-IDENTIFIED LIFE-FORM X!?

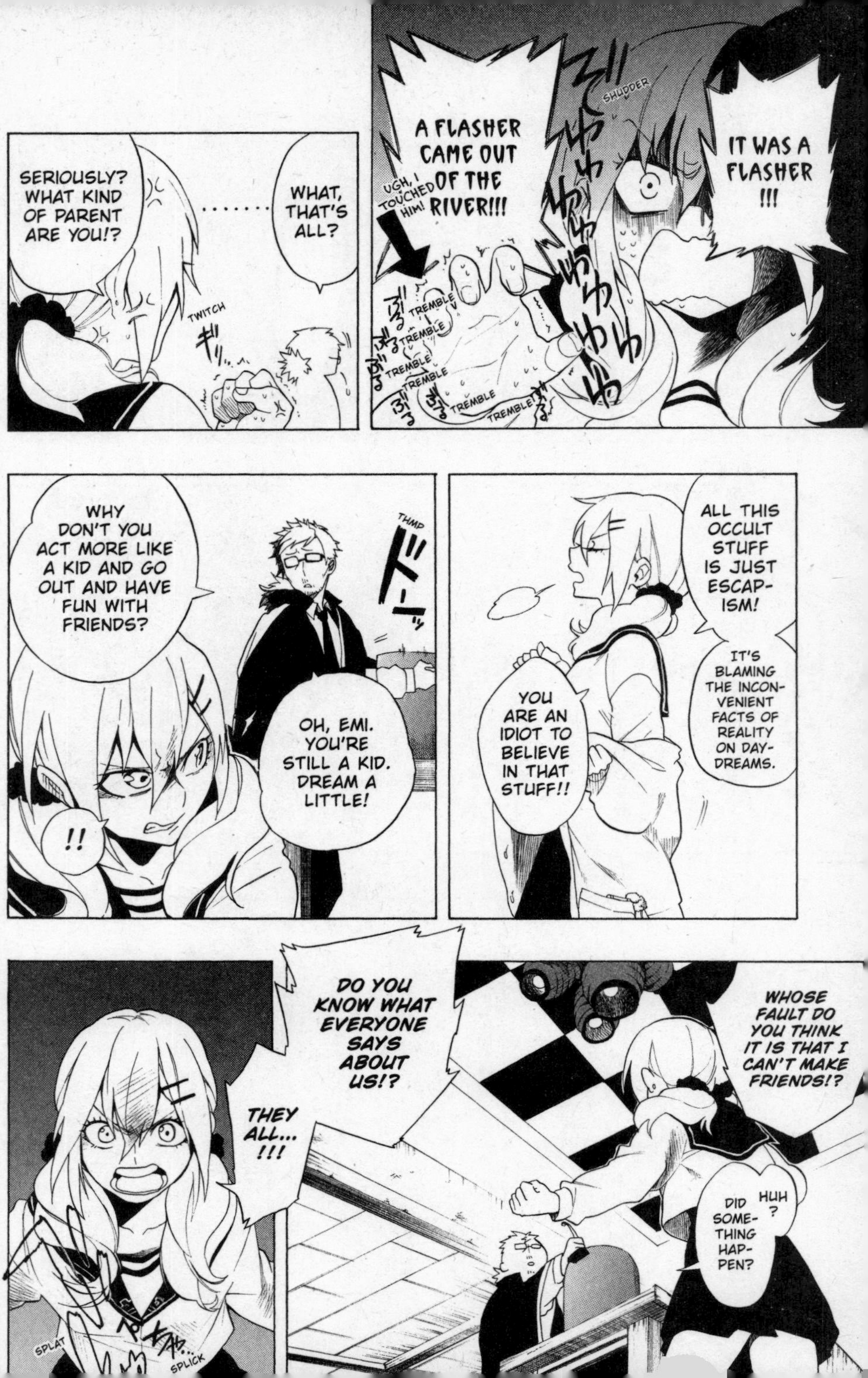
IT WAS A FLASHER !!!
SHUDDER
A FLASHER CAME OUT OF THE RIVER!!!
UGH, I TOUCHED HIM!
TREMBLE
TREMBLE
TREMBLE
TREMBLE
TREMBLE
TREMBLE
WHAT, THAT'S ALL?
……
SERIOUSLY? WHAT KIND OF PARENT ARE YOU!?
TWITCH
ALL THIS OCCULT STUFF IS JUST ESCAP-ISM!
IT'S BLAMING THE INCON-VENIENT FACTS OF REALITY ON DAY-DREAMS.
YOU ARE AN IDIOT TO BELIEVE IN THAT STUFF!!
THMP
WHY DON'T YOU ACT MORE LIKE A KID AND GO OUT AND HAVE FUN WITH FRIENDS?
OH, EMI. YOU'RE STILL A KID. DREAM A LITTLE!
!!
WHOSE FAULT DO YOU THINK IT IS THAT I CAN'T MAKE FRIENDS!?
HUH ?
DID SOME-THING HAP-PEN?
DO YOU KNOW WHAT EVERYONE SAYS ABOUT US!?
THEY ALL... !!!
SPLAT
SPLICK

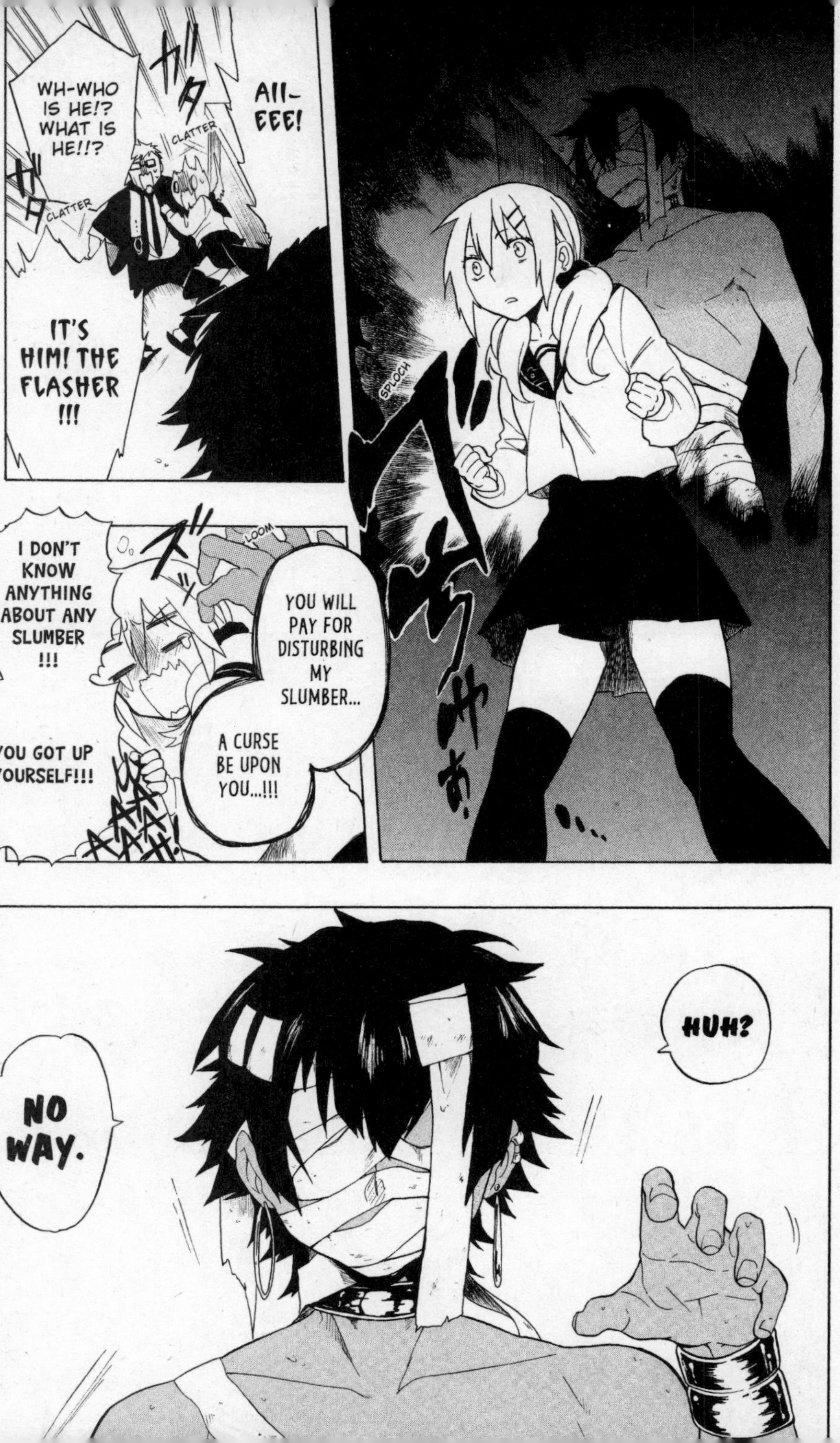
SPLOCH
...
AII-EEE!
WH-WHO IS HE!? WHAT IS HE!!?
CLATTER
CLATTER
IT'S HIM! THE FLASHER !!!
LOOM
YOU WILL PAY FOR DISTURBING MY SLUMBER...
A CURSE BE UPON YOU...!!!
I DON'T KNOW ANYTHING ABOUT ANY SLUMBER !!!
YOU GOT UP YOURSELF!!!
HUH?
NO WAY.

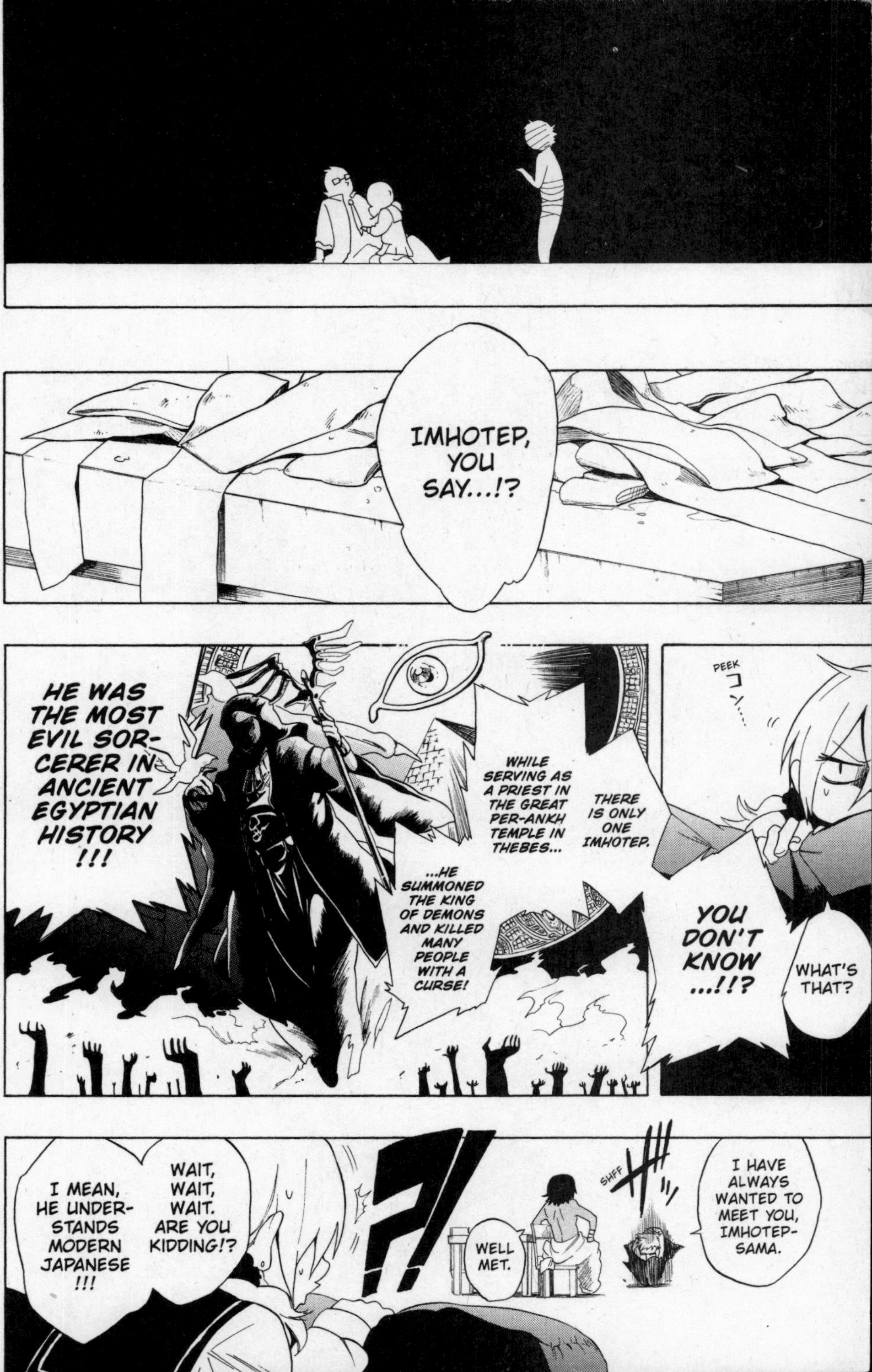
IMHOTEP, YOU SAY...!?
PEEK
WHAT'S THAT?
YOU DON'T KNOW ...!!?
THERE IS ONLY ONE IMHOTEP.
WHILE SERVING AS A PRIEST IN THE GREAT PER-ANKH TEMPLE IN THEBES...
...HE SUMMONED THE KING OF DEMONS AND KILLED MANY PEOPLE WITH A CURSE!
HE WAS THE MOST EVIL SORCERER IN ANCIENT EGYPTIAN HISTORY!!!
I HAVE ALWAYS WANTED TO MEET YOU, IMHOTEP-SAMA.
SHFF
WELL MET.
?!
WAIT, WAIT, WAIT. ARE YOU KIDDING!?
I MEAN, HE UNDERSTANDS MODERN JAPANESE!!!

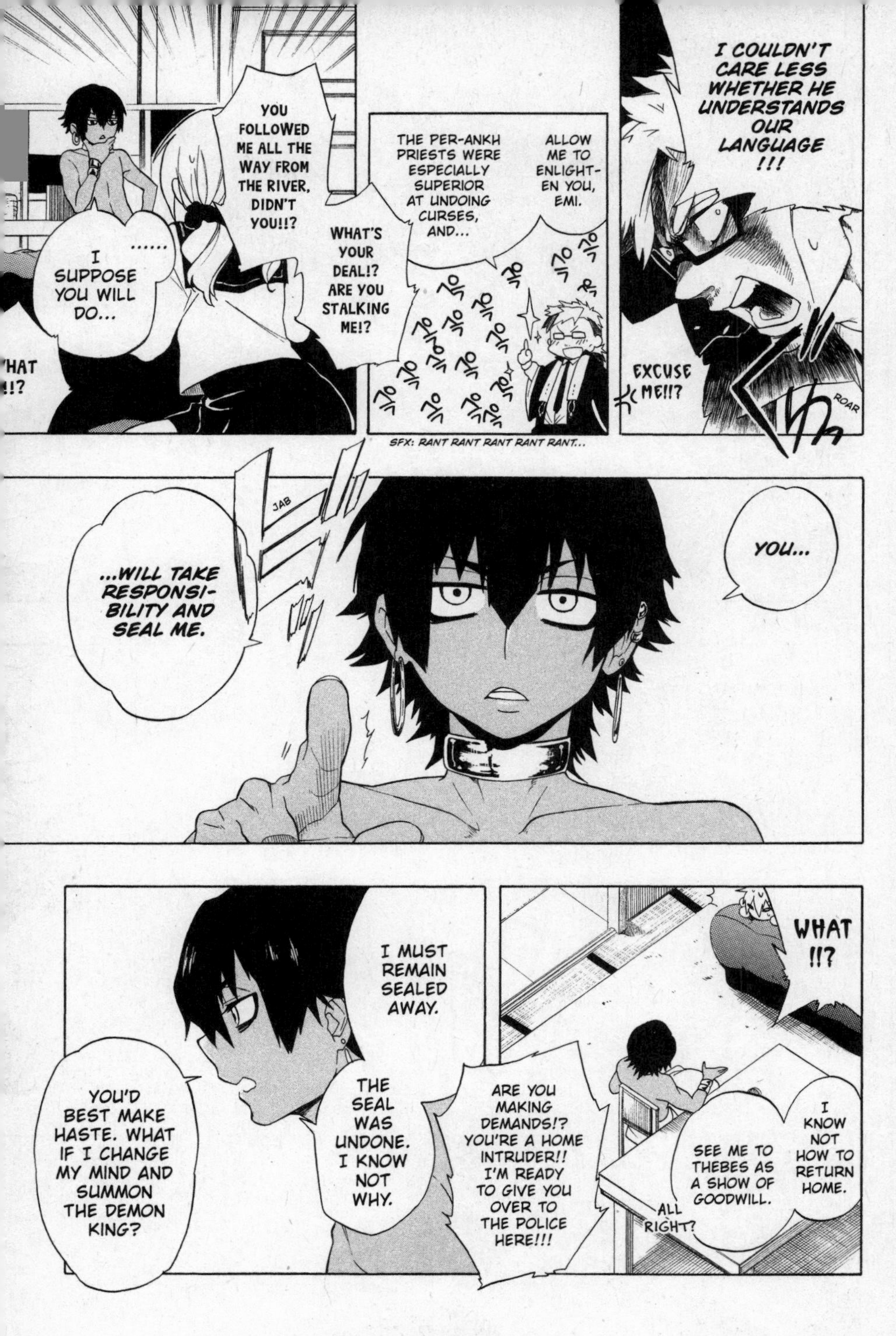
I COULDN'T CARE LESS WHETHER HE UNDERSTANDS OUR LANGUAGE !!!
EXCUSE ME!!?
ROAR
ALLOW ME TO ENLIGHTEN YOU, EMI.
THE PER-ANKH PRIESTS WERE ESPECIALLY SUPERIOR AT UNDOING CURSES, AND...
WHAT'S YOUR DEAL!? ARE YOU STALKING ME!?
SFX: RANT RANT RANT RANT RANT...
YOU FOLLOWED ME ALL THE WAY FROM THE RIVER, DIDN'T YOU!!?
...... I SUPPOSE YOU WILL DO...
YOU...
...WILL TAKE RESPONSIBILITY AND SEAL ME.
JAB
WHAT !!?
I KNOW NOT HOW TO RETURN HOME.
SEE ME TO THEBES AS A SHOW OF GOODWILL.
ALL RIGHT?
ARE YOU MAKING DEMANDS!? YOU'RE A HOME INTRUDER!! I'M READY TO GIVE YOU OVER TO THE POLICE HERE!!!
I MUST REMAIN SEALED AWAY.
THE SEAL WAS UNDONE. I KNOW NOT WHY.
YOU'D BEST MAKE HASTE. WHAT IF I CHANGE MY MIND AND SUMMON THE DEMON KING?

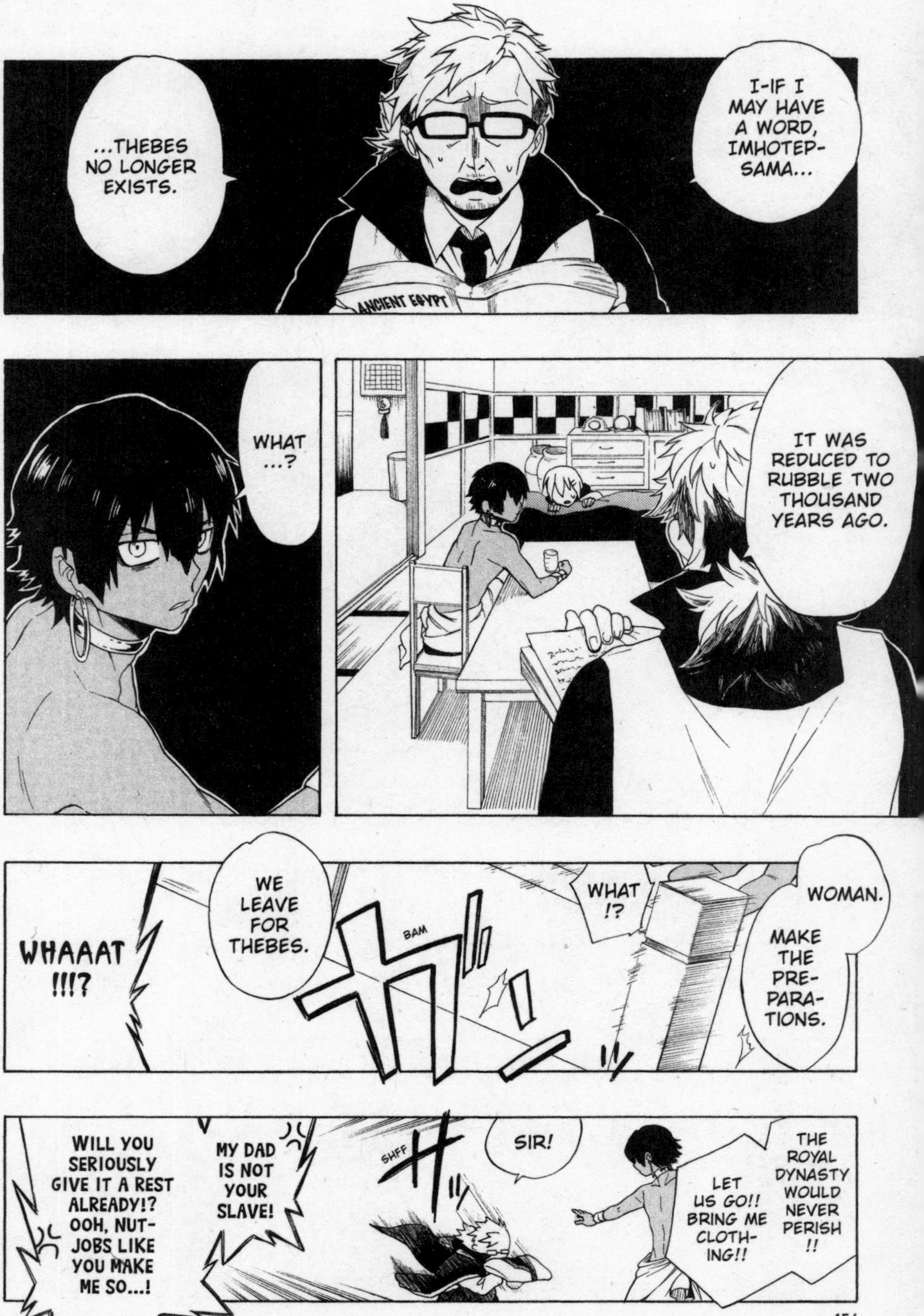
I-IF I MAY HAVE A WORD, IMHOTEP-SAMA...
...THEBES NO LONGER EXISTS.
ANCIENT EGYPT
IT WAS REDUCED TO RUBBLE TWO THOUSAND YEARS AGO.
WHAT ...?
WOMAN.
MAKE THE PREPARATIONS.
WHAT !?
BAM
WE LEAVE FOR THEBES.
WHAAAT !!!?
THE ROYAL DYNASTY WOULD NEVER PERISH !!
LET US GO!! BRING ME CLOTHING!!
SIR!
SHFF
MY DAD IS NOT YOUR SLAVE!
WILL YOU SERIOUSLY GIVE IT A REST ALREADY!? OOH, NUT-JOBS LIKE YOU MAKE ME SO...!

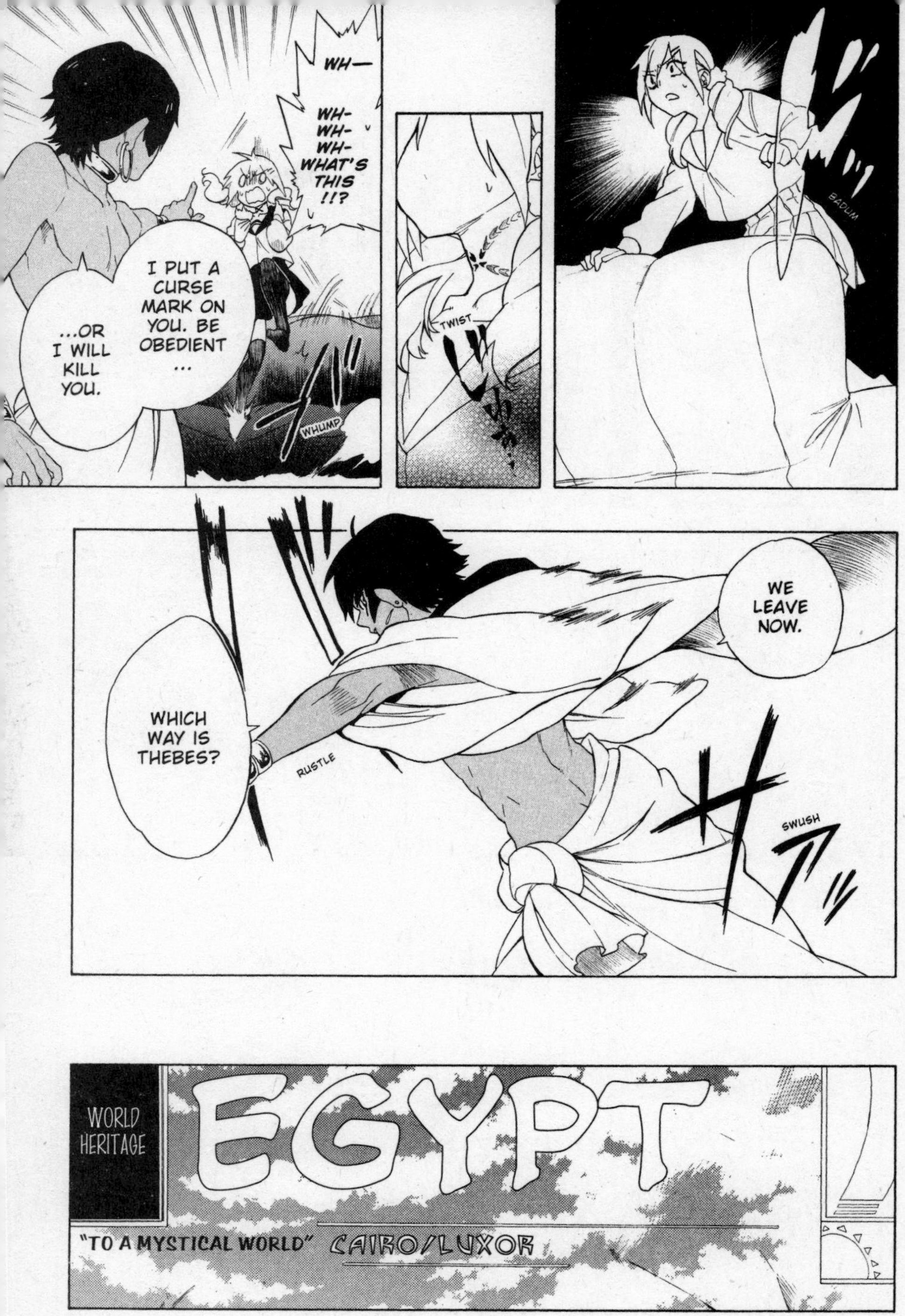
BADUM
TWIST
WH—
WH-WH-WH-WHAT'S THIS !!?
I PUT A CURSE MARK ON YOU. BE OBEDIENT ...
...OR I WILL KILL YOU.
WHUMP
WE LEAVE NOW.
WHICH WAY IS THEBES?
RUSTLE
SWUSH
EGYPT
WORLD HERITAGE
"TO A MYSTICAL WORLD" CAIRO/LUXOR

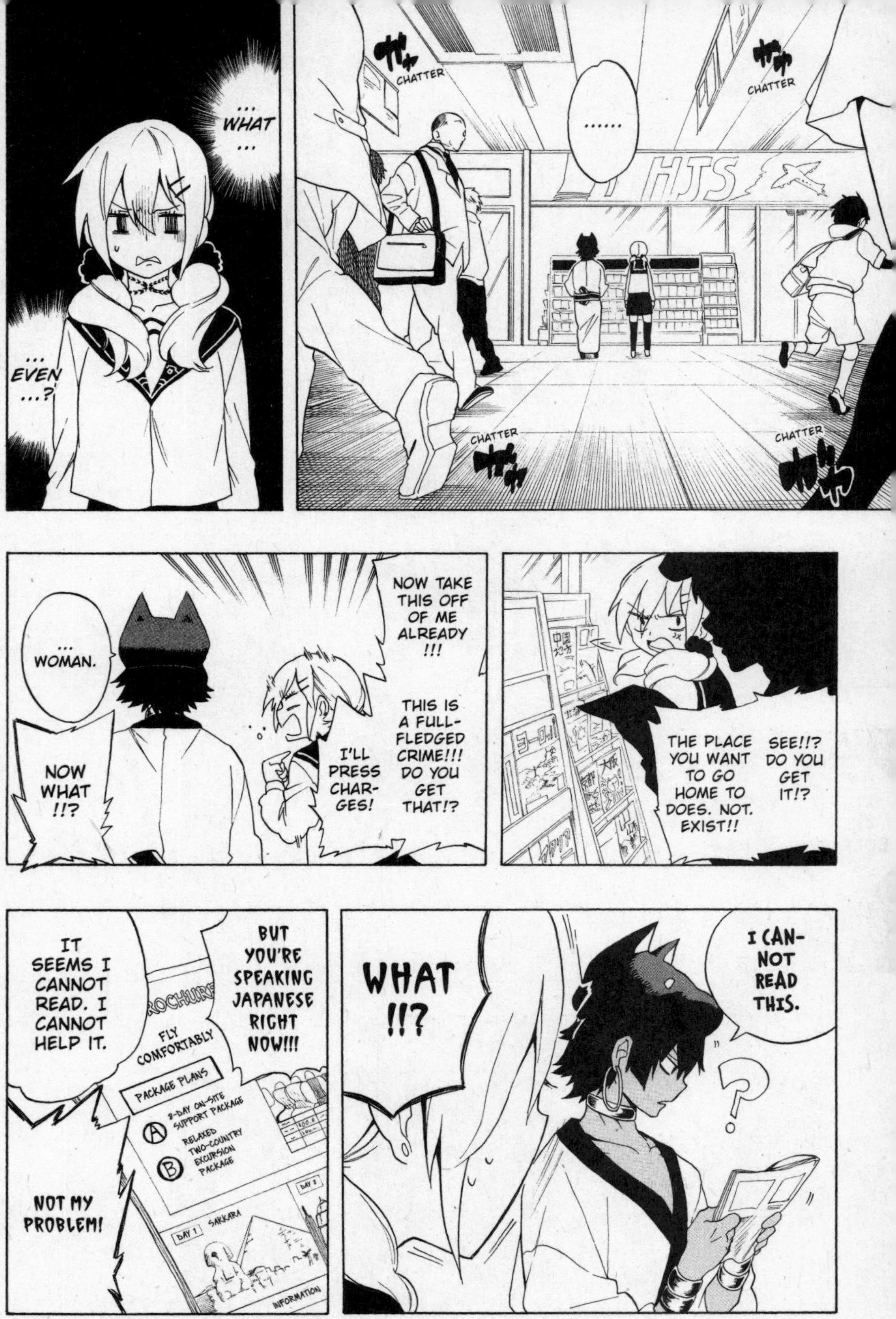
CHATTER
CHATTER
......
HJS
CHATTER
CHATTER
...WHAT...
...EVEN...?
SEE!!? DO YOU GET IT!?
THE PLACE YOU WANT TO GO HOME TO DOES. NOT. EXIST!!
NOW TAKE THIS OFF OF ME ALREADY!!!
THIS IS A FULL-FLEDGED CRIME!!! DO YOU GET THAT!?
I'LL PRESS CHAR-GES!
...WOMAN.
NOW WHAT!!?
I CAN-NOT READ THIS.
WHAT!!?
BUT YOU'RE SPEAKING JAPANESE RIGHT NOW!!!
IT SEEMS I CANNOT READ. I CANNOT HELP IT.
ROCHURE
FLY COMFORTABLY
PACKAGE PLANS
A 8-DAY ON-SITE SUPPORT PACKAGE
B RELAXED TWO-COUNTRY EXCURSION PACKAGE
DAY 1 SAKKARA
DAY 2
INFORMATION
NOT MY PROBLEM!

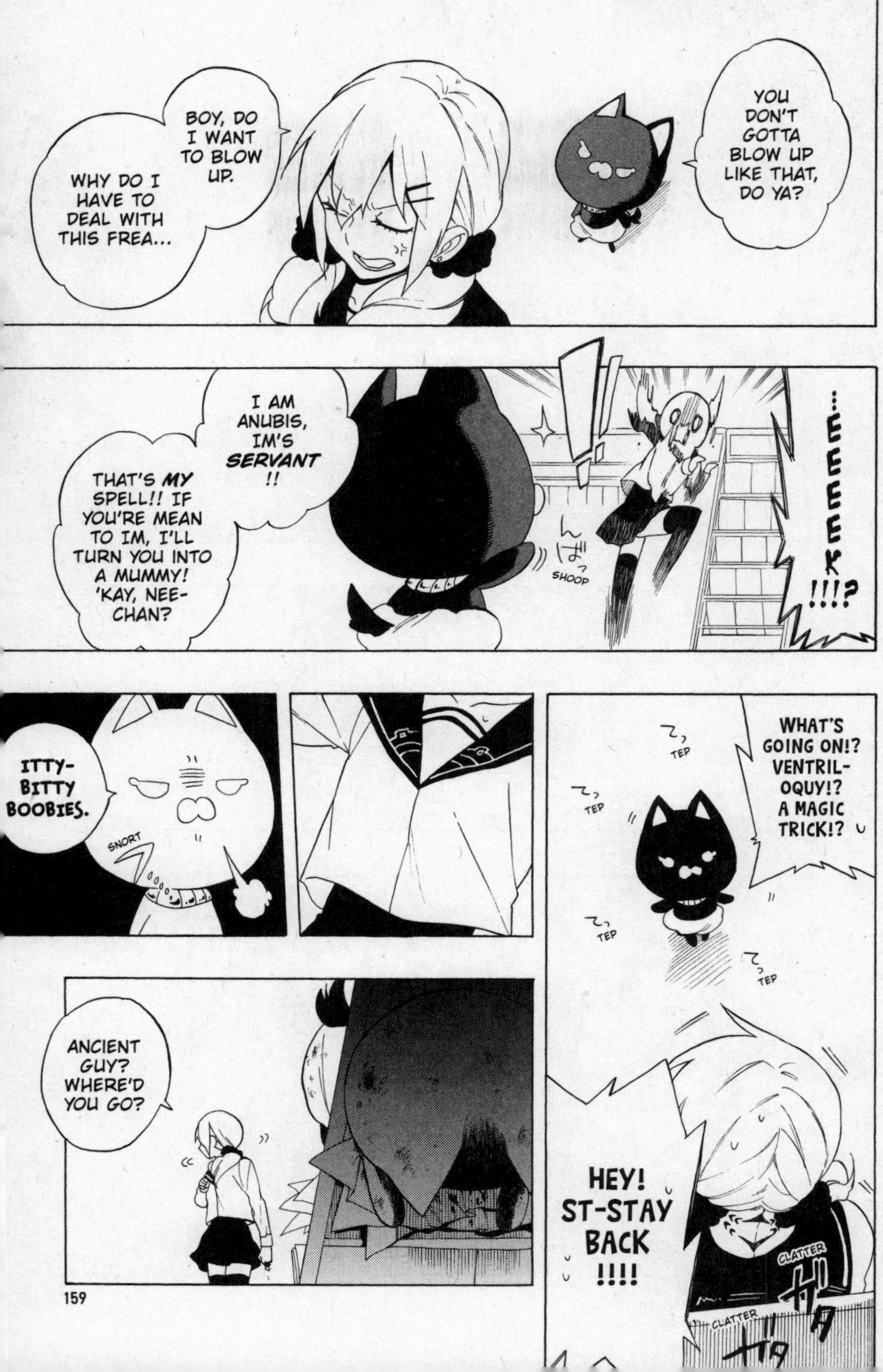
YOU DON'T GOTTA BLOW UP LIKE THAT, DO YA?
BOY, DO I WANT TO BLOW UP.
WHY DO I HAVE TO DEAL WITH THIS FREA...
EEEEEK!!!?
SHOOP
I AM ANUBIS, IM'S SERVANT!!
THAT'S MY SPELL!! IF YOU'RE MEAN TO IM, I'LL TURN YOU INTO A MUMMY! 'KAY, NEE-CHAN?
WHAT'S GOING ON!? VENTRIL-OQUY!? A MAGIC TRICK!?
TEP
TEP
TEP
TEP
HEY! ST-STAY BACK!!!!
CLATTER
CLATTER
ITTY-BITTY BOOBIES.
SNORT
ANCIENT GUY? WHERE'D YOU GO?

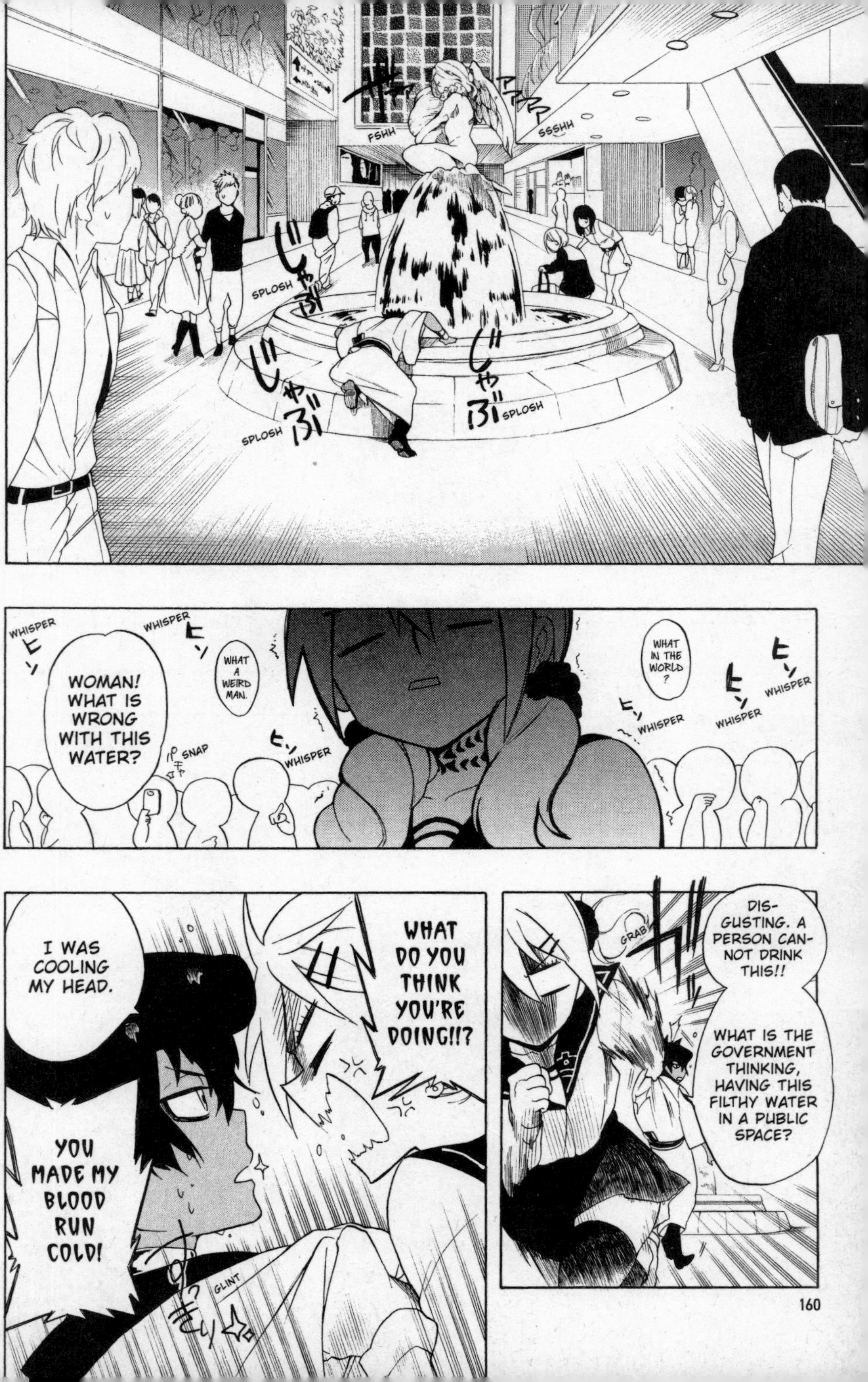
FSHH
SSSHH
じゃぶ
SPLOSH
じゃぶ
SPLOSH
じゃぶ
SPLOSH
ヒソ WHISPER
ヒソ WHISPER
WHAT IN THE WORLD?
ヒソ WHISPER
ヒソ WHISPER
WHAT A WEIRD MAN.
ヒソ WHISPER
SNAP
WOMAN! WHAT IS WRONG WITH THIS WATER?
ヒソ WHISPER
ヒソ WHISPER
GRAB
DIS-GUSTING. A PERSON CAN-NOT DRINK THIS!!
WHAT IS THE GOVERNMENT THINKING, HAVING THIS FILTHY WATER IN A PUBLIC SPACE?
WHAT DO YOU THINK YOU'RE DOING!!?
I WAS COOLING MY HEAD.
YOU MADE MY BLOOD RUN COLD!
GLINT

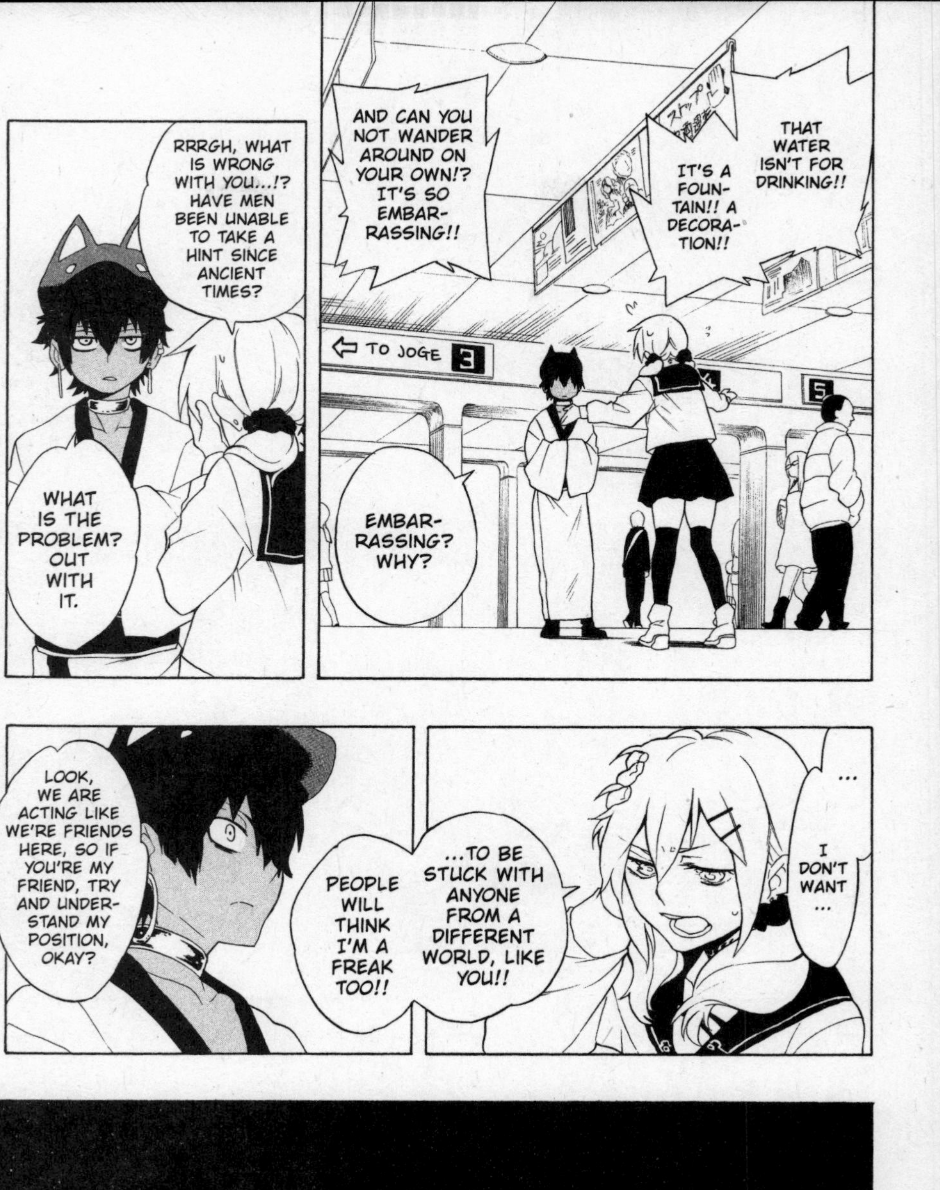
THAT WATER ISN'T FOR DRINKING!!
IT'S A FOUNTAIN!! A DECORATION!!
AND CAN YOU NOT WANDER AROUND ON YOUR OWN!? IT'S SO EMBARRASSING!!
TO JOGE 3
5
EMBARRASSING? WHY?
RRRGH, WHAT IS WRONG WITH YOU...!? HAVE MEN BEEN UNABLE TO TAKE A HINT SINCE ANCIENT TIMES?
WHAT IS THE PROBLEM? OUT WITH IT.
...
I DON'T WANT ...
...TO BE STUCK WITH ANYONE FROM A DIFFERENT WORLD, LIKE YOU!!
PEOPLE WILL THINK I'M A FREAK TOO!!
LOOK, WE ARE ACTING LIKE WE'RE FRIENDS HERE, SO IF YOU'RE MY FRIEND, TRY AND UNDERSTAND MY POSITION, OKAY?

PLEASE UNDERSTAND,
MY FRIEND.

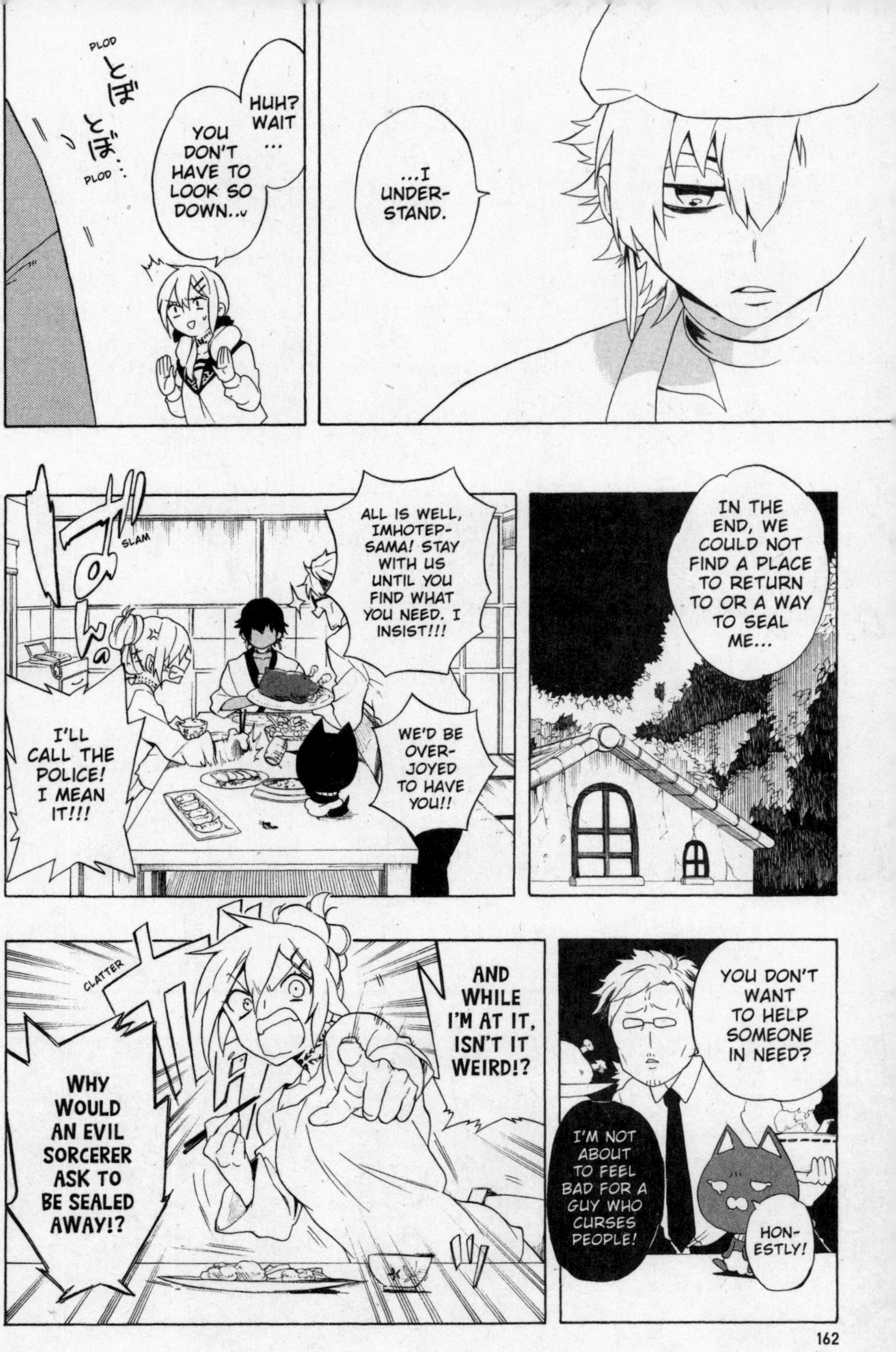
...I UNDER-STAND.
HUH? WAIT ...
YOU DON'T HAVE TO LOOK SO DOWN...
とぼ
PLOD
とぼ
PLOD
IN THE END, WE COULD NOT FIND A PLACE TO RETURN TO OR A WAY TO SEAL ME...
ALL IS WELL, IMHOTEP-SAMA! STAY WITH US UNTIL YOU FIND WHAT YOU NEED. I INSIST!!!
WE'D BE OVER-JOYED TO HAVE YOU!!
SLAM
I'LL CALL THE POLICE! I MEAN IT!!!
YOU DON'T WANT TO HELP SOMEONE IN NEED?
I'M NOT ABOUT TO FEEL BAD FOR A GUY WHO CURSES PEOPLE!
HON-ESTLY!
AND WHILE I'M AT IT, ISN'T IT WEIRD!?
CLATTER
WHY WOULD AN EVIL SORCERER ASK TO BE SEALED AWAY!?

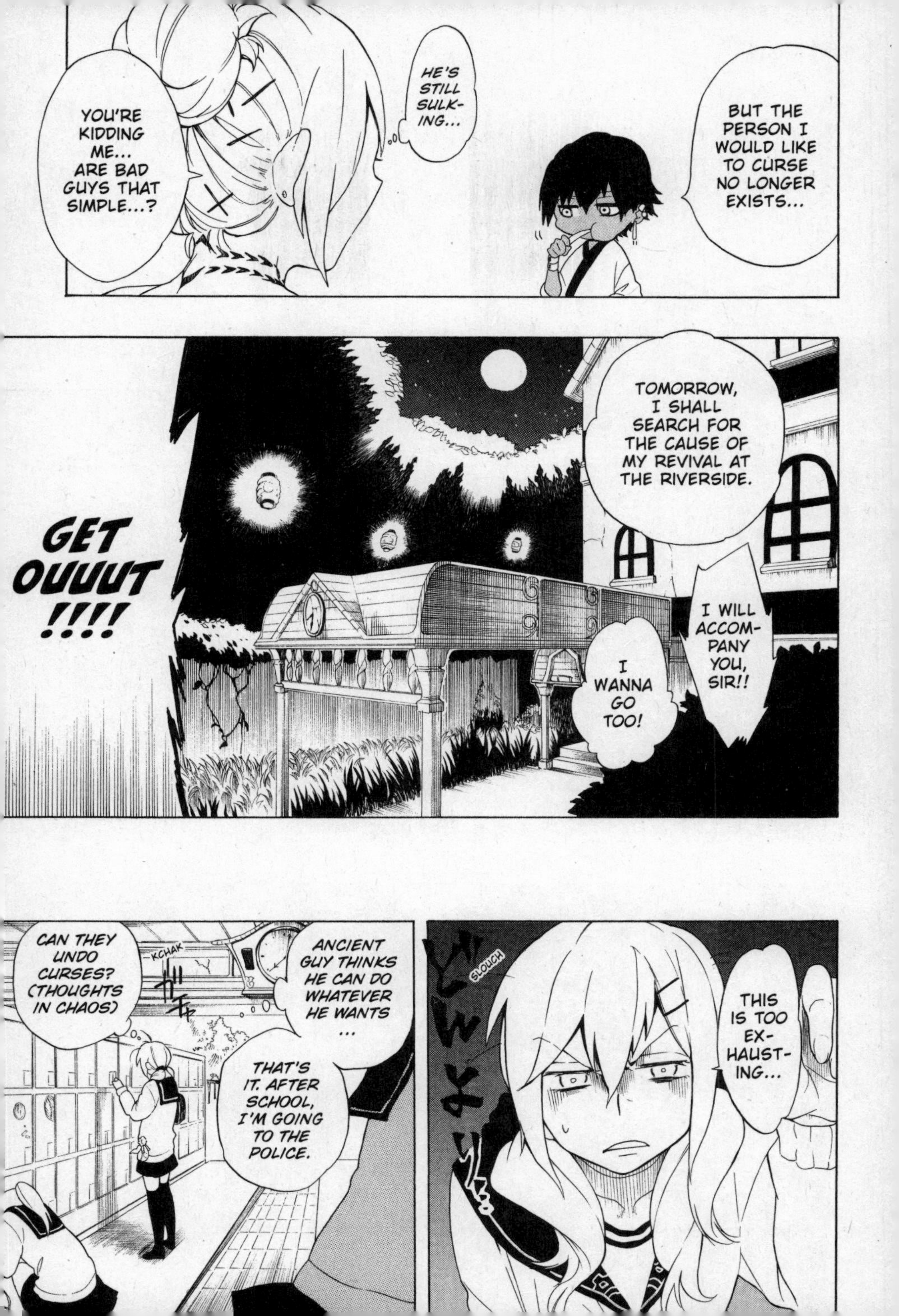
BUT THE PERSON I WOULD LIKE TO CURSE NO LONGER EXISTS...
HE'S STILL SULK-ING...
YOU'RE KIDDING ME... ARE BAD GUYS THAT SIMPLE...?
TOMORROW, I SHALL SEARCH FOR THE CAUSE OF MY REVIVAL AT THE RIVERSIDE.
I WILL ACCOM-PANY YOU, SIR!!
I WANNA GO TOO!
GET OUUUT !!!!
SLOUCH
THIS IS TOO EX-HAUST-ING...
ANCIENT GUY THINKS HE CAN DO WHATEVER HE WANTS ...
THAT'S IT. AFTER SCHOOL, I'M GOING TO THE POLICE.
CAN THEY UNDO CURSES? (THOUGHTS IN CHAOS)
KCHAK

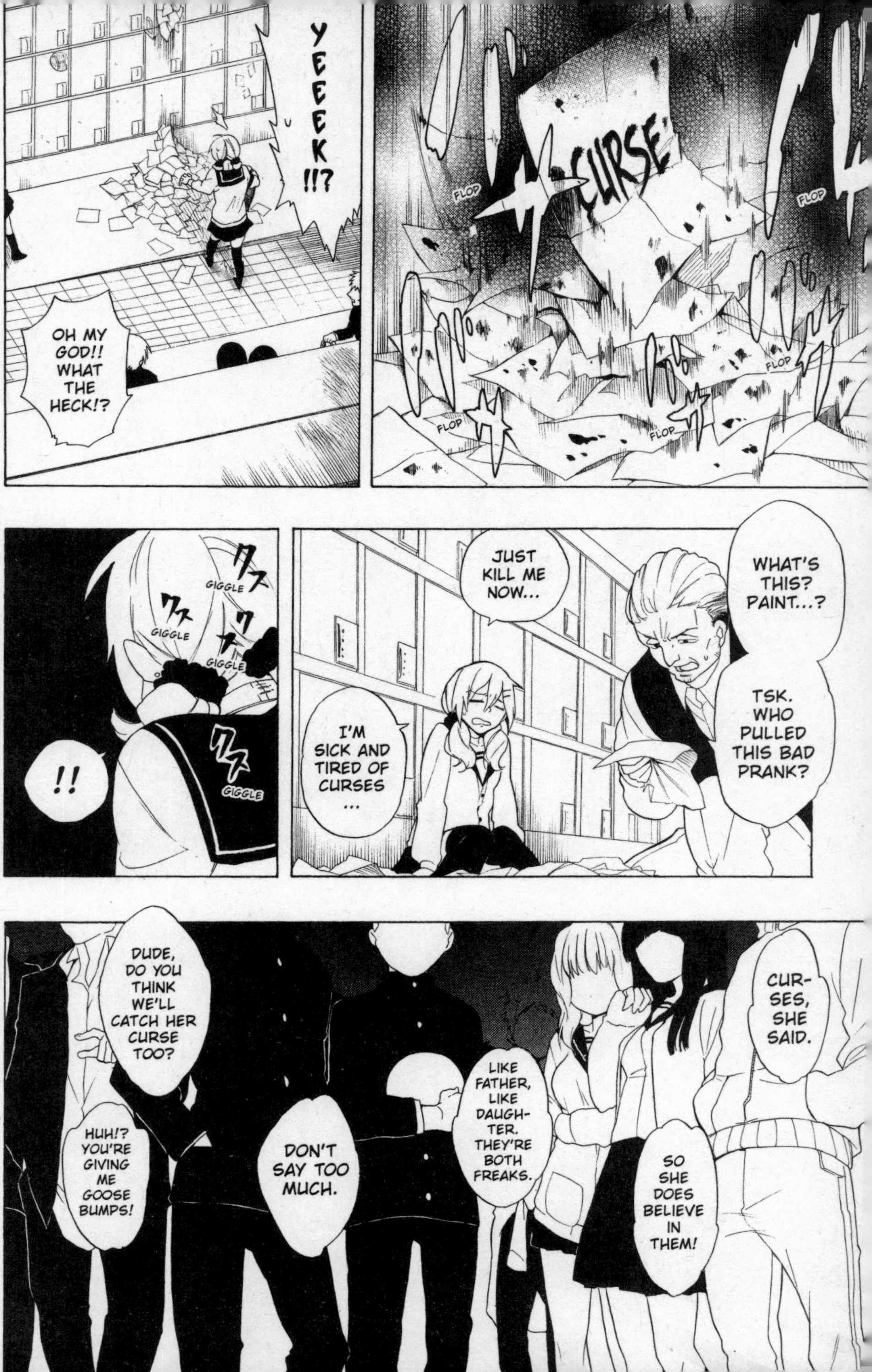
FLOP
CURSE
FLOP
FLOP
FLOP
FLOP
YEEEK!!?
OH MY GOD!! WHAT THE HECK!?
WHAT'S THIS? PAINT...?
TSK. WHO PULLED THIS BAD PRANK?
JUST KILL ME NOW...
I'M SICK AND TIRED OF CURSES...
クス GIGGLE
クス GIGGLE
クス GIGGLE
クス GIGGLE
!!
CUR-SES, SHE SAID.
SO SHE DOES BELIEVE IN THEM!
LIKE FATHER, LIKE DAUGH-TER. THEY'RE BOTH FREAKS.
DON'T SAY TOO MUCH.
DUDE, DO YOU THINK WE'LL CATCH HER CURSE TOO?
HUH!? YOU'RE GIVING ME GOOSE BUMPS!

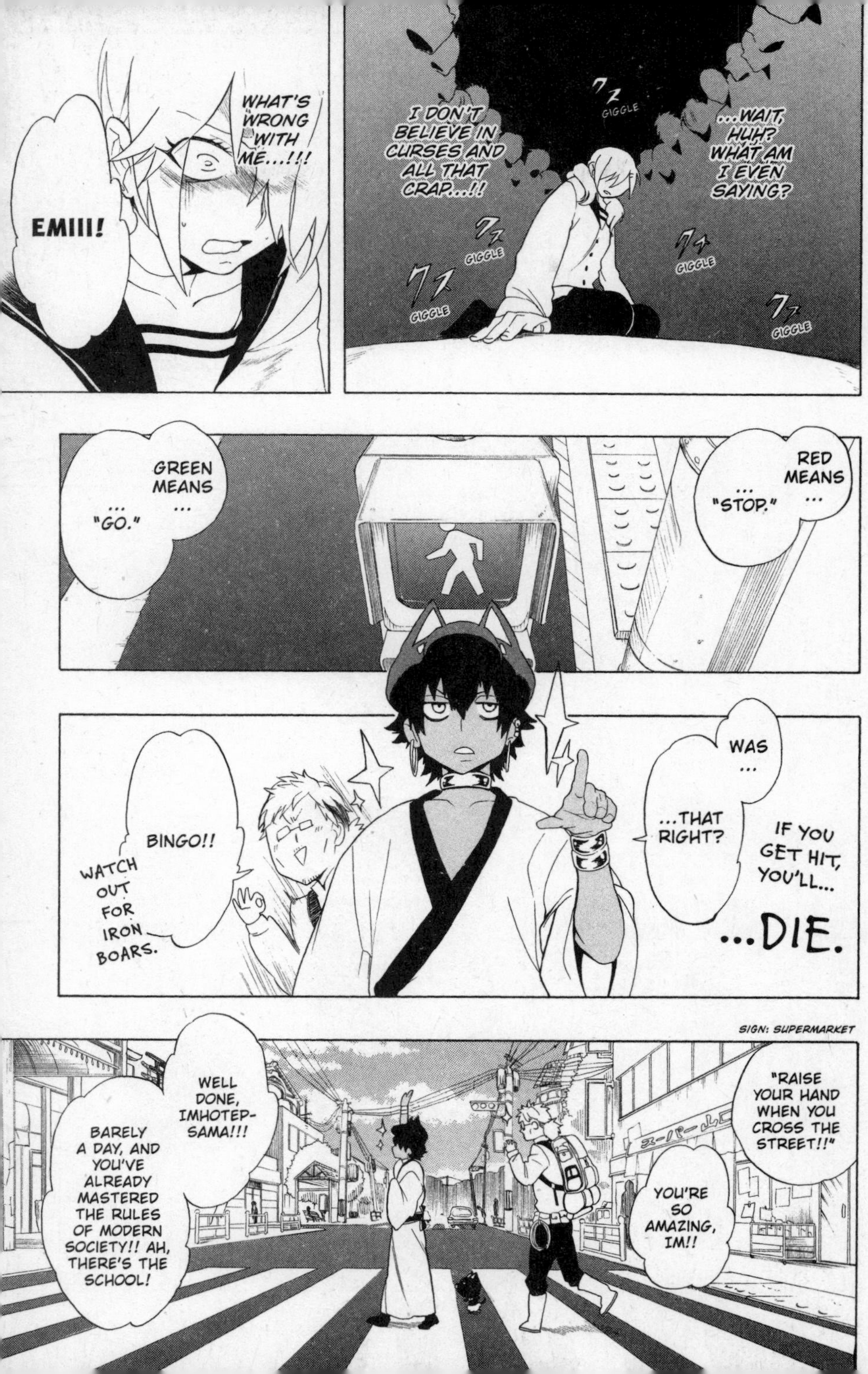
I DON'T BELIEVE IN CURSES AND ALL THAT CRAP...!!
...WAIT, HUH? WHAT AM I EVEN SAYING?
GIGGLE
GIGGLE
GIGGLE
GIGGLE
GIGGLE
WHAT'S WRONG WITH ME...!!!
EMIII!
RED MEANS ...
... "STOP."
GREEN MEANS ...
... "GO."
WAS ...
...THAT RIGHT?
IF YOU GET HIT, YOU'LL...
...DIE.
BINGO!!
WATCH OUT FOR IRON BOARS.
SIGN: SUPERMARKET
"RAISE YOUR HAND WHEN YOU CROSS THE STREET!!"
YOU'RE SO AMAZING, IM!!
WELL DONE, IMHOTEP-SAMA!!!
BARELY A DAY, AND YOU'VE ALREADY MASTERED THE RULES OF MODERN SOCIETY!! AH, THERE'S THE SCHOOL!

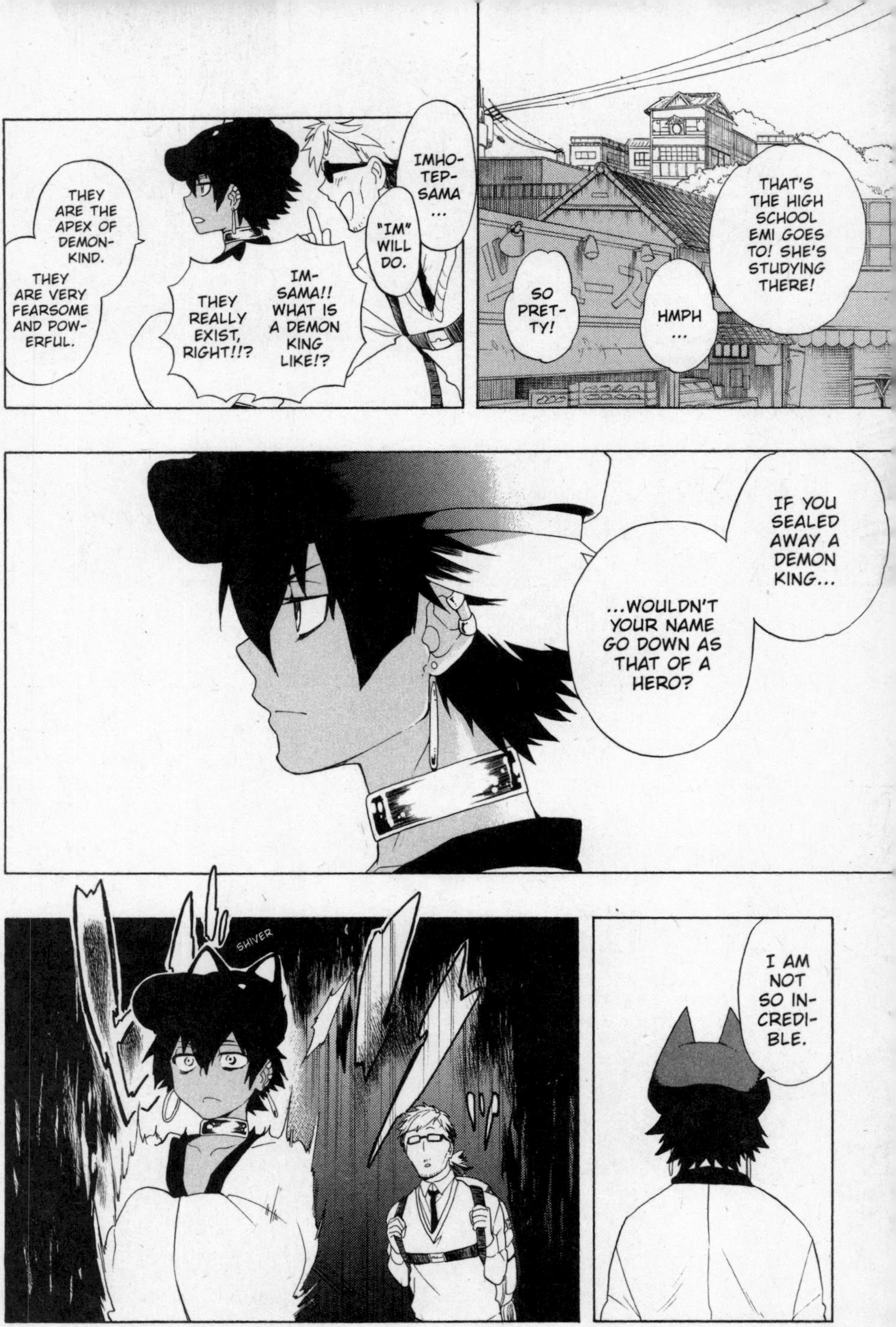

THAT'S THE HIGH SCHOOL EMI GOES TO! SHE'S STUDYING THERE!
HMPH...
SO PRETTY!
IMHOTEP-SAMA...
"IM" WILL DO.
IM-SAMA!! WHAT IS A DEMON KING LIKE!?
THEY REALLY EXIST, RIGHT!!?
THEY ARE THE APEX OF DEMON-KIND.
THEY ARE VERY FEARSOME AND POWERFUL.
IF YOU SEALED AWAY A DEMON KING...
...WOULDN'T YOUR NAME GO DOWN AS THAT OF A HERO?
I AM NOT SO INCREDIBLE.
SHIVER

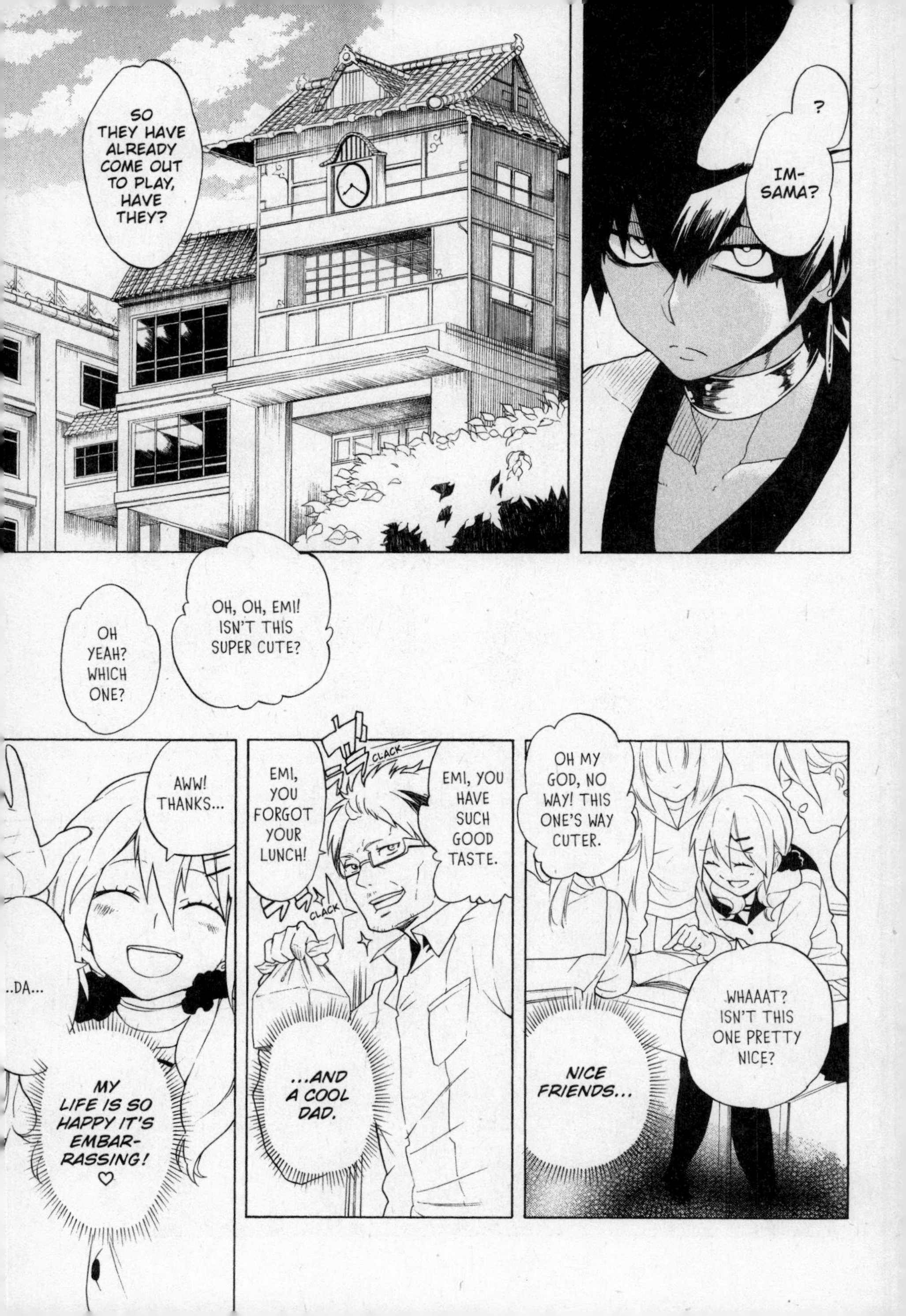
?
IM-SAMA?
SO THEY HAVE ALREADY COME OUT TO PLAY, HAVE THEY?
OH, OH, EMI! ISN'T THIS SUPER CUTE?
OH YEAH? WHICH ONE?
OH MY GOD, NO WAY! THIS ONE'S WAY CUTER.
WHAAAT? ISN'T THIS ONE PRETTY NICE?
NICE FRIENDS...
EMI, YOU HAVE SUCH GOOD TASTE.
CLACK
EMI, YOU FORGOT YOUR LUNCH!
CLACK
...AND A COOL DAD.
AWW! THANKS...
...DA...
MY LIFE IS SO HAPPY IT'S EMBARRASSING! ♡

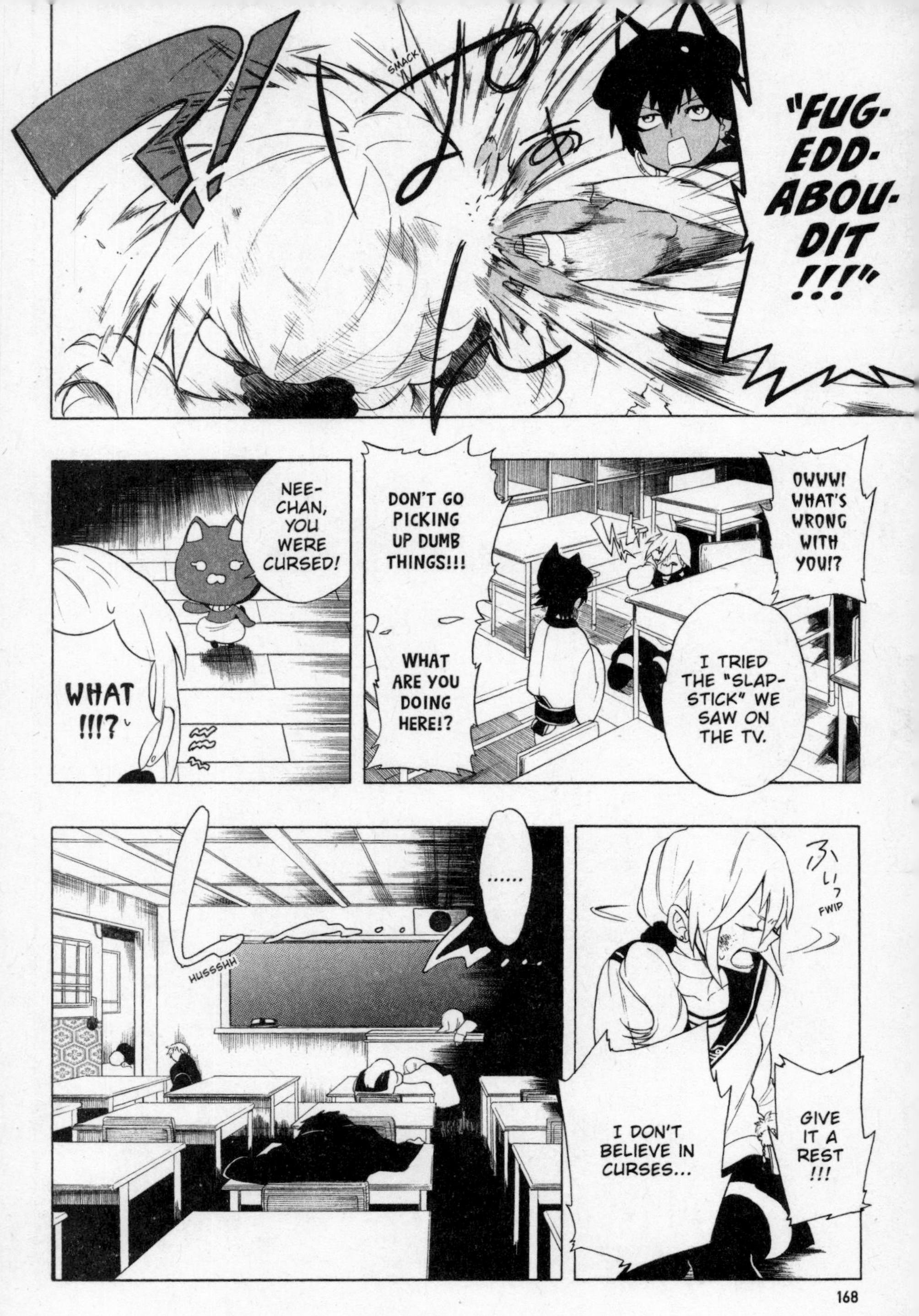
SMACK
"FUG-EDD-ABOU-DIT!!!"
OWWW! WHAT'S WRONG WITH YOU!?
DON'T GO PICKING UP DUMB THINGS!!!
I TRIED THE "SLAP-STICK" WE SAW ON THE TV.
WHAT ARE YOU DOING HERE!?
NEE-CHAN, YOU WERE CURSED!
WHAT!!!?
FWIP
GIVE IT A REST!!!
I DON'T BELIEVE IN CURSES...
......
HUSSSHH

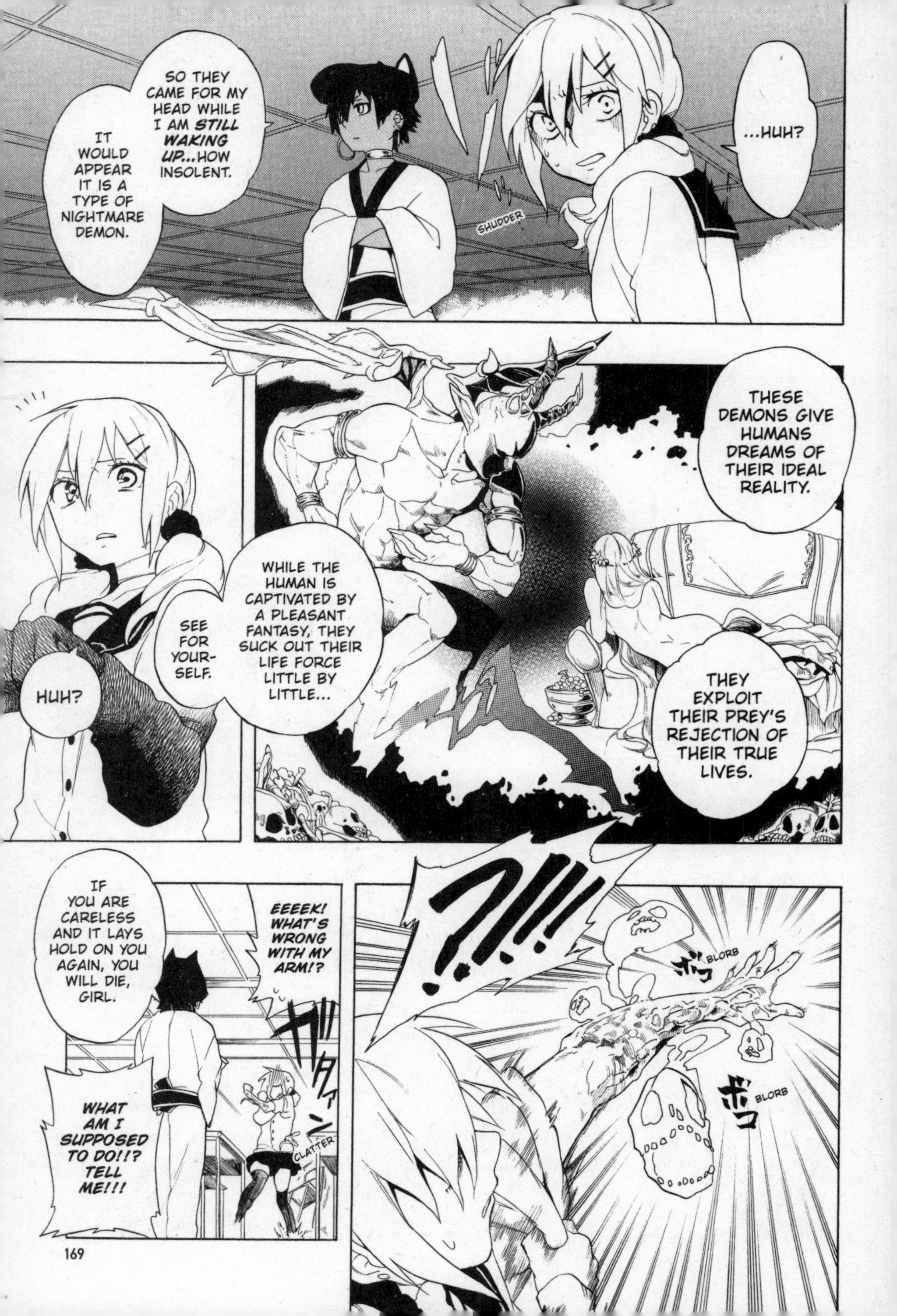

...HUH?
SHUDDER
SO THEY CAME FOR MY HEAD WHILE I AM ***STILL WAKING UP...*** HOW INSOLENT.
IT WOULD APPEAR IT IS A TYPE OF NIGHTMARE DEMON.
THESE DEMONS GIVE HUMANS DREAMS OF THEIR IDEAL REALITY.
WHILE THE HUMAN IS CAPTIVATED BY A PLEASANT FANTASY, THEY SUCK OUT THEIR LIFE FORCE LITTLE BY LITTLE...
THEY EXPLOIT THEIR PREY'S REJECTION OF THEIR TRUE LIVES.
SEE FOR YOUR-SELF.
HUH?
?!!
BLORB
BLORB
IF YOU ARE CARELESS AND IT LAYS HOLD ON YOU AGAIN, YOU WILL DIE, GIRL.
EEEEK! WHAT'S WRONG WITH MY ARM!?
WHAT AM I SUPPOSED TO DO!!? TELL ME!!!
CLATTER

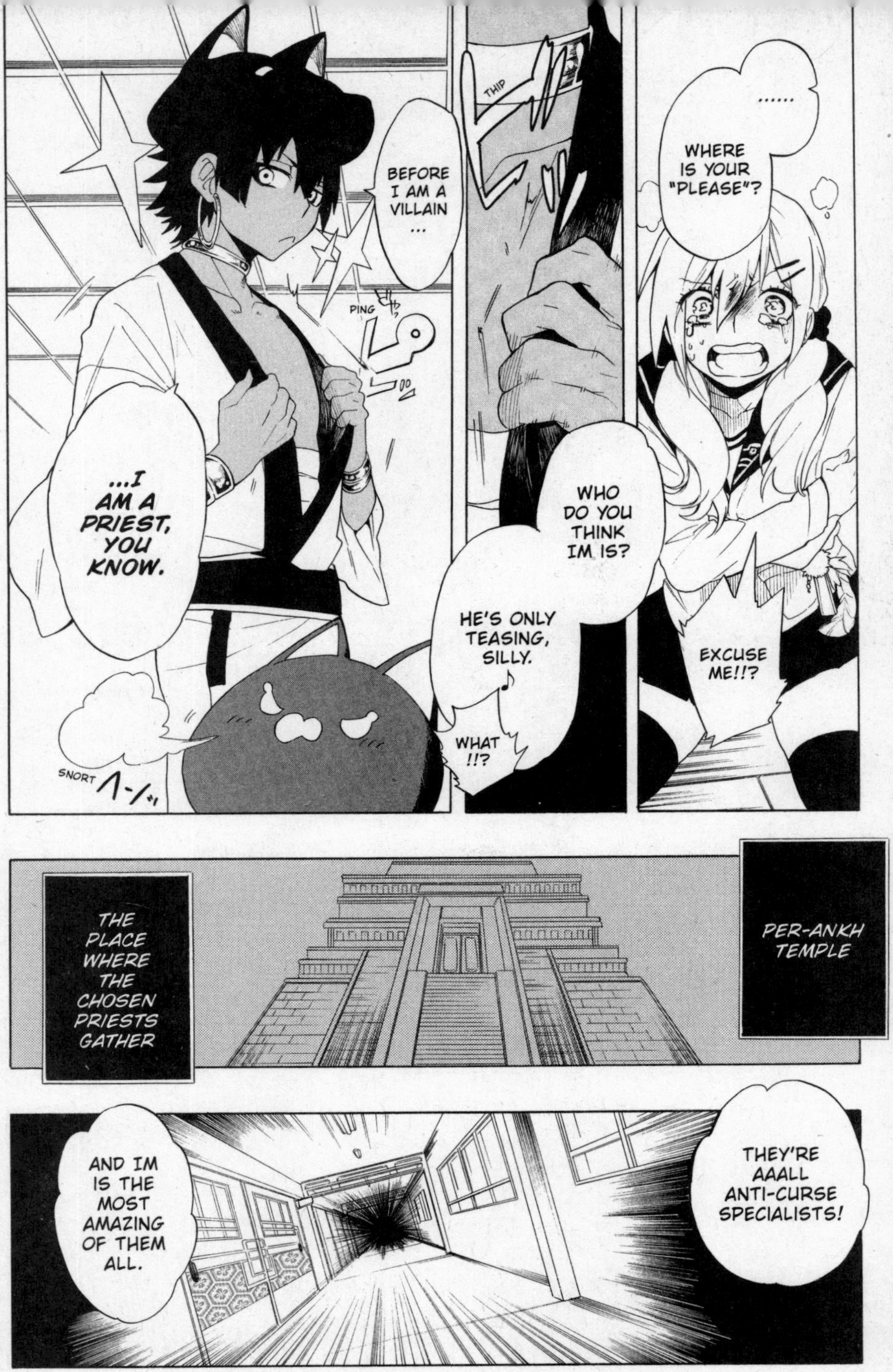
......
WHERE IS YOUR "PLEASE"?
EXCUSE ME!!?
THIP
WHO DO YOU THINK IM IS?
HE'S ONLY TEASING, SILLY. ♪
WHAT !!?
BEFORE I AM A VILLAIN ...
PING
...I AM A PRIEST, YOU KNOW.
SNORT
PER-ANKH TEMPLE
THE PLACE WHERE THE CHOSEN PRIESTS GATHER
THEY'RE AAALL ANTI-CURSE SPECIALISTS!
AND IM IS THE MOST AMAZING OF THEM ALL.

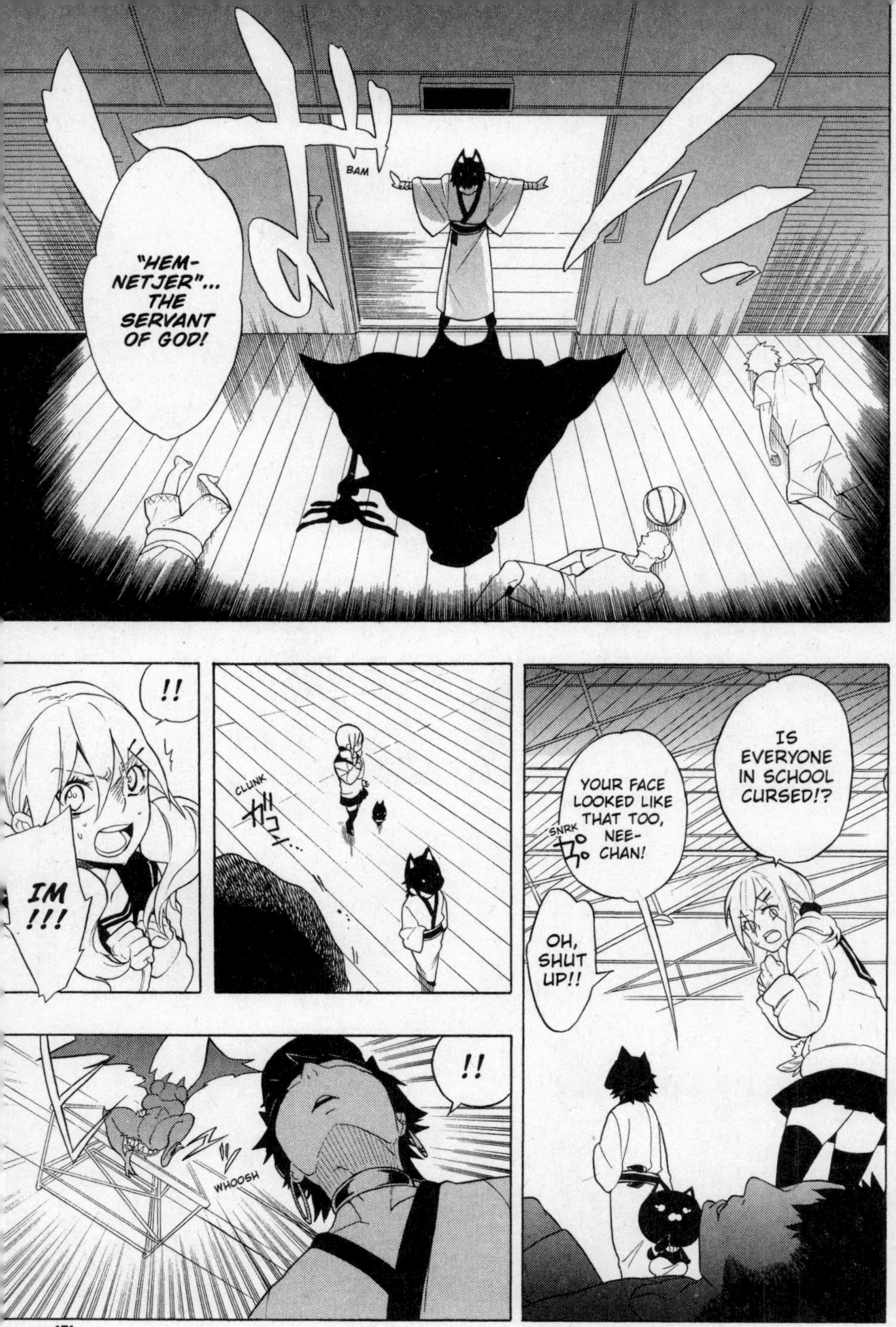
BAM
"HEM-NETJER"... THE SERVANT OF GOD!
IS EVERYONE IN SCHOOL CURSED!?
YOUR FACE LOOKED LIKE THAT TOO, NEE-CHAN!
SNRK
OH, SHUT UP!!
CLUNK
!!
IM !!!
!!
WHOOSH

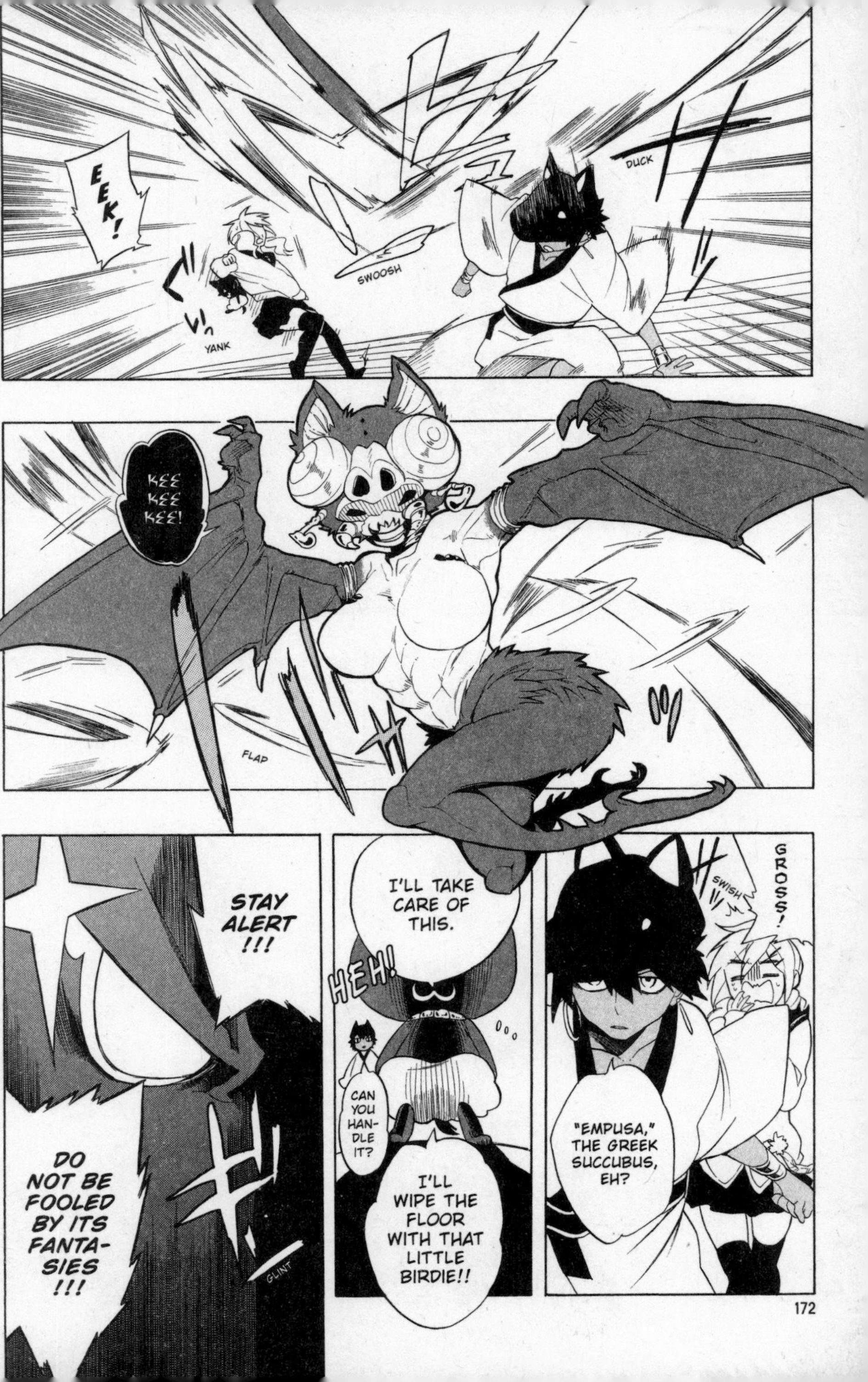
DUCK
EEK!
SWOOSH
YANK
KEE KEE KEE!
FLAP
GROSS!
SWISH
"EMPUSA," THE GREEK SUCCUBUS, EH?
I'LL TAKE CARE OF THIS.
HEH!
CAN YOU HAND-LE IT?
I'LL WIPE THE FLOOR WITH THAT LITTLE BIRDIE!!
STAY ALERT!!!
DO NOT BE FOOLED BY ITS FANTA-SIES!!!
GLINT

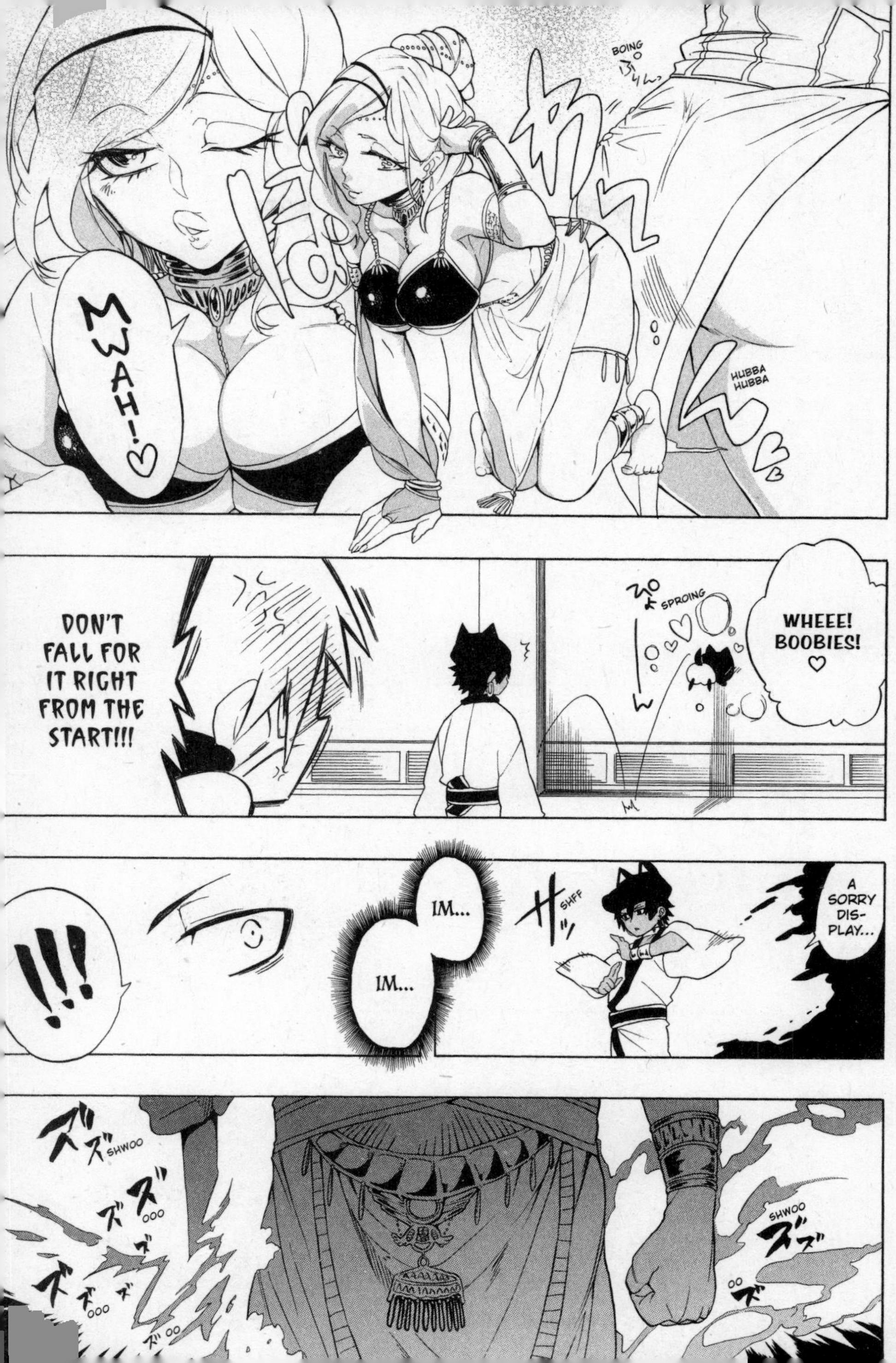
BOING
HUBBA HUBBA
MWAH!♡
WHEEE! BOOBIES! ♡
SPROING
DON'T FALL FOR IT RIGHT FROM THE START!!!
A SORRY DIS-PLAY...
SHFF
IM...
IM...
!!!
SHWOO
OO
SHWOO
OOO
OOO
OO

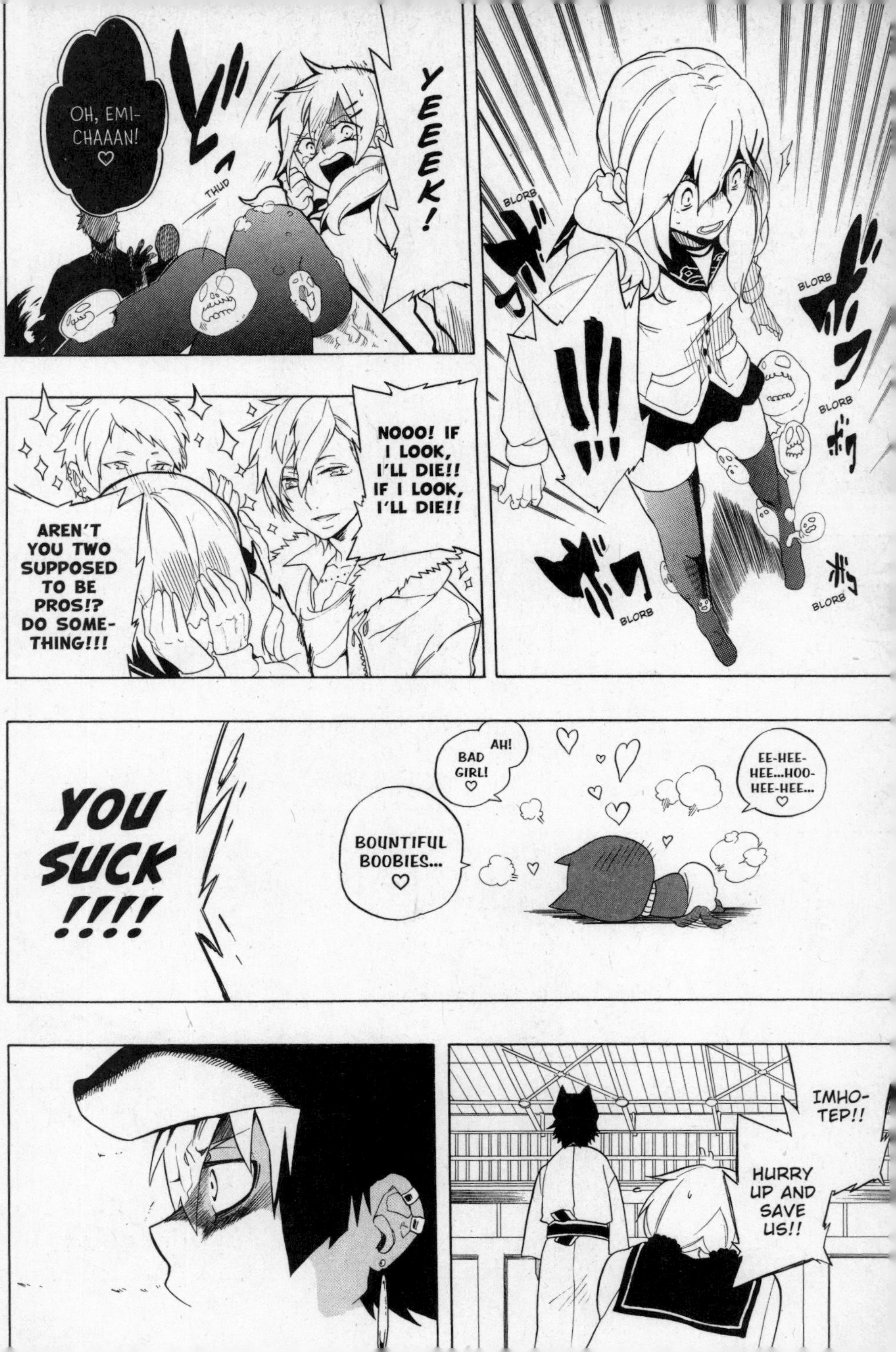
BLORB
BLORB
BLORB
BLORB
BLORB
YEEEK!
OH, EMI-CHAAAN! ♡
THUD
NOOO! IF I LOOK, I'LL DIE!! IF I LOOK, I'LL DIE!!
AREN'T YOU TWO SUPPOSED TO BE PROS!? DO SOME-THING!!!
EE-HEE-HEE...HOO-HEE-HEE... ♡
AH! BAD GIRL! ♡
BOUNTIFUL BOOBIES... ♡
YOU SUCK!!!!
IMHO-TEP!!
HURRY UP AND SAVE US!!

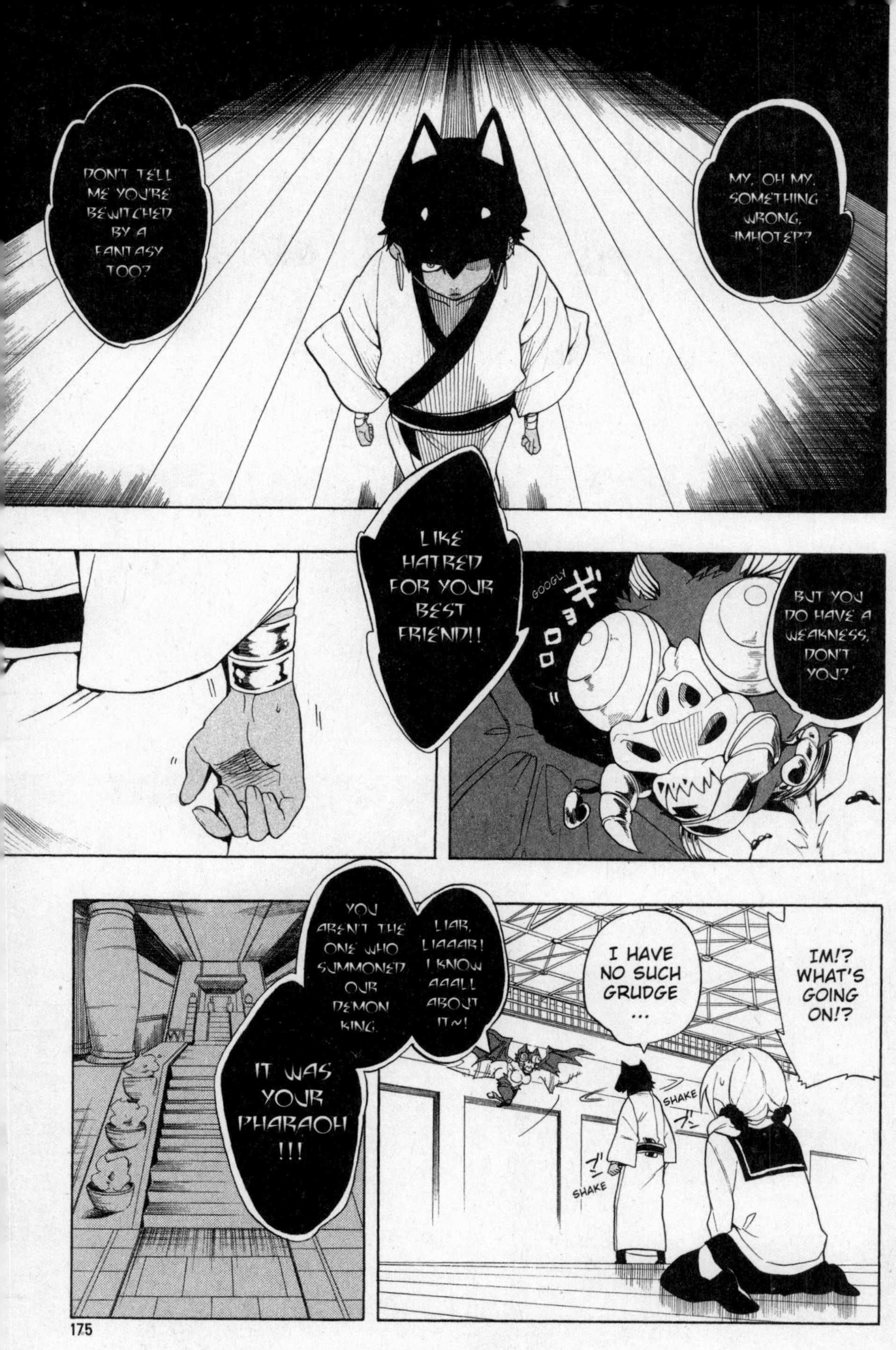
MY, OH MY. SOMETHING WRONG, IMHOTEP?
DON'T TELL ME YOU'RE BEWITCHED BY A FANTASY TOO?
BUT YOU DO HAVE A WEAKNESS, DON'T YOU?
GOOGLY
LIKE HATRED FOR YOUR BEST FRIEND!!
IM!? WHAT'S GOING ON!?
I HAVE NO SUCH GRUDGE ...
SHAKE
SHAKE
LIAR, LIAAAR! I KNOW AAALL ABOUT IT~!
YOU AREN'T THE ONE WHO SUMMONED OUR DEMON KING.
IT WAS YOUR PHARAOH!!!

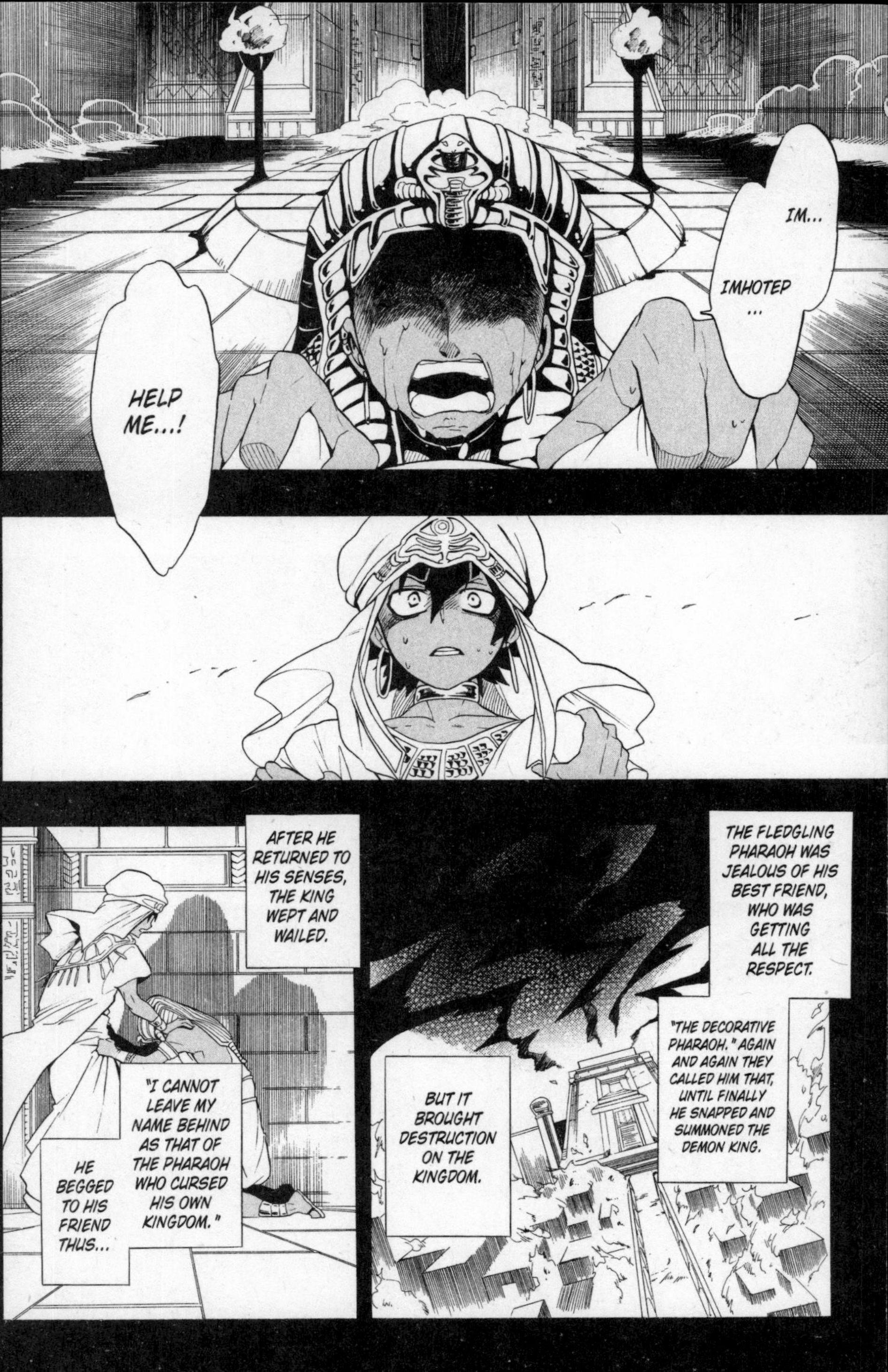
IM...
IMHOTEP ...
HELP ME...!
THE FLEDGLING PHARAOH WAS JEALOUS OF HIS BEST FRIEND, WHO WAS GETTING ALL THE RESPECT.
"THE DECORATIVE PHARAOH." AGAIN AND AGAIN THEY CALLED HIM THAT, UNTIL FINALLY HE SNAPPED AND SUMMONED THE DEMON KING.
BUT IT BROUGHT DESTRUCTION ON THE KINGDOM.
AFTER HE RETURNED TO HIS SENSES, THE KING WEPT AND WAILED.
"I CANNOT LEAVE MY NAME BEHIND AS THAT OF THE PHARAOH WHO CURSED HIS OWN KINGDOM."
HE BEGGED TO HIS FRIEND THUS...

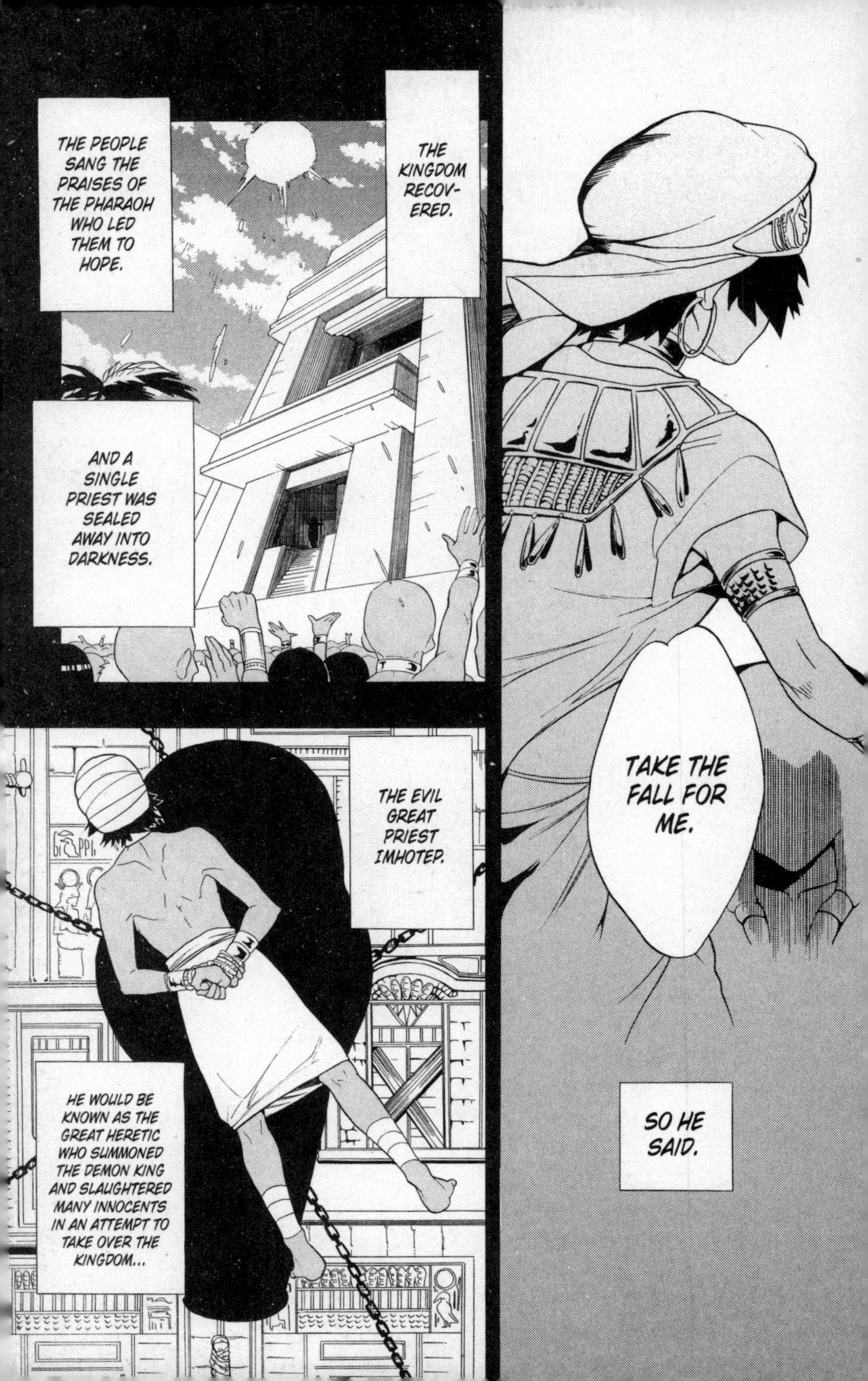
TAKE THE FALL FOR ME.
SO HE SAID.
THE KINGDOM RECOVERED.
THE PEOPLE SANG THE PRAISES OF THE PHARAOH WHO LED THEM TO HOPE.
AND A SINGLE PRIEST WAS SEALED AWAY INTO DARKNESS.
THE EVIL GREAT PRIEST IMHOTEP.
HE WOULD BE KNOWN AS THE GREAT HERETIC WHO SUMMONED THE DEMON KING AND SLAUGHTERED MANY INNOCENTS IN AN ATTEMPT TO TAKE OVER THE KINGDOM...

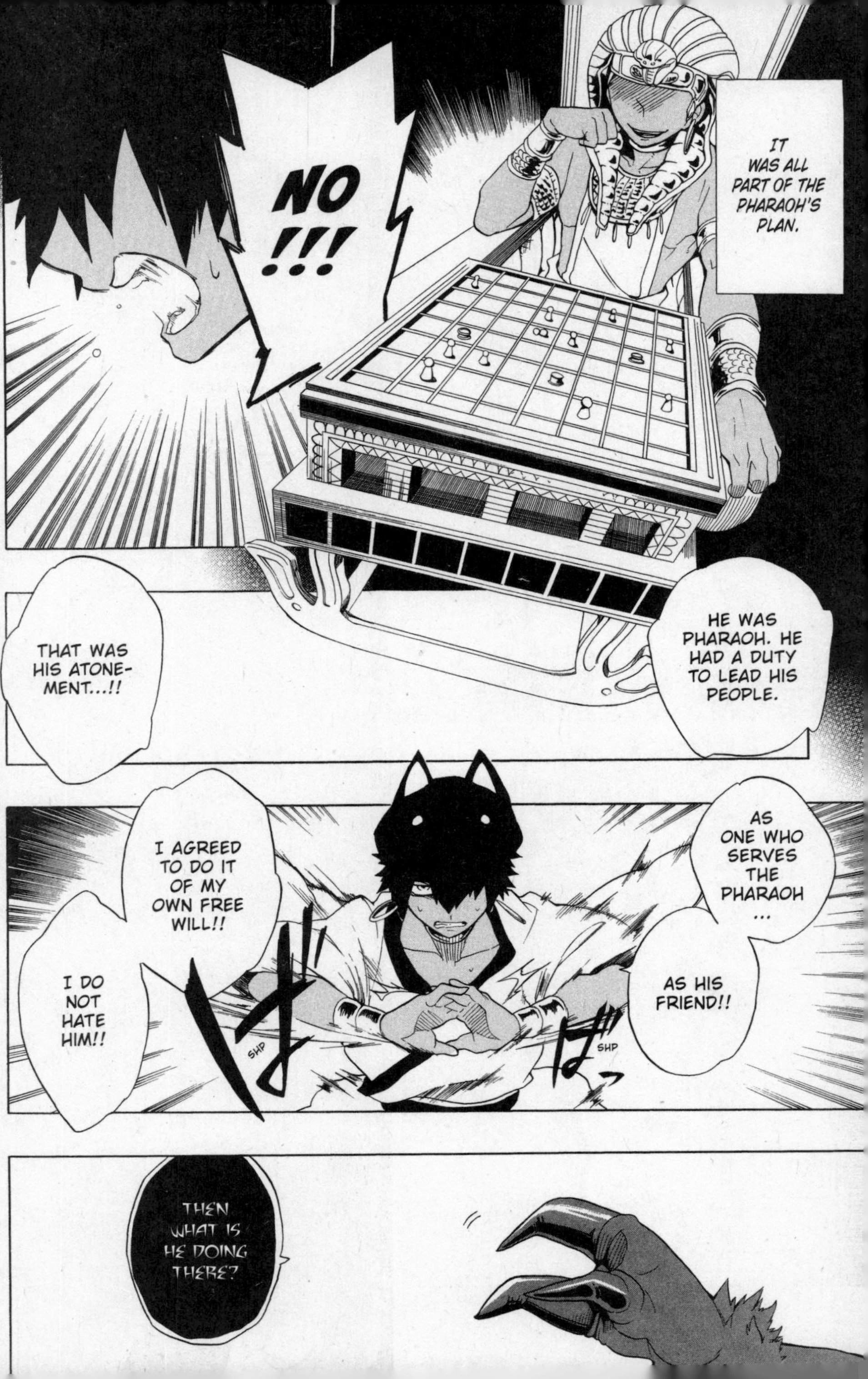
IT WAS ALL PART OF THE PHARAOH'S PLAN.
NO!!!
HE WAS PHARAOH. HE HAD A DUTY TO LEAD HIS PEOPLE.
THAT WAS HIS ATONEMENT...!!
AS ONE WHO SERVES THE PHARAOH...
AS HIS FRIEND!!
SHP
I AGREED TO DO IT OF MY OWN FREE WILL!!
I DO NOT HATE HIM!!
SHP
THEN WHAT IS HE DOING THERE?

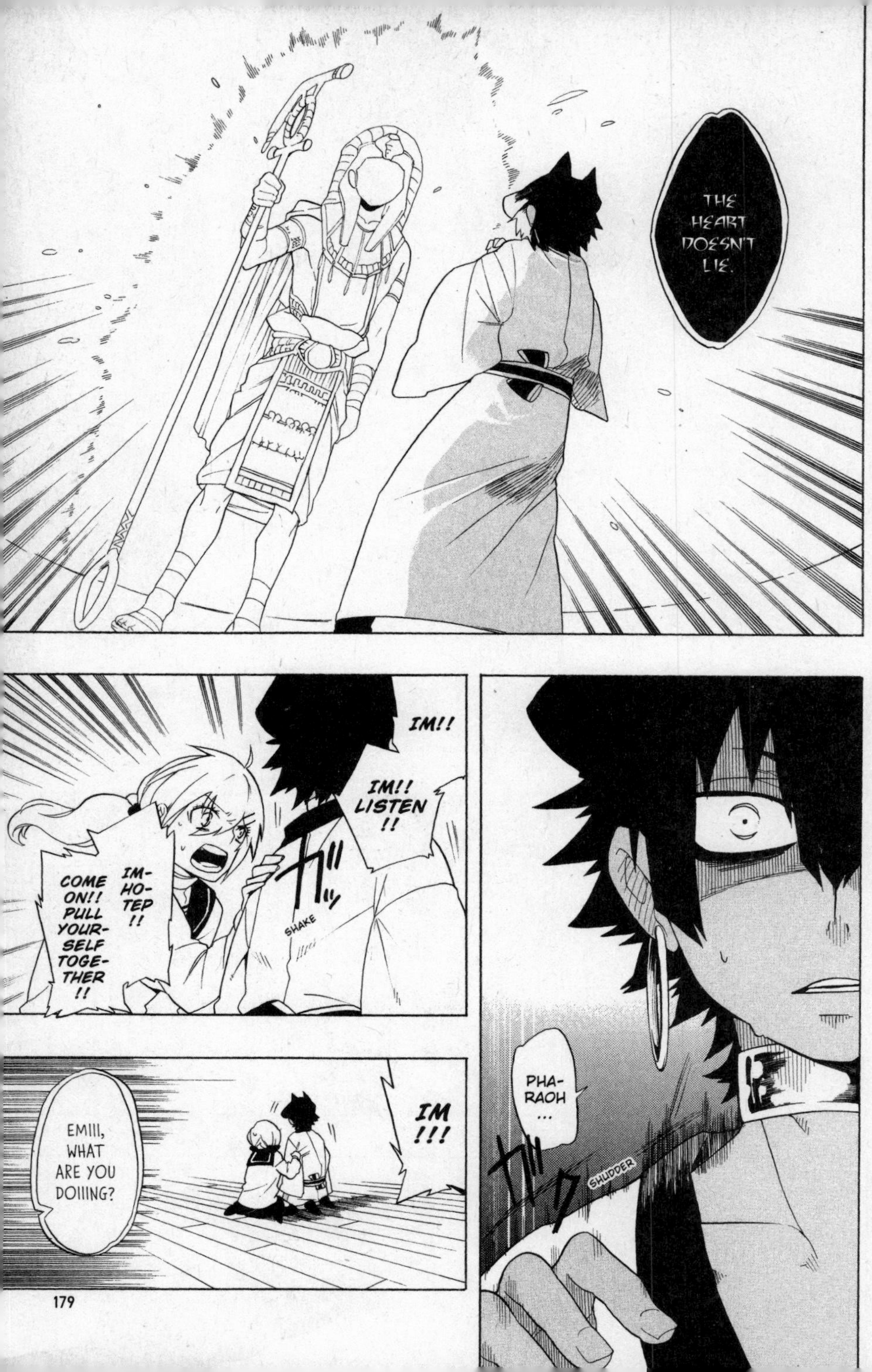
THE HEART DOESN'T LIE.
PHARAOH...
SHUDDER
IM!!
IM!! LISTEN!!
IMHOTEP!!
COME ON!! PULL YOURSELF TOGETHER!!
SHAKE
IM!!!
EMIII, WHAT ARE YOU DOIIING?

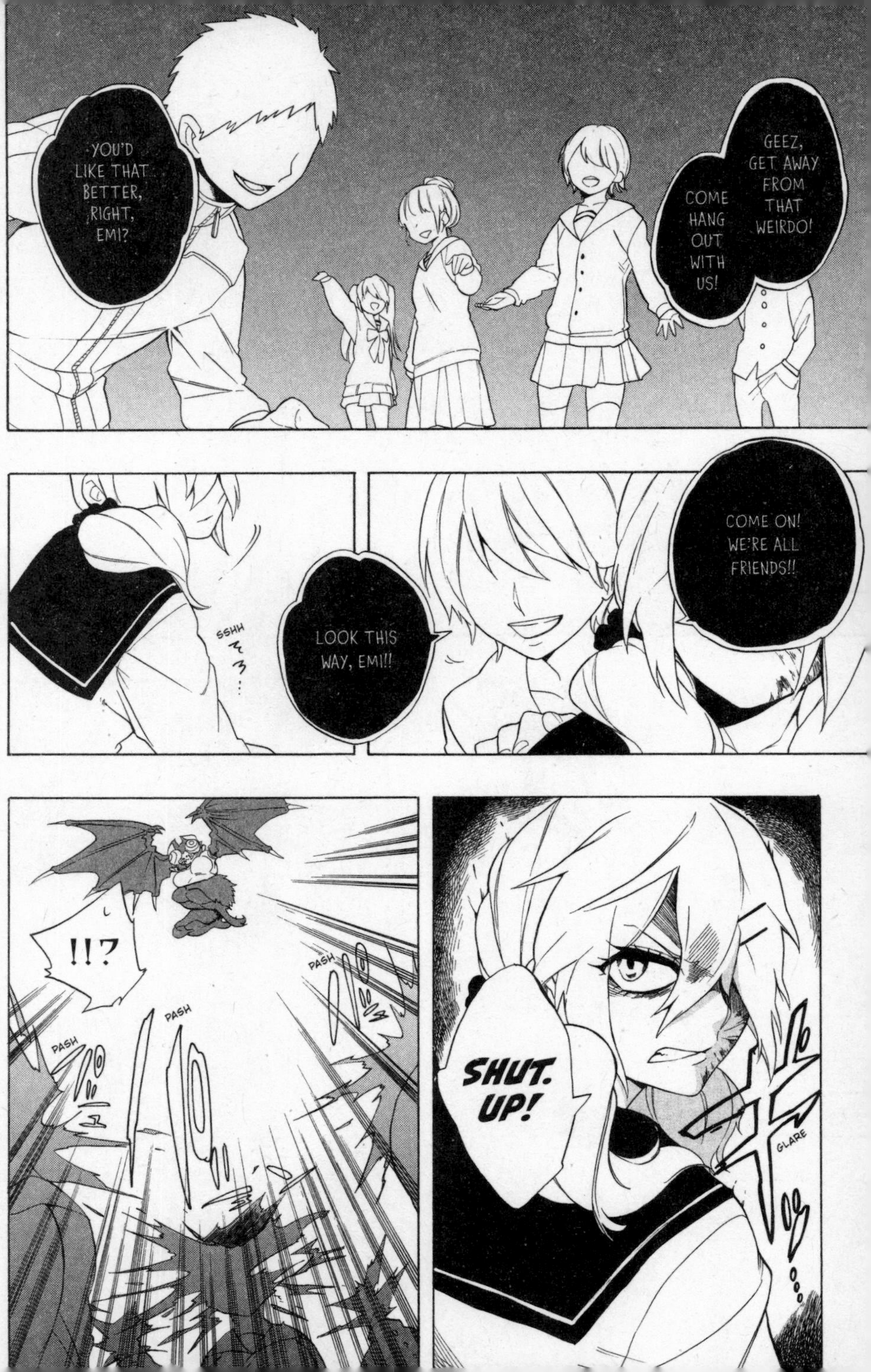
GEEZ, GET AWAY FROM THAT WEIRDO!
COME HANG OUT WITH US!
YOU'D LIKE THAT BETTER, RIGHT, EMI?
COME ON! WE'RE ALL FRIENDS!!
LOOK THIS WAY, EMI!!
SSHH
SHUT. UP!
GLARE
!!?
PASH
PASH
PASH

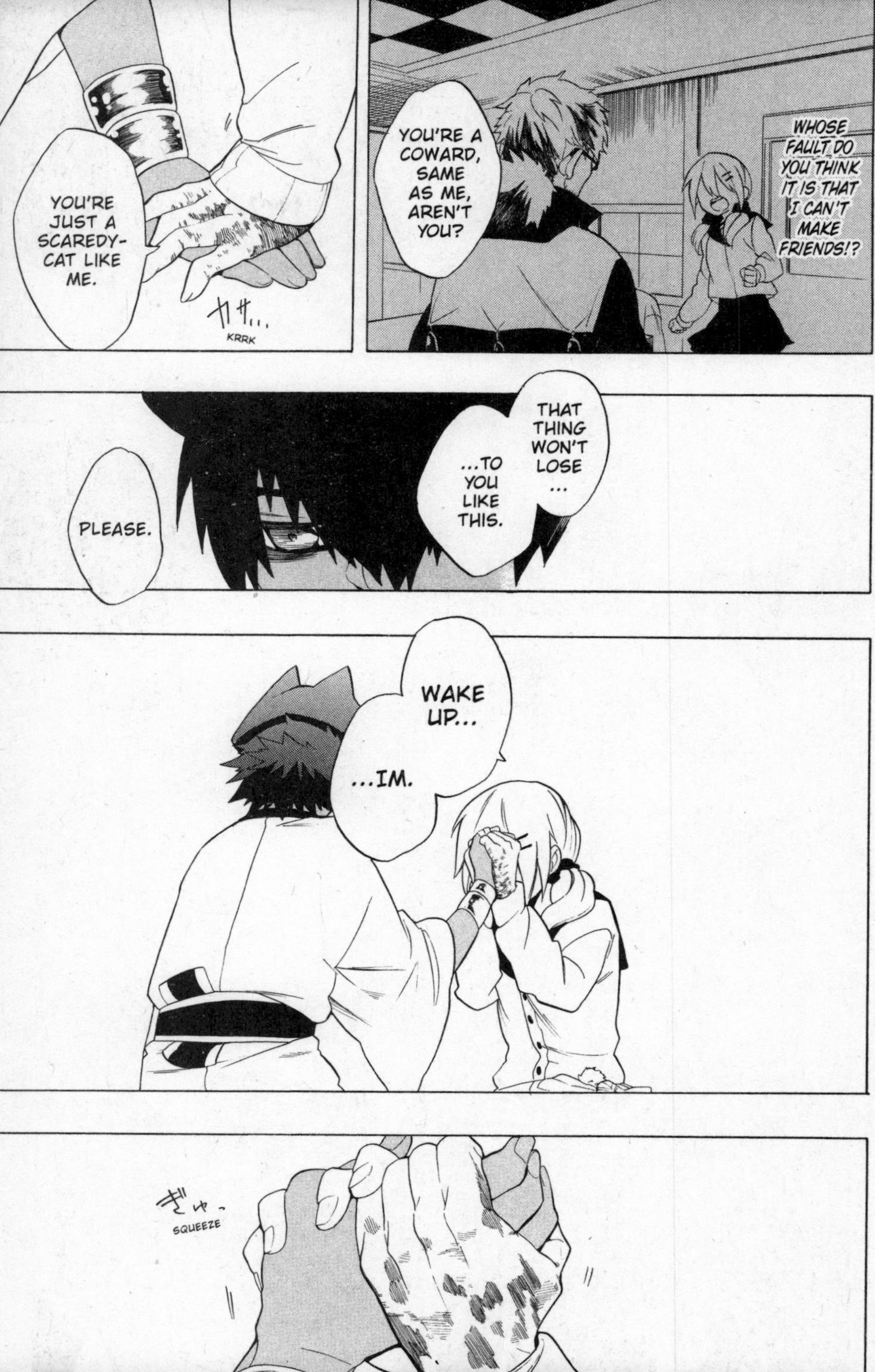
WHOSE FAULT DO YOU THINK IT IS THAT I CAN'T MAKE FRIENDS!?
YOU'RE A COWARD, SAME AS ME, AREN'T YOU?
YOU'RE JUST A SCAREDY-CAT LIKE ME.
カサ…
KRRK
THAT THING WON'T LOSE...
...TO YOU LIKE THIS.
PLEASE.
WAKE UP...
...IM.
ぎゅっ
SQUEEZE

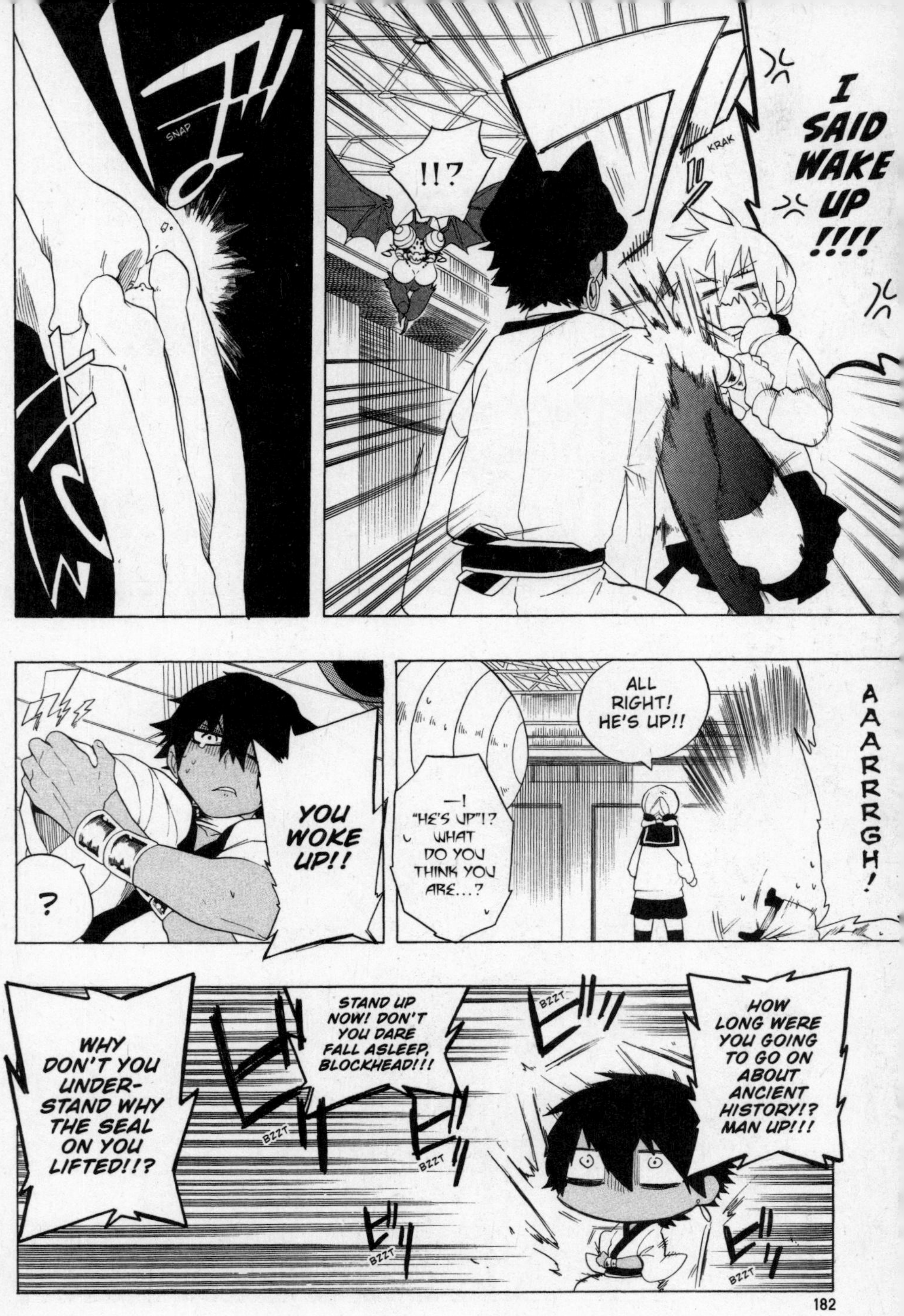
I SAID WAKE UP!!!!
KRAK
!!?
SNAP
AAARRRGH!
ALL RIGHT! HE'S UP!!
—! "HE'S UP"!? WHAT DO YOU THINK YOU ARE...?
YOU WOKE UP!!
?
HOW LONG WERE YOU GOING TO GO ON ABOUT ANCIENT HISTORY!? MAN UP!!!
BZZT
BZZT
STAND UP NOW! DON'T YOU DARE FALL ASLEEP, BLOCKHEAD!!!
BZZT
BZZT
BZZT
WHY DON'T YOU UNDER-STAND WHY THE SEAL ON YOU LIFTED!!?

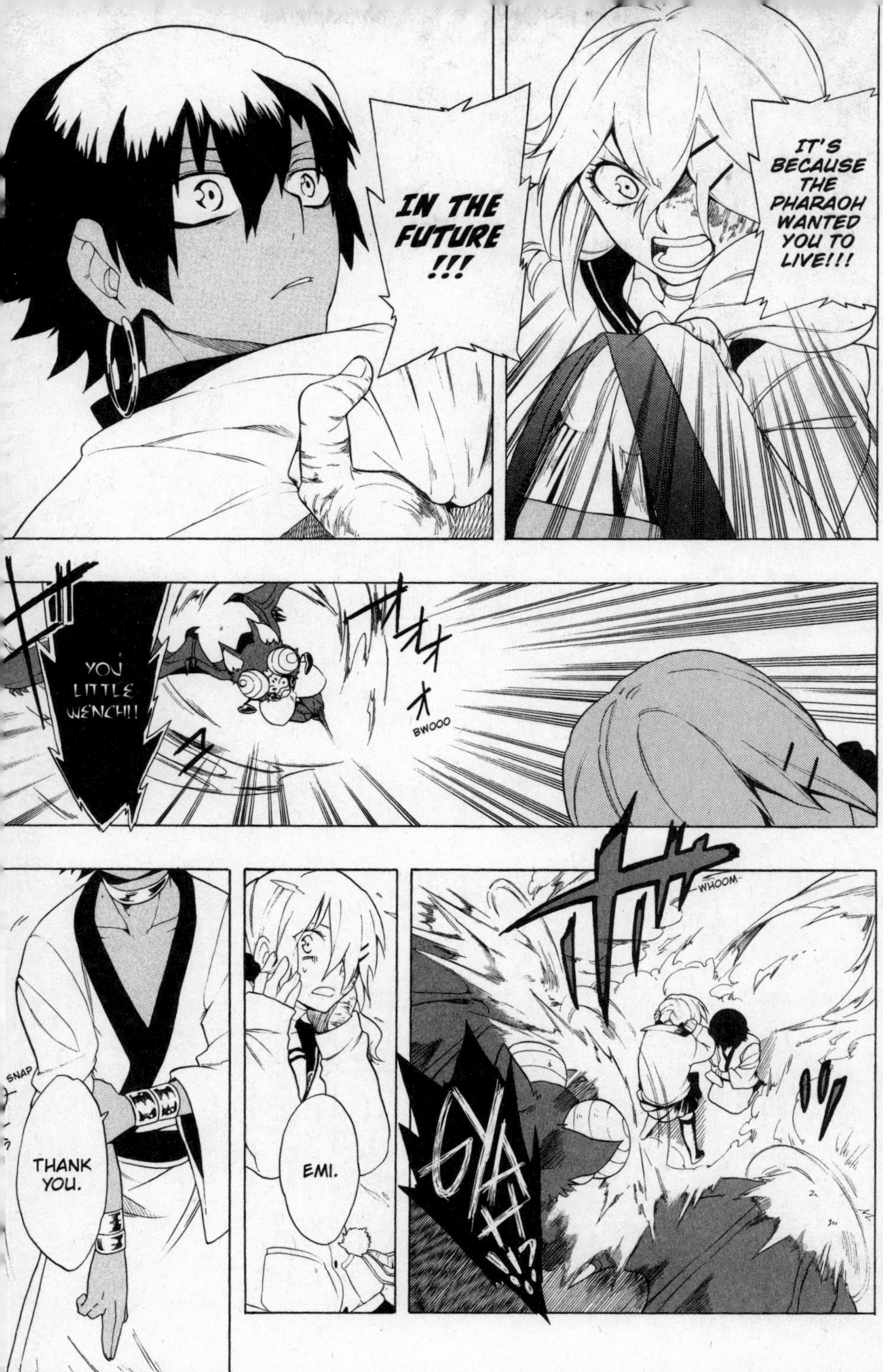
IT'S BECAUSE THE PHARAOH WANTED YOU TO LIVE!!!
IN THE FUTURE!!!
YOU LITTLE WENCH!!
BWOOO
WHOOM
GYAH!!?
EMI.
THANK YOU.
SNAP

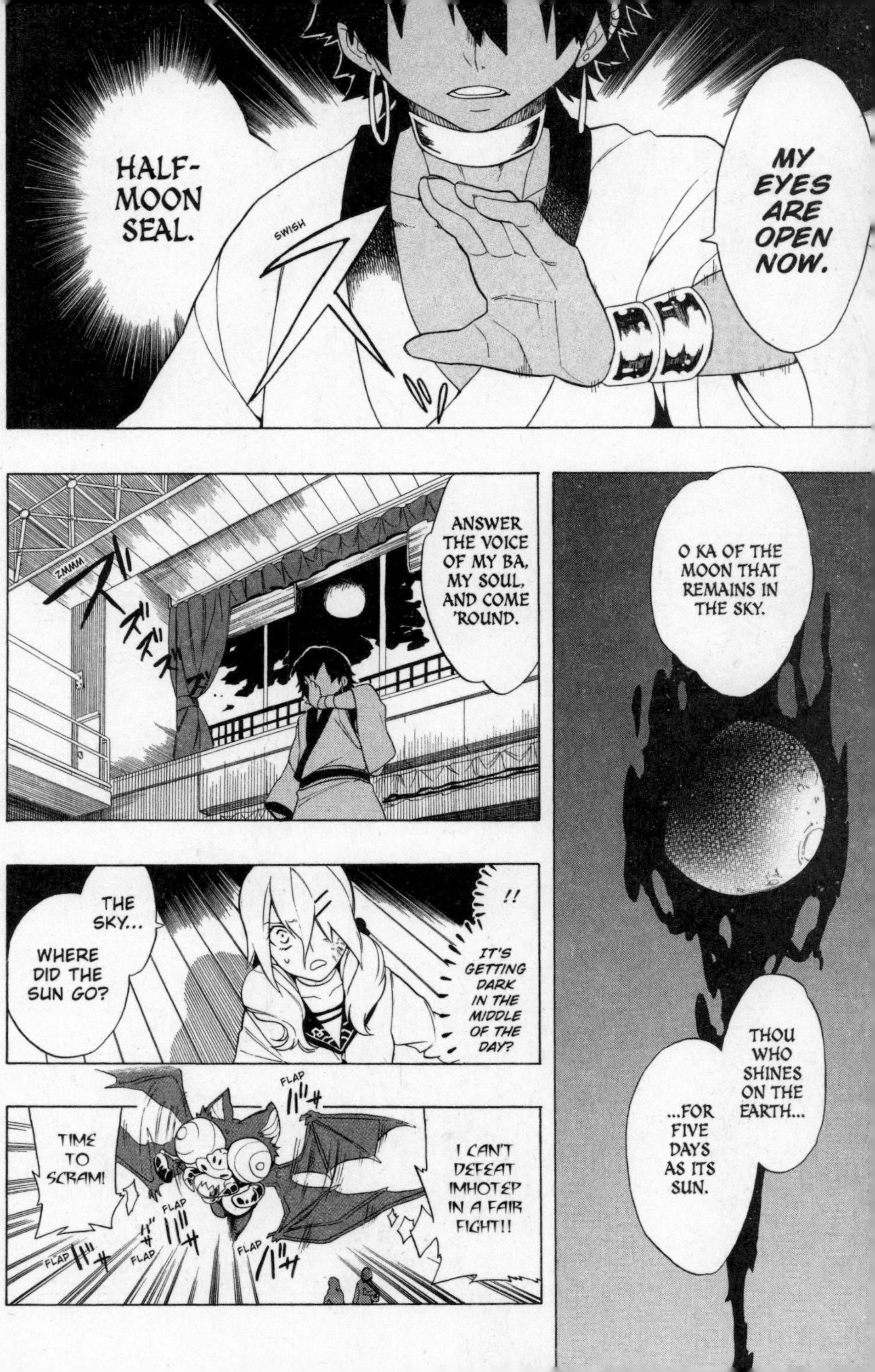
MY EYES ARE OPEN NOW.
HALF-MOON SEAL.
SWISH
O KA OF THE MOON THAT REMAINS IN THE SKY.
THOU WHO SHINES ON THE EARTH...
...FOR FIVE DAYS AS ITS SUN.
ANSWER THE VOICE OF MY BA, MY SOUL, AND COME 'ROUND.
ZMMM
!!
IT'S GETTING DARK IN THE MIDDLE OF THE DAY?
THE SKY...
WHERE DID THE SUN GO?
FLAP
I CAN'T DEFEAT IMHOTEP IN A FAIR FIGHT!!
TIME TO SCRAM!
FLAP
FLAP
FLAP
FLAP

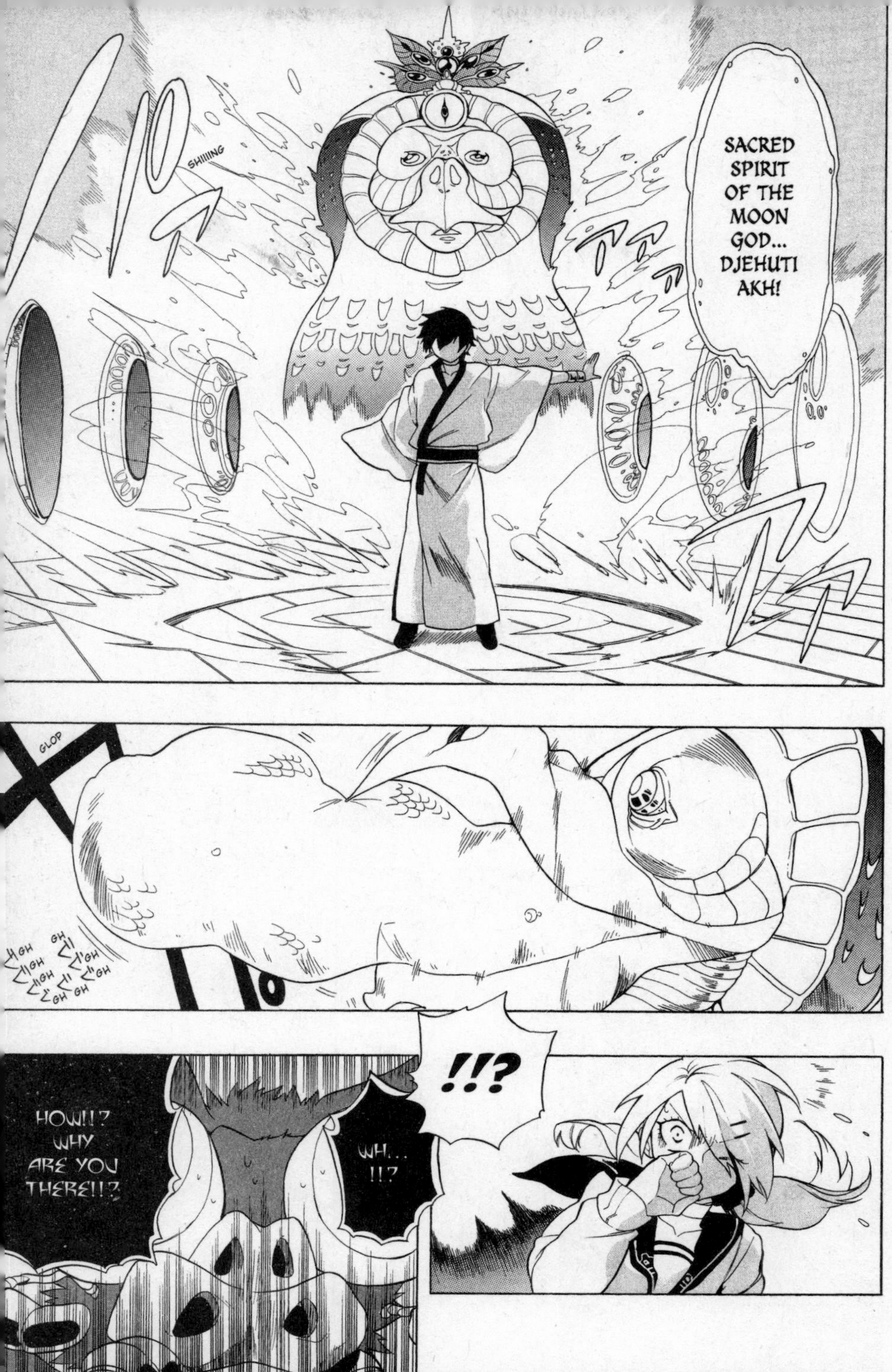
SACRED SPIRIT OF THE MOON GOD... DJEHUTI AKH!
SHIIING
GLOP
!!?
WH... !!?
HOW!!? WHY ARE YOU THERE!!?

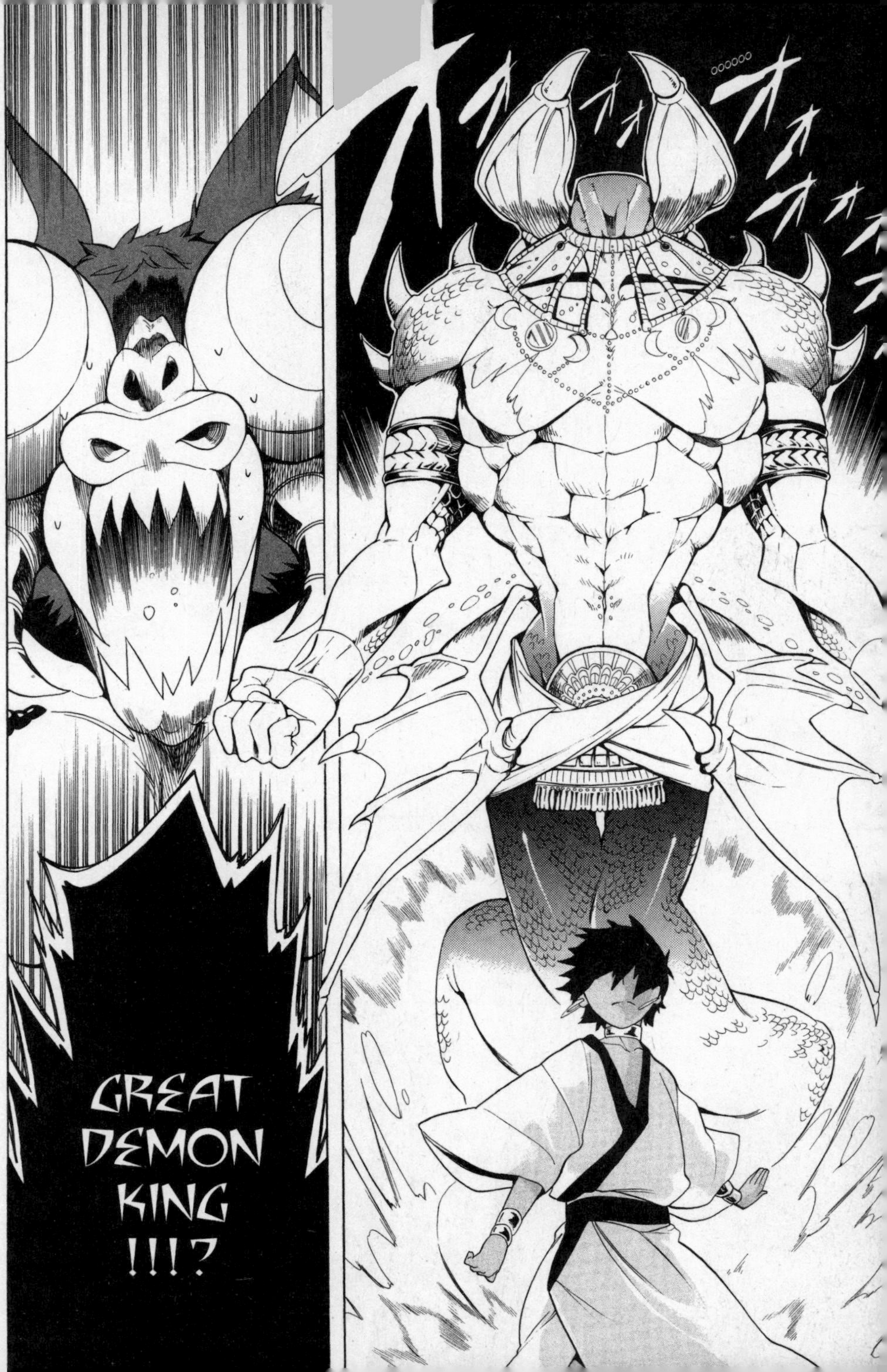
OOOOOO
GREAT DEMON KING !!!?

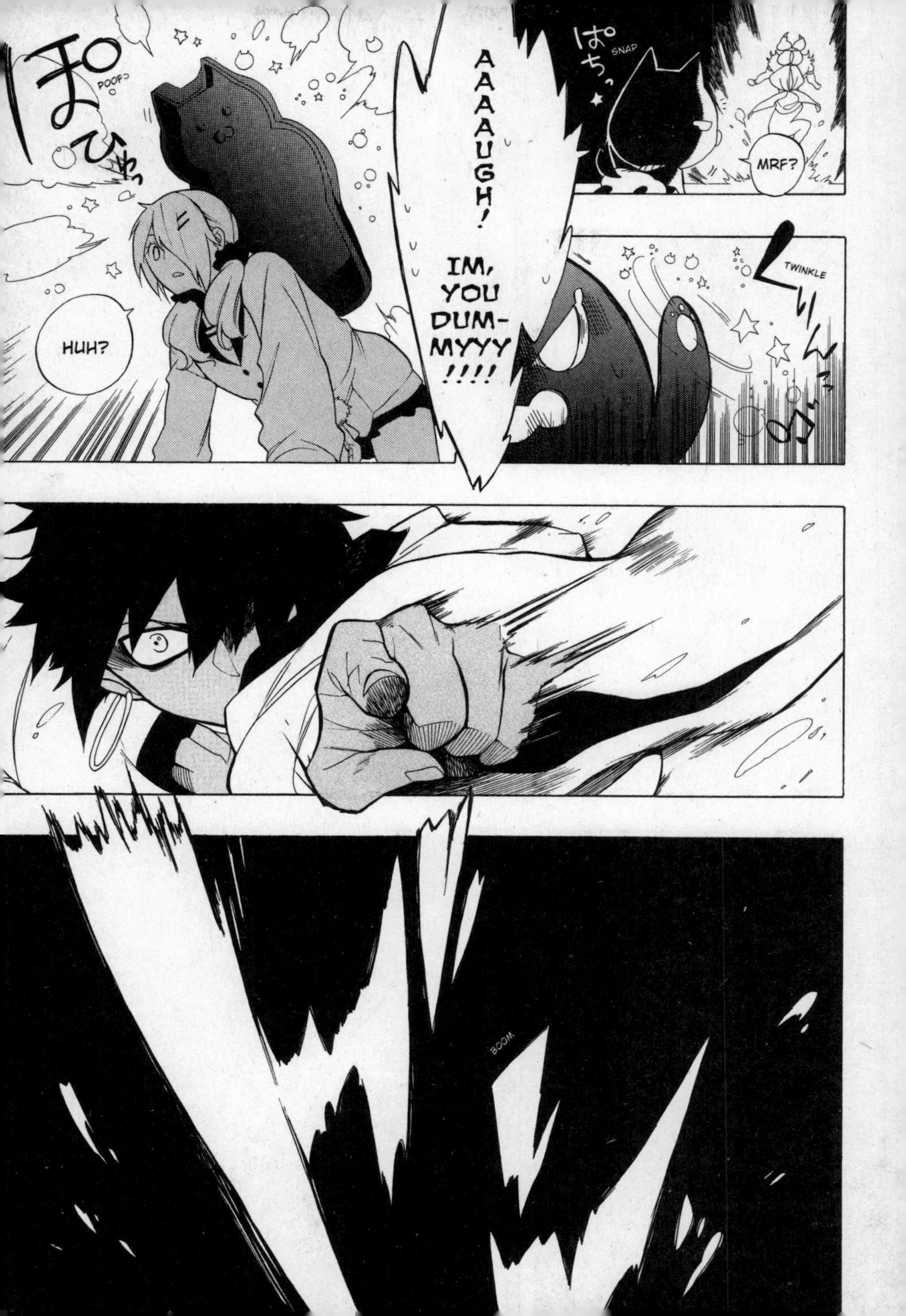
MRF?
ぱちっ
SNAP
TWINKLE
POOF
HUH?
AAAAUGH!
IM, YOU DUM-MYYY!!!!
BOOM

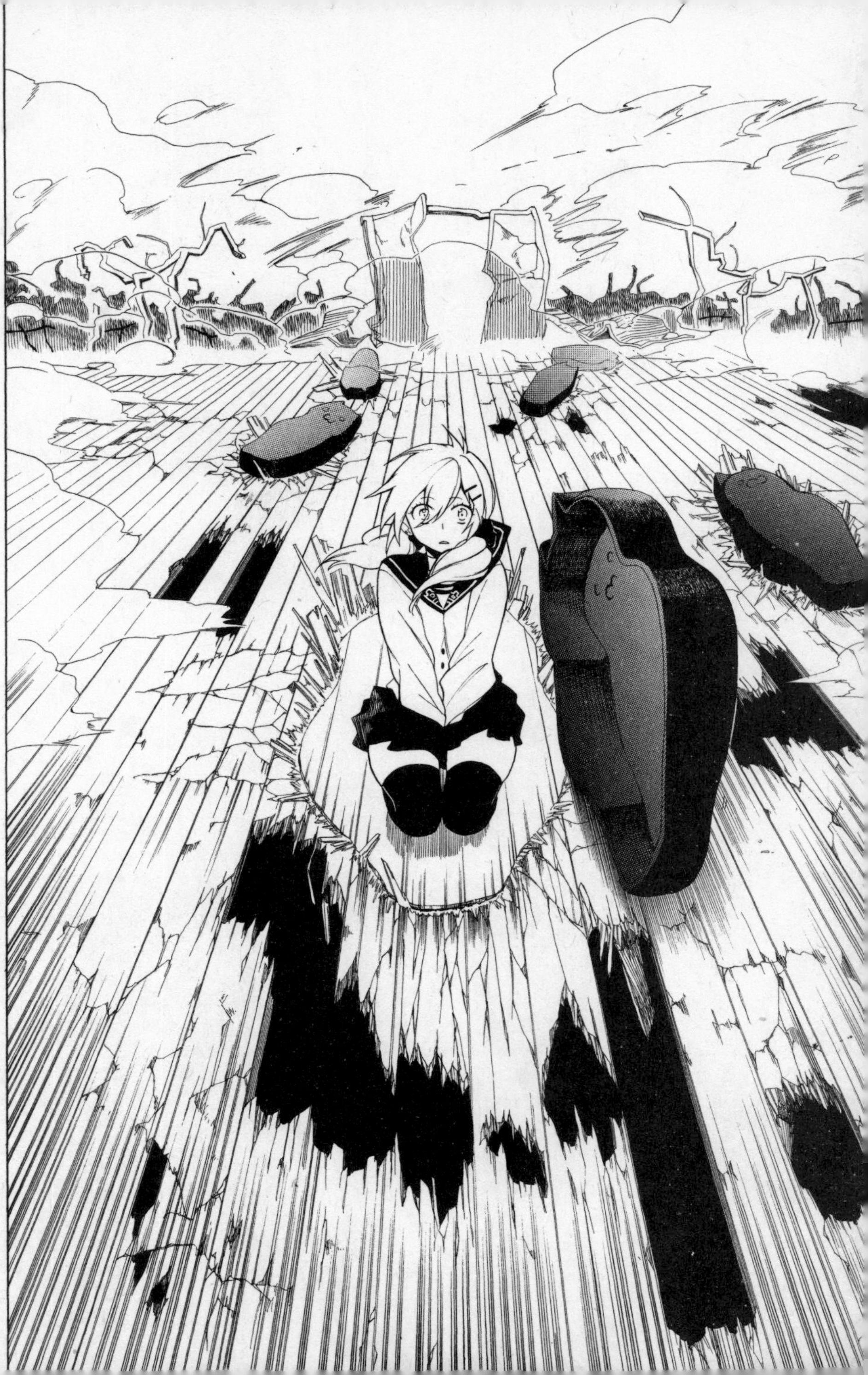

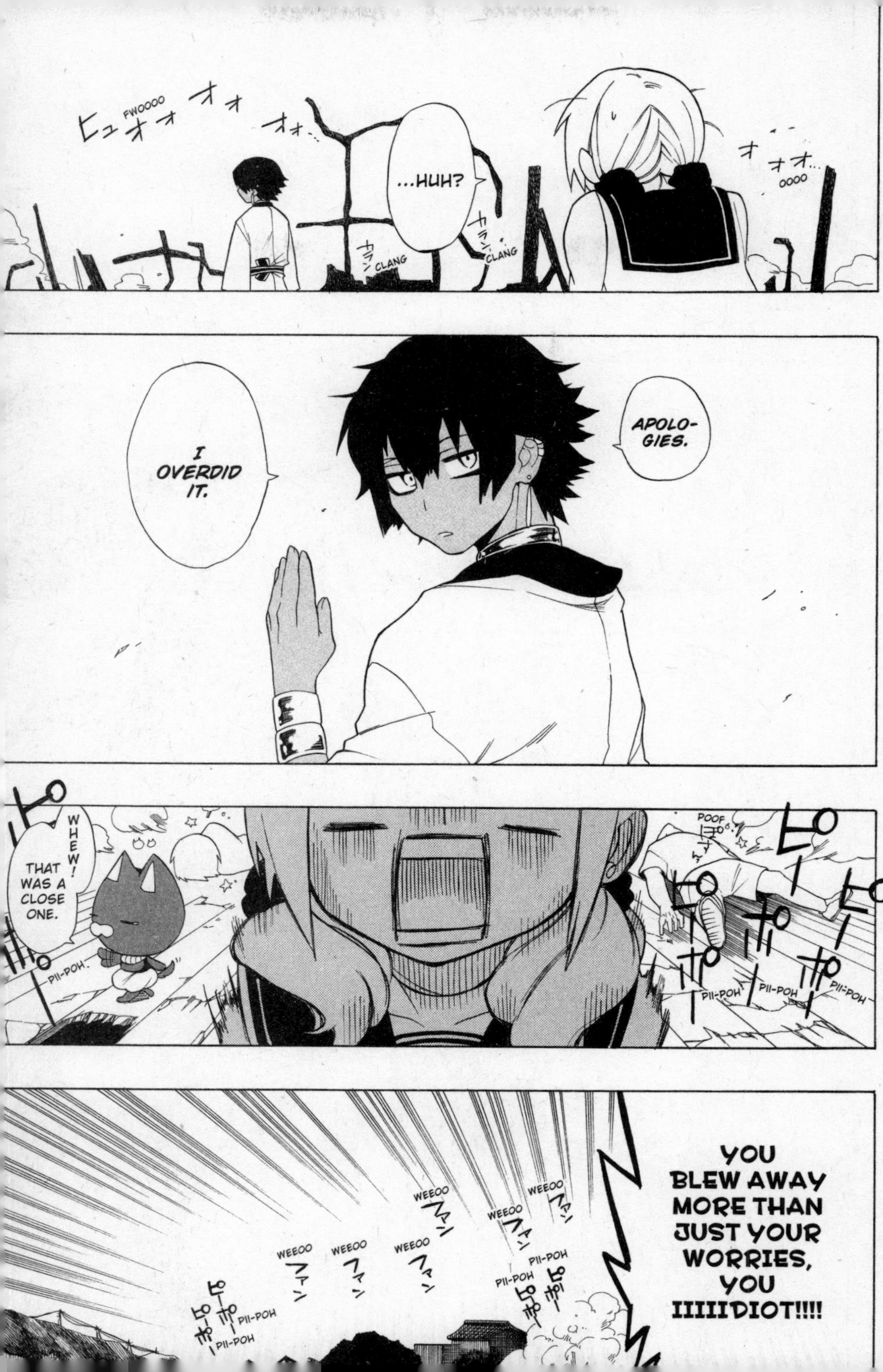

オオオ... OOOO
...HUH?
カラン CLANG
カラン CLANG
ヒュオオオオオォ... FWOOOO
APOLOGIES.
I OVERDID IT.
POOF
PII-POH
PII-POH
PII-POH
WHEW! THAT WAS A CLOSE ONE.
PII-POH
YOU BLEW AWAY MORE THAN JUST YOUR WORRIES, YOU IIIIIDIOT!!!!
WEEOO
WEEOO
WEEOO
WEEOO
WEEOO
PII-POH
PII-POH
PII-POH
PII-POH

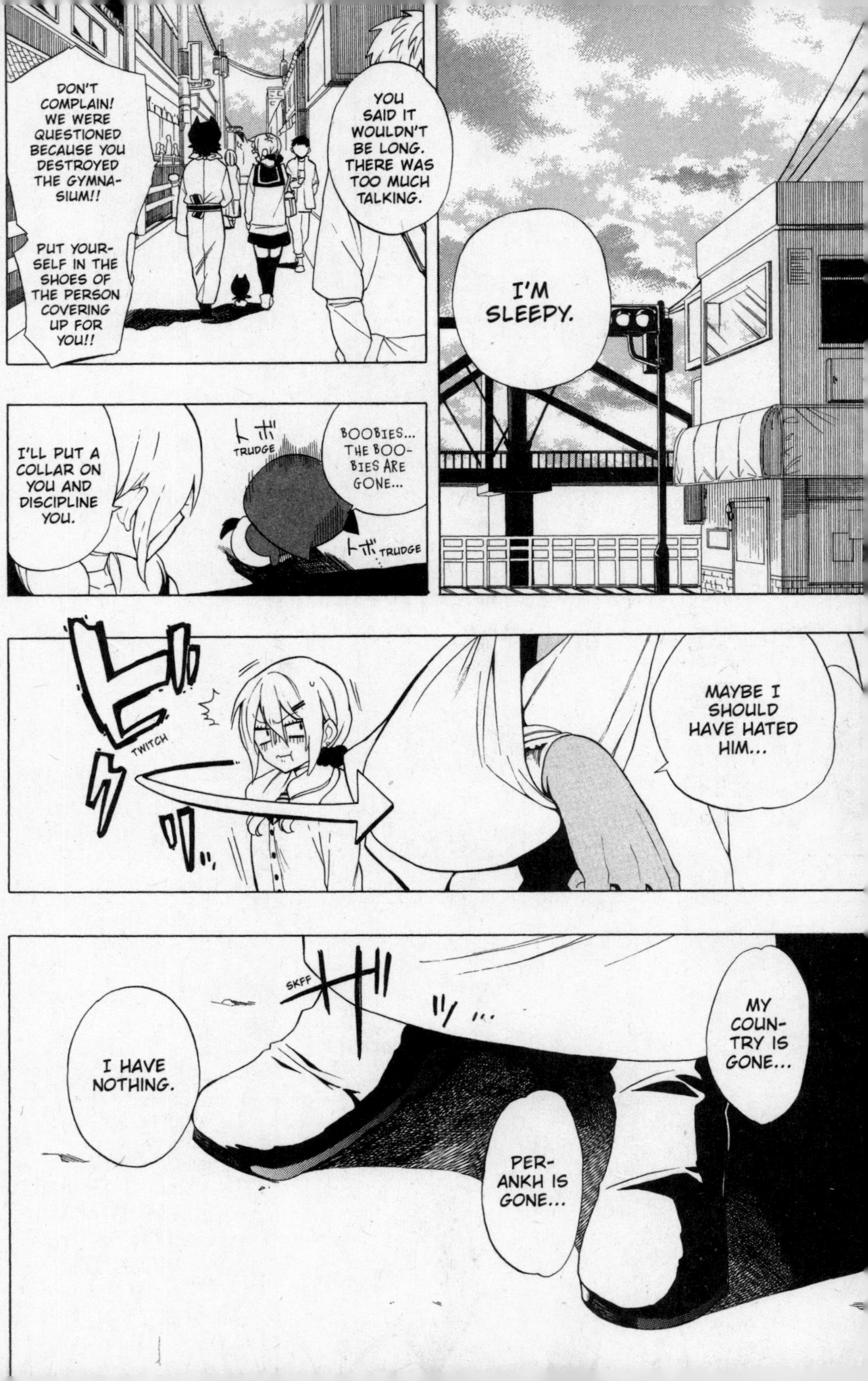
I'M SLEEPY.
YOU SAID IT WOULDN'T BE LONG. THERE WAS TOO MUCH TALKING.
DON'T COMPLAIN! WE WERE QUESTIONED BECAUSE YOU DESTROYED THE GYMNASIUM!!
PUT YOURSELF IN THE SHOES OF THE PERSON COVERING UP FOR YOU!!
BOOBIES... THE BOOBIES ARE GONE...
トボ TRUDGE
トボ TRUDGE
I'LL PUT A COLLAR ON YOU AND DISCIPLINE YOU.
MAYBE I SHOULD HAVE HATED HIM...
TWITCH
MY COUNTRY IS GONE...
PERANKH IS GONE...
SKFF
I HAVE NOTHING.

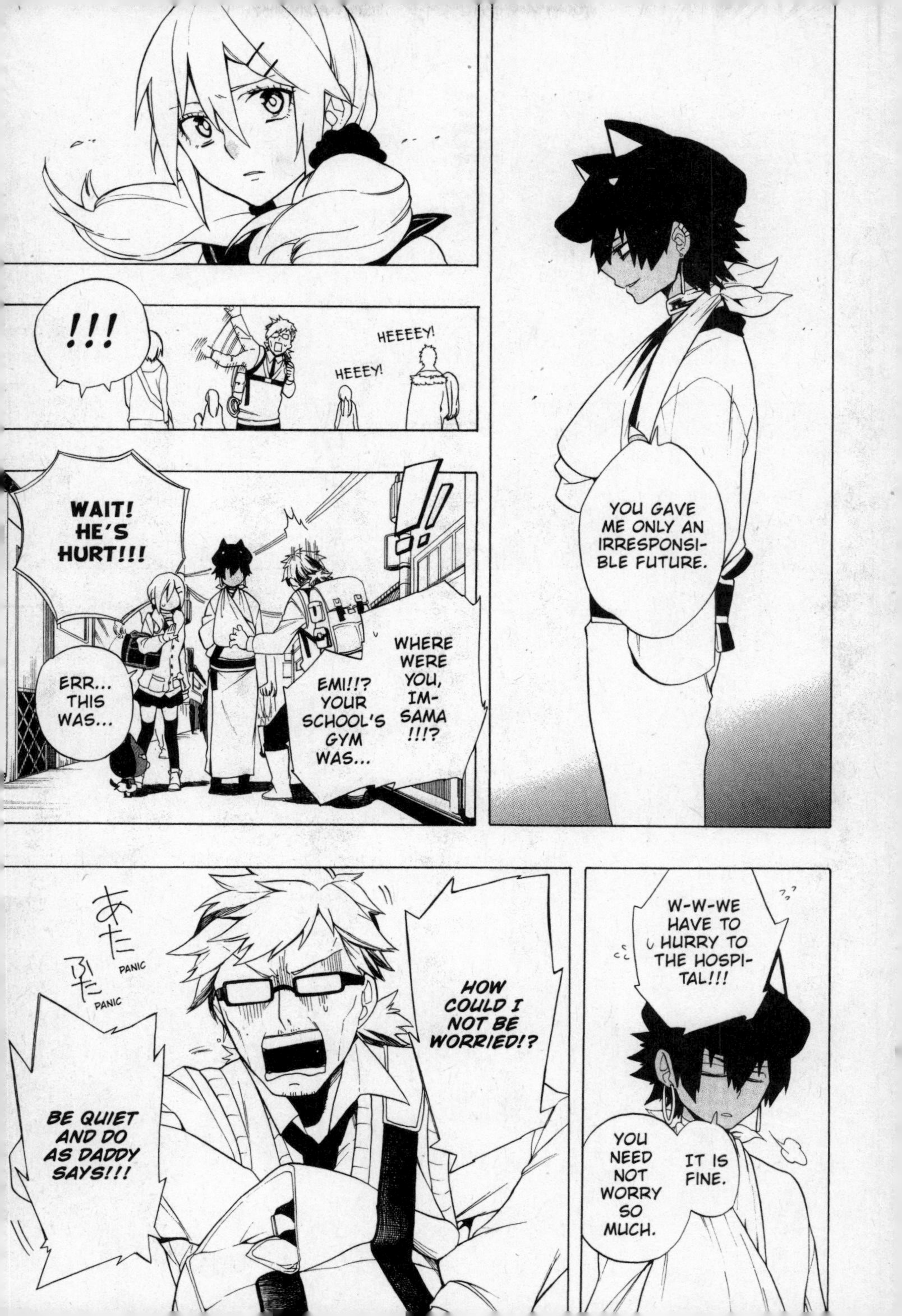
YOU GAVE ME ONLY AN IRRESPONSIBLE FUTURE.
HEEEEY!
HEEEY!
!!!
WHERE WERE YOU, IM-SAMA!!!?
EMI!!? YOUR SCHOOL'S GYM WAS...
WAIT! HE'S HURT!!!
ERR... THIS WAS...
W-W-WE HAVE TO HURRY TO THE HOSPITAL!!!
IT IS FINE.
YOU NEED NOT WORRY SO MUCH.
HOW COULD I NOT BE WORRIED!?
あたふた
PANIC
PANIC
BE QUIET AND DO AS DADDY SAYS!!!

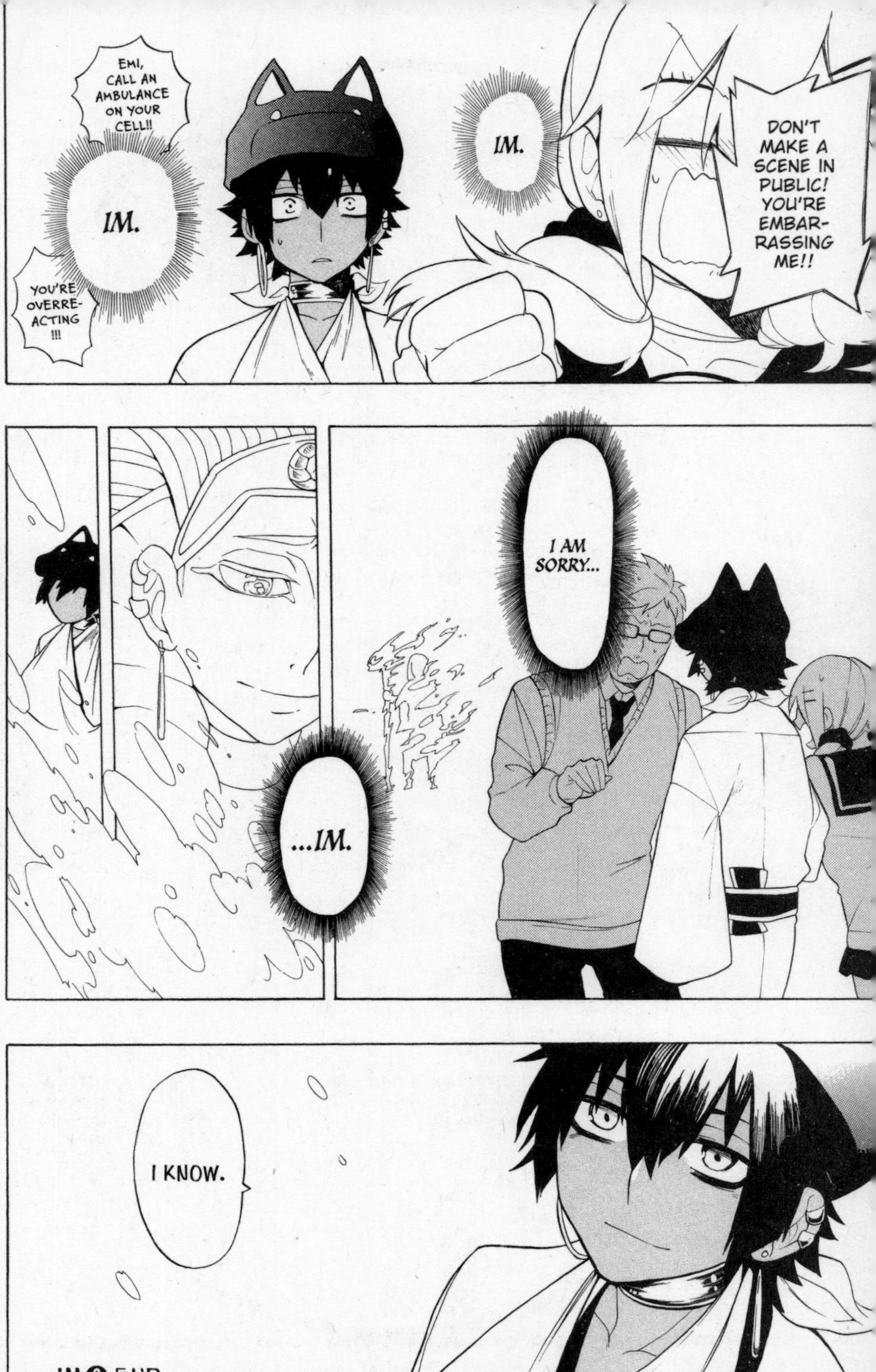
DON'T MAKE A SCENE IN PUBLIC! YOU'RE EMBARRASSING ME!!
IM.
EMI, CALL AN AMBULANCE ON YOUR CELL!!
IM.
YOU'RE OVERREACTING!!!
I AM SORRY...
...IM.
I KNOW.

AS PUBLISHED IN MONTHLY SHOUNEN GANGAN 2015 ISSUES 6 TO 8, 2013 ISSUE 2

IM 2 END

TRANSLATION NOTES

Common Honorifics

no honorific: Indicates familiarity or closeness; if used without permission or reason, addressing someone in this manner would constitute an insult.

-san: The Japanese equivalent of Mr./Mrs./Miss. If a situation calls for politeness, this is the fail-safe honorific.

-sama: Conveys great respect; may also indicate the social status of the speaker is lower than that of the addressee.

-kun: Used most often when referring to boys, this honorific indicates affection or familiarity. Occasionally used by older men among their peers, but it may also be used by anyone referring to a person of lower standing.

-chan: An affectionate honorific indicating familiarity used mostly in reference to girls; also used in reference to cute persons or animals of either gender.

-sensei: A respectful term for teachers, artists, or high-level professionals.

-oniisan, nii-san, aniki, etc.: A term of endearment meaning "big brother" that may be more widely used to address any young man who is like a brother, regardless of whether he is related or not.

-oneesan, nee-san, aneki, etc.: The female counterpart of the above, nee-san means "big sister."

Page 28
Youma: one of the Japanese words for "monster."

Page 64
Djoser is prounounced "joe-sir." (The "d" is silent.) The real Djoser and Imhotep were in fact contemporaries—Djoser was a pharaoh, and Imhotep served as his vizier.

Page 151
In contrast with Emi's cursed life, her name is written with the characters "blessed" and "happiness." Her parents must have given her the name hoping she'd live happily.

The **Tsuchinoko** is a snakelike creature in Japanese folklore whose existence is questioned, à la Bigfoot.

A BONUS FOR NO ONE ♡♡

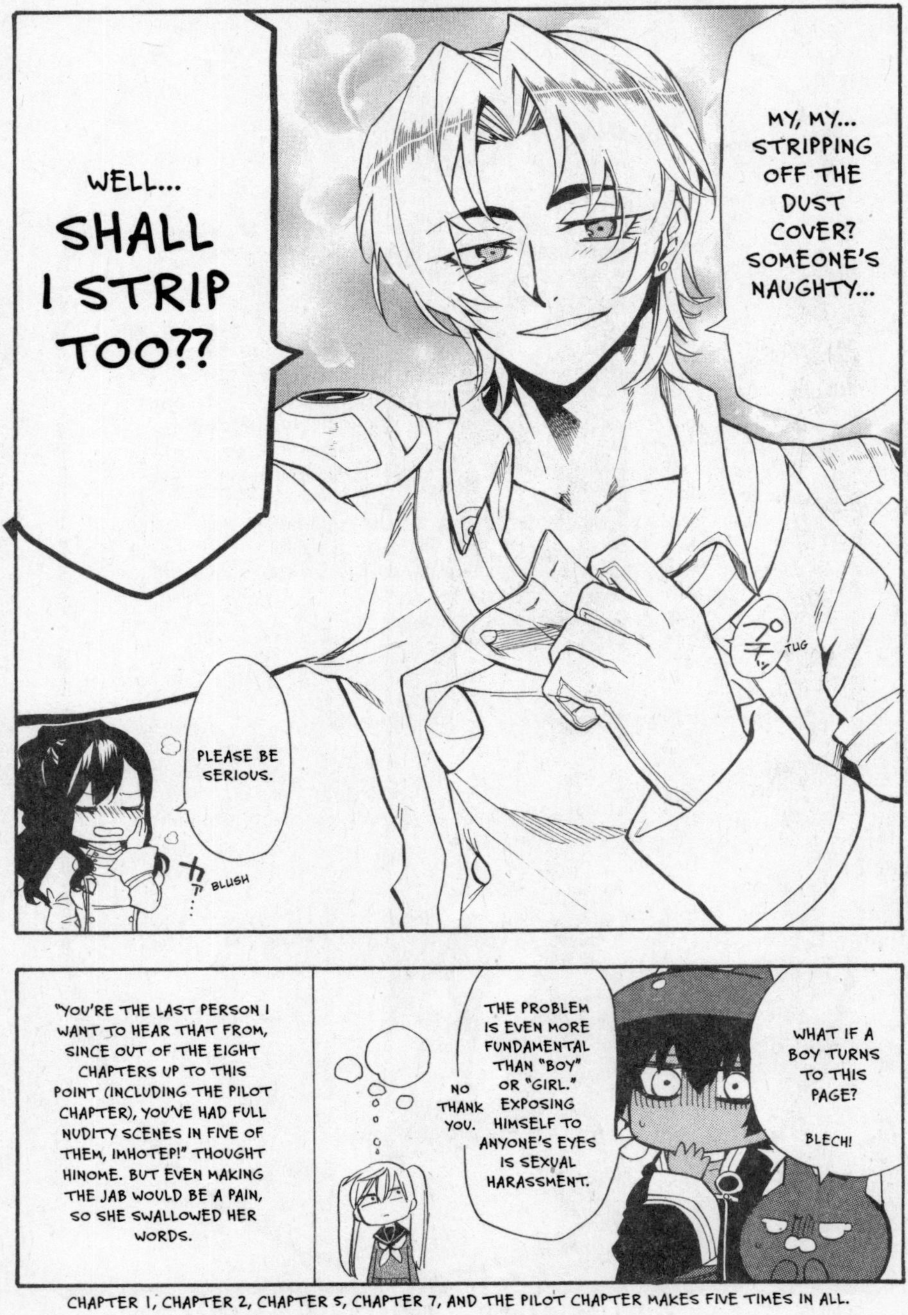
MY, MY... STRIPPING OFF THE DUST COVER? SOMEONE'S NAUGHTY...
WELL... SHALL I STRIP TOO??
TUG
PLEASE BE SERIOUS.
BLUSH
WHAT IF A BOY TURNS TO THIS PAGE?
BLECH!
THE PROBLEM IS EVEN MORE FUNDAMENTAL THAN "BOY" OR "GIRL." EXPOSING HIMSELF TO ANYONE'S EYES IS SEXUAL HARASSMENT.
NO THANK YOU.
"YOU'RE THE LAST PERSON I WANT TO HEAR THAT FROM, SINCE OUT OF THE EIGHT CHAPTERS UP TO THIS POINT (INCLUDING THE PILOT CHAPTER), YOU'VE HAD FULL NUDITY SCENES IN FIVE OF THEM, IMHOTEP!" THOUGHT HINOME. BUT EVEN MAKING THE JAB WOULD BE A PAIN, SO SHE SWALLOWED HER WORDS.

CHAPTER 1, CHAPTER 2, CHAPTER 5, CHAPTER 7, AND THE PILOT CHAPTER MAKES FIVE TIMES IN ALL.

SUDDENLY, TWO HEROES ARRIVED FROM THE FUTURE...

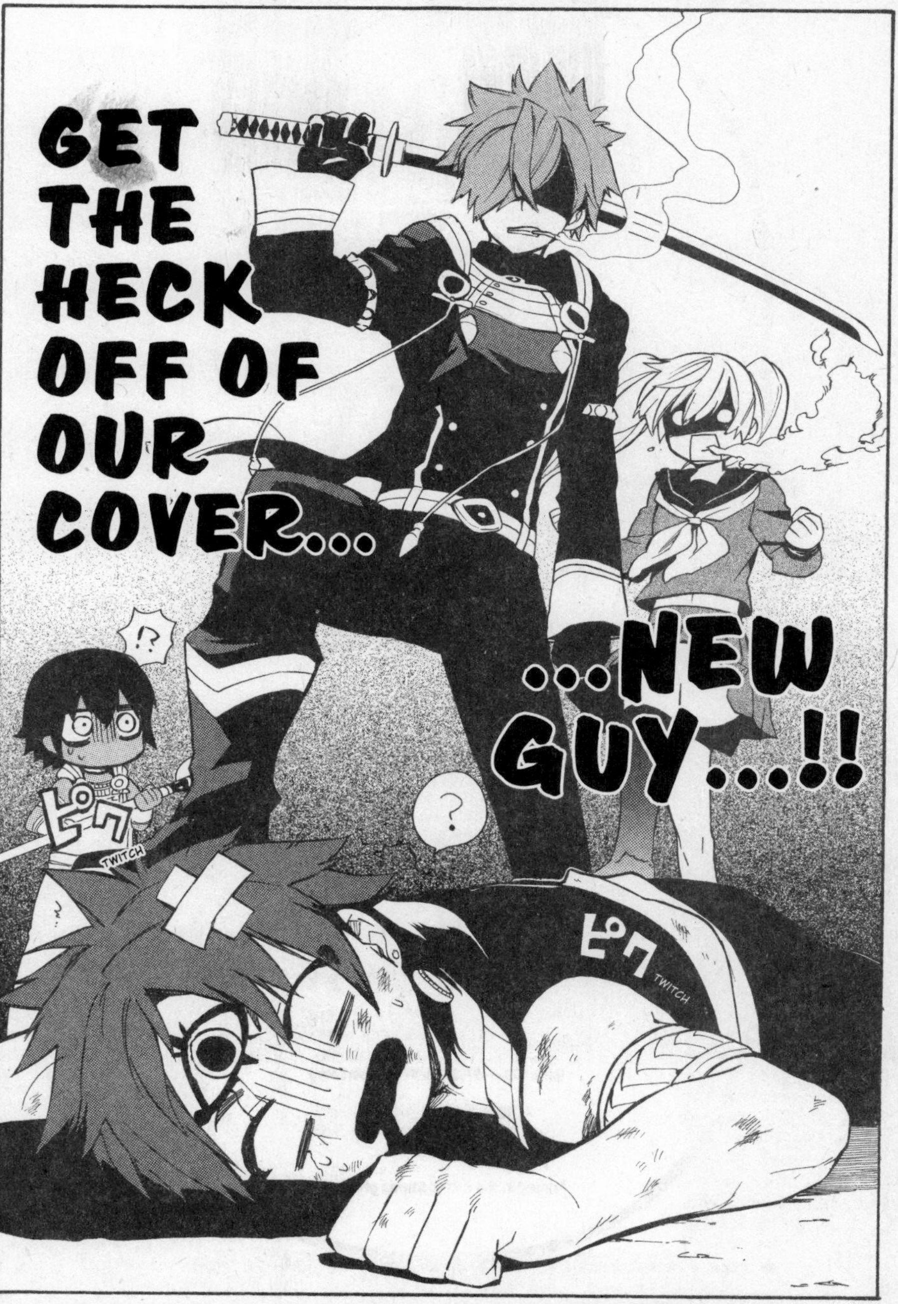
GET THE HECK OFF OF OUR COVER...
...NEW GUY...!!
!?
ピク
TWITCH
?
ピク
TWITCH

THUS, THE WORLD WAS SAVED. **IM: THE END!!!** (KIDDING)

Great Priest Imhotep 2

by MAKOTO MORISHITA

Translation: Amanda Haley
Lettering: Rochelle Gancio

IM Vol. 2 ©2015 Makoto Morishita/SQUARE ENIX CO., LTD.
First published in Japan in 2015 by SQUARE ENIX CO., LTD. English translation rights arranged with SQUARE ENIX CO., LTD. and Yen Press, LLC through Tuttle-Mori Agency, Inc., Tokyo.

English translation ©2017 by SQUARE ENIX CO., LTD.

Yen Press
150 West 30th Street, 19th Floor
New York, NY 10001

Visit us at yenpress.com ❧ facebook.com/yenpress ❧
twitter.com/yenpress ❧ yenpress.tumblr.com ❧
instagram.com/yenpress

First Yen Press Print Edition: March 2020
Originally published as an ebook in August 2017 by Yen Press.

Yen Press is an imprint of Yen Press, LLC.
The Yen Press name and logo are trademarks of Yen Press, LLC.

Library of Congress Control Number: 2019953326